PRAISE FOR THE P.A.N

"Hickman has masterfully (and magically) brought the legend of Neverland into the 21st century with this fun and fast-moving reimagining of the Peter Pan saga." -Natalie Murray, Author, *Emmie and the Tudor King* and *Emmie and the Tudor Queen* (5-star rating)

"The PAN is addictive and engaging," -Lyndsey Gallagher, Author, *The Midwife Crisis* (5-star rating)

"Right off the bat, I was sucked into this world." -Candace Robinson, Author, *Lyrics & Curses* (5-star rating)

The P.A.N.

Book One in the Pan Trilogy

JENNY HICKMAN

Midnight Tide
PUBLISHING

Published by Midnight Tide Publishing.

www.midnighttidepublishing.com

Interior Formatting by Elissa Carr/Book Savvy Services

Book Title/ Jenny Hickman. – 2nd ed.

ISBN : 978-1-7356141-0-6

eBook ISBN: 978-1-7356141-1-3

For my fellow dreamers who wish they could fly

You're as much
a part
of this story
as I am.
Welcome to Neverland.

— Peter

ONE

"I get to go home when you're finished with tomorrow's tests, right?" Vivienne assumed, feeling hopeful for the first time since she had been admitted to the hospital.

"I'm afraid not," the doctor said, adjusting the glasses on his nose. "Your diagnosis is still inconclusive."

She slumped against the pillow and picked at the surgical tape surrounding the IV on the back of her hand. The four other doctors in white coats and stethoscopes muttered their agreement.

On her way to school on Monday, she had felt a bit light-headed. Nothing new considering she had skipped breakfast. She'd felt anxious as well, but that was because she had only spent twenty minutes cramming for her history test. Halfway through first period, waves of dizziness and nausea had crashed over her. Before she could get to the school nurse, her world had gone black.

Now she was sitting in a stuffy hospital room being stared at like she was an exhibit at the zoo. The rotten smell from the wilting flowers at her bedside was turning her stomach, and if the doctors didn't stop scribbling on their clipboards and tell her *something*, she was going to scream.

As if he heard her mental freak-out, the doctor in the glasses told her that he was sure she had nothing to worry about. Then he escaped with the rest of his colleagues.

"I'm here! I'm here!" Lynn burst through the curtains, reeking of perfume and cigarettes. She collapsed onto the chair and dropped her purse on the floor. "Sorry it took me so long. Traffic was nuts," she said, shrugging free from her coat and brushing her permed hair back from her face.

"Is that a new coat?" Vivienne asked. It wasn't the faded brown one her foster mother usually wore.

"Got it at Goodwill." Lynn picked some lint out of the faux fur-lined hood. Her neon-pink nails did nothing to distract from the nicotine stains between her fingers. "It was too cheap to pass up."

The coat she had bought Vivienne three years earlier had a broken zipper and was too short in the arms. "New purse too?"

"They were both on sale. Nice, huh?" Lynn returned Vivienne's nod with a gap-toothed smile. "Are you feeling any better?"

"I haven't puked since yesterday. So that's a win."

"It sure is. I talked to the doctor on my way in here. They said you're going to be staying for a little bit longer."

The last thing Vivienne wanted was to discuss her health with Lynn. "How's Lyle?" Her foster brother had texted a few times, but hadn't made any effort to see her.

"He's fine. Maren's good too."

Vivienne's foster sister was probably too busy with cheerleading practice or organizing homecoming to realize she was even *in* the hospital.

They chatted about nothing for another ten minutes before Lynn claimed she needed to get home to cook dinner. Which was crap. It was bingo night. She would probably leave straight from the hospital for the church hall.

Vivienne didn't mind. She preferred being alone to making idle conversation. Once Lynn was gone, she tried taking a nap. But sleeping was impossible with people coming in and out of the room like it was an airport.

When she opened her eyes, there was a dark-haired teen lounging on the other side of the dividing curtain. His black hoodie and dark jeans stood out like an ominous shadow against the sanitary white walls.

The door opened, and a nurse came in wearing the same sympathetic smile as every other nurse.

"Someone was awfully thirsty," she said cheerfully, refilling the jug of water on the rolling tray table. Her dark ponytail swung from side to side as she moved around the bed.

"Yeah. They told me to drink a lot of water." Vivienne glanced back at the guy. He was looking out the window now. The nurse didn't acknowledge him. Which was odd. Right? Sure, he was on the other side of the curtain, but he wasn't invisible.

The nurse babbled about her weekend plans while she took Vivienne's temperature and blood pressure. "Do you need anything before I go?" she asked, throwing her rubber gloves into the biohazard bin. "My shift is almost over, so I won't be back in to see you tonight."

"I think I'm good. Have fun in Vegas."

"You can guarantee it!"

The nurse bounced out the door. When Vivienne turned back to the dividing curtain, the guy was staring at her. His eyes narrowed, and his head tilted to the side, but he kept silent.

She was about to say something when yet another nurse slipped between the curtains. Her purple scrubs were a welcome break from all the blue ones.

"I have some good news for you, Vivienne," she said after glancing at the clipboard. "They're moving you to another facility to see a specialist."

That was supposed to be *good* news? "I thought I was staying here." The doctor had said that, right?

"No. You're leaving tonight." In an efficient yet detached manner, the nurse unhooked Vivienne from the various machines. "Get up and get dressed. Someone will be along shortly to bring you to the lobby for transfer."

This didn't feel right. The hospital wouldn't release her without her guardian's consent. "Where's Lynn?"

The nurse launched into an explanation about forms being signed and hospital procedures and stuff she probably should

3

have been listening to, but she found her attention drifting back to the guy behind the—

He was gone.

The clipboard cracked against the bed rail. "Are you even listening to me?"

"Sorry. I thought I saw someone over there." Vivienne nodded her chin toward the empty chair. Had he been there at all?

The nurse walked to the hanging material and gave it a swift tug.

Vacant bed. Empty chair. Open window. Where had he gone?

"There's no one else in the room but us." After scribbling a note in Vivienne's chart, and with and a curt reminder to get dressed, the nurse left.

Hopefully the specialist would be able to tell Vivienne why she was hallucinating now too.

She traded the unflattering hospital gown for her ripped jeans and gray T-shirt. When she yanked her hoodie out of her backpack, a small square of glossy paper drifted to the bed. She picked up the photo of her brother and sister and smiled.

Adventures with William and Anne made up the bulk of Vivienne's scant childhood memories. Bedtime stories, pancake Saturdays, trips to the lake—

She sighed and tucked the photo between the pages of her history book.

"Are you dressed yet?" a male voice asked from behind the curtain. "It's getting late, and we really must be on our way."

His British accent made her smile. She'd always had a thing for accents. "Yeah, I'm all done." She reached for the privacy curtain to see what her escort looked—

The guy from the corner was leaning with his shoulder against the door frame. And *wow*. Just wow. High cheekbones, sharp jaw, straight nose, and his mouth . . .

She knew it was rude to stare, but she couldn't help it.

He wasn't just handsome. He was beautiful.

"It's about time they unhooked you," he said. "I thought I was going to have to do it myself." His head tilted and his brows pulled together as he studied her outfit. His eyes were the most unusual shade of green, deep and rich, like a field in the height of spring. "Do you have anything darker to wear?"

"Darker?" She looked down at her yellow hoodie. Did the color really matter? "Um...no?"

"It'll have to do then. Are you ready to leave?"

"With *you*?" She gripped the bed rails at her back to keep herself steady.

The corner of his lips lifted into a half-smile. "I can hardly let you go on your own."

Either she was missing something or this guy was in the wrong room. "Who *are* you?"

He moved past her to where her things were strewn on the bed and started collecting her books. "If you hurry up, I'll tell you."

A mysterious guy no one else could see wanted her to come with him? That sounded like a *great* idea.

She grabbed the plastic cup from the table and drank until the cool water was gone. "As intriguing as your offer is," she said, feeling steadier, "I'm going to stay here and wait for the doctor."

Instead of leaving, he continued tucking things into her backpack. When he had finished, he gripped her wrist firmly with his cold, slender fingers.

"What the heck?" When she tried to pull away, his hold tightened.

Tossing her bag over his shoulder, he yanked her toward the door as if she was a second piece of luggage. He poked his head into the hall—presumably checking for witnesses—then towed her into the stairwell.

"Let. Me. Go!" She tugged free and stumbled backwards. Her shout echoed in the hollow space.

"You can go if you'd like." He waved his hand toward the door before checking the silver watch at his wrist. "The so-called *specialist* they're sending you to is going to kill you. But you can absolutely go."

Did he say someone was going to *kill* her? That couldn't be true. She was a boring, seventeen-year-old kid from Ohio. Why would anyone want her dead?

"Or"—he pulled up his hood and winked at her—"you can come with me."

She didn't believe him, but going back to the room didn't sound very appealing either. "How do I know *you're* not going to kill me?"

"Because I'm trying to save you."

"So, what? You're like…my guardian angel?"

The grin he gave her was full of dark promises. "Something like that."

She only followed him up the next three flights of stairs because she was curious.

The higher she climbed, the more her head spun, and the more her head spun, the more she felt like she was going to pass—

Her shoe caught on a stair, and she crumpled onto the landing. The cold floor felt good against her overheated cheek. If she kept her eyes closed, maybe the water and chicken tenders in her stomach wouldn't make a second appearance.

The guy cursed. "Are you all right?"

"No." If she moved, she was going to get sick. And she *refused* to puke in front of him.

"Are you nauseated?"

She nodded.

"Here." There was a crinkling sound, and he pulled a peppermint candy from his pocket. "Eat this. It should help."

"Taking candy from a stranger? No thanks."

"My name is Deacon." He forced the candy into her palm. "There. We're no longer strangers."

Despite her reservations, she unraveled the candy and popped it into her mouth.

"Better?" he asked a moment later.

"A bit. Thanks." She ignored the hand he offered and rose unsteadily to her feet. Her stomach revolted, but her dinner stayed down.

"Do you think you'll manage," he asked, nodding his chin

toward the next flight of stairs, "or do you need me to carry you?"

"Yeah…you're *not* carrying me."

"Not yet anyway."

"Not ever"

A smile. "Not *yet*."

Vivienne rolled her eyes and told him that she could make it on her own. She clutched the handrail through another wave of dizziness, then resumed climbing. They had to be getting close to the roof. "I don't have a lot of experience escaping murderers or anything," she said, stopping to catch her breath, "but if we're trying to get away, shouldn't we be going *down* instead of *up*?"

"One would think so."

"Where will we go when we get to the top?"

"You'll see." A chuckle. "Actually, you won't see. But I'll tell you about it later."

Before she could ask what the heck that meant, they reached the emergency exit. Deacon ignored the red and white warnings posted everywhere and shoved the door open.

Yellow lights attached to the brick walls eased the severity of the falling darkness, and cool September air filled her lungs. She followed Deacon past the helicopter resting on the helipad.

"How do you feel about heights?" he asked casually.

She wasn't particularly fond of them, but she didn't have a phobia. "Why does it matter?"

He glanced back at her, and his lips curled into a smile. "Because we're going to jump off the roof."

"Ha-ha. Very funny."

He dropped to his knees and peered over the ledge.

Wait. Was he being *serious*? No . . . that was crazy. That was . . . Why was he looking down? Her arms started to itch, and her head felt loopy as she crouched beside him. "What are you looking at?"

"The people who are trying to kill you."

She steadied herself against the wall and gripped the bricks until the grittiness cut into her fingertips. Two black vans waited at the main entrance, along with several men in black suits. Two more men ran out the door, followed by a woman in purple scrubs. After a brief conversation, one man went back into the hospital while a second set off around the building. The rest of them looked like they were guarding the automatic doors.

It was strange, but that didn't mean they were trying to —*hold on*. Was that guy looking at her?

She ducked back down.

Deacon touched her arm. "What's wrong?"

"I think one of them saw me."

He swore under his breath and started digging through his pockets. "Then we've run out of time."

She pressed her fingertips to her temples and tried to make sense of the last fifteen minutes. "What the heck is— Why are you taking off your shirt?" she choked.

The black T-shirt showcased his toned arms and chest. "Take yours off as well."

"If you want to get me undressed, you're going to have to ask nicer than that."

His grin flashed in the darkness. "*Please?*"

She slipped out of her yellow sweatshirt and handed it to him. The air chilled her bare arms.

"Here." He tossed his balled up top at her, told her to put it on, and then stuffed her sweatshirt into the backpack.

She pulled Deacon's hoodie over her head, thinking the whole time how she should *not* be wearing some stranger's shirt, but also . . . *Wow*. It smelled amazing. "Happy now?"

"Immensely." He motioned for her hand. "Now give me your arm."

"Why?"

"Because you're wearing pants."

Could this day get any weirder? "You know that makes no sense, right?"

"It does to me." Deacon yanked on her wrist and shoved the sleeve over her elbow. She felt a sharp pinch, and a bead of dark blood welled in the crook below her bicep.

"Did you just…?" *Woah*. She blinked once. And again. Did Deacon have a twin? Because there were definitely two of them.

And they were both cute. Annoyingly cute. Had she always had this many hands? Where were her legs? Had they fallen off?

Deacon's features faded as he whispered, "Think of your happiest memory."

It was a weird thing to say. But Deacon said a lot of weird stuff. Reflexively, she thought of her brother and sister and smiley-face pancakes.

Warm, comforting heat gathered around her, and instead of resisting, she succumbed to the darkness.

Two

"What the hell is going on? Paul just interrogated the shit outta me and kept asking if I'd heard from you."

"I was afraid that would happen." Deacon sighed and adjusted the earpiece in his ear. "HOOK showed up at the hospital."

"I leave you alone for two days and all hell breaks loose," Ethan muttered. "How'd they know about her?"

He nestled deeper into the bank of the steep rooftop and winced when the shingles scraped his neck like sandpaper. "I haven't a clue."

"Where are you now?"

"On her neighbor's roof." The car illegally blocking the fire hydrant shuddered to life before sputtering toward the intersection.

"Do you have a death wish?" Ethan bit out. "Why'd you bring her home if HOOK knows about her?"

Deacon may have flouted the rules, but he wasn't going to do anything to jeopardize his mission. "The hospital roof wasn't the best place to convince her to accompany me."

"You must be losing your touch, Prince Charming. You've convinced girls to do a lot more for a lot less." A chuckle. "I suppose now's as good a time as any to tell you Lee caught wind of what's happening."

"Brilliant." Just bloody brilliant. Could this day get any worse?

Once the narrow alley below was clear, Deacon sat up and scooted closer to the grimy gutter.

"It doesn't stop there."

Sure, why would it?

"Paul wants you to cut your losses and come back," Ethan went on. "Expect the call any minute."

That was one call he planned to ignore. "If I go now, they'll take her." He searched Vivienne's dark window for signs of life within. How much sleep did she need? It had been hours.

"She's young—"

"I don't care if she's seventeen or seventeen hundred. We have to keep her DNA out of their hands."

"You'll need to convince her quickly, because Paul's sending extraction—"

"Tell him to hold off. We'll both be on our way by sundown." Deacon pressed the button on his earpiece. Then he jumped across the gap, landed on the third-story window ledge, and slid the glass aside.

Vivienne woke from the strangest yet most realistic dream. She had been soaring over the city in the arms of a handsome angel with white feathered wings. Instead of being afraid, she'd felt free.

She stared at the roses on her sun-dulled wallpaper and tried to separate fact from fantasy. Had she really followed a stranger to the roof? Were people really trying to kill her? Or had she been hallucinating the whole time?

If someone had been after her, why was she home, sitting in her lumpy bed?

She was still wearing the clothes from the day before, but her shoes had been removed and placed beside the nightstand.

Weird. All of this was too weird.

After a scalding shower, a blue bruise and a patch of sticky residue were the last visible signs left of the ordeal at the hospital. She wrapped herself in her Bounce-scented robe and returned to the tight space that had served as her sanctuary for the last four years.

Feeling better than she had all week, Vivienne searched the sparse contents of her closet before throwing a pair of black leggings and an oversized sweatshirt on her bed. When she slid the door closed, her reflection stared back; smudges of blue bruises ran beneath her wide brown eyes. Her face was a ghastly greenish-gray, making her look more zombie than teenager.

She reached for the tie at her waist and—

"You should probably leave that on."

She jerked around so fast she rammed her shin against her desk chair. Deacon sat on the ledge of her opened window, raising his dark brows, fighting a smile.

"Otherwise," he went on, looking pointedly at her bare knees, "I'll be too distracted to do my job." He was still wearing his black hoodie and skinny jeans.

Her face caught fire, and she gripped the lapels of her robe until her knuckles turned white. "And what job is that? Breaking and entering?"

"Among other things." He moved to investigate the framed photos decorating her desk. His lips lifted as he slid his finger along Vivienne's short blue dress in the picture of her and her friend Jamie at prom.

She stomped over and slammed the frames so the photos were face-down. The stack of college letters she had been avoiding tumbled to the floor. "You need to stop talking in riddles and give me some real answers. Otherwise, I'm going to—"

"What are you going to do?" Deacon leaned forward until they were nose to nose.

"I'll scream."

His brows quirked upwards. "No one is home."

Crap. He was right. Lyle and Maren were at school, and Lynn was at the office. "Well…then…I'll call the police."

"If you want me to leave you alone, all you have to do is say the word and I'll be gone."

She *should* want him to leave her alone. But she was too curious for her own good. "I want you to give me answers."

"Have lunch with me and I'll answer every question you have."

Her stomach responded for her. When was the last time she'd eaten? "Are you paying?" Her bank account was ten dollars away from a negative balance.

"What kind of gentleman would I be if I didn't?"

"The kind who breaks into other people's houses and creeps around bedrooms that aren't his."

"Touché." Chuckling, he went back to the window. "I'll meet you out front."

"I have a door, you know."

"What fun is that?" He slipped beneath the raised pane and . . . *jumped*.

She ran to the window and scanned the gravel three stories below. *Nothing.* And there was no ladder either. It was like he had disappeared.

Which was impossible.

Vivienne threw on the clothes she had laid on her bed earlier and raced down the stairs. Deacon was waiting for her on the porch steps, petting the neighbor's cat.

"How did you—?"

"Food first. Then answers." When he grinned at her, it felt like she had swallowed a bunch of fireflies and they were lighting up and buzzing around in her stomach.

Annoyed by her body's reaction, she breezed past him and down the stairs.

They ended up at a twenty-four-hour diner six blocks from Lynn's townhouse. Vivienne had been there once before with Lyle. Not the nicest restaurant, but the food had been good. The place wasn't busy, but there were enough people around in case Deacon ended up being a serial killer or something.

And witnesses were extra important because she had forgotten her phone back at the house.

Deacon held open the silver swinging door and let her pass.

She chose a booth near the fire exit in case she needed a quick escape. Not that she had any hope of outrunning him.

A waitress shoved a menu at Vivienne, then fluttered her lashes at Deacon and placed the second menu in his hands. "Can I get you something to drink, handsome?"

"I'll have water, please, Mary Beth."

The girl startled at his casual use of her name. "Do we know each other?" With a slight shake of his head, he pointed at the shiny name tag on the girl's striped uniform. "I always forget I'm wearing this stupid thing," she giggled.

"I hate to interrupt"—Vivienne kept her eyes on the laminated menu—"but I'd like some water too."

The waitress said she'd be right back and sauntered to the kitchen.

"Okay, *handsome*," she teased, "you owe me an explanation." Everything on the menu looked amazing. "And a burger. And fries. And maybe even dessert."

Deacon slid his menu to the end of the table and told her to order whatever she wanted—something he would probably regret saying.

The waitress came back carrying two ice waters in tall, plastic cups. She plopped them on the table, fished straws from her faded apron, and flipped open her notepad. "What can I get ya?"

"I'll take a cheeseburger and a large fry," Vivienne said. "And maybe some cheese sticks. And some nachos."

Deacon raised his brows over his wide eyes but kept quiet.

"Are you finished?" the waitress asked with a smirk.

"Until dessert." Vivienne was starving, and no one was going to make her feel bad about eating.

The waitress turned to Deacon and started flirting again. By the time he ordered, he had a napkin with the girl's phone number on it.

"That's *all* you're getting?" Vivienne asked when the girl finally left. "A chocolate milkshake?"

"I had lunch earlier."

"Then why did you insist on bringing me to eat?"

"Because I wouldn't have been able to hear myself think over the racket your stomach was making."

She shrugged. He wasn't wrong. "All right. Let's do this. How do you—?"

"Before you start firing questions my way, let me start at the beginning. When I've finished, you can interrogate me all you'd like."

"I usually throw in a little torture when I interrogate people."

"I might enjoy that," he said with a wicked smile.

Her stomach took a break from growling to do that annoying firefly thing again.

The smile faded from his lips. "What do you know about your parents?"

Her parents? What did they have to do with this?

Vivienne didn't remember much about her mom because Christine Dunn had always been working. She freed a napkin from the dispenser and spread it across her lap. "I never knew my dad, but my mom's name was Christine."

"And the rest of your family?"

"I had a brother named William and a sister named Anne. They all passed away when I was six." She tore the napkin into tiny pieces then brushed them to the floor. She grabbed another napkin.

"I'm very sorry to hear that." He sighed. "Your parents were special."

"They were *special*?" That could mean a million different things.

"Yes. And so are you."

"As flattering as it is to be called special, I'm pretty sure you have the wrong girl." The second napkin met the same fate as the first.

He leaned back and crossed his arms. "I have the right girl."

"How am *I* special?" Vivienne was the average of the average; there was nothing outstanding or remarkable about her. While she had done well in school, her good grades had been preceded by long hours of study and hard work. She wasn't athletic, nor was she the last one picked for teams in gym class. People had called her cute before, but never beautiful.

Vivienne was painfully ordinary.

"Do you remember your episode? The one that sent you to the hospital?"

"You saw the video, didn't you?" she groaned, dropping her head into her hands. Someone had recorded her stumbling down the hall like a drunk past the entire JV soccer team, tripping over a backpack, and ramming head-first into a locker.

Her foster sister had created a remix from it.

"Video? Vivienne, *I was there.*"

Was he saying he attended her high school?

"I've been keeping tabs on you for a while," he explained.

The fine hairs at the nape of her neck tingled, and her arms started to itch. "So you've been stalking me..." Of course he was a stalker. He knew her name. He knew where she went to school—where she *lived*. He had broken into her house. He had been waiting for her in her—

"I prefer the term *guardian angel*." His lips lifted into a mocking smile.

She kicked him beneath the table. "Not. Funny."

"It was a joke," he laughed, rubbing his shin. "I'm *not* a stalker. I was simply keeping a close watch for any indication that you were unwell."

That made him a good guy, right? Some of the itchiness subsided. "How did you know I was going to have an episode *before* it happened?"

"Your parents had the same experience."

"So you're saying that whatever is wrong with me is hereditary."

"There's nothing wrong with you," he said, rolling his eyes. "People like you and I possess a rare genetic mutation that activates around our eighteenth birthday. Your episode was caused by this gene activating."

The waitress chose that moment to interrupt. Vivienne would have told her to go away, except she was carrying a tray of delicious, greasy goodness. After arranging the plastic baskets in front of Vivienne and giving Deacon his milkshake, she hurried off to get the table of teens that had just walked in.

Burgers. Whoever created them deserved some sort of medal. Seriously. So good. She thought of Deacon's claim as she chewed. It *could* be true, she supposed. It didn't really make sense, but that didn't mean it was a lie. She grabbed a cheese stick and dipped it in marinara sauce.

Across the table, Deacon took a long sip of his whipped-cream-crowned shake.

If his claim *was* true, then she didn't have to worry about her health. "Why didn't the doctors know about my...condition?" Was that the right word?

"They weren't doing the right tests."

"And the specialist in Virginia?" she asked, crunching a nacho covered in guac. Deacon's shoulders stiffened, and his eyes narrowed. She'd definitely hit a nerve. "Would he—or she"—because women could be murderers too—"have done the right tests?"

A nod. "And the moment your test came back positive, they would've given you something to end your life."

He was serious. Whether it was true or not, Deacon believed what he was saying.

"Why would anyone want to kill me over a mutated gene?" She grabbed a fry and swirled it in ketchup.

"Our genetic mutations give us special abilities."

"Like what?"

His eyes darted from one table to the next as he withdrew a small, worn book from his pocket and slid it across the table.

She wiped the grease from her fingers before reaching for the tattered hardback. Why the heck was he giving her a copy of *Peter Pan and Wendy*?

And why did it look so familiar? Some long-forgotten memory prickled at the recesses of her mind. She traced the golden lettering embossed on the green leather.

"*This* is your explanation," he said. "This holds the answers to *all* your questions."

She lifted the book and turned the soft leather between her hands. "A fairy tale?"

"A fairy tale that explains how I survived the jump from your window—and the reason you're in grave danger."

There was only one ability that corresponded with both the story and the leap he had taken earlier, but it was too ludicrous to say aloud.

Deacon leaned forward and whispered, "I can fly."

Vivienne snorted. When he remained stone-faced, she sobered. "Wait. Are you...you're *serious* right now? Come on. That's absolutely crazy. It's *insane*. It's—"

"Vivienne?" He reached across the table and placed his hand over hers. "You can fly too."

THREE

H ow could he say that with a straight face? *You can fly.* Like it was nothing more than a passing comment about the weather. Vivienne searched his serious expression for some indication of a joke but found none. "You're kidding, right? Like...you have to be joking."

"I'm not kidding or joking or lying or any of the other things your rational mind is thinking right now." Deacon ate a spoonful of whipped cream and closed his eyes with a sigh of satisfaction.

"I'm out." She balled up the napkin on her lap and tossed it on the table. "I have listened to every other crazy thing you've said, but this is too much."

Deacon's spoon clattered to the floor, and he caught her hand. "Please, don't go until I've finished. I understand it's hard to believe—"

"It's *impossible.*"

He squeezed her hand. "Will you please sit down? What's the harm in indulging me for a few more minutes? You haven't even finished your lunch."

After a sidelong glance at the exit, Vivienne silenced the warning in her core, sat down, and resumed eating. "You need to see a psychiatrist." Maybe she did too.

"How do *you* think we got off that hospital roof?"

The fry in her hand fell back into the basket. "You're telling me that we *flew* off the hospital roof?" It took every ounce of willpower she possessed to keep her volume at a level whisper.

He could have dropped her. She could have *died*. She could have—*wait*. She didn't honestly believe him, did she?

Vivienne flashed back to the rooftop, trying to make sense of things. She remembered him asking to see her arm and then a pinch and then . . . nothing. "You *drugged* me, didn't you?"

"A necessary precaution. The moment we were in the air, you would have panicked and endangered both of us."

She forced her gaze from him to the book on the table, willing some logical explanation for the very illogical things he was saying. "You're claiming to be some sort of flying mutant who spends his free time saving people."

"We aren't mutants, Vivienne." Deacon pushed his sleeves over his forearms and rested his elbows on the table. "We possess a *genetic mutation*, the Nevergene, that gives us the advantage I spoke of, along with a few others."

"What else is there?" Could he walk through walls or blend in with his surroundings like a human chameleon? Or did he have x-ray vision? She crossed her arms over her chest just in case.

"Most of us don't age."

"Flying immortals. Why not?" If Vivienne chose to believe the first, she may as well go along with the second.

He drummed his fingers against his glass. "The term 'immortal' implies we cannot be killed."

"Who's going to kill you? Captain Hook?" The idea of a curly-haired, one-handed pirate chasing Deacon around an exotic island made her chuckle.

Deacon's expression hardened. "HOOK is real."

She stopped laughing. "He is?"

"HOOK stands for The Humanitarian Organization for Order and Knowledge, and they are bent on destroying every single one of us by stealing our DNA and deactivating our gene. HOOK agents were the ones who came for you at the hospital.

Which reminds me..." He checked the fancy silver watch on his left wrist. "We need to be going."

"Going where?"

A smile. "To Neverland."

"Yeah...I'm not going with you." She had followed him onto a roof and into a diner. But she drew the line at Neverland.

"Why not?" He frowned at what was left of his milkshake.

Where did she begin? "It should be pretty obvious. But the turning point for me was when you claimed you could fly."

"I can prove it to you."

She nearly choked on the last bite of burger. "You're going to *show* me?"

He slurped the dregs of his milkshake through the striped straw. "Will you come with me if I do?"

"Well, I'm not coming with you if you *don't*, so..."

"I suppose I don't have much of a choice."

After paying the bill—and leaving the waitress a hefty tip—Deacon steered Vivienne out the exit by the elbow.

Surveying the street, he escorted her down a gloomy road to the right of the diner. After about five minutes of searching, they ended up in an alley in the warehouse district, surrounded by low, windowless brick buildings.

A nervous prickle against her skin warned her not to follow him into obscurity, so she waited closer to the sidewalk.

Deacon walked to the farthest, darkest corner until she could barely see his outline. "Are you coming or not?" he called.

Part of her wanted to run back to Lynn's and lock her door —and barricade her window. But Deacon had gotten her off the roof *somehow*.

If she didn't go with him now, she would never know the truth.

Her skin started to itch, but she ignored the warning and followed him into the darkness. "Okay, I'm here. Now what do I do?"

"*You?*"

"You said I could fly, didn't you?"

He raked a hand through his dark hair and started pacing. His footsteps crunched on the gravel. "Can't I just show you?"

She had seen illusionists on television. If he wanted her to go anywhere else with him, he had to do better than some cheap magic trick. "Nope. I want to do it myself."

She couldn't wait to hear what excuse he came up with—

"Fine." Deacon winced and rubbed his ear like it was sore, then started digging through his pockets.

"What do I do?" she asked again, flapping her arms up and down because . . . well, it made sense.

"First"—Deacon reached out to stop her—"you need to get rid of all your skepticism. And then you need to take this." In his palm sat a dark pill, about the size of a vitamin.

"I'm not taking drugs." She knocked his hand away. "But at least that explains your hallucinations."

A sudden and overwhelming disappointment settled over her. Although she hadn't believed Deacon's story, somewhere inside of her had been a glimmer of hope. For a few brief moments, she'd thought there could be some hidden secret that made her remarkable.

"I'm not hallucinating," he grumbled, "and *technically* it's not a drug. At least not in the way you mean."

"It's *technically* a funny looking pill handed to me by a guy who is still *technically* a stranger."

"Your body needs an adrenaline spike to fly," he explained. "You don't know how to do it on your own, so you need to take this. Just stick it under your tongue and wait for it to dissolve."

"Unless Tinkerbell appears and sprinkles me with a magic wand, I'm *not* taking it."

"It's only stinging nettles and sugar and"—he mumbled something incoherent—"in a fancy pill."

"What was the last thing you said?"

He coughed the word, "Epinephrine," into his fist.

"You want me to swallow the stuff used to stop an allergic reaction?" Just when she thought this couldn't get any crazier . . .

"No, *Vivienne*." A grin. "I *said* I want you to put it under your tongue."

"You first, smartass." And if he didn't keel over, she'd consider it.

Deacon popped the pill into his mouth. Then he pulled another out of his sweatshirt pocket and handed it to her. Vivienne removed the lint stuck to the pill, broke it in half, and slipped the smaller piece into her pocket. Then, against her better judgment, she tucked the other half beneath her tongue.

The taste was earthy and leafy, like an unwashed salad, but also sweet, like the lettuce had been sprinkled with sugar and cinnamon. Ten slow seconds later, flames of adrenaline burned within her chest, and she staggered backwards. Her entire body tingled as if there was a swarm of ants dancing over her skin. Then she felt lighter, as if the easy breeze dancing between them could carry her away like an errant leaf.

"How do you feel?" he asked, shifting his weight from one foot to the other.

"Like I'm standing in the middle of a bonfire covered in ants."

His mouth curled into a slow smile. "And your mood?"

"Less skeptical."

"Good. Now clear your mind."

With so many questions swirling through her head, it was tough. But with a little effort, all that remained was the darkness, the fire, and Deacon's steadying commands.

When he told her to isolate your happiest memory, she pictured the Darling children thinking "happy thoughts" before soaring around their nursery ceiling.

"Make sure it's not superficially happy," he qualified. "It needs to be the kind of memory that brings so much joy it cannot be snuffed out by even the darkest sorrow."

She sifted through her past and realized the last time she was *that* happy was long ago, before the tragic fire had stolen hope from her world.

"There."

Vivienne's eyes snapped open. Everything looked the same as it had a second ago.

Then Deacon told her to look down.

HOLY CRAP. Her toes. Weren't. Touching. The. Ground.

Like . . . not *at all*.

She had to be eight inches up at least. Not exactly flying; levitating really. But close enough.

How could this be happening?

How did it work?

Why the heck was she sinking back down?

The soles of her shoes connected with the ground, and her skepticism returned with a vengeance. "What happened?"

Deacon's broad grin grew wider. "You flew."

"But why did I stop?"

"If I had to guess, I would say your brain got in the way."

Maybe half of the pill hadn't been enough. Maybe she needed to take the whole thing. She reached a hand into her pocket, but Deacon stopped her. "I want to do it again."

"And you will—*if* you come with me. What do you say, Vivienne? Will you leave all of this behind"—he opened his arms in the darkness—"to join our family?"

Family.

Vivienne's memories of a true family were few, but they were strong, and they were safe. The sense of love and acceptance that came with being part of something bigger than herself was what she wanted more than anything else in the world.

All she could do was nod.

"Yes!" Deacon spun into the sky. When he landed, his eyes sparkled with excitement. It felt like his smile had the power to clear the shadows around them. "We need to leave right away. We're already days behind schedule."

"I can't leave right now." She retreated toward the streetlights. "I need to go home, pack, and tell Lynn what's happening." And get her phone, some money, her toothbrush—

He settled his hands on her shoulders and bent so their eyes were level. "Someone alerted HOOK to your whereabouts. Who do you think it was?"

Right. People were trying to kill her.

"It wouldn't have been Lynn. She'd never do that to me." Lynn wasn't very maternal, but that didn't mean she was a villain.

"I'm not saying she's the one who made the call."

"Good. Because—"

"It could have been Lyle, or Maren, or any number of your friends and acquaintances."

"That doesn't make me feel any better." She wrenched her sleeve to her elbow to scratch her arm. Lyle? No way. Not possible. Maren though . . . *she* was another story. If anyone in Vivienne's life was a villain, it was Maren.

"It wasn't supposed to." He gave her a slight shake. "I need you to understand the reason you're not allowed to return home. It's all or nothing."

"Give me a second to think, okay?"

She shouldn't do this, right? It was insane.

But she wanted to. She peered through her lashes at Deacon. She really, *really* wanted to.

"Come with me to Neverland, Vivienne. I promise you won't regret it."

Deacon held out his hand, and she placed her palm in his.

FOUR

Vivienne squinted against the harsh fluorescent lights at the Greyhound Station. A man in the line next to them shoved his duffel bag closer to the ticket counter with his foot. Nobody, including herself, looked happy to be there.

She tugged on the back of Deacon's sweatshirt and asked him again why they were at the bus station.

"As I told you five minutes ago, we're taking the bus."

She hadn't believed him. Taking the bus was so . . . normal.

Deacon smiled at the tired-looking young woman behind the counter. "Could we have two tickets for the half eight bus to Cleveland, please?"

The woman clicked the keyboard in front of her and, before she could ask for the balance due, Deacon handed her a fifty-dollar bill.

The girl dropped the change in his palm and gave him two tickets from the printer. Deacon thanked her and turned toward the seating area.

"Why don't we fly instead?" Vivienne asked, taking the ticket he shook at her. "And why are we going to...*Cleveland*?" It was just her luck. She had been invited to freaking Neverland and didn't even get to go out of state.

"Airports have too many cameras and security checkpoints. And don't worry, Cleveland isn't our final destination."

At least that was something.

Vivienne stuffed her hands in her pockets, and her fingertips grazed the remaining half of the pixie dust pill. "I didn't mean fly on a *plane*."

He assessed her from the crown of her head to the black Converse on her feet. "You're not dressed appropriately."

Her hands smoothed the hem of her ivory sweatshirt. The clothes she wore were now her sole possessions. "Maybe I can find something darker in one of those souvenir booths." Of course, there was the problem of paying for new clothes. But if Deacon let her borrow some money, she would pay him back . . . eventually. Did Neverland do part-time jobs?

"You'd still be too heavy for me to carry all that way."

And yet he thought it had been a good idea to jump off a roof with her in his arms. She meandered over to the vending machine. Chocolate sounded really good right now. "Without flying, it feels like I'm just blindly following a cute guy with a copy of *Peter Pan* to Cleveland."

He leaned his shoulder against the machine and grinned. "You think I'm cute?"

"Shut up. You know what I mean." She added that slip to the list of mortifying things that had happened to her this week.

"Look, the fact is, you cannot fly properly yet. And I didn't save you from HOOK only to watch you break your neck from a fall." He put some coins in the slot and indicated the keypad.

She caught a glimpse of her frowning reflection in the machine as she pressed A6. The metal bar holding the chocolate in place spiralled until the treat landed with a clunk. She grabbed it from the bottom of the machine and thanked him.

"I still owed you dessert, remember?" he teased, dropping onto one of the metal chairs below a smudged window.

She curled onto the chair beside him and tucked her foot beneath her before opening the chocolate bar. Feeling generous, she offered him some. He shook his head, and she took a bite.

"Tell me all about Neverland. I want to know *everything*."

"There's actually very little I'm allowed to tell you right

now," he said carefully, his brows coming together. "But imagine limitless possibilities and all the necessary resources to help you achieve your dreams."

Vivienne's dreams had died a long time ago. But maybe she could get new dreams. Better dreams.

"The rest you'll have to see for yourself tomorrow, when you become a PAN."

Two teens stopped to look out the window. When they left, he shifted closer and leaned in—wow, he smelled good. Like expensive cologne and fresh air.

"PAN stands for People with Active Nevergenes." His whisper raised goosebumps on her arms. "Neverland was created to give us a safe place to hone our skills and to learn how to live without exposing our secrets."

"No offense, but it kinda sounds like I'm joining a cult." She took another bite of chocolate. The caramel center stuck to her teeth.

"Did I mention we have human sacrifices every Wednesday?"

Okay. He was funny. And hot. And British. Did he have *any* flaws?

Stifling a laugh, she shoved his shoulder. "Stay in my room on Wednesdays. Got it." *Wait.* Was she going to *have* a room? What if they all lived in some big communal building like an *actual* cult? "Assuming I have a room," she added.

The corner of his mouth lifted, and he rubbed his shoulder like it was sore. "All new recruits are given flats. So, yes. You'll have a room."

If she was a recruit then, "Does that make you a recruiter?"

He nodded. "I'm responsible for finding lost children and bringing them to Neverland."

She imagined Deacon as a dark angel in the night sky, combing the countryside and searching orphanages for lost brethren.

A man called their route over the crackling loudspeaker.

"That's us," Deacon said, shooting to his feet and grabbing her hand like it was the most natural thing in the world. "Come on."

She tossed her empty wrapper in the trash and ran with him to the bus. They sat at the back, nearest the window. "Can you tell me anything about the other recruits?"

"The last one I found had been in a foster home in Oklahoma."

"And did she go along willingly?"

"*He* was much easier to convince than you were." Deacon smiled and nodded to an older gentleman. The man tipped his wool hat at them before settling across the aisle and opening a book.

"I would have been a lot easier to convince if you had brought me straight there."

A woman and her toddler sat in front of them. The boy peered through the gap in the seats, and Deacon waved at him.

"Kidnapping unconscious teenagers is bad for publicity." There he was again with that grin, stirring up the fireflies. She really needed to get it together. "And when you blacked out at school, you got a pretty bad knock and needed medical attention."

He touched the hairline above her temple, and suddenly she felt warm and gooey and she hated it. She wasn't the kind of girl to swoon over some guy. Even if he smelled good and had the bone structure of a movie star.

"And if HOOK had come to my house?"

He draped his arm across the back of the seat. She liked the cocky lift to his chin when he said, "Then I would have saved you a second time."

It was still hard to fathom someone wanting her dead. She offered him a small, shy smile. Seriously. Those fireflies needed to take a break. "How'd you know where to find me in the first place?"

"We knew your parents, remember?"

The fireflies turned to lead. "And did you know my family died twelve years ago?"

Deacon's pained expression was the only answer she needed.

They had known.

Known her parents were gone.

Known that she was rotting away in the system.

They had *known*.

Every inch of her itched and burned, and no matter how hard she scratched, it didn't relieve the itching—

"Vivienne?"

She shoved her hair back from her shoulders so she could scratch her neck. "They knew what happened—that I was all alone—and they didn't even bother to come and get me? Why? Why now? Why wouldn't they just turn a blind eye like they have for the past twelve years?"

The little boy peered through the seats, and his mother snatched him onto her lap.

"Keep your voice down," Deacon hissed, twisting to block her view of the exit. "This is a lot for you to process and you're not thinking straight. I know how you feel."

"Were you in the system too?"

"No, but—"

"Then you don't know shit about how I'm feeling." She had been forced from one home to another, lugging everything she owned in a black trash bag. And right when she got settled, made a few friends, she had to do it all over again.

The man across the aisle snapped his book shut and glared at them.

Deacon reached for her arm, but she jerked back.

"Move out of my way, Deacon. I want to get off the bus."

"There are rules we have to follow," he rushed. "It's how we survive. Once you're there, you'll understand."

She didn't want to understand their stupid rules. She didn't want to hear another word about Neverland or genes or cute guys with stupid accents. "Get out of my way."

"Vivienne—"

"If you don't get out of my way right now, I'm going to start screaming and—"

Deacon cursed and slid out of the seat. She ignored the people staring at her as she raced down the aisle and out into the fresh air. The bus shuddered to life and the air brakes released, but she didn't turn around. And she didn't stop running until she reached Lynn's street.

Where were the fiendish men swarming the townhouse steps? Where were the mad scientists who wanted her dead? The normalcy in the air contradicted every word Deacon had said since they first met.

"Vivienne?" Lynn called from the kitchen. "If that's you, could you come in here for a sec?"

Vivienne poked her head around the corner and choked on the smell of burnt chicken. "Did you need me for something?" she coughed.

"Where have you been?" The dinner in the frying pan sizzled and popped, filling the room with steam and smoke. "I've been trying to call you all day."

"I went out for food with my friends. Forgot my phone upstairs."

Lynn flipped the switch for the fan. Her hair tumbled from the polka dotted scrunchie on top of her head. "I got a call from the hospital saying you left without being properly discharged."

"I *was* discharged."

Lynn lifted a penciled-in eyebrow.

"A nurse came in, unhooked me, and told me to get my stuff ready to go." She skipped the part about the woman working for an evil organization. "Then I waited for an escort, who brought me home." Not a complete lie.

Lynn pursed her lips, making the maroon lipliner stand out against her faded lipstick. "I'll call again before work and get it straightened out then. It's my long shift tomorrow," she said, wiping her hands on the stained towel hanging from the oven handle, "so I won't get to see you on your birthday."

Vivienne had completely forgotten about her eighteenth birthday.

"I hope you'll consider staying here at least until summer." Lynn had said the same thing at the last meeting with the social worker.

"That's still the plan," Vivienne assured her. It wasn't like she had anywhere else to go.

"Good. Oh! I almost forgot." She rummaged through a blue plastic bag next to a collection of unpaid bills stacking up on the counter. "Ah! Found it." The card she pulled out had crumpled corners.

Vivienne thanked her and turned toward the stairs.

"Aren't you having dinner with us?" Lynn asked, shuffling back to the chicken on the stovetop. "I'm making your favorite."

Chicken stir fry *was* her favorite dish that Lynn cooked, but that didn't mean it was any good. "I already ate, remember?"

"Oh yeah. I'll fill a bowl and leave it in the fridge in case you change your mind."

Back in her bedroom, Vivienne changed into pajamas and curled up under the covers with her phone. She made a conscious choice not to set her alarm for school the next morning. After everything that had happened, she refused to face the monotony of another day in high school.

FIVE

Deacon wanted more than anything to chase after Vivienne.

Then he got the call he had been dreading.

"You need to come home. *Now.*"

"Hello, Mother." He watched Vivienne retreat down the aisle and escape into the empty parking lot.

"Don't patronize me, Deacon. If you're not back here by morning, I'm going to send the extraction team in to—"

The bus driver started the massive engine, and Deacon fell back onto the seat. A few noisy wheezes from the closing doors and releasing brakes, and he was on his way to the first stopover in Cleveland. "There's no need for drama. I'm on my way back as we speak."

"You should have left the moment HOOK showed up. If they had captured you and found out who you were—"

"I had everything under control."

"That's debatable," she muttered. "Thankfully, it's over now."

The next time he looked out the window, Vivienne was gone. "Yes, it is."

It was over. He had failed.

"Travel safe, and I'll see you soon. I love you."

He ended the call and shoved his back against the window with a loud curse.

He'd been so close. He'd had her.

Then he'd said too much and lost her.

The woman in front of him glared from the gap between her seat and the window. Deacon mumbled an apology and went to make the necessary calls to report his progress—or lack thereof.

An uneasy feeling in the pit of his stomach stopped him.

He stuffed his mobile into the pocket of his jeans and pulled up his hood. What he wanted to do was climb out the window and stretch his muscles with a lengthy, head-clearing flight back home. Instead, he allowed himself to take a long overdue—but in his mind, undeserved—nap.

The next morning, Vivienne rolled over in bed and scrolled through her social media accounts.

The inspirational quotes about heartbreak on Lexie's page meant she and Johnny had probably broken up . . . again.

There was a home football game tonight and a dance afterwards.

No, thanks.

One DM from Jamie asked how Vivienne was feeling.

She ignored it.

Had life always been this boring?

The answer was yes. It had been boring and dull and downright depressing until a guy named Deacon had flown into her life. Had she made the right decision?

There was no point dwelling on it.

Still . . . had she?

She dropped her phone on the mattress and sighed. Last night it had been so clear, but today, everything was all muddy.

Lying around in bed feeling sorry for herself wasn't helping, but showering sounded like too much effort. She compromised and threw a sweatshirt on over her tank top and tights and pulled her hair into a ponytail.

The other half of the pill Deacon had given her last night fell out of the pocket and onto the carpet. He had been so sure she couldn't fly without it, but was that true?

Determined to prove him wrong—even though he'd never know the difference—she dropped the pill back into her pocket and cleared a space at the end of her bed to practice.

Adrenaline. It was the first step. She did some jumping jacks and ran back and forth until her heart was racing. Then she closed her eyes, emptied her mind, and imagined carving pumpkins at Halloween with William and Anne. Her skin started to feel warmer then started to itch and—

She was doing it! Her toes were barely off the carpet, but with lots of practice, she could be flying properly in no time. Who needed Neverland?

"What're you doin' home?"

Her ankle rolled when she dropped to the ground. "Lyle!" She pressed her hand against her hammering heart.

Her foster brother laughed and pushed his light brown hair out of his eyes. He had the same small gap between his front teeth as Lynn, accompanied by a smattering of freckles across his sunburned nose. "What's the matter, Viv? Afraid Mom will find out you're playing hooky?"

"It's my birthday. What's your excuse?" She rubbed at the invisible insects swarming beneath her skin until the tingling subsided.

"It's high school. Do we really need an excuse to skip?"

He had a point. "Just don't let Maren know. She'll rat us out."

"Yeah, she's a terrible human being." He stepped over her backpack and flopped onto her bed. "Probably the worst person I know."

She had to agree. Maren was the worst.

"So…whatcha doin' up here with that guilty look on your face?" He propped himself on his elbows and narrowed his eyes at her.

"Nothing. I'm still not feeling right."

"Sorry for not comin' to see you when you were sick." A

wince. "I haven't been in a hospital since Dad...well, you know."

Lyle's dad had died from cancer long before Vivienne had met him. "It's fine. I was asleep for most of it anyway."

She gathered her dirty laundry into a heap beside the door with great intentions. But the thought of bringing it all the way downstairs and washing and drying and folding it, then hauling it all back upstairs . . . Tomorrow. She would do it tomorrow.

Lyle picked up the bus ticket from her nightstand. "Are you going somewhere?"

"I *was* going to go to Cleveland," she said, snatching it from him and tucking it into her pocket, "but changed my mind."

"Good. Because I'd never forgive you for leaving me alone with Maren." He stretched to his feet and patted her on the shoulder. "I'm gonna watch some trash TV, if you're interested."

"Maybe later."

Instead of leaving, he meandered over to her desk. The frames were still face-down from the day before. "Are you gonna read these"—he picked up one of the envelopes scattered on the floor—"or are you starting a collection?"

"Are you gonna go away," she mimicked, "or are you gonna annoy me all day?"

"Geez. Someone's testy this morning." He made his way into the hallway. "Whatever you're up to, I'm going to figure it out."

There was no hope of that ever happening. "Go away, Lyle," she said with a laugh.

"I will...but only because it's your birthday."

After closing the door, she turned back to the stack of college application responses. Going to college wasn't nearly as exciting as going to Neverland, but she had to do *something* after graduation. She carried the pile to her bed and opened the first one. A form rejection. She tossed it toward the metal wastebasket next to her closet—and missed.

Ten minutes later, there was more trash on her floor than in her wastebasket.

With a yawn, she opened the card from Lynn and scanned

the generic message of celebration and well-wishes. Lynn's signature was the only word inscribed inside, and a crisp fifty-dollar bill had been taped to the inner fold. It was an enormous gesture considering the woman struggled to make ends meet.

Vivienne stood up and stuffed the money into her back pocket, knocking the last unopened letter to the floor.

She retrieved it and slid her finger beneath the seal.

Miss Vivienne Dunn:
   We are pleased to offer you a place at Kensington Academy . . .

Kensington Academy? She had never *applied* to—or heard of—Kensington Academy.

She grabbed her phone from the nightstand and typed "Kensington Academy" into the search engine. A website with generic stock photos of smiling students and stately professors popped up. Unsure whether or not it was the right place, she matched a picture of a rooster with its head raised toward two stars from the letterhead to the web banner.

She tapped the link to the college's phone number and waited for the call to connect.

"Kensington College, this is Michelle. How may I direct your call?"

"Hi. I got an acceptance letter from you guys, but I have a few questions." She tugged at a stray thread, unravelling her ancient quilt.

"What's your name?" the woman asked.

"Vivienne Dunn—with two n's in both."

The distinctive clicking of nails on a keyboard indicated Michelle was still on the line. "I'm afraid there must have been some sort of mistake, Vivienne. I can't find you in our system."

"That's why I called. I never applied to Kensington Academy."

"Ah. You're looking for Kensington *Academy*?"

Vivienne lifted the letter on her lap to reexamine it. "That's what my letter says."

"Please hold."

A generic recording boasting a picturesque campus, freedom

within classes, and unique job opportunities played while Vivienne waited.

"Kensington Academy, this is Julie. How may I direct your call?"

"Hi, Julie. My name's Vivienne, and I got a letter of acceptance to Kensington Academy. But—"

"Congratulations, Vivienne."

"Thanks." What had she been saying? Oh, right. "But, there's a problem...I never applied to Kensington."

"How odd. Will you give me your last name? I can check if perhaps the letter was sent to you in error."

"Sure. It's Dunn—with two n's."

"Give me one sec..." There was a moment of silence then a click, and Julie came back on the line. "Miss Dunn? There's no mistake. You've been accepted to Kensington."

"You're sure?"

"Quite sure. Your file is right here in front of me."

How was it possible that she had applied to a college she had never heard of? "I don't mean to be rude, but I think you have the wrong person."

"Vivienne Dunn—with two n's—born the twenty-fifth of September, living in Columbus, Ohio at—"

"How's this possible?"

"It seems as though your exemplary work at Southern High School caught the attention of our recruiting officer, and he thought you'd be a perfect fit for our institution. Do you remember meeting with him?"

There had been a college fair nearly a year ago, right before Christmas of Vivienne's junior year. For the life of her, she couldn't remember speaking to a representative from Kensington Academy. "I'm so embarrassed, but I don't remember—"

"I believe Benjamin Cronin was the one who spoke with you. Does that ring a bell?"

"Nope."

"Hmmm...How about a recruiter named Deacon?"

Vivienne's finger flew to the red button and ended the call. She shot to her feet, and the letter drifted to the carpet. That piece of paper was from Neverland. Did it mean she had another chance to reconsider Deacon's invitation?

The doorbell rang.

Holding her breath, she stepped into the hallway and tiptoed partway down the steps.

Lyle groaned and mumbled something about interruptions. The hinges on the front door whined open. "Can I help you?"

"My name is Lawrence Hooke, and I'm here to see your sister."

HOOK.

Vivienne paused mid-step.

"Which sister?" Lyle asked.

"Vivienne Dunn."

"I'm pretty sure she's at school."

Vivienne shuddered at the cobwebs overtaking the light fixture above her. She'd always known Lyle's disdain for authority would come in handy one day.

"We were just at your school," Lawrence said, his irritation clear, "and they told us she's been absent all week."

"That's so weird." It sounded like Lyle was smiling.

"In the interest of public safety, I really need to speak with her."

"That'll be pretty hard, cuz she's not here."

"I'll tell you what…My associate is going to come inside and take a look, just to be on the safe side."

"Yeah…that's not happening."

"I'm afraid you don't have a choice. Mel?"

As sounds of a scuffle reached Vivienne, she prayed the worn floorboards did not give away her retreat to her bedroom. She flicked off the lights and listened to the muffled conversation below.

"I'm calling the cops, man!"

Lyle. She had to help Lyle.

Except these guys weren't after him. They wanted *her.*

"Get out of the way, kid. We have Lynn Foley's permission to search the premises."

If Lynn had cooperated with these men, that meant she could be the traitor Deacon had alluded to. Deacon had told her the truth about flying. Could that mean he was also telling the truth about Vivienne not surviving what was to come next?

She refused to wait around to find out.

She grabbed her backpack, dumped everything onto the bed, and shoved some clean clothes inside, along with her wallet and the photo of her brother and sister.

"She's not down here!" a man called. "You sure she's still around? If *he* was with her at the hospital, then—"

"Go upstairs. She has to be here somewhere."

The wooden treads creaked as someone climbed the steps.

They were coming. She needed to hide. Would they look under the bed? In the closet? No, no. Those were the first places they'd look. Her gaze landed on the window, and a familiar tingling made her arms itch.

She knew exactly how to escape.

Adrenaline wasn't an issue, but should she take the pill anyway? She dug through her pocket for the second half and took it. While it dissolved, she opened the window; raindrops splattered on the sill. Dampness seeped through her leggings when she climbed onto the ledge.

Happy thoughts. She needed to think happy thoughts.

She closed her eyes, but all she could think about was the men coming for her. Dragging her away. Killing her slowly—

Happy. Happy. Happy. Thinking about her brother and sister made her happy. She focused on those memories. Christmas. The year her brother had made her a rocking horse. The fire in her chest spread to her limbs, and she knew the moment her body left the ledge.

She willed herself higher, and her internal fire responded like the burner in a hot air balloon. Although she was afraid to look down, she forced one eye open.

The *roof?* She was only as high as the stupid roof? Her heart hammered in her chest. Rain fell over her face, blurring her vision.

The light in her room flashed on.

"She's not here," the man bellowed.

"Are you sure?" Lawrence called.

"Yeah. The window's open and the screen is popped out."
The man's silhouette approached the opening.

Dizzy, Vivienne closed her eyes and whispered "Help me,"
to God, the stars, the rain—anyone and anything that would
listen.

Her adrenaline surged, jolting her up and out of sight.

SIX

From between passing rain clouds, Vivienne watched the black van drive away from her house. Adrenaline still pulsed through her veins, heating her core and holding her tingling body steady.

Her joy at escaping was replaced by a cold realization: she had no clue how to get back down.

Last night, her skepticism had cut the invisible string holding her mid-air.

Maybe if she was only a little bit skeptical, she could get down nice and easy.

"I don't believe it," she whispered to a passing bird.

The bird side-eyed her on its way to the telephone wires.

Vivienne didn't budge.

Mrs. Melkova came out of her house and hobbled toward her beat-up red Volkswagen. The car protested when she tried to start it. After coughing some black smoke from its tailpipe, it stuttered toward the stop sign.

Vivienne allowed more doubt to cloud her mind.

This isn't happening. This is a dream.

You're not special.

You. Can't. Fly.

The tingling stopped. Fear replaced her adrenaline like a leaded weight dragging her back to Earth.

She was falling too fast.

Think, Vivienne. Think.

What had Deacon said?

She had to clear her mind.

How was she supposed to do that with her stomach in her throat?

She squeezed her eyes shut and tried to picture her brother and sister.

Her skin prickled, but their faces were muddled, like they were lost in fog.

If I survive, I'm going straight to Neverland . . .

I'll see Deacon again.

Her adrenaline roared to life. She slowed down, but the roof still knocked the wind out of her. She grabbed for something, anything to keep her from tumbling to the ground. The shingles scraped her hands, but she couldn't get a good grip.

Her body went over the edge, but her fingers caught the cold, leaf-filled gutter at the back of the house.

The gutter groaned.

Happy thoughts. She really needed more happy thoughts. She could see her brother and sister's smiles as clearly as if they were standing in the puddles below her.

The gutter broke.

Vivienne's adrenaline spiked, and she was able to slow herself enough to land on her feet in the small gravel-filled patch behind Lynn's house. Adjoining fences surrounded the backyard, and a narrow metal gate led to the street at the front of the house. She decided on the former and threw her back-pack over the lowest fence.

Someone called her name—probably Lyle.

She didn't stick around to find out.

She nudged one of the weathered boards in the wooden wall and slid through. There was a chain-link fence on the other side of the neighbor's overgrown grass, and she climbed over it with minimal rattling. After conquering three more yards, she reached a street.

She sprinted until her lungs felt like bursting, then collapsed in the wet grass behind a wide oak tree. Once she caught her breath, she jogged the rest of the way to the bus station.

She dragged her phone from her pocket and called the number from earlier. Her shaking hands were scraped and bleeding.

"Kensington College, this is Michelle."

"Michelle. Thank God. I need your help. Can you connect me to Julie at Kensington Academy?"

"One moment."

She took shelter from the rain beneath an overhang and tried not to think of her wet socks slurping inside her muddy shoes.

"This is Julie."

"Julie. It's Vivienne Dunn."

"Hello again."

"Sorry about earlier. We got cut off, and I wasn't able to speak freely." The lie didn't sound very convincing.

"I see. What can I help you with?"

"I know this is going to sound insane," she whispered, turning away from a nosey woman smoking a cigarette, "but are you in Neverland?"

Julie's high laugh tinkled through the speaker. Was that a yes or no?

"If you are," Vivienne said, "I've changed my mind."

"About?"

The wind picked up, and she moved into the station. They still had the AC on full blast, and her teeth started chattering. "I want to come to Never—Kensington. I want to go there." Why was everyone staring at her? She looked like crap. So what? Move along, people.

"And how do you plan on getting to Never-Kensington?"

"By bus, I guess." She pulled out the soggy ticket Deacon had given her the day before. "But right now, all I have is a ticket to Cleveland."

"A ticket for your next destination will be waiting for you in Cleveland, but you'll need to show identification to collect it. Will that be a problem?"

"I kinda left my house in a hurry. Give me a second to

check…" She unloaded the stuff in her backpack onto the floor and found her wallet beneath her jeans. "Yeah. I have my license."

She set aside a dry top to change into when she was done and stuffed the rest of her things back into her backpack. "How will I know when I get to where I need to be?"

"A Kensington representative will meet you when you arrive at your final destination."

"Thanks, Julie." She stood, picked up her backpack, and settled the straps over her shoulders.

"Before you go, I assume you're calling on your cell phone?"

"I am." Vivienne tapped her index finger against the rubbery case.

"Turn it off and remove the SIM card and battery. The location could be traced and, if that's the case, we would prefer you to disappear in Columbus rather than somewhere closer to us."

Could she survive without her cell phone? There was only one way to find out.

Vivienne promised to do it as soon as she ended the call. Julie said goodbye and a bunch of messages came through all at once.

The first ones were from Lynn. *Called hospital. They said you need more tests.*

The follow-up messages from Lyle made her smile. *FYI. Weird stuff happening. Mom is freaking out. Hope ur ok. Maren is back. I hate her.*

She wanted to text him something reassuring, but there was no way to give "I'm leaving forever" a positive spin. Instead, she dismantled her phone and stored the pieces in her bag. With fifty dollars in her pocket and a backpack full of mismatched clothes, Vivienne started her journey to Neverland.

Deacon hadn't been himself since he got back last night. Only once had he failed to bring a mark to Kensington. And he had spent the last seven years making up for that mistake.

Every fledgling PAN since had taken him at his word and

trusted him. They had been so desperate for something else in life that their questions had been predictable and few. He had grown too complacent—and too cocky—never expecting a pretty, brown-eyed girl and her barrage of questions to leave him returning to Neverland empty-handed.

Vivienne should have been enjoying life in Kensington instead of being stuck in her dingy closet of a bedroom or stalked by HOOK. But she had turned her back on the possibilities, safety, and freedom he had offered.

He felt personally affronted by the rejection, as though she had dismissed Deacon himself and not the opportunity to live out what sounded like an elaborate fairy tale.

His ringing phone pulled him from his pathetic musings. The brunette he had picked up at the bar the night before rolled over and tugged the covers over her head.

He silenced the call before bringing his mobile into the hall-way. "Hello?"

"Why are you whispering?"

He pulled his bedroom door closed and said in a more normal tone, "Sorry about that, Julie." Of course she would be calling. He needed to answer to External Affairs about his recent failure and undergo the rigorous debriefing session. Still, he hadn't expected the call so soon after returning.

"I just got an interesting phone call."

"What time does Paul want me in?" he huffed, pinching the bridge of his nose, prepared to accept his fate.

"Paul didn't call me. Vivienne did."

Deacon had so many questions, but one was more pressing than the rest. "What did she want?"

"To know how to get here."

"*What*? That's brilliant. Just brilliant." He smacked his hand against the wall. This meant the few rules he had bent on her behalf were more likely to be overlooked.

"If she doesn't change her mind again, she should be at the bus station in Worcester tomorrow night."

"I'll meet her there." He had a few things to say to Miss Dunn.

"I was hoping you'd say that."

"Thank you, Julie." His week was turning around. He couldn't wait to hear what had convinced Vivienne to reconsider.

"What do you think you're doing?" Paul Mitter, head of the Department for External Affairs, scolded when Deacon entered his office at Kensington the following evening.

"I assume you asked me here for my debriefing session." Deacon spun the globe next to the window. The setting sun cast the campus in a beautiful golden hue. "And, in twenty minutes, I'm leaving for Union Station."

"Sit. Down."

"Somebody's in a foul mood," Deacon mumbled, meandering over to the chair. He found himself looking forward to seeing Vivienne again, which was a novelty for him.

She was cute—but so was the girl from last night. Maybe it was the whole damsel-in-distress thing Vivienne had going on. Deacon felt responsible for her; that had to be it.

Once she was safe at Kensington, his preoccupation with her would end.

"Is it any wonder?" Paul ground out. "Do you know what could have happened if you were caught by those agents at the hospital?"

"Thanks a lot, TINK." Deacon ripped the offending piece of tech from his ear. He understood the in-ear Neverkit, a helmet/earpiece/phone/altimeter/GPS, was vital to their success, but it felt like he traveled with a live-in nanny. "It all worked out in the end, didn't it?"

"*Worked out?*" Paul yanked open his desk drawer and rummaged around inside. "Is that what you call it when HOOK has the building surrounded, and you're forced to fly yourself and an unconscious mark off a hospital rooftop?"

"The mark's name is Vivienne," he corrected, resting his foot on the edge of Paul's desk so he could tie his shoe. "And she will be arriving at Kensington safe and sound in the next hour. So, yes. I would say it all worked out."

"No thanks to you." Paul pushed Deacon's foot back to the floor with the top of his pen. "We're aware of how much coercion you employed to get her here. This isn't a game. You give the mark simple facts, and if he or she chooses not to come, then so be it. We don't *force* anyone to join us."

"I didn't *force* Vivienne to come along." If anything, he had sent her running in the opposite direction. "She made the decision all by herself."

"You didn't follow procedure either, did you?"

Procedure, procedure, procedure . . . The PAN loved their procedures. "Nothing about this case went according to procedure. I had to go a little...off script."

"*Off script*? Deacon, you *live* off script. What happened in Ohio was unheard of."

He rested his chin in his palm. "Which part?"

"Every part! The hospital, the agents, the extra time you spent with the mark—"

"Vivienne."

"The extra time you spent with *Vivienne*, even after being ordered to return to Kensington."

At least Paul hadn't heard about Deacon and Ethan's near miss with the Ohio State Police. "I can explain. You see—"

"The only thing I want you to explain," Paul snarled, glaring at him through the thick lenses in his glasses, "is how HOOK knew where she was."

Deacon had been racking his brain for a logical reason for HOOK's rapid response. "I can't."

"I didn't think so. Which brings me to my next question." Paul slid his pen behind his ear. "Can Vivienne be trusted?"

"You must be joking."

"I'm asking you to take a second look at the facts." He rearranged the papers in the open file on his desk. When he found the one he was searching for, he held it up for Deacon to see. It was a timeline of events for Vivienne's case based on Deacon's location.

Curse you, TINK.

"HOOK agents were swarming the hospital *days* after she changed. That has never happened and can't be a coincidence."

Paul shook the page as though Deacon couldn't already see the bloody thing. "We need to make sure we consider every possibility."

"Consider whatever scenarios you need to," Deacon said, plucking the paper out of Paul's hand and tossing it back on the desk, "but I'm telling you, Vivienne is innocent."

Paul snapped the file shut. "Some people think your judgment on this issue is clouded."

"Those people are wrong." Deacon wanted to ask who doubted him but refrained. He didn't have the time for an extensive list of individuals who weren't satisfied with his performance.

"Maybe so, but I'm assigning someone else to meet her this evening."

Deacon stood and leaned with his fists on the desktop. "Like hell you are." He had started this and planned on finishing it. "If you take me off this case, you may as well hand in your resignation now."

Paul mimicked Deacon's stance. "Are you threatening me?"

"Now, now, Paul." Deacon clucked his tongue and returned to his chair. "Would I do something like that?"

"Fine. Go get her." Paul sat back down and ran a hand over his goatee. "Then you can bring her to a secure location until we can get a better handle on the details of her situation."

"You've had eighteen years to learn about Vivienne's *situation*," he said, fastening the button at his wrist. "I will be *following procedure* and bringing her *here*."

Paul adjusted his glasses and narrowed his eyes. "You may not have noticed—"

"I'm going to stop you right there. And unless you'd like me to call my grandad and ask his opinion, this conversation is over." Deacon stood and checked his watch. He'd finished in record time.

Paul tossed his glasses onto his desk and swore. "Fine. But you've just made it *your* responsibility to ensure she doesn't jump ship like her parents."

"Trust me, when Vivienne gets here, she won't want to leave."

SEVEN

The curved ceiling of Worcester, Massachusetts's Union Station, adorned with brilliant stained glass windows and glowing with the last of the autumn sun, was like a scene from a storybook—which was fitting considering Vivienne's reason for being there. The ornate dome marking the center of the grand hall made it feel like she had been locked inside a Fabergé egg.

She searched for her name among the signs held by expectant men and women at the exit, but no one appeared to be waiting for her. That meant it was time for another trip. She passed a family of six on her way to the ticket counter. The kids had way too much energy.

"Woah. What happened to you?" the man behind the glass asked before slurping from the straw in his extra-large drink.

"I fell." It was the same generic answer she had given the other attendants at the last four bus stations. She pulled her hood over her hair to hide the black and blue scrape on her cheek. After traveling for an entire day, she was ready to call it quits. "Do you have a ticket for me?" she asked, slipping her license through the slot. "I think a friend might have left one."

"No one's left anything here. Let me double check with my

manager." He leaned back in his chair and shouted across the room. "Hey, Sue?"

A woman stuck her head out of a back office. "What do you need?"

"There's a girl here asking if someone left a ticket for her."

"What's her name?"

The ticket agent squinted at Vivienne's ID. "Vivienne Dunn."

"One sec." Sue disappeared back into the room.

Vivienne toyed with the useless silver chain meant to keep people from stealing the station's pens; there was no pen.

Sue returned, her portly shape leaning against the door. "Tell her we don't have any reservations under her name."

"We don't have any reserv—"

"I heard her. Thanks for checking." Vivienne took back her ID and found a seat in a quiet corner to wait.

Her stomach tightened with anticipation. She had made it.

A handful of passengers climbed the sweeping staircases lined with iron railings to wait next to the rail platforms. Someone sat in the chair across from her, but she didn't bother looking up in case he mistook the acknowledgement as an excuse to make conversation.

"How are you?" he asked anyway.

She lifted her eyes and locked gazes with a man wearing a red, flat-billed baseball cap she recognized from the last bus. "Fine." She offered a polite yet tight smile before looking away.

"What brings you to Worcester?"

What part of her obviously trying to ignore him made him think he should keep talking to her? "I'm visiting my boyfriend." Maybe that would shut him up.

"Told ya she's too pretty to be single," he said to another man in a too-big football jersey approaching the group of chairs. "Let's go."

"Is that any way to treat a nice girl?" The newcomer's voice was confident and steady. "We'll keep her company until her boyfriend gets here."

"There's no need. I see him now." Vivienne stood and

waved at the familiar young man walking through the station's main doors. When he caught sight of her, he grinned.

"You're late," she said, sweeping past Deacon to the exit.

"*I'm* late?" he scoffed, falling in step beside her. "You were supposed to be here *yesterday*." He pushed the door aside and guided her to a black town car.

Once they were inside, Deacon steadied his arm against the passenger headrest and leaned toward the front seat, mumbling something to their driver. The man with thinning grey hair nodded, and Deacon turned back to her.

She had spent the entire journey brainstorming what to say when she saw him again. But at the moment, her mind was blank. "I'm sorry about what happened on the bus," she blurted. "You've been trying to save me ever since we met, and I haven't made your job very easy."

His answering smile was crooked and cocky. "I've always enjoyed a challenge."

"Well, I'm here now. So I guess that means you'll have to find a new challenge."

His dark brows came together. "Does it?"

"Does it?" she repeated, issuing a challenge of her own.

Deacon was the first to look away, but his smile remained. The city lights faded and the buildings shrank as they moved into the suburbs.

"Did you find it hard to leave Ohio?" he asked, all hints of teasing gone.

Vivienne pursed her lips and bit the inside of her cheek. "I didn't really have a choice."

"Care to explain?" A small wrinkle formed between his eyebrows as he searched her face. His stare grew more intense the longer it took for her to answer.

She turned away from him to catch her breath. Raindrops bubbled on the window, glowing like Christmas lights powered by each passing car's headlights.

What had they been talking about?

Oh, right. Ohio.

When she turned back to him, her hood slipped off. "HOOK

showed up at Lynn's, so it was either stay and take my chances or come find you."

Deacon sucked in a breath. He reached toward her cheek, then dropped his hand. "Did HOOK do that to you?"

"No. I fell on the way to the bus station."

His hands flexed into fists. "I told you they would come for you."

"You were honest with me about the other stuff too." Vivienne tried to focus on the dark landscape drifting past the vehicle. She and Deacon were sitting close enough that their knees could touch. Did she want them to?

The driver brought them to the middle of a stretch of road with no streetlights, where a set of imposing wrought iron gates sat between two brick pillars. Beyond the barrier stood a line of trees that could have been the start of a forest.

Deacon paid the driver and grabbed Vivienne's bag for her. The man drove away, leaving the two of them alone with the night.

"It's so dark." She felt a sudden and overwhelming urge to bolt. The fire in her chest sparked to life.

"We don't want people seeing what's happening beyond these walls."

"And that's supposed to make me want to go inside?"

He chuckled.

She traced the letters on the bronze *Kensington Academy* sign fastened to the wall. "You didn't tell me Neverland was a college."

"The whole college thing is a ruse." He leaned over a silver keypad beside the sign. "But it makes it easier to explain why a bunch of teenagers are hanging around together." Deacon typed in a code and the bricks opened to reveal a glowing square.

When he pressed his palm against the square, the gates clicked, jerked, and slid open. Inside, a sleek black car sat parked in a lot. He withdrew a set of keys from his pocket, and the vehicle responded with a chirp. The trunk popped open, and he laid Vivienne's bag into the recess.

She looked back at the closing gates. "That seemed too easy."

He opened the passenger door and ushered her inside. "That's because you can't see the cameras and signal scrambling devices."

She searched for signs of additional surveillance equipment but found nothing. Deacon settled into the driver's seat and pressed a button. The car roared to life.

"Before we go, can I ask you a question?"

"Of course." His hands dropped from the steering wheel and he turned, giving her his undivided attention.

"Why didn't the PAN come and get me if they knew my parents were gone?" In a sea of questions, it was the one that mattered most.

"It's generally against protocol to pick up a child whose Nevergene hasn't activated. If you had grown up in Neverland, it wouldn't have been an issue. But because you didn't..." A shrug.

"Why didn't my parents raise me in Neverland?" That sounded like the best childhood ever.

"They wanted you to have a normal childhood."

She snorted. Moving from one foster home to the next with people like Lynn serving as her guardian wasn't *normal*. It was sad. And lonely.

"Growing up in Neverland," he went on, running his hand along the leather gear shift, "isn't always what's best."

"Are you speaking from personal experience?"

"We're not talking about me." He twisted away and shifted into drive. "We're talking about *you*. And *you* are late."

Driving away from the gates felt like leaving the world behind. She stared into the darkness, wondering what was on the other side of the forest.

For the first time she could remember, Vivienne felt like anything was possible.

The car followed the gravel driveway winding its way through the trees. The wilderness parted, and elegant iron lamps circled the driveway in front of a brick structure that looked like a manor home straight from the pages of a novel.

The building was several stories high, with multiple rows of windows on each level. In the middle was a portico and a magnificent arched black door. The whimsical facade stretched high into the sky until it arced in two different directions like the wings of a bird poised to take flight. The imposing structure shielded the rest of the campus from view.

Deacon leaned forward and followed Vivienne's gaze through the windshield. "Impressed?"

"More like intimidated."

"It's just a building."

Deacon was wrong. It was a chance for a new life.

After retrieving her bag from the trunk, Vivienne followed Deacon up the flagstone stairs to the carved wooden door. Tiny fairies were etched into the panels, their arms and wings outstretched to whatever magical realm slept beyond the barrier.

Deacon lifted the brass knocker shaped like a rooster and knocked twice.

The building remained eerily quiet.

He pounded again, this time with more force. "Come on, Julie! Open up!"

There was a scraping noise from the other side, and the door flew open. A teen with frizzy red hair appeared in a whirl of warm cinnamon-scented air. "*You* are late," she snapped, narrowing her eyes at Deacon. When she saw Vivienne, her face lit up. "And *you* are very welcome."

Julie brought Vivienne into a balmy reception hall with black and white tiled floors, arched windows, and painted coffered ceilings. In the center of the cavernous room, a sweeping staircase encircled a crystal chandelier that looked like it belonged in a palace.

Deacon's hand fell to the small of Vivienne's back, sending shivers up her spine. "Vivienne, this is—"

"I'm Julie. She's Vivienne. Introductions done. Now tell me what happened to your poor face." Julie may have been speaking to Vivienne, but she was glaring at Deacon.

"Don't look at me," he said, dropping his hand. "I had nothing to do with it."

"It's true," Vivienne told her. "I fell."

Julie's features softened and her smile returned. "My good-ness, girl. You look just like your mom. Sound like her too."

"I-I do?" The comment was so unexpected it brought tears to her eyes. She hadn't met anyone who had known her family since the fire.

"You sure do. We were found the same year."

If what Julie said was true, she would be close to fifty years old, which was hard to believe because she looked the same age as Vivienne.

"When she and I first met, we—"

"How about we save the stories for a time when Vivienne *isn't* ready to collapse from exhaustion?" Deacon drawled, nudging Vivienne and Julie past an ornate couch toward an antique desk. The computer on top looked out of place next to the vintage lamp and the stack of old novels.

"Dash gets cranky when he's kept waiting," Julie said, swiping at her frizz and offering Vivienne a conspiratorial wink. "Which is ironic, because he is *always* late." She tugged on one of the dimmed wall lights shaped like a candelabra, revealing a door in the paneled wall behind the desk.

"Why does she call you Dash?" Vivienne asked when Julie disappeared into the secret room. She wondered if the other lights around the hall opened up hidden doors as well.

"My full name is Deacon Ashford," he said, his voice barely rising above the grandfather clock ticking beside them. "A friend back in London shortened it once and it stuck."

"It's much nicer to do this during daylight hours," Julie muttered, emerging with an olive-green folder in her hand. "Are you listening, Dash?"

"We would've been here yesterday if she hadn't been such a skeptic."

"Good for you, Vivienne. Make him work for it. Those pretty green eyes of his usually get him whatever he wants, whenever he wants it."

Although it sounded like Julie was teasing, it felt like there was a lot of truth in what she said.

"Don't listen to her," Deacon whispered, his warm breath

tickling the shell of her ear. "She's an old busybody who can't seem to mind her own business."

"What did you say?" Julie hissed.

Deacon straightened and gave her a sheepish smile. "Nothing, Julie. Do you have the paperwork ready?"

Julie muttered as she dragged papers from the folder and spread them across her desk. She explained each one before asking Vivienne for her signature. The documents seemed pretty straightforward; there was a lot of stuff regarding confidentiality and safety. Vivienne didn't understand all of it, but there was no mention of human sacrifices or blood oaths, so she figured she was okay to go ahead and sign them.

She handed Deacon the pen so he could sign as a witness. Julie added her signature, pressed the sheets with a heavy wooden stamp from beside her computer, and filed the pages in the folder.

"We're all set here," Julie said, slipping the folder back into the secret room and closing the door. "Dash, you can head on home."

Deacon picked up Vivienne's bag from the checkerboard tiles. "I don't mind showing Vivienne to her flat."

"Yeah, that's not happening." Julie took the backpack and slung it over her shoulder. She linked her free arm with Vivienne's and hauled her toward the hallway. Lights came on as they walked, revealing a line of mahogany doors on both sides and an arched window at the end.

Vivienne glanced back once, but Deacon was already gone.

Outside the last door, Julie came to an abrupt stop. "There's someone who needs to speak with you before I bring you to your apartment," she said, opening the door on the left and stepping aside.

Inside, a gentleman sat at a round table. His grey polo shirt matched the hair at his temples and his goatee. He motioned for Vivienne to enter and sit. His eyes, over the thick rims of his glasses, never left the papers scattered in front of him.

The deep green plaster walls were covered in mismatched frames, filled with black-and-white photos. She recognized

Tower Bridge from one of the larger frames and wondered if the rest of the pictures were also from London.

Julie assured her it wouldn't take long before making the introductions. The man's name was Paul Mitter, and he was the head of External Affairs at Kensington. Whatever that meant.

Vivienne sat in the chair closest to the thick gold curtains and waited while Paul collected his pages into a pile. She hid a yawn inside the neck of her sweatshirt. God she was tired.

"I apologize for having to fit this in tonight," he began, "but I will do my absolute best to keep this brief. One of my jobs is to vet new members *before* they arrive at Kensington. However, the presence of HOOK at the hospital tells me that your case requires a bit more investigation." Paul pulled a yellow legal pad from a briefcase at his feet and clicked the top of his pen. "Are you ready to get started?"

Vivienne nodded.

"Did you make contact with anyone after you were admitted to the hospital?"

"Besides the doctors and nurses, you mean?"

"Anyone *outside* of the hospital staff," he clarified.

"I texted Lyle a few times, but no one visited me except Lynn."

Paul scribbled something on his legal pad. "That would be Lynn and Lyle Foley, correct?"

"Yes."

"So, you're telling me, in all that time, not one other person stopped by to see you?"

"That's what I said." Her hands balled into fists in her lap.

He made more illegible notations. "Did you recognize any of the agents from the hospital?"

"I couldn't see them very well from the roof."

It was clear from Paul's pinched expression that he wasn't pleased with her answers. "You have no clue how or when HOOK found out about you?"

"No clue," she said, scratching her leg. "But they knew where I lived."

Paul's eyes met hers, and a glint of victory flashed across his stern features. "What do you mean?"

"Agents were at the house the day I left." Her feet tapped against the floor.

"Did they say anything to you?"

"They didn't know I was there. I had time to get out before they got to my room."

He jotted another note. "That was Friday, correct?"

"Yes."

"Were you followed to the bus stop?"

"No."

"What happened to your—?"

"My face? I fell, okay?"

He rubbed his hand over his goatee and swore. "Is there *anything* you can remember that may help us uncover your connection to HOOK?"

"One of the guys was named Lawrence."

Paul's pen dropped to the floor. "Lawrence *Hooke*?"

"You know who he is?" She didn't know why she asked. The answer was pretty obvious.

"Lawrence Hooke," he repeated, removing his glasses and tossing them onto the table, "is the current CEO for HOOK, and he's rarely seen outside of their facility in Virginia. You, my dear, are very, *very* lucky that you escaped."

EIGHT

The next morning, Vivienne stretched her travel-weary muscles and rolled over in her new bed. The contents of her backpack sat in a messy lump on top of her desk, illuminated by the light in her private en-suite.

She stretched once more before climbing onto her knees and opening the blinds covering the window above her headboard.

The view of Neverland in the raw morning light stole her breath.

She wished Lyle could see it.

Her apartment was across from the big building she had been in the night before—Julie had called it Kensington Hall. Vines climbed the aged red brick, as if nature was slowly reclaiming the structure. In the center of each of the five levels was a window twice as tall as the others. A bronze railing had been attached around the perimeter of the sloping roof, and a black door had been cut into the highest point where she imagined another window should be.

Between the big building and her apartment stretched a manicured lawn with a crushed yellow stone walkway connecting the two. In the center of the walkway, a fountain with a rooster on top bubbled in the early autumn sun. A second walkway running perpendicular to the first connected a small chapel on the left to a second stately house similar to the apartment on the right.

The buildings she could see had all been built using the same red brick, with contrasting decorative gold bricks framing the windows and corners.

There was a knock on her bedroom door, and Vivienne twisted toward where the noise had originated. "Hello?" she called, wondering how this person had gotten in.

A teenaged girl with dark, glossy curls and perfectly sculpted cheekbones poked her head into the room. She gave a small, energetic wave from the doorway. "Good morning, room-mate! I'm Emily."

Roommate? Julie had failed to mention that she had to live with someone.

"I'm Vivienne." She crossed her arms, hiding the state of her soft, hole-ridden cotton T-shirt. It was a far cry from the cute matching ensemble with lace edges that Emily wore.

"*Vivienne.*" Emily tapped her pink nails against the door-frame. "It's kind of long, isn't it? Do you have any nicknames, or do you prefer just Vivienne?" She spoke so fast it made Vivi-enne's head spin.

"Just Vivienne." Lyle was the only one allowed to call her anything else.

Emily's hand steadied. "I suppose it's too pretty to hack into a nickname."

"Thanks? Um...what time is it?" She was having trouble keeping up.

"I dunno. Eight maybe?"

Vivienne groaned and fell back against the warm mattress with a thump. She wasn't sure what time she had fallen asleep last night, but it had been late.

"I've been awake since six waiting for you to wake up," Emily went on, skipping into the room. "I've had two cups of coffee already. Or was it three? I can't remember." She hummed to herself and patted Vivienne's clothes on the desk.

Vivienne had always had more luck being friends with the boys at school, so she didn't have high hopes for getting close to Emily. But if they were going to live together, she was determined to try. She offered her a tentative smile. "Sorry. I'm not really a morning person."

"Oh, it's fine. Most PAN are the same cuz we're only allowed to fly off campus at night. I guess I'm the exception." Emily bounced her way back to the door. "I'll go away so you can wake up. If you're hungry in a bit, maybe we can grab breakfast together?"

Vivienne gave her a thumbs-up and stretched once more before swinging her legs over the edge of the bed. They were only allowed to fly at night. Emily had been so blasé when she had said it.

The small private bathroom had been stocked with generic shampoos and crisp white towels that smelled like they had come straight from a warm dryer. Her cheek looked worse than it had yesterday; the scrapes were oozing and red, the bruise more pronounced.

After a stinging shower, she found a hair dryer in the otherwise empty desk drawer, then got ready to explore Neverland.

Hanging in the closet was a pair of dark tights, a gray T-shirt, and a black hooded sweatshirt. The material was like nothing she had felt before; it was rubbery like neoprene on the outside but had the softness and warmth of fleece on the inside. Somehow, despite the layers, the garment was not bulky or heavy.

She traced the emblem embroidered on the left side of the sweatshirt, over the heart. Similar to the Kensington letterhead on her acceptance letter, a golden rooster lifted its beak toward a pair of stars.

Vivienne dressed in her Kensington gear and ventured into the common area. The living space had a small gray sectional and a rustic coffee table. Next to the TV was a floor-to-ceiling window. It reminded her of the ones in the center of Kensington Hall.

Then she noticed a handle behind the curtain. Not a window. A door.

A glass door that had nothing but air on the other side.

She pressed her hand against the cold pane to check the

three-story drop. A small silver keypad had been attached to the exterior wall beside the door.

It would be a long time before she felt comfortable using *that* as an exit.

Emily came bounding down the hall wearing the same outfit as Vivienne. "I have something for you." She held out a white tube. "It's antibiotic ointment. For your face."

"Thanks. I fell down a few days ago."

"I wasn't going to ask."

"Really?" Everyone else had.

"I figured you'd tell me if you wanted to."

Maybe she and Emily could be close after all. Vivienne brought the ointment to the mirror and smeared it on her raw cheek. It stung at first, then went numb.

"Are you hungry?" Emily asked when she gave back the tube. "Because I am starving."

Vivienne rubbed her growling stomach. "I could eat."

"Want to get food at The Glass House?"

"Is it far?"

"No way! It's right downstairs." Emily grabbed Vivienne's hand and hauled her toward the front door.

Out in the hall, frames had been attached to the greenish-blue walls. She had noticed them the night before—there were so many, it was hard not to. But she had been too tired to inspect them.

They were all of the same place: a field with low stone fences and a single tree. Some were black and white, and others were in color and taken in different seasons.

"What's with these?" She pointed to one of the shots taken in the height of autumn. The tree looked like it was on fire with brilliant orange, yellow, and red leaves.

Emily touched a black and white one with snow sticking to the tree's barren branches. "One of the lost boys is really into photography. I can't remember which one."

Between the photographs, Vivienne counted three more doors identical to theirs. Did one of them belong to Deacon? "Does everyone live on campus?"

"Only until our training is finished. Pam has her own apartment on this level." Emily pointed to the end of the hall. "Adam and Cole room together on the ground floor. And Max has the second floor to himself at the moment."

"How long have you been in Never—at Kensington?" Emily knew too much for someone who had just arrived.

"It's okay to call it Neverland." Emily flipped her hair over her shoulders. "I do it sometimes too. And to answer your question, I got here last week."

"I still can't get my head around the fact that Neverland exists."

"I'm pretty used to the idea now." Emily inclined her head toward a window. The sky beyond was a crisp, cloudless blue. "Once you see it during the day, it'll feel more real—crazy, but real."

When they reached the inner stairwell, Emily took off at a brisk jog, and Vivienne struggled to keep up. Once out of the building, Emily resumed a normal pace.

A stitch pulled in Vivienne's stomach, and she pinched her side to relieve the sharp aching. "What the heck was that about?"

Emily stretched her quads and explained that everyone on campus sprinted up *and* down the stairs. "I'm still not sure why," she said, "but I didn't want to stick out like a weirdo, so I started running too. Now I do it without even thinking."

Vivienne stood to her full height, which was up to Emily's chin, and winced at the sky. No wonder Deacon had looked so athletic. "I'd take mermaids and pirates over a bunch of sprinting immortals this early in the morning."

"You'll get used to it," Emily laughed.

The sun glinted off the dew around Kensington's picturesque grounds. Vivienne turned in a slow circle, taking it all in.

Behind their apartment, more crushed stone led to flagstone stairs built into a slight incline. At the top of the incline sat a Victorian greenhouse. A patio dotted with picnic tables surrounded the transparent structure. The Glass House, she assumed.

To its left stood a smaller version of Union Station with a

domed glass roof. Emily called it the Aviary and said they taught Aviation classes there.

Beyond it stretched a green lawn that ended at a bordering forest.

A group of loud teens approached the flagstone stairs, raced to the top step, then resumed their casual stroll. When Vivienne and Emily reached the stairs, they did the same.

There was still one building that Emily hadn't mentioned. "What's that over there?" It looked like a smaller version of the apartments.

A girl with dreadlocks and striking blue eyes strolled past wearing a black Kensington sweatshirt, short jean shorts, and black cowboy boots. Her legs looked longer than Vivienne's entire body.

"That's where Peter and the other members of Leadership stay when they're at Kensington," Emily said.

"As in...Peter Pan?"

Emily put an arm around Vivienne's shoulders and squeezed. "Exactly."

"Have you actually met him?" She had so many questions.

"Not yet. Far as I can tell, he and Leadership only show up when there's a problem."

Delighted to have her bearings, Vivienne followed Emily into the greenhouse.

The dining area consisted of twenty or so marble-topped tables surrounded by plush, high-backed chairs. In the kitchen, teenagers in chef hats prepared meals for their fellow PAN. Emily led Vivienne to an empty table equipped with two tablets. The technology felt foreign in such an antiquated space.

Vivienne patted her pockets and groaned. "I left my money in the room." A pitiful gurgle echoed from her hollow stomach.

Emily stopped scrolling long enough to tell her that everything was free.

"We don't have to pay for anything?" Vivienne's hungry eyes devoured the extensive digital menu.

"Not a penny."

Two guys sat at a table across from them. The one in the gray fedora had shoulder-length copper hair. His dark plaid pants looked too short, hiked up by the suspenders he wore over his black shirt. The only burst of color in his ensemble were the rainbow striped socks sticking out from beneath the hem.

The second guy's buzzed black hair peeked from beneath the black Kensington cap he wore. His gray thermal top spilled over his black cargo shorts.

The only thing they had in common was the mischievous glint in their eyes. She'd seen it in Deacon's eyes as well. And in Julie and Emily's.

Vivienne ordered enough food to feed an army and wondered if her eyes would ever look the same.

"Welcome to Orientation for the People with Active Nevergenes —or PAN," a smiley teenager with short black hair and a pierced septum welcomed. "My name is Penelope and I couldn't be more pleased for the three of you to be joining us today." She motioned to two empty desks using the pen in her hand and waited for Vivienne and Emily to take their seats.

There was a guy with spiky brown hair there already. He smiled at the girls but remained quiet.

Penelope touched her ear and mumbled something.

Vivienne glanced at Emily, but she looked equally confused.

"You're here because you possess the incredibly rare Never-gene," Penelope went on, "a genetic mutation that, when active, keeps you eighteen forever and"—she nodded to the windows —"allows you to fly."

Vivienne thought she saw movement outside and rose from her chair. Sure enough, a group of PAN floated above the fountain.

"Check it out!" The guy slid out of his desk and went to the window. Emily jumped to her feet and followed him. Vivienne went to the window at the back of the classroom.

The levitating teenagers waved at them before flying off in different directions. Two of them landed daintily beside the fountain. One guy, the one with the rainbow socks, spun upward and out of sight. Another girl flipped, then shot toward The Glass House. And the last boy pretended to backstroke toward the library.

"The Nevergene is unpredictable," Penelope said when they were back in their seats, "and it remains inactive in the majority of people. Our goal is to ensure one hundred percent activation, so that every PAN has the same opportunity to live—and soar— forever. To help us achieve this goal, we have teams of researchers all over the world conducting tests on PAN DNA.

"Each of you represents another piece of the Nevergene puzzle." Penelope tapped her pen against the desk. "Giving our researchers access to your DNA could lead to a breakthrough. You could be the one to help us save our friends and family who possess inactive Nevergenes."

Hearing her talk about DNA made Vivienne's hands tingle. "HOOK wants our DNA too."

"Hold up." The guy straightened in his chair and twisted toward her. "No one told me Captain Hook was real."

"I see your recruiter has been very informative, Vivienne." Penelope wiggled her pen between her fingers. "Who brought you in?"

The way she said it made it sound like Vivienne had done something wrong. "Deacon Ashford."

"No surprise there..." Penelope sighed and went to the whiteboard to write HOOK in bold red letters. Using the marker as a pointer, she explained about the Humanitarian Organization for Order and Knowledge. "For decades they have been using PAN DNA to try and unlock the secret of eternal life for profit," she said, replacing the marker in the tray and returning to the front of her desk.

"HOOK conducts unsanctioned experiments on PAN, then neutralizes their test subjects with a poison they've developed to *deactivate* Nevergenes. If a PAN's Nevergene has been active for over ten years, the results can be fatal." She crossed her arms and looked pointedly at Vivienne. "So, HOOK and Neverland are interested in PAN DNA for two very different reasons. In addition to working tirelessly to artificially *activate* Nevergenes, we're developing an antidote that would keep us safe from

HOOK's poison. And, unlike with HOOK, DNA donation in Neverland is not compulsory."

Emily raised her hand. "You just want us to give blood?"

"That and a cheek swab," Penelope confirmed with a nod.

Emily gave her a thumbs up and said she was in.

"Yeah…" The guy scratched his neck. "I guess if you think it'll help, I'm in too."

"It will. Thank you, Max." Penelope turned to Vivienne.

"I've had enough needles stuck in me this week," she said, touching the fading bruise on the back of her itchy hand. "I may hold off for right now, if that's okay."

"That's entirely up to you." Penelope's smile never wavered. She set a small red booklet on each student's desk. "Unlike donating, following Neverland's rules is mandatory. To stay safe, we stay hidden. And to stay hidden, we follow the rules."

Vivienne lifted booklet. *Neverland Policies* was printed in bold black letters on the front.

"These policies have helped us hide from outsiders and from HOOK for over a century. One of the rules states that only Kensington-approved cellular devices can be used on and near campus. Did you bring your cell phones?"

"Don't go anywhere without it," Max said, pulling his phone from his back pocket.

Although it was currently in pieces, Vivienne had brought hers out of habit. She found the bits in the front of her backpack and reassembled them on her desk.

Penelope brought four black bags printed with the Kensington crest from behind her desk and asked them to trade their phones for orientation bags.

"What? Why?" Max clutched his phone to his chest.

"We don't want HOOK tracing them to our location."

"But HOOK doesn't know about me."

Penelope leaned close; the smile that had been on her face since the beginning of class disappeared. "Are you willing to bet your own life—and the life of every other PAN in Kensington—on that?"

Max shook his head and handed over his cell phone.

Penelope took the phone and gave him a bag. "Don't worry, there's a new one inside of this."

Emily looked down at the dark screen in her hand and asked about all her photos. Vivienne had been wondering the same thing.

"You can save everything to your new laptop after our technicians disable them."

"We get computers?" Emily shoved her phone away, and Penelope replaced it with a bag.

After a brief hesitation, Vivienne set her phone on the desk too. The orientation bag Penelope handed her was heavier than she'd expected.

Penelope opened a fourth bag and started pulling out the contents one item at a time. "Your new phones come pre-loaded with all imperative phone numbers, including Kensington's main line and the extension for extraction, Neverland's version of 911." She pressed a button on the phone and the screen turned on. "We've also stored contact details for your fellow classmates and your recruiters, if applicable."

Vivienne's stomach flipped when she scrolled to find Deacon's number in her small list of contacts. Was he out finding more PAN, or was he close by? Would she see him again soon? She secretly hoped so.

Penelope explained that they wouldn't be allowed to access their social media accounts on their phones or laptops unless they were outside of the state. "Vivienne, because of the situation at the hospital, it would be best if you deleted your accounts altogether. We'll organize a secure location for you to do so in the next few weeks."

Vivienne nodded, uncomfortable with the way Emily and Max stared at her.

"What's she talking about?" Emily whispered.

"Tell you later."

Penelope continued digging through the bag. "You each have a copy of *Peter Pan and Wendy*, signed by Peter."

Vivienne's hand trembled when she opened the front cover of her book. After the title page was a picture of Kensington's crest. Below the crest was a handwritten note.

You're as much a part of this story as I am.
Welcome to Neverland
-Peter

She traced Peter's bold signature and tried to picture what he looked like. Definitely short. Red hair. Pointy ears, like an elf.

Penelope cleared her throat, and Vivienne closed the cover with a snap.

"You'll get to choose a watch from the catalogue." Penelope showed off the silver one on her wrist. It looked similar to the one Deacon had worn. "All Kensington watches have an altimeter fitted to let you know how high you're flying. You also have a schedule of classes for the next few months—the remainder of your high school curriculum will be covered in the mornings, and PAN-based classes are held in the afternoons."

Max groaned.

Vivienne felt the same way. When she'd left Ohio, she had assumed high school was a thing of the past.

"You'll find some additional Kensington shirts at the bottom, and I have a credit card for each of you that gives you access to Neverland funds." She passed around cards stuck to a piece of paper. "You can use them at any ATM or as a regular credit card for purchases. If you buy anything online, use the address listed on this sheet as your mailing address."

Vivienne pressed her thumb against the name embossed on the card, leaving an indentation of the words *PANE Aviation, Inc.* on her skin.

Emily slipped her card into her copy of *Peter Pan.* "Is there a spending limit on these?"

"No. And I trust that none of you will take advantage of it."

"Wouldn't dream of it." Emily hid her smile behind her hand.

"Since the administrative stuff is out of the way, I'm giving you this list of career paths." Penelope passed Vivienne a stack of spiral-bound books. Vivienne took one, then handed the rest to Emily. "I encourage you to find roles that foster your individual passions. I'm passionate about teaching, so I teach. Emily? What are you passionate about?"

"Um..." Emily tapped her nail against her lips. "I like shopping."

"Would you believe we have personal shoppers in Neverland?" Penelope stepped in front of Max's desk. "What about you?"

"I dunno about passion," Max said with a shrug, "but before I came here, I wanted to join the state police."

"It sounds like extraction may be your calling." Penelope moved next to Vivienne. "And you?"

"I don't know." Vivienne scratched the back of her hands, but the motion only made the itching worse. Penelope kept staring at her like she was waiting for a better answer. Vivienne shoved her sleeves up to her elbows and scraped her burning arms.

Couldn't she move on? Talk about something else?

"What made you decide to come to Neverland?"

The unbearable tingling under her skin forced Vivienne to rip off her sweatshirt. Her ponytail came loose, and she collected her hair tie from the floor. "I said I don't know." Her nails left angry red streaks on her arms.

"Close your eyes and take three deep breaths."

Vivienne stopped scratching. "What?"

"Breathe..." Penelope's eyes fell closed. "In through your nose...and out through your mouth."

Vivienne felt her face turn red, but she followed Penelope's instructions. After she exhaled the third breath, the itchiness subsided. "Thanks."

"The tingling was always the worst part for me too," Penelope said in a soothing voice. "Your body is adjusting to surges of adrenaline from your fight-or-flight response. It'll even out soon enough."

Vivienne pulled her sweatshirt back over her head to hide her raw skin.

"I'm going to ask you again, and if you feel your adrenaline spike, try to breathe through it." After Vivienne nodded, Penelope asked her why she had come to Neverland.

With her eyes fixed on the desk, Vivienne took a deep breath. "Because I wanted to belong somewhere."

"You belong right here." Penelope gave her red hand a reassuring squeeze. "It sounds like you should check out our recruiting program."

That made her think of Deacon, and her adrenaline spiked for an entirely different reason.

"All right everyone, I want you to leave your things here and come with me. It's time to get you linked to Neverland's security system."

NINE

They followed Penelope to a door concealed in the paneling near the reception area. Behind the door, she pulled the string on a single exposed bulb and started down a narrow stairwell with creaky wooden treads.

"Someone needs to fire the maid," Max muttered, swiping at one of the many cobwebs hanging on the chipping plaster walls.

Vivienne gulped the musty air and moved closer to Emily. If she saw a spider, she was going to end up embarrassing herself even worse than she had upstairs.

"They're fake," Penelope said when they reached the concrete pad at the bottom. "We don't want outsiders thinking we use this area for anything important."

At the end of a short, damp passageway, light seeped from beneath a wooden door with a dented silver knob.

Deacon had been kidding when he said there were human sacrifices, right?

This looked like the place to avoid on Wednesdays, just in case.

On the other side of the door was a corridor barely big enough for the four of them. Vivienne stayed between Emily and Max in case there were cobwebs on the cement walls—fake or not.

Penelope pulled the string attached to another hanging bulb.

The tight space felt smaller in the dark; Vivienne's adrenaline surged. She squeezed her eyes shut and took a deep breath. Before she could take a second breath, she heard a mechanical hum.

Her eyes snapped open in time to catch a glowing blue screen emerging from the wall. Penelope bent, and the screen scanned her eye, then the wall to their left disappeared, revealing a massive, state-of-the-art laboratory.

There wasn't a cobweb in sight.

"Hey, Penelope," a guy greeted with a smile as broad as his shoulders. "Are these the newest PAN?" His southern accent and deep voice were as smooth as apple butter.

"They sure are." Penelope waved the newcomers into the room. "Max, Emily, and Vivienne, this is Robert, head of R&D at our on-campus lab."

"Hey, y'all." Robert's black hair had the slightest hint of a curl. "Welcome to my little paradise within paradise."

"What's happening down here?" Emily touched one of the microscopes on the table beside her.

"We're responsible for helping Neverland survive in secrecy by creating and modifying Nevertech. But we also maintain the security system on campus and"—Robert indicated a row of frosted windows behind him—"house a large microbiology sector for research."

"Research on the Nevergene, right?" Vivienne said. A woman opened the door to the back section, and she tried to catch a glimpse of what was going on inside.

"They mostly handle the inactive Nevergene problem in the London lab." Robert tucked his hands into his lab coat pockets. "Here, we're trying to improve our ageless injection and analyze the adverse effects of HOOK's poison."

"Why do we need an ageless injection?" Vivienne asked.

"You and I don't. But we need to administer an injection to anyone without an active Nevergene who marries a PAN."

74

Vivienne's mouth dropped open. Surely he wasn't saying . . . You can keep normal people from getting older too?"

"I wish." Robert picked up a vial of pink liquid from the desk beside him. "So far, we've only been able to keep them from *looking* older." Robert replaced the vial and clapped his hands. "How about we get movin' so we can get y'all back out into that beautiful sunshine? Who's first?"

When no one volunteered, Vivienne lifted a hesitant hand. "I'll go first."

"Great," Robert said with a smile. "Vivienne, right?"

She nodded.

"I knew it!" He smacked his thigh. "You look just like your momma." He told the others to have a seat and asked Vivienne to follow him.

"You knew my mom?"

"Sure did. But I knew your dad better. He worked here in the lab before they moved to Ohio."

If her dad had moved to Ohio, what had happened to him?

Vivienne followed Robert past teenage workers hunkered over tables and wondered how many of them had known her family. "What'd he do here?"

He snapped on a pair of rubber gloves from a box on his desk. "Your dad was studying the way HOOK's poison deactivates Nevergenes." He scooted a silver tray with vials and needles in sanitary packages closer to where Vivienne stood and asked if she had eaten breakfast.

"Yeah. At The Glass House. Why?"

"I don't want you getting woozy after giving blood."

The smell of alcohol lifted to her nose when Robert ripped open the antiseptic swab. "I'm not giving blood."

He set the antiseptic back on the tray and frowned. "Why not?"

Vivienne crossed her tingling arms over her chest. *Breathe in. Breathe out.* "I just think I should wait."

Robert picked up a giant Q-tip in a sanitary packet. "What about a cheek swab?"

Vivienne shook her head.

"All right then..." He moved the tray to the other side of the

75

desk. "Will you let me scan you for biometric access, or do you want to wait on that too?"

"Yeah. That sounds okay."

After scanning her retinas, fingerprints, and palms, Robert stood and walked to a table against the wall. He came back lugging what looked like an antique astronaut helmet. The bulky piece of equipment was attached to a thick rope of woven electrical cords.

"This beauty scans your head, face, and neck so we can create a customized earpiece and helmet for you."

She touched the blacked-out visor. "Will it be as big as this one?"

"Goodness, no. Could you imagine trying to go unnoticed with this thing on your head?" Robert clicked some buttons on his keyboard and plugged the helmet into the USB port.

With Robert's assistance, she lifted the monstrous contraption over her head until the heavy base rested on her shoulders. Inside the helmet was a gray screen. A vertical line of green lights flashed in her peripheral vision. The helmet began beeping, and the green line ticked pixel-by-pixel across her vision and toward the back of her head before returning to where it had started.

Then the green line disappeared and was replaced by a red line, horizontal across the visor. It blinked from a point below her nose, went down to the base of the contraption and then back up again.

The red light disappeared, and a muffled voice from outside of the helmet told her to take it off.

A computerized image of her features appeared as digitized dots on Robert's computer screen. An assistant handed her a laminated sheet of text and a microphone and told her to read what was on the paper.

She touched the mic to her lips. "Hey there. Hello. Are you asking a question? Pizza, please. Yes. No. I would like to have that for dinner. Would you? Emergency. Your name." She returned the mic.

He handed it right back. "No, you need to say your name."

She lifted the microphone closer to her mouth. "Vivienne Dunn."

"Perfect." He collected his things and moved back to where Emily was waiting.

After everyone was scanned, probed, pricked, and recorded, Robert asked each of them to choose a four-digit PIN for access to Kensington's gates and the stairless entries.

With the extensive process finished, they returned to their classroom on the second floor. Penelope was reading a book with her ankles propped on her desk.

When she saw them, she closed the book and set it aside. "I know you all must be hungry and anxious to get to know one another, so we'll finish up for the day. But before I let you go, there's one more thing I want to tell you. All of these things"— she lifted her orientation bag—"can be replaced. But you cannot be. If you're ever in trouble and need a quick exit, leave *everything* behind. You are in charge of *you*. You're not responsible for your fellow PAN. You're not responsible for any of this insignificant technology. You are responsible for keeping yourself safe."

Vivienne and the others collected their backpacks and orientation bags and headed for the door.

"That...was...*awesome!*" Emily gushed. "Like, a million times cooler than I expected. Did you guys see all those gadgets downstairs? Robert told me they have these things that are like tiny drones for spying on HOOK. And that ageless injection? Wow. Just wow."

The lab had been pretty cool. Still, it all seemed a little too good to be true.

The warm sun glinted off the rooster's sightless bronze eyes. The recesses along the feathers had turned blue from age and weather. As with the crest on Vivienne's sweatshirt, its beak lifted toward two stars, built like a halo around the figure. Water cascaded down the base, bubbling quietly as it fell into the shallow pool at the bottom.

Vivienne watched Max throw a smile toward Emily and

increase his pace. Emily matched his stride easily with her long legs. When he had challenged her to a race across campus, Vivienne doubted he had expected Emily to keep up.

By the time she reached them at The Glass House, they were both doubled over, red-faced and breathing heavily.

"Who won?" she asked, holding the door open for them.

Max raised his hand. "That would be me."

"Only because you got a head start," Emily muttered, shoving him into the dining room.

Vivienne went to an empty table in the far corner. The wall of glass behind them overlooked the forest, giving her a new view of the far side of the Kensington campus. She set her backpack and bag on the floor beside her chair but kept her eyes on the colorful leaves. "How big do you think the forest is?"

Emily picked up the tablet in the center of the table. "It's exactly a mile from the first tree to the wall around Kensington." When she finished placing her order, she handed Vivienne the tablet.

"How could you possibly know that?" Max asked, knocking on the marble top with his knuckle.

Vivienne scrolled through the menu, listening for Emily's answer. Did she want soup or a salad? Or a cheeseburger? Oh! They had pie. How long had it been since she had eaten pie?

Was she hungry enough to order all of it?

"I'm a second-generation PAN." Emily explained that her grandmother was one of them, and that her dad's Nevergene had never activated.

Vivienne ordered and slid the tablet across the table to Max. "Have you known about Neverland your entire life?"

"No way. My parents only told me about Kensington when my Nevergene activated."

"Did they come with you?" Vivienne had lost her family so long ago it was hard to imagine what it would be like to have her brother and sister nearby.

"Yeah. They have a house about ten miles from here. I could've stayed with them, but I thought living on campus would be way more fun."

"Did you have a recruiter, Max," Vivienne said, feeling at a disadvantage, "or did you find out about this place from your family too?"

"Recruiter. I got put into the system after my grandma died. Two weeks ago, I got really dizzy and felt like crap. Then this guy shows up to the house telling me I'm part of Peter Pan's gang or whatever."

Vivienne went to rest her hand on her cheek and winced. She had forgotten about her sore face. "And you went with him, even though all of that sounds crazy?"

Max shrugged and spun the tablet on the table. "I figured it had to be better than the place I'd been living since I lost Grams. Plus, he told me I would find out what happened to my family if I came with."

Emily scooted her chair closer to the table. "Are you guys bringing anyone with you?"

"We're allowed to do that?" Vivienne rushed.

Max nodded. "My recruiter told me that if we're on our own, we can invite someone to come with us." He fished around inside his bag and withdrew the red rule book. "There's probably something about it in here."

Vivienne dumped the contents of her bag onto the table and found her own copy of *Neverland Policies*.

"I'm borrowing this." Emily pulled the spiral-bound book of career paths from beneath Vivienne's *Peter Pan*.

"No photographs with PAN, no photographs of Neverland," Max said from behind his booklet. "Flying outside Neverland during daylight hours is strictly prohibited unless we're under threat. Man, these people love saying no." He closed the booklet and found his own list of career paths.

"We're a secret society," Emily said, leafing through pages like she was looking for something. "They're hardly going to let us do whatever we want."

"It says here"—Vivienne dragged her finger along the words as she read aloud—"'A PAN may nominate one individual to join him/her in Neverland after the outsider has been vetted and received unanimous approval from the Leadership committee.'" The only person she wanted to invite was Lyle. But how did she nominate him?

Deacon soaked in the September sun from the roof of Kensington Hall. The breeze carried the crisp smell of autumn, but the air was still fairly mild for so close to October.

Across campus, Vivienne emerged from The Glass House with two other PAN he assumed were also new recruits. He ran to the gutter and dove over the edge, landing with the slightest crunch in the gravel next to the fountain.

Vivienne waved at him and turned to say something to her friends. They continued to the apartment building, and she jogged to where he waited.

"I see you're still stalking me," she said. Her cheek looked worse than it had the night before, and her hands were red and marked. Her hormone levels must have been running high.

"Would you believe me if I said seeing you was a coincidence?" Ethan was supposed to be meeting him for lunch.

"Nope." She laughed and brushed her hair over her shoulders. "I'm mad at you, by the way. You should have told me I was allowed to bring someone to Neverland."

"Should I have told you before we jumped off the hospital roof"—he kicked some gravel toward the fountain—"or after you left me on the bus?"

Her defiant brown eyes narrowed. "How about you tell me now?"

He explained the complicated procedure for nominations. With each step, her frown deepened. It was possible to bring in outsiders, but not easy. "Once your case is cleared by External Affairs, you'll be able to submit your nomination to Leadership."

"Really?" Her eyes brightened for a split second before she frowned and started chewing on her lip. "Paul didn't say anything about it when I met with him."

She'd met Paul? Why the hell hadn't he been told? "When did you meet with him?"

"After you left last night. He kept hinting that I knew something about the HOOK agents that I wasn't telling him." She adjusted her grip on her bag, exposing more marks on her raw arms. "It made me feel guilty, even though I didn't do anything wrong. At least I don't think I did."

"You didn't do anything wrong. Paul is an ass."

That brought the smile back to her lips. "Well, he didn't seem to want me here, that's for sure. So I doubt he'd be into me bringing a friend."

Lucky for her, it wasn't up to Paul. The final decision was Peter's. "I had no idea he would subject you to an interrogation before you had a chance to rest or settle in."

Vivienne scratched at her wrists. "It's fine."

"No. It's not." He hid his fists in his pockets. "If you'll excuse me, I just realized I forgot to give Julie something last night." Deacon turned and stalked back to the Hall. He went directly to Paul's office and knocked, but didn't wait to be called inside.

Paul set the mug in his hand on the notepad in front of him and groaned. "Oh, great. You're back."

"Why did you interrogate Vivienne last night?"

Paul leaned back in his chair and returned Deacon's glare. "You know my job is to—"

"I know very well what your job is. My mother gave it to you."

Paul shot forward and smacked his palms against his desktop. "If you're pissed that I'm making sure a new recruit isn't going to damn us all to hell, then that's your problem. But I'm not putting my family and friends in jeopardy."

Deacon dragged on the ends of his hair. "I already told you she was clean!"

Paul's mouth lifted at the corners even as his eyes narrowed behind his glasses. Why did he look so smug? Deacon felt his bravado wane.

"Did Vivienne tell you that Lawrence Hooke was at her house before she left?"

"*What?*" The last time Lawrence Hooke left Virginia, Vivienne's parents had ended up dead.

"Vivienne claims that she escaped before Lawrence searched the property, but we can't corroborate her story." Paul settled back into his chair. "For all we know, she was meeting with him to report on you and your failed attempt to bring her to Neverland."

Paul thought this was *his* fault?

Deacon had done his bloody job.

Vivienne had been sitting beside him on the bus, safe from HOOK, willing to give up her life and come to Neverland.

Until she realized that she had been abandoned.

"I *failed* because Neverland allowed Vivienne to rot away in a system where she felt alone for over a decade." His nails dug into his palms when he squeezed his hands into fists. "But I suppose that wouldn't have been an issue if Neverland hadn't failed her parents first."

TEN

B y the end of Vivienne's second day in Neverland, she had gotten used to the youthful instructors looking like they belonged in a seat next to her. That night, she stayed up until 3 a.m. reading *Peter Pan and Wendy* from cover to cover.

When she allowed herself to sleep, her dreams were ravaged by pillaging pirates, mischievous mermaids, and fickle fairies.

Joseph, a young man of eighteen—fifty-five times over—opened their history class the following day by asking how many of them had read the book the night before.

Three hands lifted toward the ceiling.

"Every single time," he murmured, a smile on his smooth face. "I usually begin our first class by discussing J.M. Barrie and his role in all of this." Joseph grabbed a marker from the desk drawer to write the author's name on the white board.

"Peter was a fan of Barrie's earlier novel, *Sentimental Tommy*. The two were introduced in London in 1898 and became friends." He snapped the lid back on the marker. "Remember, there were no smart phones back then, so literature was key to communication. Peter thought that if there were others like him who heard stories about a boy who could fly, they may be compelled to contact the author"—Joseph pointed back to Barrie's name—"who would direct them to Peter."

Emily paused her note taking to ask if it worked.

"Albert and Henry were found this way." Joseph returned to the board to write their names. "Two may not seem like a lot, but there were only seven PAN at the time, and adding two more to the ranks was a huge success."

Vivienne raised her hand. "I keep coming back to Peter. In the book, he's a little kid who can fly, but our Nevergenes don't activate until eighteen."

Joseph sat on the corner of his desk and held his copy of *Peter Pan* in the air. "At its heart, this book is a fairy tale. But, as with most stories, there is a modicum of truth behind it. This fictional Peter Pan"—he pointed to the boy flying on the cover —"is an amalgamation of Barrie's brother David, who died tragically on the eve of his thirteenth birthday, and our Peter, the first PAN on record who could fly and will forever look eighteen."

"But how did Peter find out he could fly?" Max asked.

Joseph set the book down on the desk. "There was an accident and he fell off of something very high. Instead of landing and getting hurt, he flew."

Vivienne lifted the pages then let them fall like a flip book. "What did Peter—?"

"Let's move away from Peter for the minute and focus on..." Joseph stopped when Max's hand shot into the air. "Yes, Max?"

"Are the lost boys real?"

"The lost boys were the first People with Active Nevergenes that Peter found. Most of us are descendants of the original members."

Vivienne opened to the inscription in her book. "Will we ever get to meet Peter?"

"Of course you will." Joseph stood and walked back to erase the whiteboard. "He's based in Harrow, but he comes to Kensington a few times a year."

Max leaned forward and asked what Peter did now.

"He serves as the head of Leadership." Joseph drew a circle and wrote *Peter* in the middle. Then he drew seven lines from the center circle. "Leadership is a panel of seven PAN—eight if you count Peter—who act as the governing body for all the Neverlands."

Vivienne studied the drawing and wondered where she fit into the fantastical world. "Are there records of us all some-where?" Maybe she would be able to find information about her dad.

"We keep records of every PAN we know, and you'll learn your own family history during your genealogy meeting. But Peter and his team are working to identify others who carry the Nevergene and are not related to the original lost boys." Joseph tossed the marker into the tray.

"What's the deal with the crocodile?" Vivienne asked.

Joseph went to the low bookshelf beneath the window and picked up an old alarm clock. "In the book, the crocodile lurks in the background, tick-tick-ticking, until finally, it eats the villainous Captain Hook." He twisted the knob on the back of the clock, and it started to tick. "Like the fairy tale pirate captain," he went on, "HOOK is bent on poisoning every PAN alive, taking away our ability to fly or killing us outright. And Peter has been searching for a plan to end HOOK's existence—a crocodile, if you will, to stop them for good."

"What's the plan?" Emily clutched her book to her chest.

All three students leaned closer to where Joseph stood. "We don't know yet." He returned to his desk and set the clock on top of his book. "But we keep these Charlie Bell clocks around campus to remind us that HOOK's time is nearly up."

The week built to a climax in Vivienne's final class on Friday: Aviation. The flight instructor was an attractive blond teen named Joel who looked like he belonged at the starting line of a triathlon.

Three slender balconies lined the walls of the Aviary. There was a set of stairs beside the main entrance, but Vivienne imag-ined they went unused considering the space was used for teaching people to fly.

Ornate coving linked the walls to the ceiling. The dome was

fitted with panes of stained glass colored like patches of the sky, held in place with white decorative supports. According to Emily, the glass could retract with a press of a button.

After brief introductions, they joined Joel for a run up and down the stairs. The excitement she had felt before class was quickly replaced with muscles protesting movement and lungs gasping for oxygen. When Joel allowed them to stop, they collapsed onto the cool, refreshing floor. Thick blue-gray veins twisted along the white marble tiles, reminding her of rivers in winter.

"Any time you come to a *flight* of stairs, you need to run, not walk," Joel said, wiping his face with the bottom of his sweat-drenched T-shirt. "Most pursuers won't be fit enough to catch you. And they'll think that once you get to the top, there will be nowhere left to go."

"It's a good thing we're learning to fly." Max wiped the sweat from his forehead. "Because right now, I don't think I can walk."

Joel clapped his hands and told them it was time to start.

Start? Vivienne and her trembling legs were ready to finish.

"First step," Joel said, handing out blue pills, "pixie dust under the tongue until they dissolve."

The name made Vivienne chuckle.

Emily smelled it first, then shrugged and put it beneath her tongue. Her nose wrinkled, and she frowned. "Tastes gross."

Vivienne turned the dark blue pill in her fingers before doing the same. She didn't mind the taste.

"I'm going to need all of you to close your eyes and clear your mind. Focus on breathing in and out."

"All I can focus on is my legs," Max whined.

"I know you're hurting," Joel said without an ounce of sympathy, "but you have to learn to overcome physical pain and all outside stimuli if you're going to fly."

The hollow room grew quiet until only the sounds of breathing and the occasional rustle of clothing remained.

"Now, think of your happiest memory."

Vivienne's hypersensitive skin began to prickle and itch. Instead of giving in to the urge to scratch, she breathed deeper.

Fed by the increase in oxygen, the fire within her chest expanded until it reached every inch of her body. She thought of visiting the playground with William—the one with the wavy slide. As she lifted upward, her eyes opened, and her chest swelled with pride when she saw how far above the ground she hovered.

Max floated unsteadily near her waist, as if he was dangling from an invisible string. His arms flailed at first, then steadied. Emily giggled from a few feet below him.

"Hey, Joel?" Vivienne called from the third balcony. "How do we get down?" She didn't feel like bruising her face again.

"Just turn it down." He said it like the answer should have been obvious.

"Turn what down?"

"Your adrenaline."

Turn it down. Vivienne closed her eyes and imagined a valve over her heart, pumping adrenaline into her floating body. She twisted it to the right and felt her tingling subside. When she opened her eyes, she had reached the first balcony. She turned the imaginary valve slowly; her adrenaline seeped from her limbs and collected inside her chest for safe keeping.

Joel gave her a high-five when she landed next to him. "Now it's time for me to explain a few *ground* rules. Just because you *can* fly doesn't mean you *should*. Consider this an escape mechanism instead of your default mode of transportation. When you take off and land, be aware of your surroundings and check for prying eyes, cameras, or low-flying aircraft."

Max stepped forward and asked if they would always have to take pixie dust beforehand.

Joel retrieved a small bag of pills for each of them from the larger bag at his feet. "After a lot of practice, the need for these will become obsolete. Even so, you're advised to keep it on your person for the rare occasions when you need an extra boost of adrenaline." Joel zipped the bag and let it drop to the floor. "Now, how about we try lifting off once more before we call an end to class?"

The following week consisted of endless stairs and squats. That Friday, they added a two-mile run around campus to the start of the class. Endorphins, Joel explained, were an essential element of flying, and being in peak physical condition was vital for completing long-haul flights.

At the end of week three, Joel brought them to the stairs in Kensington Hall. After climbing five stories at a brisk pace, their reward was a fresh October breeze on the rooftop. It took only a few minutes for Vivienne to cool down.

Beside her, Emily rubbed her bare arms. "A-are we d-done, Joel? I'm f-freezing."

"We're done," he said with a mischievous smile, "but you're not going back the way you came up. Follow me." He took off running and dove over the edge.

Heck. Yeah. Vivienne wanted to do *that*.

She definitely wasn't ready yet, but when she was, she was going to dive off of everything.

"I'll go first." Max's voice held a tremor as he spoke. He popped a pill beneath his tongue and made it to the edge before he froze. "Never mind...It's farther down than it looks."

Vivienne and Emily locked eyes and seemed to come to the same conclusion in tandem. They flanked Max like two sentinels at their posts.

"Do you have a pill I can borrow?" Emily asked.

Vivienne plucked two pills from her pocket. She handed one to Emily and took the second one herself.

"You can do this!" Joel yelled, cupping his hands around his mouth like a megaphone.

A small group of PAN had gathered on the patio of The Glass House, and a few more were emerging from the Hall. All of them shouted words of encouragement.

"I know they're trying to help," Emily said, her voice trembling, "but having more people watching isn't doing anything for my motivation."

Around the corner of the Aviary, a tall guy with dark hair jogged into view. A jolt of adrenaline buzzed through Vivienne when she saw Deacon. He conquered the space with long, confident strides and stopped in front of the fountain. The sleepy fireflies in her stomach woke up. She hadn't seen or spoken to him since her second day in Neverland. More than once, she'd been tempted to text him. But every time she started typing, she chickened out.

"Let's go together," she said, tightening her hands into resolute fists at her side.

Max croaked, "If you say so," and inched closer to the ledge.

"We've been flying for weeks," she reminded them. "We're practically professionals at this stage."

"I know you're being sarcastic," Emily laughed. "But it's working."

"Good. Now close your eyes...Think of your happiest memory." She thought of the time she and Anne had burned an entire batch of Christmas cookies. "Focus on your fire inside, not what's waiting at the bottom...And go." She took a deep breath and stepped into the sky.

The sensation of being supported by the air wasn't any different from how she'd felt standing on the solid rooftop.

"We did it!" Max punched a fist into the sky.

"Thanks to this girl." Emily smacked her in the arm.

"Yeah, I'm great. Didn't you guys know that?"

Emily snorted, and Max chuckled.

Feeling lighter than ever, Vivienne twisted her imaginary valve and dropped fast enough to make her stomach flip. When she landed, Joel was waiting with a proud smile and a fist bump. She knocked her fist against his but searched the crowd for—

Deacon. At the back. Grinning.

When their eyes met, he gave her a wink.

And Vivienne had a new happy memory.

ELEVEN

"I can't believe you came!"

"Keep it down," Deacon snapped, pulling the neck of his jacket higher and descending the concrete stairs into a poorly-lit basement. "I'm not here as a participant, but as an objective observer."

Ethan jabbed him with his elbow. "Whatever you say, rebel."

Deacon scanned the gathering for familiar faces—and saw far too many. He slipped to where cinder blocks had been stacked like stools against the cold, slightly damp wall.

"Sitting in the back isn't going to keep people from noticing you're here," Ethan said with a chuckle, taking the blocks next to him.

Sure enough, the handful of bystanders nearest to Deacon all nodded, waved, or pointed at him. This wasn't going to end well. But since he was already here . . .

"I'd like to thank everyone for coming," a strong voice announced from the far corner. "It's amazing how much we've grown over the past year. One day soon, Leadership will have no choice but to take notice of the growing unease and dissatisfaction in Neverland."

Although there were murmured responses, it was hard to tell whether or not they were all in agreement. Deacon shifted for a better view of the speaker's face. Lee Somerfield's brown hair was a good deal greyer and the lines on his forehead more pronounced than the last time Deacon had seen him.

Deacon's reason for exploring Neverland's largest rebellious faction was twofold: First, he found himself questioning many of Neverland's rules, and was searching for like-minded individuals to help bring about change. The world was a different place than it had been a century ago, and it was time their archaic policies were updated.

Second, he was bloody bored since his mother had told him there would be no new missions until the spring. He had already made two trips to London in search of distractions and didn't feel like making a third.

"I used to be one of you," Lee said sadly, "and then my brother and I were captured by HOOK." He touched the black marks on the crook of his arm, his veins stained by HOOK's poison. "Because my Nevergene had activated only nine years before they neutralized me, the poison only left me grounded." He raised his eyes toward the murky window near the wooden beams above his head. "Unfortunately, Nicholas was five years older than me…and I was forced to watch him transform from a lively teenager to a gray, wrinkled corpse in a matter of minutes."

Deacon shuddered. He glared at the drafty window above him, but knew the chill was a result of his recent brush with HOOK. His own Nevergene had activated seven years earlier, so if he had been caught, he would have survived the poison. But would he ever be happy again if he was grounded? It only took one look at Lee to know the answer to that question.

"What drew me to Neverland, what I remember loving about it when I was a naive eighteen-year-old kid, was the sense of community. It was a place where children could grow up in homes with their ever-young parents instead of having aging roommates or being forced to move every four years to avoid suspicion. We could freely explore the fantastical aspects of this life. We could truly belong.

"But HOOK, and their mission to unlock the Nevergene's secrets at any cost, forced our community to become a safe-house. Fueled by greed, they disguised themselves as a humanitarian project to find the key to eternal life. And they've been preying on us ever since.

"I ask you now, what has Leadership done to deal with HOOK? What is their response when PAN are poisoned, *murdered* for our secrets?" Lee kicked one of the unoccupied blocks beside him. The crash made the people around him jump. "They don't do a damn thing because they're too preoccupied with telling *you* what to do. They've saddled us with rule after rule, claiming it's for our *safety*. Everyone here knows Leadership has just created a Neverprison!"

Lee's point received a resounding cheer from the audience. Deacon sank lower on his cinderblock chair.

"They're obsessed with power," he growled, "and would rather hide away on their thrones than fight for us."

"You said this was a meeting about change," Deacon whispered to Ethan. "So far all I've heard is a bunch of Leadership bashing."

Ethan shrugged. "There's a bit of bashing too."

"We need to show them that we're no longer content to remain in the shadows, following their red rule book!" Lee dragged a copy of *Neverland Policies* from one pocket and a lighter from the other. Then he lit the book on fire. Cheering echoed off the walls, and smoke filled the room. He kept it aloft until the flames were nearly to his fingers. When he could hold it no longer, he threw it on the ground.

"We need to show them that we're not afraid to fight!" *Stomp.* "We need to show them we will not be ignored any longer." *Stomp.*

"You've been preaching this for two decades, Lee. But you haven't taken action either."

Everyone's heads swiveled toward a young woman standing in the center of the crowd with her hands on her hips.

Deacon thought Audrey was spot on. Lee had become as complacent as Leadership. And it seemed like he was losing sight of the original purpose of the faction: to take down HOOK.

"You're right, Audrey." Lee gave what was left of the book a final stomp. "I have been busy making plans." He lifted an old Charlie Bell into the air. "Time for action is drawing near, and we need to be ready when it presents itself."

"You think we should go on the offensive?"

Deacon craned his neck to see who had spoken. "What's Joel doing here?"

Ethan kept his eyes forward when he answered. "Joel's been coming longer than I have."

Lee tossed the clock once. Caught it. Then smashed it against the wall. The glass face exploded, and the metal clanged. "We need to hit HOOK where it'll hurt most: their main research facility in Virginia."

This time, the cheering was deafening.

The crowd disbanded quicker than Deacon had expected, and everyone funneled toward the single exit. "Come on." He pulled Ethan by the sleeve. "I want to get out of here before anyone—"

"Deacon. It's been a while."

Deacon managed to appear relaxed as he turned with a nod. "Hello, Lee."

"Are you stopping by in an official capacity," Lee said, throwing his coat over his shoulders, "or are you as interested in anarchy as the rest of your fellow PAN?"

"I will admit, it was interesting—you made some valid points. I have one question though," Deacon drawled, loosening a bit of mud stuck to the unfinished walls. "If you're so sure of Leadership's inaction, why are you hiding in this musty basement?"

"Maybe you could ask Peter to lend us the Aviary for our next meeting."

"Ask him yourself. I'm sure he'd love to hear from you."

"Don't worry," Lee said, his mouth curling into a malevolent smile. "He'll be hearing from me soon enough." He turned to walk away, then stopped and twisted back around. "I wonder what your mother would do if she knew you were here?"

Deacon knew exactly what his mother would do—and he had a feeling that Lee did too. "I make my own decisions."

"If you say so…"

Lee Somerfield was an arrogant ass who deserved a kick in the bloody teeth. Deacon stomped up the stairs, pulled up the hood of his sweatshirt, and turned toward home.

"You need a drink," Ethan called, jogging to catch up.

Deacon stopped mid-stride. A drink sounded wonderful, but, "I don't really feel like socializing."

"Come on," Ethan whined, clapping him on the back. "We both know you're not gonna sleep when you get home."

He had a point. "Fine. One drink." Deacon crouched, then shoved away from the earth.

Ten minutes later, they landed in the trees behind the parking lot of their favorite bar. The clientele was middle-of-the-road, and it was mostly deserted on weeknights. Plus, the staff had stopped asking for ID two years earlier.

Deacon pulled aside the door with faded beer stickers plastered over the window and stepped inside the warm, stale room. Joe saluted them from behind the bar. He'd been working there for as long as Deacon could remember.

"You guys here for the usual?" Joe asked, throwing a rag toward the sink. Lights filtered through the bottles of liquor on the shelves behind him.

"Please." Deacon removed his sweatshirt and settled it over the back of his stool.

Ethan nudged his shoulder and asked what he thought of the meeting.

"I certainly don't plan on going back."

A group of four men in their mid-twenties stumbled through the door, laughing and shouting curses at each other. Three of them fell into the booth nearest the door, and the fourth, a short man with a barely-there mustache and a buzz cut, weaved unsteadily to prop himself up against the bar.

"Here you go, boys." Joe set a glass of scotch in front of Deacon and a glass of whiskey and Coke in front of Ethan. Deacon handed over his credit card, and Joe asked if they wanted to start a tab.

"I'm afraid we've time for only one drink tonight." The last thing he wanted was to be hungover tomorrow.

Joe nodded and went to the till.

"Yeah, but what about the stuff Lee said?" Ethan asked, picking up where they'd left off. He clinked his glass against Deacon's and took a sip. "He's right about a lot of it, you know."

"I can see why people are drawn to his ideas." And if Lee had stuck to berating the rules and HOOK, Deacon probably would have given him more credit. But the moment he started on Leadership, he had lost Deacon's support.

"I'm surprised you weren't standing beside Lee, cheering him on. You hate the rules almost as much as he does."

Joe slid a black checkbook toward him, then turned to serve mister mustache.

"I wouldn't say I *hate* them." He understood why some rules were necessary. A select few, anyway. He leaned across the bar for a pen so he could sign the receipt and leave Joe a tip.

"You sure as hell don't follow them," Ethan snorted, taking another drink.

Deacon relished the way the cold liquor scalded his throat. "I adhere to the no-photos policy."

"That's only because you don't want Leadership knowing what you're up to." Ethan swiped a cherry from the plastic container. "If I tried half the shit you've done," he said, popping the cherry into his mouth, "they would've kicked me out years ago."

"That's because no one likes you."

"If you weren't so pretty, no one would like you either." Ethan's mobile started ringing and he cursed. Instead of answering, he silenced it and abandoned it on the bar.

Deacon glimpsed the screen before it went black. "How's Nicola?"

"Pissed off." Ethan knocked back his drink, slammed the glass onto the bar, and wiped his mouth with his shirtsleeve. "She caught me texting Brittany the other day."

Brittany, Brittany, Brittany . . . Who the hell was—"The girl from the nightclub with the phoenix tattoo?"

Ethan's brows shot up. "How do you know about her tattoo?"

He hid his smile in his glass. "She showed me."

"I hate you," Ethan groaned, dropping his head in his hands. "I *really* hate you."

Deacon never understood why Ethan insisted on wasting his time with outsiders when he had Nicola. "Why do you hate me? I'm single and can do what I like." Ethan, on the other hand, was supposed to be trying to make it work with Nicola.

"Gwen would disagree."

"Gwen and I have an arrangement." His least favorite rule in Neverland was the one regarding relationships. Leadership had this insane notion that, if an inter-PAN relationship didn't last forever, the breakup could jeopardize their beloved secrets. He'd been seeing Gwen on and off for years, and the PAN's existence was still as secret as it had been a century ago. "She understands I'm not interested in anything serious."

"That makes two of us." Ethan waved at a pair of girls smiling at them from across the narrow room. Their tight dresses dipped low, and their tighter skirts rode high. "What do you say? Shall we go make some new friends?"

The group of men in the booth stopped the girls for a chat.

"Looks like someone beat you to them."

Which suited him down to the ground. He wasn't interested in meeting yet another girl who would never know his real name. His life had enough secrets, and he hated bringing more of them into the bedroom.

"Those dudes look like tool bags. That one guy's mustache looks like he drew it on with a pen."

Deacon laughed into his drink. "You're just jealous."

"Of the mustache? No way." Ethan rubbed his chin. "But the one beside him has a pretty sweet goatee. I'd love a goatee. Or a beard. I'd look great with a beard."

Deacon looked over again only to find the girl in a short black dress and red heels staring back at him. She waved and whispered something to her friend in the green dress. Mr. Mustache reached for her hand, but she shook him off. There was some drama going on there that he did *not* want to get involved in.

"Hold on...They're coming over." Ethan grabbed his shoulder and gave him a shake. "You gotta play along, man.

Girls love your stupid accent. You can be Oliver Cavendish, my boring cousin from England. I'll be Spencer Miller—you can call me Spence."

"Cavendish?"

"Yeah. Sounds über-British, right?"

Deacon finished his drink and set it on the counter. "Sorry, Spence. I'm just not feeling it tonight."

"Too late, Oliver." Ethan nodded to someone behind him.

"Hey, guys," the girl in black said, resting her elbows on the back of Deacon's stool. "I'm Ashton, and this is my BFF Maci." The dark-haired girl giggled and waved.

"Spence and Oliver." Ethan dragged over two more stools and offered them to the girls. "Can we buy you ladies a drink?"

"Two Mic Ultras, please." Maci tugged her skirt toward her knees, but it rode back up her thighs when she climbed onto the stool.

Ashton didn't bother to adjust her skirt at all. "Where are you guys from?"

Ethan waved toward Joe, then ordered a round of drinks for all of them.

"I'm from Surrey," Deacon said, hating these stupid games, "and Spence is from Oklahoma."

"Oh my God." Ashton's silver-lined blue eyes widened. "You're from *England*?"

Ethan sniggered and passed each of the girls a bottle of beer.

"I am."

"Your accent's hot."

He sighed.

"Hey, kid," a voice said behind him. "How old are you?"

No one in Neverland was too concerned with age for obvious reasons. Unfortunately, it wasn't the same for outsiders. At nearly twenty-five, the question had already become tiresome. He could only imagine how he would feel in another hundred years.

Deacon turned to find Mr. Mustache glaring at him. "I'm twenty-one."

The man's eyes narrowed into slits. "You sure about that? You look a lot younger."

"What can I say? I have good genes."

Ethan snorted.

Ashton shoved the man's shoulder. "Leave him alone, Stan. He didn't do anything to you."

"The two of you know each other?" Brilliant. Just the sort of drama he tried to avoid. It wasn't Ethan's fault, but he was going to blame him anyway.

"She's my girlfriend, kid," Stan snarled, grabbing for Ashton's elbow.

She shook him off and hissed, "*Ex*-girlfriend."

"I don't think she wants you to touch her, Stan," he drawled, feeling his adrenaline stir beneath his skin.

"Go back to your own damn country and mind your own damned business."

"Is there a problem over here?" Joe asked, wiping down the bar as he approached.

Stan pointed at Deacon and Ethan with his beer bottle. "Have you checked their ID's?"

"Didn't need to. They've been coming in ever since they turned twenty-one."

God bless Joe. He didn't know about the PAN, but he knew enough that if he kept them happy, they'd keep his tip jar full.

"My mistake." Stan not-so-discreetly knocked Deacon's wallet into a puddle of unknown origin on the floor.

Deacon closed his eyes and took a steady breath. *It's not worth it. It's not worth it.* He would pick it up, finish his drink, and go home. He would *not* hit Stan. "I'm sure you didn't mean to do that." Whatever was on his wallet was sticky and smelled like piss.

"What if I did?"

In his peripherals, he saw Ethan stand up. Push his sleeves to his elbows. Shouldn't he be trying to diffuse the situation instead of encouraging it? Deacon needed better friends.

"I really don't need this tonight." He tried to go back to his stool, but Stan blocked him. "Excuse me. That's my seat."

"Come on, Stan. Leave 'em alone," Ashton pleaded, her blue eyes wide and frightened.

"Shut the hell up, Ash." Stan puffed out his chest and shoved Deacon toward the wall. "Is it? Is it your seat?"

It's not worth it. It's not worth it. "Hey, Spence, let's go."

Ethan chugged his beer, and Deacon pulled his sweatshirt free. "Ashton, Maci." Deacon nodded to the two girls, feeling guilty for leaving them alone with the prick. But what other option did he have? "It was a pleasure meeting you both."

"What the hell, dude?" Stan slammed his bottle on the counter. "*Stop* talking to my girlfriend."

Another shove, this time between his shoulder blades. His sweatshirt landed in the disgusting puddle. *Don't hit him. Do NOT hit him.* "If you put your hands on me again—"

Stan went to shove him a third time and, oh god, his fist was already flying through the air, and there was nothing he could do now but watch it connect with the asshole's nose. A crunch. And blood. Shit there was a lot of blood. He'd definitely broken Stan's nose. Shit. Shit. Shit.

Stan caught his elbow, twisted his arm behind his back, and slammed his chest against the bar. He knew better than to move from the hammer lock, even though the pressure felt like it was going to snap his bloody shoulder.

Joe shouted something as he rounded the bar.

Stan reached into his back pocket and pulled out a . . . *Shit.* That was a badge.

Shit.

TWELVE

"As we discussed last week, this fairy tale was originally a play." Joseph tapped his book against his knee. "And Barrie used grossly oversimplified caricatures in order to segregate the different factions in his version of Neverland—like the pirates and Tiger Lily's tribe."

"Isn't that a nice way of saying it's racist?" Emily asked, popping the lid on her pen. "Because that's all I see when I read about Tiger Lily."

"Yes." Joseph took a deep breath. "Barrie was the quintessential upper-class Victorian white male. We could hide behind the idea that perhaps he was simply depicting Neverland from a Penny Dreadful point of view—those were cheap fantasy novels popular at the turn of the century. But the fact is, he took non-white cultures and rolled them into one racist trope. Even the term *Piccaninny* is a Victorian racial slur."

Vivienne had loved the story as a kid, but she hadn't realized how racist it was until she read it as an adult. "Can't someone change it?"

Joseph slipped his book into his leather briefcase. "The copyright on *Peter Pan* has been granted in perpetuity. It's protected and cannot be changed." He looked up and smiled sadly. "As described in the text, the tribe is an amalgamation of people considered to be *other*—which misses the point of Neverland entirely. We call everyone outside of our Never-circle..." Joseph raised his eyebrows and waited.

"Outsiders," Vivienne and her friends said in unison.

"Exactly. But in the world's eyes—if they knew about us —*we would be the outsiders*. The others."

"That's how I've always felt," Max said, his eyes fixed on the notebook in front of him. "Like I didn't belong." He looked up and smiled. "Till I came here, that is."

Vivienne returned Max's smile. "Me too."

Emily swatted his arm. "Same."

"What does Peter think about all of this?" Vivienne asked.

"That's something you can ask him yourself when you meet him."

She tried not to be disappointed by Joseph's vague answer. It was the same one he always gave when one of them asked a question regarding their mysterious founder.

Joseph checked his watch. "I'm afraid we'll have to continue this on Monday. Have a great weekend."

Vivienne settled her backpack over her shoulders and followed Max and Emily outside. She didn't bother joining their argument over who could fly faster and refused to be the judge when Max suggested a race. Instead, she went back to her apartment to re-read the portions of text about Peter.

Later that afternoon, she found Emily sitting at the kitchen table, flipping through a tabloid.

"Do you ever get the feeling," Vivienne said, sitting across from her and reaching for the box of cereal Emily had yet to put away, "that everyone is avoiding our questions about Peter?"

"Oh, yeah. Totally." Emily shoveled in another bite. "It's super weird."

"Almost as weird as cereal for dinner," she teased. High fructose corn syrup was the first ingredient listed on the side panel of the colorful box.

"If I'm going to have a teenage metabolism forever, I may as well take advantage of it."

Emily had a point. Vivienne grabbed a handful and popped a few colorful circles into her mouth. She had forgotten how good artificial flavoring and sugar tasted together. Lynn only bought corn flakes or cereal with raisins in it. "Did you and Max have your race?"

Emily smiled as she chewed. "Yup."

"And you obviously won." She grabbed more cereal, then closed the box.

"Yup."

Emily was fast—the fastest of the three of them. She even gave Joel a run for his money over short distances. As Vivienne returned the box to the cupboard, the calendar hanging on the wall caught her eye. A sense of unease settled over her. "What's today's date?"

"I'm pretty sure it's the twenty-third, but don't hold me to it."

October twenty-third was important for some reason, but Vivienne couldn't remember why. She tapped the date on the calendar, willing the information to emerge from the empty white box. "Is there anything happening this weekend?"

"Not that I know of."

What couldn't she remember? She closed her eyes and rested her head against the wall. The twenty-third was . . . Her eyes snapped open. "It's Lyle's birthday!"

How could she have forgotten? They'd bought tickets to see this weird grunge band he loved. Who would he take in her place? Her stomach twisted with guilt.

She had avoided thinking about Ohio for that very reason.

"Who's Lyle?"

Vivienne's heart sank. "My foster brother."

"You never told me you have a foster brother! Is he cute?"

"I don't even know how to answer that question." He was cute, she supposed. But she had never thought of him that way.

"If he wasn't your foster brother, would you date him?"

"I don't know…maybe?"

Emily finished her last bite of cereal and brought her bowl to the sink. "Are you going to get your hot brother a card or something?"

"Gross. Please, don't call him my hot brother. That's just wrong."

Emily giggled. "Cards are kinda lame, but at least he'd know you're thinking of him."

Would that be against the rules? If she sent him something from out of state, from somewhere far away, maybe it would be okay. She could let him know she was still alive. That she missed him.

In spite of what Paul and Deacon believed, Lyle was her ally and not her enemy. She spent the rest of the evening arguing with herself over whether or not she should send him a card. When she finally went to sleep, she had decided a card wasn't good enough.

She wanted to talk to him.

Vivienne paused in the hallway outside Emily's door. She still wasn't sure if she was doing the right thing by inviting her friend to be an accomplice, but she really didn't want to go alone.

So she stuffed her worry beneath her guilt and knocked.

Everything was going to be fine. No one was going to find out.

Emily told her to come in. When Vivienne opened the door, her roommate was glaring into her bursting closet like all the clothes offended her.

Emily turned around and offered her a wide smile. "Why are you up so early?"

Vivienne typically slept until at least ten o'clock on the weekends. "I need to buy some new outfits."

It wasn't a lie. The only clothes she had were the things she'd stuffed into her backpack and the few bits Kensington had given her. She was sick of doing laundry every other day.

"Just get one of the personal shoppers to buy stuff for you." Emily swept the makeup strewn across her desk into a shimmering pink bag.

Vivienne slid the hangers from one side to the other. Most of the stuff still had tags.

"I was going to ask them, but then I remembered you want to be one and thought maybe we could go together."

"Are you serious? Please tell me this isn't a joke! I've wanted to dress you ever since we met. You'd look amazing in deep, rich colors that show off your flawless skin. And something tighter than those baggy old sweatshirts that make you look like you don't have a figure at all."

"Wow. I didn't realize my wardrobe was such a problem for you."

Emily dragged a handful of hangers from her closet and handed them to her. "These are yours."

"You already bought me stuff?" Vivienne was as horrified as she was touched.

Emily went to the stack of jeans on the closet shelf and grabbed two pairs from the bottom of the pile. They had tags on them as well. "I like to shop. A lot."

That was an understatement. Was there a day since they'd met that Emily hadn't bought something? She didn't think so.

"What kind of best friend would I be," she went on, collecting T-shirts and a pair of cute pearl earrings from the cache under her bed, "if I didn't pick up a few things for you as well?"

"I don't really know what to say." All the stuff looked like things she would wear. Nothing too gaudy or revealing. Simple and—holy crap. *Expensive.* "Emily! This white T-shirt cost fifty dollars!"

"It's a really pretty one."

"It's a plain white T-shirt." One that would probably end up with a ketchup stain.

Emily rolled her eyes and told her that when she tried it on, she would understand.

Right. The excuse of shopping didn't really work anymore. Unless—"I assume you didn't buy me underwear."

"Since you asked…" Emily went to her drawer. Then she started giggling. "Just kidding! I thought that may have been crossing the line."

Vivienne really didn't care about her underwear. It wasn't

like anyone else was going to see them anyway. "Do you want to go shopping with me then?"

"No. I think I'm all shopped out."

"Oh...okay."

"I'm kidding! Geesh. The only time I'm ever going to turn down a trip to the mall is if I'm dead."

It didn't take much to convince Emily to go on a road trip to Albany, New York. She had her bag packed in less than twenty minutes.

Vivienne put on a pair of the jeans Emily had given her, along with the white T-shirt. She couldn't explain it, but Emily was right. It was a really nice top. Not worth fifty bucks, but it was nice. She transferred all her new clothes straight into the suitcase Emily let her borrow and threw in the old sweatshirt Emily hated just for fun.

The car they rented was left idling at the Kensington gates and, after signing a few forms, they were on their way to New York. Emily was serious about her role as a DJ, and never let a full song play its way from start to finish without switching to one she claimed was even better.

Multiple playlists and light conversation filled the first hour. Halfway to Albany, Vivienne's phone buzzed from the center console. She pressed a button on the steering wheel to answer the call, thankful Emily had taken the time to sync their phones to the car's Bluetooth.

"Hello?"

"How are you this morning?" Deacon's melodic accent poured through the car's speakers.

She did her best to ignore Emily's silent "Who is that?" to her right. "Great. How are you?" The firefly dance party in her stomach wasn't as easy to ignore. She scanned the highway signs ahead and focused on not hitting the eighteen-wheelers on either side of the car.

"I'm quite well. Are you going to be around later?"

Emily's eyes widened, and she wiggled her eyebrows. Vivienne turned away from the rude faces. "Why?"

"I was thinking of grabbing some lunch with a few friends

on campus around half twelve. You're welcome to come along if you'd like."

After all these weeks, why did he have to choose today to call her? "I would, but I'm out of town at the moment."

"What do you mean you're out of town?" he clipped.

Smiling at her co-pilot, Vivienne said, "My roommate and I took a road trip."

Emily craned her neck to speak into the microphone concealed above the driver's seat. "*Hiiiiii* there."

"This is Emily, right?"

"That's me." Emily squeezed Vivienne's shoulders. "And you are?"

"I'm Deacon." He cleared his throat. "Has Vivienne not mentioned me before?"

Mentioned him? Why would she have mentioned him to Emily?

"Nope. She must want to keep you all to—"

"She doesn't know what she's talking about," Vivienne blurted. Emily gave her a sly smile that said she was in for an interrogation when the call was over.

Deacon chuckled, stirring those fireflies. "Where are the two of you headed?"

She flicked the blinker and passed a slow car in front of them. "We're going shopping in Albany."

"Are you staying the night?" His voice sounded strange. Tight and . . . annoyed? Why would a shopping trip annoy him?

"What kind of road trip would it be if we didn't stay?"

"Indeed."

Her GPS said something the same time Deacon asked about the hotel they had booked.

"Sorry, but I have to go. My GPS is going nuts here. I'll talk to you later." She clicked the button on the steering wheel in time to hear the woman's voice tell her to take a left turn up ahead.

A satisfied smile played on Emily's pink lips. "Who's *Deeeacon*?"

"My recruiter." Vivienne turned up the radio, hoping the pop music would distract Emily from her inquisition.

Emily turned it back down. "Is he hot? Cuz he sounds hot."

"Yeah, he's pretty cute." Vivienne turned it back up.

Emily turned it off. "He's obviously from the Harrow Neverland."

"I guess so. I didn't ask."

"I bet you're sorry you chose today to care about fashion."

"It's not a big deal."

"Not a big deal?" Emily shook Vivienne's shoulder. "Mister Sexy Voice totally just asked you out!"

"No, he didn't." Grabbing lunch with friends wasn't a date. Was it? No. It was stupid to even think that way. Deacon was probably supposed to check on her as part of his job.

"Think what you want, sister. But he seemed pretty darn disappointed that you weren't around to meet up."

Vivienne adjusted her dollar-store sunglasses and tried not to sound disappointed when she said, "Deacon doesn't care whether I'm there or not."

Deacon tossed his phone onto the duvet and stalked toward his chest of drawers.

Just when he thought his week couldn't get any worse, this happened. He'd been forced to call Paul to pick him up from the police barracks after the disaster at the bar. Luckily, there were enough witnesses to say the fight wasn't his fault, and no charges had been filed. That hadn't appeased Paul, but Deacon was convinced nothing made the man happy.

He told himself not to make any rash decisions, that Vivienne had brought Emily along with her for a simple overnight getaway.

She was happy at Kensington; she was excelling and thriving. There was no logical reason to worry she would return to her life in Ohio. Still, that was what his fear boiled down to: that Vivienne would reject Neverland.

He hadn't been able to do anything about her leaving on the

bus, and he wouldn't be permitted to stop her if she decided to leave again.

There was nothing he could do.

He pulled his running gear out of the drawer, intent on putting Vivienne out of his mind.

Except now she knew too much . . .

And if HOOK caught her when she went back to Ohio, there was no telling what they would do to her in order to get her to talk.

When he slammed the drawer shut, he tweaked his sore shoulder and cursed. His car keys fell onto the floor. He picked them up and pressed the button on his nearly invisible earpiece. "Hey, TINK."

A woman's voice responded in his ear, "Hello, *Deacon*."

"I need directions to Albany, New York."

THIRTEEN

"I'm beat." Vivienne dropped onto the plush mattress in their spacious hotel room and turned off the blinding lamps attached to the wall next to the bed.

Emily plugged her phone cable into the charging port by the desk, then sprawled beside her. "We only went to a few stores."

A few stores? Vivienne pressed a button on the digital alarm clock on the nightstand. "We were at the mall for six hours!"

Emily snorted and called her an amateur.

"The only thing keeping me awake right now is hunger." They had eaten at the food court when they had first arrived, but the chicken nuggets and waffle fries were nothing more than a distant memory.

"What kind of food do you want?"

"The fast kind that doesn't require me to shower or change my clothes."

"But we bought so many cute pieces today! Why don't you wear the black dress?"

Emily had insisted they bring every single bag in from the car. Vivienne was afraid she was going to force her to do a fashion show.

"Let's compromise." Vivienne plucked an outfit out of the closest bag and tossed it in her direction. "You put on something fancy; I'll run across the street to the diner, get us a table, and order every appetizer on the menu."

"Will you save me some cheese sticks?"

Vivienne paused with her hand on the doorknob. "I refuse to make a promise I can't keep."

"Fine." Emily stuffed the fluffy black sweater back into the bag and pulled her phone free from the cord. "I'll come with you now."

They got to the restaurant and ordered enough food for five people. They chatted about everything and nothing. Vivienne managed to keep Emily talking about her family so she didn't have to talk about her own.

They'd grown up so differently. Emily had lived in the same house her whole life. Had kept the same group of close friends since kindergarten.

It made Vivienne wonder what her life would have looked like if she hadn't been orphaned. Would she have grown up in the white two-story house with blue shutters? Would she—

Emily's phone started ringing.

"It's my mom," she groaned at the screen.

"Aren't you going to answer it?"

"I guess I should." She scooted out of the booth and took her conversation to the waiting area.

Vivienne dipped the larger chip crumbs into what was left of the salsa. Then she considered the final cheese stick. She cut it in half to share with Emily but ended up eating both halves. With no sign of her friend returning, Vivienne pulled her phone from her purse and flicked through the apps before opening the camera roll. The only picture she had was of a pair of hideous shoes Emily had tried to make her buy.

"Sorry about that."

Vivienne turned off the screen. "Everything all right?"

"My mom was just checking in." Rolling her eyes, Emily tucked her phone back into her purse. "She's so needy sometimes."

Vivienne smiled. She'd give anything to have a needy mom checking up on her. "Yeah, but I bet it's nice having them so close."

"It is. And I love that my mom and dad know about Neverland and Peter. But sometimes I wish I had been the one surprising them instead of the other way around."

"I wonder what my foster family would say if I told them I'm part of Peter Pan's secret society of flying teenagers." Maren would be so jealous. The thought made her smile. Lynn would want to know that she was being safe. And Lyle . . . "Lyle would insist on coming along to see for himself."

"The two of you seem close," Emily said thoughtfully, toying with a bit of straw paper left on the table.

"We were." When she had first moved to Lynn's, Maren had made fun of her for being so short. Lyle had picked up a handful of dirty leaves and dumped them onto his sister's head. From that point forward, they had been inseparable . . . Until she ditched him to come to Neverland.

"Why don't you invite him to Kensington?" Emily scooted what was left of her chocolate cake to the edge of the table.

Vivienne had spoken to Paul about the possibility. He'd told her that until the whole HOOK thing was sorted, she couldn't invite anyone. "HOOK showed up when my Nevergene activated, and—"

"*What?*" Emily's cake clattered to the floor. "I can't believe you never told me!"

"It never came up." It was a poor excuse, but it was the only one she could think of. Vivienne helped Emily clean up the mess with her own napkin. When they were finished, a waitress came by with a tray to take away all the dirty dishes.

Emily asked how HOOK found out about Vivienne.

"Nobody knows."

"Do they think Lyle is some sort of spy?"

"He's *not* a spy." But according to Paul, he was still a suspect.

When they got back to the room, Vivienne suggested renting a movie, but Emily said she was too tired. Which was perfect. The sooner she fell asleep, the sooner Vivienne could sneak away.

"I'm a little offended that, after everything we bought today," Emily said, glaring at her from the other bed, "you're still wearing that ugly sweatshirt."

Vivienne pushed the covers aside and stared down at her OHIO sweatshirt. Emily was right. It was ugly. But it had belonged to William, so Vivienne would be wearing the thing until it disintegrated. "I don't see anything wrong with it."

"I hate it."

"I'm going to buy you one just like it for Christmas so we can match."

"No you won't."

Emily's horrified expression made her giggle. "Just watch me."

Once Emily fell asleep, Vivienne slipped out of her bed and pulled on her shoes. The door clicked behind her, and she took the elevator to reception. She went outside and crossed the parking lot to the convenience store next door. The plan was to pick up a prepaid phone and a few snacks in case Emily woke up and asked where she'd gone.

The door jingled when she opened it. She grabbed a small bag of chips and a bar of chocolate and brought them to the counter to ask the clerk if they had any prepaid phones.

The pock-faced teenager looked at her with dead eyes, not bothering to move from where he slumped against the register. "We only have flip phones."

"That's perfect. May I have one?"

He huffed at the inconvenience of being forced to move and lumbered to a locked cabinet behind him. "Do you want a blue or black one?"

The bell above the door jingled. Vivienne glanced at the couple who came in, then back at the clerk. Why was she so nervous? It wasn't like she was doing anything illegal. "It doesn't matter."

"Uhhh…" He stared into the cabinet.

"Just give me a blue one." She paid for everything and went back outside. The air felt thick and heavy, like it could start pouring any minute. After adding minutes to the phone, she dialed her foster brother's number.

"Hello?" Lyle answered with the same amount of wariness that he applied to daily life.

Vivienne inhaled a shaky breath. "Hey, Lyle."

"Holy shit." His voice lowered to a whisper. "Is that you, Viv?"

She swiped at her welling tears. It was so good to hear his familiar voice. "Who else would it be?"

"Where the hell are you?"

"It's kind of a long story." She balanced on the edge of the curb and thought of everything that had happened over the past month. She wanted to tell him so badly but was already risking enough calling him. Soon. She would tell him soon.

"Come on. You go missing the same day a bunch of creepy guys come looking for you and all you're going to give me is, 'It's kind of a long story?'"

Her skin began tingling. "Speaking of those creepy guys… Did you know who they were?"

"Not a clue. But they came to school looking for you every day for a whole week after you went missing."

She shivered and pulled the neck of her sweatshirt higher. "Did they ever come back to the house?"

"They've been here a couple of times since, asking us if we've heard from you. But mostly, they end up talking to Mom."

"If they come back again, are you going to tell them I called?"

"Seriously, Viv? I never ratted you out before, why the hell would I start now?"

She smiled at the starless night. "I miss you."

"I miss you too." A door shut in the background. "Can you tell me where you're hiding?"

"Not yet." Vivienne meandered toward the hotel. "But I can wish you a belated happy birthday."

Lyle chuckled. "Well, this was a great birthday present."

"I'll try to call again soon." She ended the call and tossed the phone into the trash can outside reception.

The hotel's automatic doors opened to the lobby when she

got close. She wasn't going to be able to sleep for a while with all the adrenaline—

Deacon smiled at her from the couch next to the lobby's marble fireplace.

What the heck was *he* doing here?

"You've gotta stop following me. It's getting creepy."

"Maybe you need to stop running away." Deacon stood and slid his hands down his thighs, straightening his dark pants. They rode low on his hips, revealing a hint of black elastic beneath. She tore her eyes from his waist. The last thing she needed was to think about Deacon Ashford in his underwear.

"Running away? I told you that Emily and I were going shopping."

His head tilted to the side and he narrowed his eyes at her sweatshirt. "You don't strike me as the kind of girl who enjoys shopping sprees."

If only she had taken Emily's advice and worn something prettier. He slipped a finger through one of the holes in her sweatshirt. "I hope you bought a new top."

She could feel his skin against her bare stomach, stirring up the fireflies. When he withdrew his hand, she had to fight the urge to bring it back. He sank onto the couch and patted the seat beside him.

"About twenty of them," she said, dropping onto the cushion. "Shopping with Emily is like running a marathon. As you can tell from this ancient thing I have on, I've never been too concerned with what I wear."

"Then why did you agree to come?"

Crap. She'd set herself up for that one. "I guess I wanted a chance to feel like a normal teenager for a day."

"And do you feel normal now that you've had some retail therapy?"

She gave him a sidelong smile. "No."

"You'll never feel like you used to."

How could one person be so good looking? It wasn't fair.

"Why are you *really* here, Deacon?" He had to know she wasn't going to run away. She had nowhere else to go. "And how did you find us?"

His brows came together and his mouth flattened. "I may have asked a friend to track your mobile phone."

First the invitation to lunch, and now this? What the heck was going on?

He brushed her hair over her shoulder and traced the neckline on her top, and every single muscle in her body tensed. Her heart was hammering so loudly she was sure he could hear it, and she was afraid if she moved, he'd take his hand away and she'd die. But if he didn't stop touching her, she was going to catch on fire.

"And I already told you," he said quietly, "I'm making sure you're not going to run off again."

Vivienne didn't know if Neverland would be her forever, but it was her right-now. "I'm not going anywhere."

"I suppose I look a bit silly following you across state lines."

Before she could answer, she yawned.

Deacon blinked. His hand stilled . . . and dropped. "You're tired."

Tired? She wasn't tired. She'd never felt more awake. "No, I'm not." She didn't want to go. Not yet.

"Go to bed, Vivienne." His lips curled into a mischievous smile. "Emily's probably waiting for a pillow fight."

"Pillow fight?" He really did say the strangest things.

He picked up the decorative pillow between them and tossed it into the air. "Pillow fights are kind of a staple at girl sleepovers, aren't they?"

"*Very* mature." She twisted her wrist to check the time. It couldn't be midnight already . . .

"My money's on you. You're feistier than you look."

"Watch out. Otherwise, you're the one I'll be beating with a pillow." She clutched the decorative pillow at her back and launched it toward him.

He caught it with a laugh. "I'd be up for that."

Something dark twisted inside of her, urging her to play this dangerous game with him. "Do you have a room?"

His eyes widened. "Why?"

She shifted on the couch, leaned close enough to feel the

115

heat from his skin and smell his cologne, and whispered, "For our pillow fight."

His smile faltered, and his Adam's apple bobbed when he swallowed. "Seriously?"

The final pillow caught him in the side of the head. "Nope. I was only wondering if you were staying here or going back to Kensington."

He threw it back at her. "I'll stay if you stay with me."

"Is that...is that a joke?" He was joking, right? He had to be joking. Because he was *not* asking her to stay the night with him.

His lips curled into a slow smile, like he knew she was freaking out. "I don't know, is it?"

Flirt and fly away. That's what Deacon did.

But not tonight.

Tonight, she was the one who was going to leave. "Goodnight, Deacon."

She ignored the shock on his face, grabbed her bag of snacks, and ran to the elevator.

She didn't turn around. Couldn't. Because if she did, she'd be tempted to take him up on his offer.

FOURTEEN

The next morning, Vivienne expected to see a flirty text or two from Deacon. But all she got was a stupid blank screen. Stupid guys with their stupid flirting.

She really needed to get a grip.

They got back to Kensington that afternoon, and it took two trips to get all of the bags into the apartment.

"I'm so glad we're home!" Emily dumped the last of the bags onto the floor next to the first batch.

"Me too." Although Vivienne's response had been automatic, it surprised her to realize how much she meant it. She wasn't sure when it had happened, but her apartment at Kensington felt more like home than Lynn's house ever did. She stacked her new clothes on her desk before putting them away. Beneath the final sweater, she found the book of rules that Penelope had given them on their first day.

She really should have done more than skim the first few pages. Figuring now was as good a time as any, she brought it to her bed and settled in to learn all the things she wasn't allowed to do. Three pages in, her eyes started getting heavy. At five pages, the words blurred. At six, she gave up and took a nap.

Somewhere, someone was pounding, and it was interrupting the pillow fight she was about to have with Deacon. He'd made a ridiculous rule that every time someone got hit, they had to take off an article of clothing.

He winked before blindsiding her with a blow to the shoulder.

When he finished laughing, he told her it was time to take off her shirt.

Her heart thudded against her ribs as his hands fell to the hem and pulled—

"Vivienne! Can you get the door?"

Vivienne shot out of bed, sending the book she'd been reading tumbling to the floor. Her heart was racing and her forehead was sweaty and—

Holy crap. What kind of dream was *that*?

Whoever was at the door knocked again. She pulled her hair back from her sweaty face and checked herself for drool stains in the mirror before running into the living room.

She had to step over Emily's yoga mat to get to the door, but when she opened it, the hall was empty.

Her phone dinged in her pocket as a bunch of messages came through . . . from Deacon. *Open the door. Hurry up. It's freezing out here.*

Her heart picked up double time when she turned and saw Deacon waiting outside the glass door.

"Hello again," he said with a crooked smile when she opened it. He waited on the other side as though there was a landing where he hovered. His eyes fell on the bright orange mat behind her. "Did I miss yoga?"

"That's...um...that's Emily's stuff." Vivienne cleared the surprise from her voice and stepped out of his way. "What's up?"

He flew past her and into the room. "I have come to apologize," he said, checking out their living space. Vivienne was so glad Emily had cleaned up while she'd been napping. "I had no business tracking your mobile, much less following you to New York. It was incredibly stalkerish of me, and I hope you will forgive me."

Did that mean he regretted last night? Not that anything had happened. But it could have. "It's no big deal," she assured him, rolling up Emily's mat and stuffing it behind the tv stand.

"Vivienne!" Emily called from the hallway. "Max asked if we wanted to go bowl—Oh! *Hellooo.*" Her voice lifted an octave when she saw Deacon leaning against the arm of the couch, and she smoothed non-existent stray hairs into her perfect bun.

"You must be Emily." Deacon's smile broadened. "Won any good pillow fights lately?"

"Pillow fights?" Emily looked between Deacon and Vivienne, the question plain on her face.

"Don't listen to him," Vivienne blurted. The last thing she needed was for Emily to find out about last night and think there was more to it than there was. "What were you saying, Emily?"

"Max invited us to come bowling..." She tilted her head toward Deacon. "But I can totally tell him you're busy if you have *other* plans."

"Nope. No other plans. Count me in."

"I love bowling," Deacon confessed from over her shoulder.

Emily fluttered her hand in his direction. "You should totally come with us!"

"Would it be all right if my mate Ethan came too?" he asked, pushing away from the couch. "We were supposed to do something tonight."

"Yeah. Yes. Absolutely..." Did Emily just swoon? "We have a...uh...thing reserved at Par-Mat-Lanes."

"Lane?" Deacon offered.

"Yeah. A lane. Seven. Seven o'clock, I mean. Not seven lanes."

"Brilliant." A smile. "We'll be there." He turned his attention back to Vivienne and apologized again for last night.

She could feel Emily's eyes boring into the side of her head when she said, "Already forgotten. I'll see you later."

"Looking forward to it. It was nice to meet you, Emily," he called over his shoulder on his way to the glass door. He swept it open and jumped into the wind.

Emily collapsed onto the couch in an exaggerated faint. "Oh. My. God. *Vivienne.* You lying little bitch."

The door slipped from her hand and slammed shut. *"What?"*

"He's kind of cute? *KIND OF CUTE?* My friend's dog is kind of cute. That guy"—she threw a hand toward the door—"is sex incarnate. I could stare into those emerald green eyes forever." She batted her own dark lashes. "And did you notice how delicious he smells? And that formal British accent is like icing on the hunky cake. You get dibs because you saw him first, but if you don't want him, please, *please* give him to me."

As if Deacon was hers to give. The thought made Vivienne laugh. But it was a nervous laugh. Even a bit maniacal.

Emily's brows came together, and her eyes narrowed. "Why was he saying sorry to you?"

Vivienne could have told her the truth . . . but the truth would have led to more questions. Instead, she said, "He was apologizing for checking up on me so much."

"I wish someone like that would check up on me."

"They're really, really late." Emily frowned toward the bowling-pin-shaped clock at the back of the alley. "You don't think they changed their minds about coming, do you?"

"I'm not sure." Vivienne checked her phone again. Deacon hadn't texted her to cancel. Was he that kind of guy? The kind who made plans only to let everyone down? She hoped not.

"Are we going to bowl tonight or just eat?" Max asked, finishing the last of the pizza. "And if we are just eating, can we order some dessert?"

"Look!" Emily jumped to her feet and hauled Vivienne to hers. "He's here!"

"Sorry we're late." Deacon wiped the glistening rain from his unkempt hair. "Traffic was mad."

"It's okay." Emily tapped her hand on a marbled pink ball in the rack behind their chairs. "Why don't you go get your shoes and we'll get things set up here. Is…um…Ethan coming?"

Deacon cocked his head toward the entrance. "He's parking the car."

A moment later, a blond guy wearing a Kensington hoodie

and a black baseball cap sauntered in. When he removed his hat, Vivienne gasped.

"Tell me about it," Emily said with a knowing nudge. "Total babe."

He was pretty hot. But that wasn't why Vivienne was so shocked. "I know him."

"You do?"

She didn't *know him*, know him. But she remembered seeing him somewhere . . . "He was at my high school." Which meant he was probably a recruiter like Deacon.

Emily sighed. "I *really* missed out on this whole recruiting experience."

Ethan joined Deacon, leaning his elbows on the rental counter and chatting to the woman handing out the shoes.

"Who is *she*?" Emily blurted, pointing to a girl who had come in and squeezed between them.

Tall. Blonde. Jaw-droppingly *gorgeous*. Who the heck had invited a Swedish supermodel?

The girl threw her head back and laughed at whatever Deacon said. Leaned in close to whisper in his ear.

Crap. Deacon had a girlfriend. Of course he did. The two of them looked like they belonged on a red carpet together.

All the effort Vivienne had put into her appearance tonight was for nothing. Emily had picked out her skinny jeans and black V-neck T-shirt that she swore made Vivienne's boobs look amazing. She'd even let Emily do her eyeliner. Stupid. She was so stupid.

Would Emily get mad if she went home?

"That's Nicola," Max said from behind them, smiling for the first time since they had ordered pizza. "She's the queen of extraction and a total badass."

The trio at the counter turned, and Vivienne pretended like she hadn't been staring.

Deacon brought his bowling shoes to the lane and plopped onto a chair next to her. Emily gave her a sly wink.

It didn't mean anything. There was an empty seat; Deacon filled it. No big deal.

"Is that one of the new tops you bought in Albany?" he

asked, slipping out of his shoes and pushing them beneath his chair.

"Yeah."

"I like it."

He shouldn't like it. His girlfriend was sitting right beside him.

After all the introductions were made, Ethan flashed her a grin. "Good to see you again, Vivienne."

She returned the smile. "You too." She'd had two classes with him, Physics and History.

"How's everything going for you since moving here?" Nicola asked, resting a hand on Ethan's arm. The move was subtle, but there was no mistaking its possessiveness. Interesting . . . Maybe Nicola wasn't with Deacon after all.

Vivienne's mood brightened. "I don't have any complaints."

"Have you had a chance to think about careers yet?"

"Penelope said I should look into recruiting." She couldn't be sure, but she thought Deacon perked up at her announcement.

"Recruiting is for people with no imagination," Nicola said with a wink. "Extraction is where we have all the fun."

Max raised his hands and told her he was hoping to get accepted into the program.

"That's great." An appreciative smile crossed Nicola's full, glossed lips. "I look forward to welcoming you to the team."

"Hold on a minute." Deacon stood and adjusted his pants from where they had slid down his hips. "If you work in extraction, all you do is laze around waiting for someone to screw up."

"As long as you're in the field, Dash, we don't get to laze around at all." Nicola hit his leg with her elbow. She touched him a lot for someone who seemed to be dating someone else.

"Forget them both. Scouting is where it's at," Ethan drawled, leaning against the back of his plastic chair and putting his hands behind his head. "Laid back. No-pressure."

"They put you on scouting duty because you're shit at everything else." Deacon tossed one of his shoes in Ethan's direction.

Ethan swatted it to the floor and told him to shut the hell up.

Vivienne couldn't help but laugh. Maybe tonight was going to be fun after all.

Emily put everyone's names into the computer and chatted to Nicola about personal shopping. Meanwhile, everyone else discussed the teams. When Deacon suggested boys versus girls, Ethan groaned.

"No way, dude," he said. "I don't want you on my team."

"Why not? I could be really good."

"You're not."

"How do you know?"

Ethan raised his brows and kicked Deacon's foot. "Remember Georgia?"

Deacon winced.

What had happened in Georgia?

"Well, we don't want him either," Nicola clipped, selecting a purple ball from the rack. "And since we're doing boys versus girls, I'm afraid you're stuck with him, babe."

"Vivienne would let me on her team," Deacon said, nudging her knee with his, "wouldn't you Vivienne?"

"Not if you're bad." She didn't want to lose.

He chuckled, leaned closer, and whispered, "What if I promise to be very, *very* good?"

Bowling. He was talking about bowling. He had to be talking about bowling. Because if he wasn't—

She gaped at him as he got up, grabbed a ball from the rack, and asked who was first.

An hour later, the boys trailed by ten pins. Deacon had put two balls into the gutter, and he couldn't stop laughing about it. Ethan made fun of him until it was his turn and he bounced one into the abyss.

"I think you're worse at this than you are at football," Deacon teased, catching Ethan in a headlock and wrestling him to the ground.

"Dude, we're on the same team!" Ethan growled, shaking free and heading toward the bathroom.

"It's a good thing Max is here," Deacon shouted to his

friend's back. "Otherwise we wouldn't have broken double digits."

"You guys both suck," Max said with a laugh. "Next time I want Vivienne and Emily on my team." He proceeded to bowl one straight down the middle for his team's first strike.

"You know you're not much better, right?" Vivienne nodded toward the screen. Deacon's score was half of her own. "I thought you said you were good at bowling."

"I wasn't talking about bowling." He winked at her and her heart stuttered.

Flirt and fly away.

She had to remember that.

A loud shout resonated from the corner, where a drunken group of college-aged guys took up three lanes. Emily bowled seven pins, then announced that she was going to get a refill.

After seeing some of the college guys stumble toward the snack bar, Vivienne offered to go with her. She didn't feel comfortable letting Emily go on her own. Plus, she needed to get away from Deacon so she could breathe.

He was so confusing. Disappearing for weeks without a word and then reappearing again like no time had passed. And last night . . . Had it only been last night? Something had definitely changed between them.

When Vivienne and Emily approached the counter, the group of guys parted, nudging each other and whispering.

"Hello, there," one said over the top of his beer can. He took a long drink but spilled some over the Greek letters on his shirt. The name Bret was sewn onto his breast pocket.

Vivienne said, "Hi," knowing he would be more obnoxious if she refused to acknowledge him.

Bret wiped his mouth and gave her a sloppy grin. "What are you girls up to?"

"Bowling," Emily answered haughtily. "Excuse me?" She waved to the woman behind the counter and asked for a refill.

"Do you go to Worcester State too?" asked another guy with patchy stubble and a faded black eye.

"No, we don't," Vivienne told him in her most dismissive voice.

A third man with long hair pulled back beneath a bandana pushed forward. "What brings you our way then?"

Emily shook her full cup in his face and said, "Bowling."

"Are you girls looking for something to do after you're finished *bowling*?" Bret asked.

The others behind him sniggered.

"Not with you." Emily's disapproving look remained as she turned back toward their lane.

When Vivienne moved to join her, Bret caught her wrist with his clammy hand. "What about you?"

"What about me?" She attempted to tug free. Bret's friends closed ranks around him, shutting off her exit.

His fingers tightened around her wrist. "Do you wanna get outta here, tiny thing?"

Was he serious? Gross. "Yeah, no."

He yanked her wrist, and she collided into his damp T-shirt. "Aw, come on," he whined, the alcohol on his breath mixing with the stench of stale cigarettes. "I'd love to bring you back to my place."

She was more pissed off than scared, but her voice wobbled when she demanded to be let go.

"Vivienne?" Deacon called from outside the circle. "Is everything all right?"

"Vivienne?" Bret whispered. "A pretty name for a pretty girl."

She felt a steady, protective hand on her shoulder.

"I'm fine, Deacon." This time when she pulled away, the guy let her go.

Bret mimed a silent apology to Deacon before turning back to his beer on the counter. All his friends laughed, and the tense moment ended as quickly as it had begun.

Deacon led Vivienne by the waist to the lane where everyone else waited with wide eyes. "Are you sure you're all right? Because if you're not—"

"I said, I'm fine, okay?" Why was her voice so shaky? She brushed away an annoying bit of hair that had fallen into her eyes and told him it wasn't a big deal.

"Those guys are idiots." Nicola came over and linked her arm through Vivienne's. "The best thing to do is walk away."

"Dash?" Ethan stepped beside Nicola and tilted his head in question.

Deacon glanced at Vivienne before looking back at Ethan and shaking his head ever so slightly. The guys dropped the issue and went back to being terrible bowlers. When the competition finished, the girls had trounced them three games to none.

"Do you want to ride back with us?" Ethan tossed his shoes atop the pile of discarded shoes at the returns counter. "It'll be a squeeze, but Vivienne is so small we could fit her in the trunk."

"Thanks a lot." She kicked at his leg, but he sidestepped the assault with an easy laugh.

"The three of us could always call a cab so this one," Emily said, patting Vivienne's hair, "doesn't have to pretend to be luggage."

Their group headed toward the door, but Deacon didn't follow them.

"Dash?" Ethan said over his shoulder. "Aren't you coming?"

Deacon turned toward Vivienne and said, "Do you want to be luggage, Vivienne?"

"Not really." She had done it before. One of the joys of being the shortest was that she was either put in the trunk or stuck sitting on someone's lap. Her stomach fluttered. How did she casually suggest *that*?

"I'm going to walk," Deacon said with a crooked smile. "Would you like to join me?"

Emily's eyes widened, and she nodded as if she had been the one to whom Deacon had extended the invitation.

"It's a little far."

He rolled his eyes and asked Ethan to borrow his coat.

"Sure thing." They exchanged a few quiet words. Ethan didn't look happy, but he rejoined Nicola near the exit.

"Here," Deacon said, handing his own sweatshirt to her.

Vivienne pushed it back at him. "I'm not cold." They had the heating in the place jacked up way too high.

"Put it on." He offered it to her once more. "Please?" His eyes softened as the corner of his lips lifted.

He could have asked her to do just about anything and she would have said yes. Vivienne pulled his sweatshirt over her head. The moment everyone walked through the door, she became hyperaware that she and Deacon were alone.

"Are we really walking all the way back to campus?" she asked, tucking her nose inside the neck of his top and inhaling his spicy cologne.

"What do you think?"

Heck. Yes. He was going to bring her on her first proper flight! She'd flown around campus but that was it. This was going to be amazing. "Before we leave, I'm going to run to the restroom for a minute."

"I'll be right here waiting for you."

In the closet that served as the unisex restroom, Vivienne considered her reflection in the cracked mirror and unflattering fluorescent light. Pale. She looked pale. She pinched her cheeks until they were pink. Emily had curled her hair, but it had gone flat. She *really* needed a haircut. Her split ends were getting out of control. She finger-combed it, trying to breathe life back into the heavy strands.

If only she had brought some lip gloss or something.

Why did it matter?

It didn't. She wasn't going to change who she was for some guy.

Her heart shuddered and her adrenaline came to life when she saw Deacon waiting for her by the entrance. Bad idea. Falling for him was a very, very bad idea. For all she knew, he was saying the same stuff to every other girl he met. But how did she tell her heart that?

They left the building only to run into the drunken guy, Bret, from earlier, lighting his cigarette outside the door.

"Leaving already?" He took a drag of the cigarette and blew the smoke in their direction.

The acrid stench made her cough. Why was this guy such a jerk?

"School night," Deacon muttered, scanning the parking lot.

Bret did the same. "Looks like your friends left without you."

Vivienne's body felt like it was on fire. If Deacon was nervous, he didn't let it show. Two guys from across the parking lot moved closer. She recognized them from inside.

Bret clucked his tongue, leering at her chest. "Your girlfriend's awfully pretty."

"Yes, she is." Deacon laced his fingers with hers. Squeezed. "And you're lucky I didn't break your damned nose for touching her."

What was he *doing*? "Deacon, let's just go."

Bret's eyes widened. "It's not my fault your little slut was coming on to me."

Oh no he didn't . . .

Slut? This guy thought she was a *slut*?

"As if I would *ever* be interested in your ugly, drunk ass," she hissed, rage building in her chest, pulsing in her veins.

Deacon bit back a laugh.

The rest of Bret's group left their posts beside their vehicles and came toward them. Bret dropped his cigarette, making a show of crushing the butt into the gravel at his feet. "Oh, the little bitch has claws, does she?"

"Vivienne, darling?" Deacon smiled down at her as if they weren't facing a mob of drunk guys looking for a flight. "What do you think?"

"About what?" she snapped.

"Fight or flight?"

With her heart pounding in her ears and the group advancing toward them, the fire in her chest burned stronger than ever.

She wanted to fight. Wanted to be the one to teach these jerks a lesson. And she had no doubt that Deacon would take on every single one of them for her. But it was five against two —Well, more like one-and-a-half. There no way they would win.

The sky beckoned her, and she whispered, "Flight."

The woods bordering the parking lot were the safest place to lift off. Deacon hauled ass toward the trees, keeping a death grip on Vivienne's hand. Footsteps thudded behind them, but the men hadn't anticipated them running in that direction. Once they reached the shadows, he was ready to pick her up, but she let go and alighted toward the branches.

How long had she been at Kensington? Two months? It looked like she'd been flying her entire life. It had taken him almost six months to learn that kind of control.

He heard Bret curse and spew threats into the darkness, but he and Vivienne were already entering the layer of silence that lived above the trees.

The night hadn't ended as he'd hoped, but there was still time to salvage it. Having Vivienne meet his friends had been strange at first. He couldn't recall ever inviting a girl to join their group. But she'd fit right in.

And the tight black T-shirt she was wearing had nearly driven him out of his mind. He was losing it. It was just a bloody T-shirt. Then there was her reaction every time he whispered something borderline inappropriate. Wide eyes. Flushed face. Unsteady breathing. It made him want to do more than make suggestions. But she'd never said anything to indicate she'd be interested. She'd either changed the subject or left.

It was making him insane.

They flew over houses and roads and warehouses until they reached the forest bordering Kensington. Adrenaline still pulsed through his veins, searching for an outlet. The flight had been too short. He felt like he needed to fly to Boston and back.

Vivienne landed without a sound on the lawn outside her flat. She didn't immediately turn around, which struck him as odd. Why wasn't she turning around?

"Vivienne? Are you all right?"

"You're crazy!" she snapped, whipping around and charging toward him in a flash of dark hair and narrowed eyes. "What the heck was that back there?"

"Wait...are you *mad* at me?" That made no sense. "What did I do?"

Her nail dug into his chest when she poked him. Twice.

"You just had to bring it up, didn't you? You couldn't just leave it alone and walk away."

Walk away? She was the one who was crazy. "Did you want him to touch you, Vivienne?"

"What?" She dropped her hand. Retreated a step. Her brows came together as she shook her head. "No. Of course not."

If Ethan hadn't held him back, he would've handled the situation the moment the bastard had put his slimy hand on her. "And when you asked him to let you go," he said carefully, "did he do it?"

"He thought he was hitting on me." She said it like the fact excused his actions.

Deacon had hit on plenty of women, and not once had he touched one like that. "Answer the question."

"No." Her eyes dropped to her shoes. "He didn't let me go."

"And if someone doesn't speak up, what's to stop him from doing it to someone else?" A fresh wave of fury crashed over him. He wanted to hit something. Hard. "If I'd said nothing, I would've been no better than the rest of that bastard's friends."

"I've been dealing with jerks like that my entire life."

"Are you serious?"

Her nod was matter-of-fact.

Did these men not have mothers? Sisters? Bloody Grannies? Did they have no damned self-respect?

He flexed his hands at his sides. Really, *really* wanting to hit something. "Now I'm sorry I didn't insist on fighting them."

"Don't be an idiot." She shoved past him and opened the door. "I can take care of myself."

She had been brilliant when that bastard had called her a —*Dammit*. Why hadn't he punched him? For a moment, he had thought she was going to take on the lot of them.

He swore and dragged his phone from his back pocket. When the call connected, he asked Ethan if he fancied a trip back to the bowling alley.

FIFTEEN

D eacon balanced himself on the low wall surrounding the fountain at the center of campus. It had been five days since the incident at the bowling alley, and his face still hurt when he smiled. But it had been worth it.

"You have to do it." Ethan held out the black rubbish bag toward him.

"I can't." He pushed the bag aside. "If my mother finds out, she'll have my head." The incident at the bar had been his "last" last chance. She still hadn't heard about the bowling alley. And if he was lucky, she never would.

Ethan shook the bag. The contents inside made an ominous swishing sound. "But it's tradition."

Deacon winced and pain shot down his cheek. "Aren't you always the one preaching about change?" He dipped his fingers in the frigid water and touched them to his cheekbone. When he got home, he'd have to ice it again.

"You're it." Ethan shoved him toward the water. He had to grab the bag to keep from falling in.

"Can someone *please* tell me what's happening here?" Vivienne stomped in the gravel leading up to the fountain and glared at them. "And where in the world did the two of you get matching black eyes?"

When he had seen her on campus between classes, he hadn't expected Ethan to choose that exact moment to approach him with his inconvenient demands.

"We're going trick-or-treating," he explained, hoping the answer would distract her from the second question.

"You're both way too old to be dressing up and bumming candy off strangers."

Ethan's hand flew to his chest. "Bite your tongue!" He collapsed onto the fountain wall. "As long as I look like I'm a teenager, I will continue our amazing Halloween traditions."

"Maybe she's right." Deacon jumped off the wall and landed next to her. "We've been doing this for a long time. Perhaps we should retire our costumes." He dropped the rubbish bag onto the ground. What would Ethan do if he left it there?

"Enough nonsense." Ethan shot to his feet. "The tradition must live on."

"Do you remember what happened last year? My mother said—"

"Last year was a fluke." Ethan gave him a dismissive wave. To Vivienne, he said, "Deacon's mother is the enemy of fun."

Vivienne laughed. "She sounds great."

Deacon kicked the bag in defeat. Neither of them could imagine exactly how anti-fun his mother was. "Ethan, it's your job to get a group of people to come along. It's a bit weird when the two of us go on our own."

Ethan slid his arm around Deacon's shoulders and wiggled his eyebrows suggestively. "I always thought it was our special bonding time."

He escaped before Ethan could kiss his cheek.

"You'll come, won't you Vivienne?" Ethan said to her.

"I can't even remember the last time I went trick-or-treating." Vivienne hooked her thumbs beneath the straps of her backpack and frowned. "I was probably five."

Was that a yes or no?

Ethan skipped in a circle around her, kicking stones off the path in the process. "All the more reason to come see what you've been missing."

Her bottom lip pushed out when her frown deepened. "I don't have a costume."

Still not an answer . . .

Ethan suggested Vivienne borrow one of Nicola's.

She snorted. "Yeah, okay."

"What? I'm sure she won't mind," Ethan said with a shrug.

"I'm half her size."

Ethan paused and seemed to consider their obvious differences in height as if he had never noticed it before. He stretched to his toes then squatted down and looked up at Vivienne. Then he stood, placed the side of his hand next to Vivienne's forehead and drew an invisible line to his sternum. "Maybe you're a bit shorter."

"A bit?" She looked to Deacon for assistance.

He enjoyed teasing her too much to answer honestly, so he asked Ethan if he knew Nicola's exact height—in meters.

"Never mind," Vivienne muttered, rolling her eyes. "I'll find a costume somewhere. Can Emily and Max come?"

Yes. It was a yes.

Deacon threw the rubbish bag over his shoulder and told her, "The more the merrier."

He didn't care who else she invited as long as she showed up.

"Of course I'll come with you!" Emily gushed, jumping up and down in the kitchen.

"Do you know where to get costumes this late? Ethan offered to let me borrow one of Nicola's but—"

"But you would need to stand on stilts to wear her stuff?" Emily finished with a shake of her head.

"Thank you!" Vivienne gave her roommate a high five. Apparently, height was an insignificant detail to guys like Ethan and Deacon. Were they really that oblivious?

"I know just the place." Emily grabbed her backpack from beside the door. "Let's go today after class."

That afternoon, they went to the closest pop-up Halloween

store in Worcester. Emily chose a flowy princess costume with an elaborate blue ball gown and glistening tiara; the flouncy outfit suited her love of frills. After a lot of deliberation, Vivienne settled on a witch costume from the children's section. Although she wasn't thrilled with it, there hadn't been many choices in women's costumes unless she wanted to be a sexy nurse or sexy bunny. She sprung a bit of extra cash for the high-quality green face paint and broom to accompany her black dress and trademark pointed hat.

Max was thrilled with the invitation and asked if he could bring his friend from extraction. Deacon texted to let her know they would be meeting outside the school gates at six thirty the following evening. She wanted to text him back something funny, but ended up sending a thumbs-up instead.

Before leaving the apartment on Halloween night, Vivienne found two envelopes sticking out of their letterbox. She brought both of them to Emily's room where she was getting ready.

"Loving the green face," Emily said, loosening the curler from her spiraled lock. She nodded to the envelope. "What's that?"

"I'm not sure." Vivienne turned the letters over in her hand. "But there's one for you too."

"Gimme." Emily took it, and they opened them simultaneously. "It's a letter about self-defense classes."

"Mine too." Vivienne scanned the official document. They had been booked for self-defense classes at the Aviary gym three days a week. She couldn't help her suspicions that their outing at the bowling alley had something to do with the addition.

"I thought those classes weren't until after we finished high school." Emily tucked the envelope beneath her makeup bag and touched up her sparkly blue eyeshadow.

"They must've changed the requirements." Or someone with green eyes had pulled some strings.

"As exciting as this is, I must finish preparing to meet my royal subjects. Please, excuse me." Emily swirled her taffeta skirts toward her bathroom.

Vivienne went to her own closet, dragged out her Chucks,

slipped them over her red-and-white striped socks, and checked her reflection in the mirror. She didn't look half bad, and the hat was actually kind of cute.

When they arrived at the gates, Max and his friend in a life-like SWAT uniform were already there. Max was dressed like a pirate, with a painted stubble beard, a red velvet coat, and a black tricorn hat. The leather eyepatch he wore had a skull and crossbones printed on it.

"Where'd you get the costume on such short notice?" she asked him, taking a turn with his realistic-looking sword. She stabbed him with it, and he pretended to collapse.

"Ethan let me borrow it." His beard smudged when he rubbed his chin. "Where's everyone else?"

"I'm not sure." They were really late. She hadn't brought her phone, so she hoped Deacon hadn't changed their plans or canceled.

A red car rounded the corner from the road to Worcester, its headlights flashing like a searchlight over them before coming to a stop in front of the gates. Deacon, Nicola, and Ethan climbed out; the driver did a U-turn and sped off toward Worcester.

Nicola was dressed as a black cat, complete with fierce fangs and contact lenses, giving her yellow eyes elongated pupils. The tight-fitting bodysuit accentuated her athletic curves, and left Vivienne feeling self-conscious in her kid-sized costume.

Deacon's Peter Pan costume was straight out of a movie. He even wore the tights, which should have looked ridiculous. But didn't. Ethan—at least she assumed it was Ethan—wore a black morph suit.

Emily pulled at the stretchy fabric on his arms. "What in the world are you supposed to be?"

"Peter's Shadow." It was strange hearing Ethan's voice but not being able to see his face.

"I'm surprised you and Ethan didn't coordinate costumes," Vivienne whispered to Nicola. Maybe next year she and Emily could come up with something together.

Nicola rolled her hypnotic eyes. "Dash and Ethan have a

thing about dressing up together. It's weird, but I'm used to it. Last year was worse."

Vivienne watched the pair stretching in tandem, fighting a smile. Everything Deacon did, Ethan mimicked behind him. "What were they last year?"

"Mr. and Mrs. Potato Head."

"Tell me you have pictures."

"No photos, I'm afraid," she said, adjusting her pointed ears. "It's one of the few PAN policies the guys follow."

That was too bad. She would have paid good money to see it. "Which one was Mrs. Potato Head?"

"They took turns switching parts. By the end of the night, there was only one pair of eyes and a single ear between them."

Emily tapped her scepter against her palm and asked if they were waiting for anyone else.

Ethan flew above the group with his hands curved around where his eyes should be, like a pair of binoculars. "I don't see anyone else coming."

"Ethan Bates!" Nicola hissed, grabbing his ankle and yanking him back. "We're on a public road, you idiot. Don't you dare start this shit. I'm not dealing with it tonight."

"Retract those claws, pretty kitty." Ethan laughed and tried to pet her head, but she swatted him away. "Nice kitty."

"I'm going to make you hurt in ways you can't even imagine if you don't stop calling me kitty."

Deacon called for Max and waved him over, saying he had a proposition for him. Whatever that meant.

Vivienne tried not to be hurt that he hadn't even tried to talk to her yet. He seemed different when his friends were around. Not as attentive. But why would he be attentive to her? She was nothing to him. Another girl to flirt with.

After some whispering, Max nodded emphatically. Ethan laid out the route for the occasion and led everyone to the right. Vivienne ended up at the back of the procession, trying to avoid stepping on Emily's glittering blue skirt.

"I like your costume," Deacon said, falling in line beside her. "Are you feeling wicked tonight?"

Was she feeling wicked? "I guess you'll have to wait and see."

"I'd be up for a bit of devilment myself." The way Deacon's eyes landed on her lips made her mouth go dry. Surely, he wasn't suggesting—"I think you should ride into town on your broom."

Flying. He was talking about flying.

Vivienne felt herself deflate. "I haven't read the whole rulebook, but I'm pretty sure Kensington wouldn't approve." They reached a stretch of sidewalk, and she scraped the mud off her shoes.

"I certainly won't tell anyone about anything you do tonight."

He was still talking about flying . . .

But he was looking at her mouth again, and her stomach was fluttering, and if he didn't stop looking at her mouth, she was going to do something stupid and try to—"Max."

Deacon's brows came together. "What?"

"Um, what were you saying to him—to Max—before we left?" She skirted around a large puddle, but the back of her dress still got wet.

Deacon flew over it. "It's a secret."

"I'd say you're good at keeping secrets by now."

"I'm excellent at keeping all kinds of secrets."

She swallowed against the lump in her throat. Did every word out of his stupid, beautiful mouth have to sound like a proposition? "Am I allowed to ask if you had us put into self-defense classes, or is that another secret?"

Deacon groaned and raked a hand over his face. Which was a weird reaction to a pretty simple question. "Kensington gives all new recruits training in self-defense," he clipped.

"That wasn't what I asked you," she shot back. His guilty look was all the confirmation she needed. "You didn't have to do that."

He jumped and smacked a low-hanging branch. A handful of damp orange leaves fluttered around them. "Do what?"

"I don't need you to protect me," she muttered, pulling a leaf from her costume.

"I wouldn't be a very good guardian angel if I didn't at least try to protect you—or ensure you can protect yourself."

The only thing that needed protection right now was her stupid heart. "I don't want a guardian angel."

"Then what do you want, wicked little witch?"

She froze. It was a good question. And she didn't care if he was talking about something obscure. He needed to know where she stood in whatever this was. "I want someone who isn't going to fly away, *Peter Pan*."

She left him standing there and hurried to catch up. Why had she even bothered saying that? She shouldn't have opened her mouth.

Deacon flew to her side and resumed walking. "I've changed my mind."

"About what?"

"I don't like your costume."

She rolled her eyes. This guy. As if she cared whether or not he liked it. "And why don't you like my costume anymore?"

It was his turn to stop. She stopped beside him; the rest of their party continued without seeming to notice.

Deacon leaned in close enough for her to see his pupils dilate. "Because," he whispered, his warm words tickling the fine hairs along her green neck, "that damned green face paint makes it impossible for me to get away with kissing you."

HOLY CRAP.

She hadn't been imagining things. He wanted to kiss her. He'd said that, right? She wasn't hallucinating. Deacon wanted to kiss her.

Would washing her face in one of the puddles look desperate? Probably. Definitely.

What in heaven's name had possessed her to paint her face green?

Yellow halos around the streetlights gave an eerie glow to the dark night. Following the sidewalk from house to house, they filled their bags and baskets with candy. A few people said,

"Aren't you all a bit old for this?" But mostly, there was over-whelming appreciation for Deacon and Ethan's performance.

At every house, Deacon walked up first, and Ethan followed him as close as possible, mimicking his every move. After he and Ethan had collected their candy, Max, the pirate, chased them to the next porch. There were a fair number of duels fought between stops; Peter and his miming shadow always emerged the victors.

"They must have practiced this," Vivienne said to Nicola as they watched the guys wave goodbye in perfect unison.

Nicola shrugged. "They've been planning it for at least eight weeks. Two months ago, they asked me to be Tinkerbell," she said with a snort. "I'm way too tall to be a pixie."

Two houses later, Vivienne realized Deacon had gone miss-ing. Not that she was aware of his every single move. That would have been stalkerish.

How times had changed . . .

There was screaming from around the corner of the last house, but she thought nothing of it. Deacon caught up with them by the next driveway.

The odd pattern of Deacon disappearing and reappearing continued into the next hour of trick-or-treating. Once their containers were filled to the brim, the PAN agreed to call an end to their candy-collecting excursion. On the way back to Kens-ington, their party met a smaller group of three teens and ended up chatting to each other about the best houses that were giving away full-sized candy bars.

"I love your costume," a sexy angel told Deacon.

"Thank you." He removed his hat and bowed. "I like your costume as well. Very original."

Vivienne had encountered at least five other sexy angels in this neighborhood alone.

"Is the accent real or just for Halloween?"

Deacon put his finger to his lips. "It's a secret."

"I won't tell."

His eyes darted to Vivienne when he said, "I don't share my secrets with just anyone." Then he smiled back at the angel, and replaced his hat. "You have to earn them."

Vivienne wasn't jealous. Her stomach twisted and ached from all the candy. She was NOT jealous.

"And how would I do that?" The angel raked a glittery silver nail down his chest.

He grinned and whispered something into the girl's ear. Her eyes widened and she took a step back. Vivienne could only imagine what he'd said to her. It was probably funny and flirty and wildly inappropriate.

"Have you guys seen the ghost yet?" the second teen, a sexy policewoman, said. Her eyes lifted to the moonless sky, and she shuddered.

"You think you saw a ghost?" Deacon shivered.

"What did the ghost look like?" Nicola sounded serious.

"Do you really want to know, or are you going to make fun of me like everyone else?" the officer asked.

"I really want to know."

"Well, it was white and had these hollow black eyes." She spread her eyelids with her fingers. "I only saw it for a second in the sky, but it was definitely real."

"You're sure it was flying?" No longer looking at the girl spinning the tale, Nicola's eyes were fixed on Deacon and Ethan —both of whom seemed to be searching the night for signs of the supernatural. "Maybe it was something stuck in a tree."

"I told them someone probably hooked the costume to a drone or something like that," an astronaut in a realistic costume said from beneath his tinted helmet. "There's no way the ghost of Worcester is real."

"That's the most likely explanation," Deacon said with an emphatic nod.

His shadow stood behind him, nodding.

Vivienne had a new level of respect for Ethan's commitment to his role.

"Thanks for the warning." Nicola sidled next to Ethan and linked her arm with his. "We'll keep our eyes peeled for ghosts on our way home."

"You should come with us," the policewoman said to Deacon. "We're going to a bonfire, and we have beer."

Vivienne hoped he would stay so she could get over this

stupid crush. He could do whatever he wanted with those girls. She didn't care. And to show him how much she didn't care, she turned and walked away.

A moment later, there were footsteps behind her, and Deacon jogged until he caught up. "Where are you running off to, little witch?"

"I'm going home."

"You could do that. *Or*...you could stay out and get into trouble with me."

Trouble. That's exactly what Deacon was. "Fly away, lost boy. I'm not looking for that kind of trouble."

The next morning, Vivienne received two text messages from a blocked number saying there was a mandatory meeting in the Aviary at 10 a.m. She and Emily happened upon Deacon and Ethan at the entrance.

"We should probably go inside," Emily said, peering through the door. "It looks pretty crowded in there."

"Can't." Ethan nudged his chin toward the fountain. "We're waiting for Nicola."

Deacon's Kensington hat cast a shadow over his bloodshot eyes. He rubbed his temples and told Ethan to keep it down.

"Rough night?" Vivienne asked, wondering where he'd gone when he left.

"Very." He looked pale. And exhausted. And irritable. And he reeked of alcohol.

Instead of trying to make more conversation, she went to wait next to Emily, who was giving her a questioning look that she ignored.

Nicola trudged up to them a few minutes later, her face pinched and brows furrowed.

"Hey babe." Ethan tried to slip his arm around her waist, but she shoved him away.

"Don't even start," she bit out, adjusting her black sweater. "My dad is pissed, and if he sees you touching me, he'll flip."

Paul Mitter was stalking down the gravel behind her, a stern frown on his face. Wait. Paul was Nicola's dad? Now that she saw them together, she could see the resemblance. They had the same straight nose and blue eyes.

Julie ran along behind Paul, her frizzy red hair bouncing on her shoulders as she struggled to keep up.

"You," Paul growled, pointing at Deacon when he passed. "I need to speak with you in my office after this."

Deacon rolled his eyes but gave Paul a tight-lipped nod.

Ethan stepped in front of Julie, blocking her when she tried to enter the building. "What's going on, Julie?"

She narrowed her eyes and smacked her notepad against her palm. "Were you all out last night?"

"It was Halloween," he said with a laugh, "of course we were out."

Julie mumbled something about seventeen calls. "Then I have a feeling you know why you're here. Every damn year we have to deal with this immature bullshit." She pushed her frizz aside. "Your mother will get the report when she gets back, Dash. And you know what that means."

Deacon pinched the bridge of his nose and groaned again.

Inside, they took seats at the back. Vivienne glanced at Deacon a few times, but he ignored her. She shouldn't feel bad for last night. Not after seeing him flirt with those girls so openly in front of her. But for some reason, she did.

A microphone squealed at the front of the room, and Paul gave the top three swift taps. "The sooner you're quiet, the sooner we can start," he said, waiting for everyone to shut up. "I hate calling this meeting on such short notice, but I'm afraid we didn't have a choice. My Nevergene may not be active, but I was your age once too. I know the drill. Halloween is fun. You go a little crazy. Play a few pranks. But back in my day, there weren't camera phones."

He nodded to where Julie stood, and she pressed the light switch. The room darkened as much as possible with the November morning illuminating the stained-glass windows. Paul held out a remote, and the machine beside him projected an image of what looked like a ghostly figure with hollow black eyes against the far wall.

The crowd began to murmur as Paul scrolled through the images, all in varying degrees of clarity. At the end of the slide show, he played a bumpy, grainy video clip. Everyone watched the ghost flit across the night sky.

Everyone except Ethan, who was busy whispering in Deacon's ear.

Once the video played, Julie turned the lights back on.

"I expect the responsible party to come forward," Paul said, his tone unamused. "We're a secret society and having someone out there dressing up like a ghost and flying around scaring people is putting all of us in danger."

Someone near the back of the room began to chuckle, and then another person at the front joined him. Before long, the entire group was in a fit of laughter.

Paul threw up his hands and stomped out the side exit.

Vivienne glanced over at Deacon once more, but he was already walking out of the room.

Deacon felt like shit. Had it been Ethan's or Joel's idea to do shots? He couldn't remember. It didn't matter. He hated both of them.

And Paul refused to stand still. He just . . . kept . . . pacing . . . back and forth . . . in front of the bloody window . . . and the sun was burning through the glass and—Was it hot in here? He really needed some water.

"Look," Deacon said, knowing the sooner he got this over with, the sooner he could get back home and pass out, "before you ask about the ghost—"

Paul stopped moving long enough to glare at him. "That childish prank is the least of my worries."

"Then why did you just call a meeting for everyone on campus?" And why the hell had he called it so early?

"Because if there's not at least the threat of some sort of disciplinary action, this place is going to descend into complete anarchy. Peter and your mother are busy with the latest

Mermaid fiasco, and I'm bogged down figuring out Vivienne's connection with HOOK."

"I don't see how any of that pertains to me."

"It doesn't. But I heard a rumor that you've been attending Lee Somerfield's meetings."

After the incident at the bar, Deacon had hoped the meeting he'd attended beforehand had been overlooked. "I went to *one* meeting," he grumbled, slipping off the sofa arm and onto the cushions. It was comfy. Would Paul mind if he took a nap there?

"We need the young people on our side." Paul went to shuffle files until he found his yellow legal pad. "And when they see you attending meetings with a rebellious faction, it doesn't exactly serve Leadership's purpose, does it?"

Paul mustn't remember what it was like to be young. The very essence of rebellion ran through Deacon's veins. Right or wrong, when someone told him to do something, he wanted to do the opposite.

"People are going to continue attending Lee's meetings, if not out of genuine interest, then at least out of curiosity," he told Paul. "Whether I'm there or not doesn't make a damn bit of difference to anyone."

"What's done is done, and I'm hoping there's something positive we can take from it. What are your thoughts on the meeting?"

"It was...interesting." Deacon's keys fell out of his pocket, so he tossed them into the air.

"What did Lee say?"

"Mostly stuff about HOOK being the enemy." He threw his keys higher and caught them with one hand. He tossed them a third time . . . and they landed in Paul's palm.

"You stayed for an entire meeting and that's all you got from it?"

Deacon swiped for his keys, but Paul moved them out of his reach. "I'm giving you the highlights."

"What are his plans?"

"To continue growing until Leadership takes action. May I have my keys back, please?"

Paul considered the keys in his hand. "What kind of action?"

"To be honest, it seems *any* action at all would appease them." Deacon rubbed his aching temples and tried to remember what had been said. It felt like forever ago. "He also mentioned something about going for HOOK's Virginia office."

Paul dropped the keys onto his desk. "How many people saw you?"

He wasn't invisible. "*Everyone* saw me." Deacon rose from the sofa and snagged his keys.

Paul tapped him on the shoulder before he reached the door. "Do you want to call Peter, or should I?"

"You do it." Deacon had a hangover to nurse.

SIXTEEN

" And here I thought you'd given up stalking me." Vivienne hadn't seen Deacon since the day after Halloween, and his meaningless comment about kissing her had kept her awake more nights than she cared to admit.

"I didn't give up," he said, sweeping past her into the living room. "*Someone* told me to fly away."

Crap. She had hoped he'd forgotten about that. "Sorry. I was…annoyed." She refused to say "jealous" because she had no right to be jealous. Then again, she didn't have the right to be annoyed either.

With her muscles aching from self-defence, she hobbled over to where Deacon leaned on the arm of the couch. Her legs felt like jelly, and her arms felt like lead, and her shoulders were wound so tight, even shrugging was excruciating.

Deacon's lips flattened, taking away some of their fullness. "What did I do that annoyed you?"

"You were flirting and whispering with that angel." It sounded pathetic when she said it aloud. Petty and pathetic.

His brows came together, and he rubbed the back of his neck. Then he laughed and gave her a silly grin. "Do you want to know what I said to her?"

"I don't care. It doesn't matter."

He crossed his arms and waited.

"*Fine*," she groaned. "You can tell me if it'll make you feel better."

"I told her that if she didn't stop touching me, my little witch was going to put a curse on her."

His little witch?

He had told the angel to go away? Now that she thought about it, after he had whispered to the girl, she had dropped her hand and stepped away from him.

"I'm an idiot." She hid her horror behind her hands.

"It's a pity you didn't stay out. You missed a good night." He chuckled as he went into the kitchen. "Ethan fell off a roof, and Max passed out in my back garden wearing Nicola's catsuit." Deacon meandered around her kitchen, opening and closing the cabinets and drawers, peering into the fridge.

Something else about that night bugged her. "Tell me about the ghost."

"I don't believe in ghosts." A small smile played on his lips. "May I have a bottle of water?"

"You can if you answer my question."

The seal on the lid cracked when he twisted it open. He kept his eyes on hers as he raised it to his lips and took a drink. "You didn't ask me a question."

"Was it you?"

"Was what me?"

"The ghost."

"Why does it matter?" He glanced down the dark hallway. "Where's Emily?"

"Out to eat with her mom and dad. Stop changing the subject."

He walked up to her and whispered, "Boo." Endless secrets sparkled in his green eyes.

So it *was* him. The disappearing and reappearing on Halloween made sense now.

"Why are you here?" She rolled her neck, hoping the muscles stretched out before her run later. "Don't you have anyone else to haunt?"

"Why would I haunt someone else when I can haunt you?"

Deacon dropped onto the couch and draped his arm across the back cushion, giving her a pointed look. "Are you still avoiding *trouble*?"

She should be avoiding him. But after hearing what had really happened on Halloween, she wanted to jump on top of him and kiss him senseless. Should she point out that she wasn't wearing green face paint anymore? "I let you in, didn't I?"

"True. How's self-defence?"

They hadn't seen each other in weeks and he wanted to talk about classes? Great. "My entire body aches so…good?"

"Lucky for you, I know how to cure those aches."

So they were back to this again. "I'm sure you do," she snorted.

"You don't believe me?" Deacon slid onto the floor and patted the space between his knees. "Come here and I'll show you."

"No. What? *Why*?"

He rolled his eyes. "I just told you I could help."

With her heart in her throat, she sank down in front of him, holding her breath as he brushed her hair to the side. And then his hands were on her shoulders, moving in slow circles with the right pressure in the right spots, and she let out an involuntary moan because it felt *sooo* good.

"This would be a lot easier," he said against her neck, sending shivers down her spine, "if you took off your top."

"*What*?" she squeaked.

He tugged the corner of her sweatshirt. "Your top."

"Oh…um…right. Yeah."

She thought she heard him chuckle but was too mortified to turn around. Instead, she pulled her sweatshirt over her head, tossed it onto the couch, and adjusted the T-shirt she had on underneath.

Hugging her legs to her chest, she rested her chin on her knees. "You're really good at that."

"I've been told I'm really good at a lot of things."

Deacon could write a book on double entendres. "Can you not do that?"

"Not do what?" He found a knot behind her right shoulder blade and kneaded it with his knuckle.

"That thing you do where it sounds like you say one thing but really mean another."

A pause. "I always say exactly what I mean."

"Yeah, okay." When she twisted toward him, his hands dropped. "What about telling me to take off my top?"

"It's fairly self-explanatory, Vivienne," he drawled, rolling his eyes. "I wanted you to take off your top so I could help you with your sore shoulders."

"You know what I thought you meant." His mock innocence wasn't fooling her. "I thought you were saying that you wanted to see me topless."

"Is that in the cards?" A wicked smile. "Because I would absolutely love to see you topless."

"W-what?"

Heat from his chest scalded her back when he leaned forward and said, "You heard me," against the shell of her ear.

Okay . . . well *that* wasn't going to happen. She was *not* going to take off her top, no matter how good it would feel to have his hands moving on her bare skin—

Nope. Nope. *Not* happening.

He resumed working the knots from her shoulder blades. She felt him shift, then something soft pressed against the skin behind her ear. Moved lower.

Wait . . . was that his *mouth*?

Holy CRAP.

He was kissing his way down her neck and—

Heat pooled in her stomach and she leaned into him because there was no way she was going to lean away. His hands slipped around her waist to her hips, and if something didn't happen, she was going to spontaneously combust.

"You and I should get into trouble together," he said against her shoulder

"Deacon..." his name was a sigh on her lips.

She felt his smile against her skin. "Let's go to your room."

Yes. Yes. Wait. No.

He thought he could come in here after not talking to her for weeks and put his beautiful mouth on her and then she'd invite him to her room? She wasn't sure what kind of girls he usually hung out with, but that wasn't something she did.

"I...I...um...I have to go to genealogy." It wasn't a lie. She had to be there in an hour.

He released his grip on her waist.

Pulled away.

Cursed under his breath. "I didn't realize that was today. Do you need me to come with you?"

"Why would you do that?"

"Some find it helpful to have a friend join them for their first meeting."

Friend. Deacon thought they were just *friends*? She didn't know exactly what she felt for him, but it was a good deal more than friendship. He was probably one of those guys who wanted to "keep it casual." "Friends with benefits" and all that crap.

"I'll be fine on my own." She pushed away from him and stumbled to her feet.

His dark brows came together; he seemed to be breathing as heavily as she was. "Did I say something wrong?"

"Nope." She ripped her sweatshirt off the couch. "I need to go."

"Right now?" he groaned, dropping his head into his hands.

"Yep." Because if she didn't, she'd be tempted to make some very bad decisions.

"All right." He got up, raked his hand through his hair, and went to the glass door. Before he left, he twisted back to her. His eyes were wide and worried. "If I said or did something to offend you," he said, shaking his head, "I'm sorry, all right?"

She could only nod and watch him fly away.

"Vivienne?" the slender young woman in a gray dress asked after a quick glance at the stack of papers on her desk. The pendulum on the cuckoo clock on the wall swung back and forth behind the woman's head.

Vivienne stepped closer to the desk. "That's me."

"I'm Martina." She checked her watch. "You're very early."

"Sorry. I had some time to kill, so I thought I would go ahead and make my way over." She fiddled with the hair tie on her wrist. "If you want, I can come back."

"There's no need." Martina donned a long white lab coat that had been draped over the back of her chair and told Vivienne to follow her. There was a smaller door concealed in dark paneling at the back of the office. Inside was a closet-like room with a single white desk squeezed into the space along with two padded chairs.

"Do you have anyone coming to meet you?" Martina looked over the rim of her glasses toward the door. She tugged a pair of soft white gloves out of her pocket and pulled them over her fingers.

"Not that I know of."

"Very well. Have a seat and put these on." She held out an identical pair of gloves to Vivienne and said she'd be right back. When she returned a few minutes later, she was carrying a remote control and a stack of books. She placed everything on the desk and topped off the pile with an unsteady box of tissues.

Without another word of direction, the woman clipped out of the room and shut the door.

What appeared to be a loose piece of paper forgotten between the books caught Vivienne's attention. She adjusted her gloves, drew the yellowed edges free, and unfolded it. Printed on the aged poster was a faded tree with names scrolled on the branches.

At the top of the page was the name MAIMIE WARD. Below Maimie's name, written in smaller letters, was the name Howard Jones.

The twenty or so names on the family tree were unfamiliar, but when Vivienne reached the last three entries, her mind began to race, and her skin began to itch.

WILLIAM DUNN ———— ANNE JONES DUNN

Beneath their names, on the final branch, was her own name.

That couldn't be right . . . William and Anne weren't her—

The pieces of a puzzle she had been collecting since childhood shifted.

Anne, Vivienne's beautiful, vibrant sister, was really her mother.

And her absent, faceless father hadn't been absent or faceless; William, her handsome, silly brother, was really her father.

The revelations that followed could have taken five minutes or five hundred minutes. At some point, Vivienne resurfaced from drowning in her memories to grasp for an explanation. Her fingers closed around the silver remote.

Darkness surrounded her when she clicked play. A mechanical whir hummed above her head, and a single beam of light shot from a projector that had lowered from a cavity within the ceiling. There was shuffling from the machine, and then a familiar voice she hadn't heard in twelve years asked a simple question.

"Is it working?" her sister Anne asked from off screen.

Not my sister, she reminded herself. *My mother.*

The videographer panned to the left, and there sat Anne Dunn, wearing a faded black T-shirt beneath a pair of denim coveralls dotted with paint. She was exquisite in her simplicity and bearing a smile that could banish even the scariest nightmares.

Anne Dunn had always been smiling.

"Hello, Vivienne," she said, her brown eyes full of secrets.

Then her father sat on the chair next to Anne. "Hi, Viv."

Tears filled Vivienne's eyes, blurring the images. She cursed and grabbed for the tissues. She wasn't going to miss even a second with her family.

"We're so happy you made it to Neverland," Anne said. "Our only regret is that..."

William accepted Anne's shaking hand and rubbed his thumb across her knuckles. "That we aren't there to show it to you," he finished, his voice catching.

After Anne composed herself, she said, "I know you must be

confused by our choices, but please give us the chance to explain before you pass judgement. Neverland is a place of dreams, but living there without having any other choice is not something we ever wanted for you. Your father grew up at Kensington and struggled with keeping all the secrets. Like many PAN before us, when we found out about you, we decided to press pause on our lives in Neverland and move somewhere new.

"Because we don't age, we couldn't tell the outsiders that we were your parents. It wouldn't have fit our cover to have you turn nine, ten, eleven..."—Anne pointed to herself and William — "and the two of us look like we're forever eighteen. And we didn't want to move around more than necessary or rouse suspicion. So, we asked my sister Christine to come with us to Ohio to act as our mother."

The woman she knew as her mother was really her aunt.

Her entire life felt like a lie.

"What you see before you is everything we've kept for you. We love you so much and have always been so proud of you," Anne said, crossing her palms over her heart.

"We love you, Bug." Her father's familiar, forgotten term of endearment brought another downpour through Vivienne's lashes. By the time she composed herself, the video had ended, and the lights had flickered back on.

We love you . . .

Was that even true? If they had lied about so much already, why not lie about that?

Vivienne lifted the cover of the first of five books and realized they were photo albums. Didn't they have the no-photos rule eighteen years ago?

Inside were pictures of Vivienne as a baby and her mother in the hospital after giving birth. Anne proudly displayed her tiny treasure snuggled in a pink knitted blanket.

There was another one of a newborn Vivienne being cradled by her father; instead of looking at the photographer, he had been caught sharing a secret smile with his daughter as her fingers encircled his thumb.

So many first experiences were preserved within the

volumes—her first Christmas, first Easter, and first birthday. She felt removed from the blissful story they told, like she was looking at someone else's life. As her gloved fingers flipped, the memories became clearer: her third birthday and a cake decorated with ponies, a floppy yarn-haired doll her father had given her, a trip to the lake to feed ducks and sail a yellow wooden boat the three of them had made together.

The final image was from Vivienne's sixth birthday party.

Anne and William crouched on either side of Vivienne's balloon-laden chair, crooked party hats on their heads and smiles on their faces, watching their daughter shovel cake into her mouth. Vivienne's eyes were closed, as though she was relishing every last lick of the purple icing covering her lips.

Her parents' faces seemed filled with joy and adoration—and love.

What had she been thinking? Of course her parents had loved her.

She had been the center of their world until the day they died.

The rest of the pages were empty, confirming that, without a family, there was a void in Vivienne's life that would never be filled.

Wanting to see her parents again, she pressed play on the remote. Like before, the lights turned off and the machine awoke. But this time, there was a five-minute video from the hospital on the day Vivienne was born. She watched this and countless other snippets that brought to life the still images from the albums. When the final video played, Vivienne sat in the dark for some time before she felt like moving.

She was exhausted and drained and so weary she barely had the energy to get off the chair. The puffy skin around her eyes throbbed when she gave it one final wipe. Composing herself as best she could, she shoved a few more tissues into her pocket and hoped Martina wouldn't notice her slip away.

When she opened the door, there was someone waiting for her . . . but it wasn't Martina.

Leaning on the edge of the desk, Deacon watched her with a wary expression. Without smiling, he stood . . . and opened his arms. And she didn't have to think about her response. She collapsed against him, and the tears that had barely dried returned with heavy sobs.

"I know you told me not to come," he said quietly, "but I thought…Well, I didn't want you to be alone after."

He had come for her.

"I'm so glad you didn't listen to me." She loved the way his arms felt around her. Warm. Strong. Safe. "I'm sorry about earlier. I just got really confused and freaked out."

Smoothing a hand down her hair, he huffed a laugh. "You confuse the hell out of me too."

At least they had that in common.

"Did you know about my parents?"

He stiffened. "Do you mind if we discuss this outside? I promised Martina I'd lock up as soon as you finished." He let her go and offered her his hand.

Together, she and Deacon made their way down the stairs, through the empty reception hall, and out the main door. Next to the forest, one lonely lamppost shared its warm glow with the darkness. Beyond, a narrow path covered in damp leaves led into the heart of the forest.

Once her eyes adjusted, she could make out a faint light from somewhere along the wooded tunnel. "Where are we going?"

"You'll see." He led her down the lonely trail, accompanied by the autumn wind and an occasional motion-activated light that fluttered to life a few seconds before they reached it. "Our DNA is too precious for traditional burials and graves," he said, ducking beneath a low-hanging branch. "When one of us passes away, we're cremated, and the ashes are scattered in the wind."

The PAN were expected to live *and* die in secret. It didn't seem right. Didn't seem fair.

He stopped when they reached a dark clearing. One by one, the seven lamps marking the perimeter began to glow. In the center was an even brick patio surrounded by leaf-filled flower beds and gardens hibernating until spring. Somehow, not one fallen leaf had reached the bricks.

Deacon laid his hands on her shoulders and gave them a

reassuring squeeze. "This is the closest thing there is to a grave-yard in Neverland."

Vivienne pulled free from his grasp and went to the engraved red squares. It took a few minutes, but she located what served as a headstone dedicated to her parents' memory.

Her father had been sixty-four when he'd died. Her mother had been fifty-five.

But the dates gave no indication of how much life and vitality had been left in her parents when they had passed. They should have lived for *centuries*. Lived forever.

She collapsed onto one of the soggy benches and tried to process everything that had happened in the last twelve hours.

"To answer your question from inside," Deacon said, sinking next to her, "I knew about your parents."

His confession didn't surprise her. "So you knew my father grew up at Kensington."

A nod.

"And that they didn't want me to do the same."

"There's a lot to be said for their decision." He cleared his throat and adjusted his position so that he was facing her. "I, um...I grew up in the Neverland outside of London—in Harrow."

Vivienne scooted back so she could see his face more clearly. The shadows suited him. *Everything* suited him.

"It's more regimented and far stricter than it is here," he went on, picking at his nails. "Leadership is based there, and the majority of residents are much older than here at The Academy. My mother was afraid I would let our secrets slip to the wrong person, so I spent most of my youth between my parents' flat, my grandfather's home, and campus." He leaned forward and put his elbows on his knees. "They loosened up as I got older, when I knew what I could share and what needed to remain secret.

"We moved to the states when I was thirteen. Then I learned there was a good chance I wouldn't be like my mother because my father was an outsider. People treated me like I was some sort of ticking bomb, waiting to see when—*if* I would explode.

When I changed, it was such a relief. I don't know if they would've known what to do with me if I hadn't."

That sounded awful. To have such a big secret you could never tell anyone. No child should have that kind of responsibility.

"You're lucky your parents took you away," he confessed to the barren trees.

"I may be lucky they took me away," she said, clasping his fingers in hers, "but I'm even luckier that you came to find me."

SEVENTEEN

"You were home awfully late last night," Emily said from behind the fridge door. "I fell asleep waiting for you."

"My genealogy appointment ran late." And instead of sleeping when she got home, Vivienne had spent half the night staring at her ceiling thinking about the mystery that was Deacon Ashford.

"How was it?" She carried the milk jug to her bowl of cereal on the table.

Vivienne fell onto the chair across from her. Where did she begin? "Well, I found out my brother and sister were really my parents. They were both PAN—"

Emily's spoon clattered into her bowl. "They were *both* PAN?"

"Yeah. So?"

"Didn't you read the red book Penelope gave us?"

"Not yet." She had tried a few times, but it was too boring to hold her interest. "Why?"

"Neverland doesn't do divorce, which means marrying another PAN is an eternal commitment. That's a big reason so many of us marry outsiders."

Vivienne touched the printed date on the back of the milk jug. "Because outsiders have an expiration date?"

"Exactly," Emily said with a cheerful nod. "The longest I've stayed with a guy is six months. I can't imagine finding one I want to be with forever."

Neither could Vivienne. But knowing her parents had entered into such a lasting commitment gave her hope that kind of love existed.

"Plus," she went on, "I heard the guys in Neverland are only interested in one thing—and it's *not* eternal commitment."

"Who told you that?" The question came out harsher than she'd intended.

"A few girls I met were complaining about how immature all the guys on campus were. After hearing what they said, I'd rather take my chances with outsiders. At least you know they'll grow up someday."

Guys who never grow up. Deacon liked to play pranks and get drunk and flirt and—

"You're thinking about Deacon right now, aren't you?"

"What? No. Why would you say that?"

Emily cupped Vivienne's jaw in her hands and made a pouty face. "Because you look all 'I love you' and 'Be my boyfriend' and 'Kiss me with your hot British mouth.'"

"Shut up," Vivienne choked, pulling free and escaping to her bedroom before Emily could see anything else on her face. That girl was too intuitive for her own good.

She dragged her rule book from beneath a pile of laundry and flipped until she found the section about relationships.

. . . *Due to our immortal nature, romantic relationships between PAN are not encouraged and should not be entered into lightly. If two PAN decide to marry, the union requires prior approval from Leadership to ensure longevity* . . .

Not encouraged. What did that even mean? Was it off limits or just frowned upon?

When Vivienne went back into the kitchen, Emily was shoving her books and an extra sweater into her backpack. The weather had taken a turn, and the forecast didn't look good for the weekend.

Vivienne slid her fingers along the text while her heart

pounded in her ears. "Apparently we need permission to marry outsiders too."

"That's because they have to take that ageless injection Robert told us about," Emily said, struggling with the zipper. "Leadership won't give it to anyone who isn't married."

Vivienne folded the corner of the page and closed her book. None of it mattered. She wasn't looking for a relationship. With anyone.

Her phone dinged in her pocket. When she checked it, the fireflies started going berserk—and Deacon had only written one word. *Lunch?*

Trouble. Flirt and fly away. Never grow up . . .

She shouldn't text him back. Pretend she never saw it. *With you?*

Ugh. She had no self-control when it came to him.

Deacon's reply was instantaneous. *No, with Ethan.*

He was such a smartass. *Then definitely.*

Two messages came back, one after the other. *Lunch is off. Have to go murder my best mate.*

She texted him back the eye-rolling emoji and asked what time. He told her he'd be there at one.

Was it one o'clock yet?

"Is a certain sexy Brit texting you?" Emily teased, pulling her coat down from the hook.

Be cool. Don't grin like a lovesick fool. "Maybe." Vivienne smiled so wide it made her face hurt.

"Ah! Tell. Me. Everything." Emily dropped onto the chair and squeezed Vivienne's knees. "How long has this been going on? Is he your boyfriend? Have the two of you made out?"

"Nothing is going on. And no."

"No to which one?"

She rolled her eyes. "To both."

The corner of Emily's mouth lifted into a knowing smile. "Is that the story you're going with?"

"Yep."

"You're no fun at all. You know that, right?" She shoved to her feet and stomped to the door.

Vivienne laughed and wished her good luck with her genealogy appointment.

Once Emily left, Vivienne went to the cupboard for cereal, but when she opened the door, the smell of chocolate wafted from within. She grabbed the packet of chocolate chip cookies and tore the opening wider.

Leaning against the fridge, cookies in hand, she tried to figure out why the rules about relationships annoyed her so much. It wasn't like she wanted Deacon to be her boyfriend or anything. Because she didn't. He probably wouldn't make a very good boyfriend anyway.

An hour later, someone knocked on the door. Vivienne brushed the crumbs from her top and went to answer it.

Max was bent over in the hallway, tying his shoes. When he saw her, he smiled. "Hey, you got a sec?" He stood and tugged on the hem of his green T-shirt.

"Sure, come on in."

"Cookies for breakfast?" He picked up the packet she'd left on the table. "I like your style. Do you have any milk?"

"One sec." She pulled two glasses from the cupboard, poured one for each of them, and sat in the chair across from him. "What'd you want to talk about?"

He dipped his cookie into his glass and took a bite. "My family stuff. Turns out my birth mother was a surrogate. My mom was too old by the time she and my dad decided to have me."

Vivienne closed her eyes to keep things straight in her mind. "Your mom is an outsider."

"She *was*. She died when I was ten. They gave her the ageless injection when she married my dad, but we all know that doesn't stop outsiders from getting old."

"But what about your dad?" Vivienne took a drink of milk.

"He's one of us." Max scratched the back of his hands. "And he's in England."

"Why isn't he with you?"

"Because he has Alzheimer's and doesn't even know I exist."

Alzheimer's? Wasn't that something people got when they were really old? "But he's only eighteen."

"His body is eighteen, but his mind is eighty-seven." Max finished his milk and sighed. "They showed me pictures of him. He looks just like one of us, like there's nothing wrong. I thought about going to see him after Thanksgiving."

Vivienne wished she could spend even one more hour with her parents.

Max ran his hands through his hair and rested his elbows on the table. "I mean, he won't know who I am, but I want to meet him at least once."

"I definitely think you should—"

The front door flew open and cracked off the doorstop.

Emily stood in the doorway, her face red and splotchy. And she was . . . crying?

Vivienne sprinted over, checking for cuts or bruises or blood or some visible reason why her roommate was sobbing. "What happened? Are you hurt?" Should she call a doctor? Was there one on campus?

Stumbling forward, Emily ripped off her coat and scraped her nails along her arms, leaving angry red streaks on her skin. "My dad's a damn liar and I *hate* him."

"Okay, you need to take a breath." Vivienne wrapped her arm around Emily's waist. "Come sit down and tell us what happened."

"Us?" Emily stiffened. "Who else is here?"

"Just me," Max said, grabbing a glass from the cupboard and filling it from the faucet. He carried it over, his eyes wide with concern, and handed it to Emily.

Vivienne sat next to her on the couch, and Max took a seat across from them on the edge of the coffee table. Emily didn't say anything. She just sat there, staring at her shoes. Vivienne glanced at Max; he nodded as if to say, "Go on."

"Emily?"

"You want to hear some crazy shit?" Emily leveled angry, tear-filled eyes at her. "My dad neutralized himself."

"*What?*" Vivienne's adrenaline spiked, and her own arms

started itching. "I thought your dad's Nevergene wasn't active," she said hesitantly, not wanting to make things worse.

"Yeah. Because *he,*" she spat, wiping her eyes with the back of her hands, "deactivated it on purpose."

Max pulled a pack of tissues from his pocket and handed them to her.

That made no sense. Why would someone with an endless life want to give that up?

"Dad told me he didn't want to have a life without..." Emily ripped a tissue in two then pressed her fists to her eyes. "He didn't want to live without my mom."

Vivienne hugged her, not knowing what to say. Deacon had been so amazing after her appointment; she felt like she was failing Emily when she needed her most.

"He wouldn't stop apologizing for...for abandoning me," she sniffled. Tears fell on Vivienne's shoulder.

"But he didn't abandon you," Vivienne pointed out. "They've both been with you for your entire life."

"You don't get it," Emily snapped, pushing away. "He neutralized himself *after* they had me. There was only a small chance that my Nevergene would activate, and my dad made the selfish choice to have one lifetime with mom instead of chancing an eternity with me."

Max asked where he'd gotten the poison.

"Does it even matter?" Emily blew her nose into what was left of the tissue and cursed. "This is all a bunch of shit."

Max put his hand on her knee. "It sounds like you should go talk to—"

Emily knocked him away. "No way."

"Emily..." Vivienne reached for her but stopped. Maybe she didn't need comfort. Maybe she needed time to be pissed off.

"Didn't you guys *hear* what I said?" Emily's hands clenched in her lap. "I'm never going back home. *Ever.* I don't care what they say to me. They can have each other for the rest of their short ass lives. I don't need them." She rocketed to her feet and stomped toward the bedrooms.

A swirling November wind lifted what remained of the leaves into cyclones along the gravel path. Deacon enjoyed the fall best of all, and the darker evenings meant longer flights. He tucked his hands into his pockets and waited for Vivienne to show up. For the first time in a long time, he wasn't the one who was late.

The main door to the flats opened, and Vivienne came running out, her dark hair tangling about her shoulders. He hadn't slept for worrying about her.

He wasn't sure how she'd act after last night . . . after yesterday.

He couldn't have been more clear about what he wanted. She had seemed into it at first, but he'd pushed his luck by suggesting they go to her room. At least he knew her cut-off point now.

"Hey, Deacon." There were circles beneath her eyes and her smile looked forced.

"What's wrong?"

"Nothing's wrong. Not with me anyway." She brushed her hair back from her flushed face. "Emily just had her genealogy appointment."

Emily Liller's father had been one of the ones who had volunteered to help with HOOK's research in exchange for their "treatment." One of only two individuals in PAN history who chose to give up his immortality for love. Some people probably thought it was romantic. Deacon thought it was foolish. He couldn't imagine anyone worth being grounded for, let alone losing their life over.

"How is she?" he asked.

"Pretty upset."

Barry, Ricky, and Jason nodded to him on their way to The Glass House. Deacon didn't miss the looks of appreciation they shot Vivienne before going inside. He should've offered to order takeaway.

"Do you need to go back to your flat so you can be with her?"

This time her smile seemed more genuine. "As long as I bring home fries, she'll be all right."

The Glass House was nearly full, so they sat across from one another at one of the smaller tables near the door. In the center of the table, a display frame listed the hours for the upcoming holidays—not that the hours made a difference to him. He'd be gone the day after Thanksgiving.

"So…this is different."

He slid the tablet across to Vivienne so she could order first. "What do you mean?"

"We've never shared a meal before," she said, keeping her eyes on the menu as she scrolled.

"Of course we have." Her order was still up when she handed him the tablet. Eggplant parmesan for lunch? Actually, that sounded good. He ordered the same.

"No we haven't," she insisted.

"In Ohio, remember? You ordered half the menu."

Vivienne rolled her eyes and leaned back in her chair. "That didn't count."

"Why not?"

"Because I was half afraid you were going to murder me."

Had she really been afraid? He'd been friendly enough, hadn't he? Confusing as hell of course, but that was the nature of recruiting. He was only permitted to give certain details before the mark was in Neverland. The joys of secrecy. "And do you make a habit of dining with murderers?"

"I usually turn them down, but I made an exception for you." She grabbed for the frame. Her neck and jaw turned pink. "Do you have any plans for the holidays?" she rushed.

The holidays . . . not what he wanted to focus on right now. He wanted to know what other exceptions she'd be willing to make for him—the ones that were making her blush. "I'm going to London with family for Christmas."

"Sounds magical," she sighed, her smile soft and whimsical.

Magical? Hardly. "You don't know my family," he muttered, picking at the skin around his nails. "My holiday will end up being more like a board meeting than a celebration."

Her brows came together and she rested her chin on her hand. "Why don't you spend Christmas here instead?"

If only . . . "My mother would be devastated if I didn't show."

"How long will you be gone?"

"A month. Maybe more." It wasn't negotiable, so he'd never really concerned himself with the timeframe before. But for some reason, right now, a month seemed like a long time to be away.

"I've never been overseas."

Deacon had seen her file. Before he'd come to take her away, she'd never even been out of Ohio. "We'll have to go someday."

"Together?" she choked, her eyes wide.

Travelling with someone who had never been out of the country might make the whole experience feel less monotonous. "Would you like that?"

"Yeah. Sounds fun." Her ferocious blush negated her nonchalant response. "Can we go to Buckingham Palace?" He nodded. "Big Ben?"

"I'll bring you wherever you want to go."

"You know where I really want to go most?" she said, scooting closer to the table and leaning forward as though what she was about to say was a big secret. "I want to see the Peter Pan statue in Kensington Gardens."

"That can be our first stop."

Although she would be disappointed. The statue wasn't very impressive. But a walk along the Serpentine was usually enjoyable. They could grab dinner, maybe stop by the West End for a show and—

What was he doing? He didn't make plans.

"I'm going to hold you to that, you know." She held her hand across the table toward him.

He gave it a firm shake, and said, "I hope you will."

EIGHTEEN

Vivienne frowned at her red-nosed reflection in the bathroom mirror before turning off the light. If it hadn't been Thanksgiving, she would have been asleep hours ago. She had felt great the night before, but since she woke up that morning, her nose wouldn't stop running, and her throat felt like she had swallowed a cactus.

She allowed one longing glance toward her bed before collecting her coat, hat, and scarf from the living room. "Emily? Are you ready to go?"

"Coming!" The hall light turned off, and Emily appeared in her new red wool coat and black hat. Her nose wrinkled when she made a face. "You don't look so good."

"That's because I feel like crap." Vivienne pulled one of the balled-up tissues from her coat pocket and blew her nose. The pressure in her head eased a fraction.

For what felt like the hundredth time, Emily asked her if she wanted to stay in bed.

"I'll stay here if you go to your mom and dad's for dinner."

Emily hadn't seen her parents since her genealogy meeting. She almost seemed back to her normal, bubbly self, but every once in a while, Vivienne would catch her with tears in her eyes.

"Not happening."

Vivienne wrapped her scarf around her neck and face and dragged her hat over her hair. Once she was bundled, they trudged down the stairs and out into the blustery snow. It took them twice as long as normal to reach The Glass House, but when they did, Vivienne was glad she had forced herself out of the apartment.

The Glass House had been transformed with miles of pine garland and a massive fir tree decorated with colorful lights and antique baubles. Gold place cards marked the seating arrangements at the long trestle table lined with wooden benches and high-backed chairs. With an aching head, Vivienne found her seat between Max and someone named Alex McGee.

Emily kept circling the table until she reached a chair at the far side. "Ugh. We're so far away from each other," she whined.

Vivienne tried not to make it obvious that she was scanning the nametags as she walked over. The card next to Emily's had Deacon's name printed on it.

"Wanna swap so you can sit next to lover boy?" Emily picked up her place card. "I don't mind."

"Don't be silly. It's not a big deal."

"Yeah. Okay." She rolled her eyes. "You two have been texting *all* week. I don't think he wants to sit beside me."

Vivienne hadn't seen him since their lunch together, but he'd texted her nearly every day. Still, she didn't want to look pathetic, so she told Emily she didn't care and went back to her own seat, deflated.

The room filled with boisterous PAN, but she knew the moment Deacon walked in with Ethan and Nicola. They all waved to her from across the room. She returned the greeting and watched Deacon locate his seat between Ethan and Emily. He frowned, and his eyes flashed to hers. She shrugged. The last thing she wanted was for him to think she was desperate.

After everyone was seated, the campus pastor said a blessing for the meal. Four succulent turkeys suited to a vintage holiday postcard were brought from the kitchen and spaced evenly among the vast variety of side dishes. Every type of potato imaginable, along with two dozen different pies, completed the spread.

Max came in, stomped the snow from his shoes, and threw his coat on top of the pile next to the tree. Vivienne waved at him and pointed to the chair to her right. Dusting the snow from his hair, he jogged over and plopped down.

"Sorry I'm late. My stupid alarm didn't go off." He stabbed a piece of turkey and flopped it onto his plate. Quieter, he asked how Emily was doing.

Vivienne watched Emily smiling and laughing from across the table. "She's still refusing to talk to her parents." Emily put on a brave face, but Vivienne heard her crying in her room at night.

"I figured, since she's here for this." Max piled his plate with every dish within arm's reach, dumped gravy over all of it, then shouted for Barry to pass the stuffing.

"I don't think I'll have to eat again until Christmas," the guy next to her said. He wore a gray button-down shirt half tucked into his black jeans and a pair of leather boots with loose laces.

"Tell me about it." One thing was for certain: her cold hadn't diminished her appetite. Max handed her a bowl, and Vivienne made room for candied carrots on her already full plate.

"I'm Alex." His smile lines and hint of stubble made him look older than nearly everyone else at the table.

"You're not one of us, are you?" she said, handing Alex the carrots.

He set the bowl on the hotplate in front of his dinner. "And here I thought my disguise would work," he teased, smoothing his free hand over his cheek.

"If you wanted to disguise yourself in Neverland, you probably shouldn't have gone with a beard."

"I've always pitied you immortals for not being able to grow facial hair."

"I dunno. I'm pretty thrilled I'll never grow a beard. I'm Vivienne, by the way."

"You're only half-right, *Vivienne*." The candlelight danced along the sun-kissed streaks in Alex's caramel-colored hair. "I'm one of the unfortunate souls with a lazy Nevergene."

"I'm so sorry." She wasn't sure what else to say, so she shoveled some turkey into her mouth.

He shrugged and spread his napkin onto his lap. "How do you like Neverland?"

Her eyes found Deacon, and her heart gave an answering thump. Deacon said something to Ethan that made everyone around them laugh. "It's pretty great."

"I'm very happy to hear that."

"Do you live around here?" she asked, helping herself to more mashed potatoes. He didn't look familiar.

"No." Alex handed her the gravy boat before she could ask for it. "But the holidays aren't the same on a California beach as they are in the blustery snow in Massachusetts."

A glimpse of the blizzard swirling on the glass above them sent chills sliding beneath Vivienne's shirt. "I don't know. A bit of heat would be nice right about now." Snow was fine, but heat and sunshine were better.

His piercing blue eyes narrowed. "You're not a Mermaid, are you?"

What kind of a question was that? "Not that I know of," she laughed, pretending to check beneath the table for a tail.

A grin. "Everyone knows Mermaids hate the cold." Thankfully, she was saved from having to respond when Alex asked where she was from.

"I've lived in Ohio my whole life."

He pointed to the snow-covered ceiling with his fork. "Then you should be used to this weather."

"Just because I'm used to it doesn't mean I like it." The mashed potatoes were so buttery she could feel the extra calories in each bite.

"All right, Vivienne from Ohio, here's a question for you: what's your favorite kind of pie?"

That was an easy question to answer. She had loved the same kind of pie for the last ten years. "Peanut Butter." She cleared her scratchy throat and drank some water to ease the pain.

Alex shook his head as he reached for the salt shaker. "Wrong answer."

"You asked my opinion. There is no wrong answer."

"Wrong again."

"Okay, *Alex from California*," she drawled, "what's the *right* answer?"

"Pumpkin."

Pumpkin? Gross. "I hate pumpkin pie. It is the worst kind of pie in the history of pies."

He looked horrified. "I can't...Are you *serious* right now? I can't even talk to you anymore. I wish I could say it was nice to meet you, but you're obviously a terrible human being who has awful taste in pie." He twisted so his back was to her and leaned his elbow on the table between them.

What was happening? Ridiculous. This guy was ridiculous. She caught his smile when he reached for his glass of wine. A ridiculous guy with cute dimples.

"And what makes you the resident pie expert?" she asked, poking him in the arm.

"*Shhh!* Not so loud," he snapped, looking around them before scooting closer and saying in a quiet voice, "I don't want everyone thinking I associate with people as awful as you."

She leaned forward and matched her voice to his. "What makes pumpkin so much better than peanut butter?"

"It's a vegetable. Which means you can eat more of it, obviously." He rolled his eyes, but she could tell he was fighting a smile.

"I'm not a doctor, but I'm pretty sure that pumpkin pie isn't any healthier than any other kind of pie."

"Well, I *am* a doctor, and I say it is. And since I'm the expert, I'm right."

She snorted. "You honestly expect me to believe you're a doctor?"

His brows came together, and his eyes widened. "Why wouldn't you believe me?"

"You don't look like any doctor I've ever met."

"And what about my looks is so un-doctorly?"

For one, he was hot. And even though he looked too old to be a PAN, he looked way too young to be a doctor. And he was too fit. Most of the male doctors she'd met had been overweight and balding. But she couldn't say any of that out loud, so she went with, "You're not wearing any glasses."

He held up a finger, reached into his breast pocket, and pulled out a pair of tortoise shell glasses. Somehow they made him even cuter. "How about now?"

"I'm still not convinced. Maybe you should say something doctorly."

He sat up and rubbed his stubbled chin. "As an incredibly smart and important doctor, I travel to hospitals to assess teenage patients with a handful of specific symptoms—unexplainable spikes in adrenaline, dizziness, loss of consciousness, high levels of unknown hormones, those kinds of things. Doctors who aren't as smart as I am sometimes misdiagnose an activating Nevergene as pheochromocytoma or paraganglioma, even though there's no tumor present. I double check to make sure they're not PAN."

Vivienne had no idea what pheo-chrom-whatever or para-gangly was, but they sounded complicated.

"Was that doctorly enough for you?" He winked, removed his glasses, and replaced them in his pocket.

"Wow. You're awfully full of yourself."

"I was trying to impress you." He flashed her a grin before taking a sip of wine. "Did it work?"

"Maybe a little," she admitted.

Alex proved to be good company—which was a relief, considering Max spent most of the meal talking with his friend Barry about extraction. She appreciated his easy conversation because it kept her distracted from the amount of laughing Deacon and Emily and the rest of her friends were doing across the table. Seriously. What was so funny?

She ate until even the smell of food made her feel like bursting. The combination of a full belly, a terrible cold, and the warm atmosphere left her yawning so much her jaw ached.

"Am I boring you?" Alex asked after one particularly drawn out yawn.

"It's not you, I promise," she said from behind her hand. "This cold is kicking my butt."

"You should go home and rest—and drink lots of fluids."

"I think you're right."

"Of course I'm right. I'm a doctor, remember?"

"It was really nice meeting you, Dr. Alex." It surprised her how much she meant that.

He rose from his chair and caught his napkin before it slipped onto the floor. "Would you like me to walk you home?"

"There's no need. I'll be there in two minutes."

"Alex McGee!" Julie shouted, approaching them with another woman in tow.

Vivienne touched his arm. "Thanks for keeping me company."

He put his hand over hers. "Any time you need company— or pie—I'm your man."

Out of all the people in the whole bloody world, why did Vivienne have to sit next to the person Deacon hated most? Growing up, Alex McGee had spent his summers in Harrow with his great-grandad, which meant Deacon had been stuck entertaining him. Deacon's mother had this mad notion that the two of them could be friends. As if he'd want to be friends with an arrogant asshole who thought he knew everything. Alex was dull and prattled on constantly about his "theories" regarding the Nevergene—and that was before he'd been accepted into medical school.

Now he was sitting next to Vivienne, making her smile and laugh. What the hell was so funny? He'd never heard Alex say anything even remotely funny. Vivienne must've felt sorry for him. That had to be why she was laughing like he was the funniest man in the world. Because there was no way she was interested. Alex was so . . . infuriating.

If Deacon hadn't been running late, he would've switched out the place cards before everyone else had arrived. Why hadn't Vivienne changed them? Didn't she want to sit with him? Had she forgotten it was his last night in Kensington?

Dammit, that woman was confusing.

Thankfully, Julie caught sight of Alex and flagged him

down, which left Vivienne on her own, searching the stack of abandoned coats next to the Christmas tree.

"Where are you running off to?" Deacon asked, tapping one of the tree's star-shaped ornaments with his finger. The bauble spun around, throwing sparks of light over Vivienne's face.

"I'm going home." Her voice sounded huskier than usual.

The spinning star stopped in his clenched fist. "Already? Why?" It wasn't even nine o'clock.

"I feel like crap," she said, pulling on her black coat and zipping it to her chin, "so I'm going to bed."

"You're sick?" Now that he saw her up close, he noticed the dark circles beneath her eyes. And her nose was a bit red.

"It's just a cold." Vivienne wrapped a scarf from her coat pocket around her neck. "But the doctor told me I should get some rest." Her eyes darted to where Alex was speaking with Julie and Pam.

Bloody doctor . . . "I suppose I'll see you next month then." He found his own coat beneath Ethan's blue one. They'd be leaving for the bar as soon as Nicola stopped chatting to Emily.

Vivienne's brows came together over her wide eyes. She pushed the woolly material down to say, "I totally forgot you were leaving tomorrow."

She'd forgotten about him already? He hadn't even left—

Vivienne threw her arms around his waist, knocking him off balance and nearly into the tree. She was so soft and warm, and her hair smelled like vanilla, and—*Shit*. Ethan was staring, and Nicola was glaring. The two of them needed to mind their own business.

He extricated himself from the warmth of her arms and slipped into his own coat.

Trussed up like a child waiting for a snowball fight, Vivienne stuffed her gloved hands into her pockets and smiled. "Are you going to miss me?"

He *was* going to miss her. So he wasn't sure why he said, "Are *you* going to miss *me*?"

She rolled her eyes and told him to have a safe flight and then turned for the door. He knew his friends were still watching and why the hell hadn't he just said yes? It was a simple, three-letter word. Y-e-s.

"Let me walk you home," he blurted before he could consider the consequences.

"I'm pretty sure I can make it on my own."

"That's not the point." He caught her by the waist and herded her to the door.

Once they were outside in the snapping wind, some of his irritation subsided. Vivienne huddled into herself and waded through the snow that had dumped down during dinner.

"Did you forget that we can fly?" The snow was soaking into his shoes and getting his socks wet. He hated wet socks.

"I'd rather walk."

All right. If she wanted to walk, then he'd walk. Soggy socks and clammy feet be damned. His hands were freezing by the time they reached her flat. Instead of using the glass door, Vivienne kept going to the main entrance. He pulled the icy handle and held open the door for her.

"I made it," she said, stomping the snow from her boots, "so you're free to go."

"What kind of gentleman would I be if I left you this far from your flat?"

She snorted. "It's just upstairs."

"Exactly." And she was unwell. And he didn't want to say goodbye yet.

A wrinkle formed between her furrowed brows. "Are you going to tell on me if I don't run?"

She had a lot to learn about him. "A gentleman never tells."

Her cheeks flushed before she turned away. Climbing the stairs without running felt achingly slow, but eventually, they reached her flat on the third floor and he waited for her to say—

"Do you want to come in for a minute?"

That. That was what he had been waiting for. "Absolutely."

His mobile buzzed from his pocket, but he ignored it. Whoever it was could wait.

"I mean, I'm sure you have better things to do—"

"I don't have any plans." It was a lie, of course. It had become a tradition to meet Ethan and Nicola for a farewell drink after Thanksgiving dinner. They could go on their own for all he cared.

To say Vivienne's apartment was festive would've been an understatement. Snowflakes dangled from the ceiling, three Christmas trees blinked out of sync—one in the living room, one in the hall, and one on the kitchen counter—and a host of Rudolph/Santa/Angel/Snowman decorations had been displayed around the place.

"Someone likes Christmas." He didn't even own a wreath.

"Don't blame me for any of this. It's all Emily's fault. She's obsessed with the holidays." Vivienne unraveled the scarf from her neck and peeled off her coat. Both landed on the floor beside her snow-crusted boots.

He picked them up and settled them on the hook before removing his own shoes.

"You don't have to take those off if you don't want to. I don't really mind."

He looked down at his icy laces then back to Vivienne. "My socks are wet."

"Oh. Okay." A shrug. "I'm going to change. I'll be back in a sec."

If he had been at home, he would've put his socks on the rad. Instead, he draped them over his shoes and hoped they dried quickly.

He watched her disappear into the room on the left side of the hallway. With nothing better to do, he went over to the sofa. The tree in the corner flashed rapidly before slowing to a lazy blink before holding steady before fading and repeating the sequence over and over. His mobile buzzed again.

What was he doing? He shouldn't be here. Not when she was sick. Not when he was leaving tomorrow.

He stood to collect his shoes, and then Vivienne came back . . . wearing a pair of shorts so tiny they barely peeked from beneath the ridiculous Ohio sweatshirt she seemed so fond of.

Aaand he sat back down.

She swiped the remote from the coffee table and curled onto

the corner cushion like a cat ready to nap. "Did you enjoy dinner?"

A rerun of some sitcom he couldn't recall the title of came on the tele when she turned it on.

"No. I didn't enjoy dinner."

"Really?" Her brows came together, and she toyed with one of the holes at the bottom of her sweatshirt. "I thought the food was pretty good. What I could taste anyway."

"Oh, the food was divine." Chef Audrey would have it no other way. "It was the company that I found lacking."

Her head tilted, sending her hair cascading over her shoulder, making him think of the last time he'd been in this room with her.

His stomach tightened. He should definitely not think of last time. The way she'd sighed when he'd touched her or the way she'd leaned into him or the way her heavy breathing had made her chest—

She was sick. She was sick. She was sick.

"You looked like you were having fun," she said, jolting him back to the present.

Had she been watching him? The thought made him happier than it should.

"It may have looked that way," he told her, "but I wasn't."

"Why not?"

Because she'd been sitting by Alex and not him. "I think you already know the answer to that."

Vivienne smiled at him even as she dropped her head and closed her eyes. She didn't look very comfortable squished in the corner, so Deacon reached for her legs and settled them across his lap. A blush painted her cheeks, but she didn't open her eyes.

She had a freckle on her knee. And another just above it, on her thigh. He "drew" a line between them, loving the way her skin broke out in chills.

"What're you doing?" she whispered, her eyes wide.

He continued connecting the dots, gauging her reaction. "Does this bother you?"

She shook her head.

"Are you sure?" He found a freckle right below the hem of her shorts. "Because you look awfully flushed."

"I'm just sick."

Little liar. "Is that right?"

"Yep."

He leaned toward her slowly, hearing her breath catch in her throat. "Are you having trouble breathing, Vivienne?"

"I'm…just…sick."

He pressed a kiss to her neck and had planned on stopping there. But then she sighed and lifted her chin, and she smelled so good, and she caught him by the hair and held his head to her. And he wasn't going to *not* kiss her if she wanted him to kiss her, so he made sure to sample every inch of exposed skin from her ear to her throat. If she wasn't sick, he'd be exploring her mouth. But this would have to do.

"Your pulse is racing," he whispered, sucking a bit harder where her neck met her shoulder.

"That's just because," she moaned, "I'm sick."

The dingy, neon glow in the narrow bar reflected Deacon's mood. If Vivienne had stayed awake, he would've been there instead. But it felt creepy to stick around after she'd passed out on the sofa. Plus, he had wanted to get out before Emily got home.

Ethan waved him over to where he and Nicola waited next to one of the high-top tables. As if he hadn't seen Ethan's hideous orange turkey sweater from the doorway. "Where the hell have you been?" he asked, slurring his words already.

"My socks were wet, and I needed to swing by my place to get new ones."

"You and your damned socks." He rolled his eyes and took another drink of his whiskey and soda. After asking Deacon for his order, he squeezed beside a middle-aged woman waiting at the bar.

Nicola punched him in the arm. Hard. "I saw you leave earlier. You'd better not be doing what I think you're doing."

Her hair was down for once, twisted in curls over her bright red top.

She knew him better than most—which wasn't always a good thing.

"I fail to see how it's any of your concern," he said, rubbing his sore shoulder. The woman was freakishly strong.

"I know you, Dash. And I know you're going to do the same shit you always do. I'm not going to stand by and—"

Ethan turned around and shoved a glass of scotch into his hand. "You're a drink behind. Bottoms up."

The first sip burned, but then his throat went numb and the rest slipped down like water. He slammed the empty glass on the table and ordered another.

"That's my boy!" Ethan cheered, finishing his drink as well. "I'm gonna feel *shitt-ay* tomorrow. But not nearly as bad as you. What time is your flight?"

"Half seven."

"I'll probably be just getting to bed," he laughed, pulling Nicola by the belt loops on her jeans, "*if* I'm lucky."

"If you keep drinking at that pace," she mumbled, "you're not getting lucky at all."

Joe waved at them from behind the bar, another round ready and waiting. Ethan collected their drinks, clinked his glass against Deacon's, and muttered some convoluted toast about turkeys and airplanes that didn't make a bit of sense.

Nicola cleared her throat, catching Deacon's attention over her bulbous glass of pink gin and strawberries. "Any plans while you're in London?"

"The usual, I suppose." Be miserable for a month and then come home.

She narrowed her eyes and hummed.

"Do you have something to say to me, Nicola?"

"Yeah. I think you're being shady as hell and it pisses me off. I like Vivienne and—"

"You don't know what you're talking about."

"Oh, really? So you don't plan on seeing Gwen when you get to London?"

He hadn't given Gwen a second thought in weeks. He'd

seen the messages on his phone that she'd sent earlier, but hadn't felt like responding. Was he going to see her? He didn't honestly know.

"That's what I thought," Nicola snorted.

The door opened and a snowy cyclone spun through the entrance. When Deacon saw who had come in, he swore into his drink. This night was going downhill fast.

"Would you look who it is," Ethan welcomed, clapping Alex McGee on the shoulder.

"I see you guys are still hanging out in this dump." Alex nodded toward Nicola. "Nicola, lovely to see you, as always."

"You too, Alex." She combed her fingers through the ends of her hair and offered him a smile that would've left Ethan seeing red if he hadn't been playing with the googly eyes on his sweater. "Are you in for long?"

Alex settled his jacket on the back of the free stool at their table. "I was planning on heading home before Christmas," he said, scraping a hand across his damned five o'clock shadow, "but now I'm thinking I may stick around until January."

For as long as Deacon had known Alex, the man had never stayed beyond December. He couldn't shake the feeling that the decision had something to do with—

"What's Vivienne's story?"

Shit. Not good.

With her eyes on Deacon, Nicola said, "What do you mean?"

"I mean, she's cute and I'd like to know if she's seeing anyone."

Ethan snorted. His eyes darted to Deacon, and his lips curled into a smile. "Ask Dash."

Alex turned to him. "Well?"

How was he supposed to answer that? "Yes, she's single, but if you so much as talk to her, I'll rip out your throat" sounded a bit intense. But so did telling Alex that Vivienne was something more to him than she was.

Because they were just two people attracted to each other, having fun.

"Well what?" he said.

"Does she have a boyfriend?" Alex pressed, retrieving his wallet from his pocket.

Beside Alex, Nicola and Ethan watched with too much interest.

Deacon took a deep drink of his liquor and wiped his mouth with the back of his knuckles. "Not that I know of."

"That's a shock."

Deacon didn't want to talk about Vivienne anymore. "How's Tootles these days?"

"He doesn't remember any of us now. They moved him to Scotland last month."

"Who's serving on Leadership in his place?" Nicola asked.

"Mom doesn't have time, so she asked me to do it instead." Alex tapped his credit card on the table and offered to get the next round.

"I don't want anything," Deacon told him. "I'm done." Done with drinking. Done with his mates. Done with this whole bloody night.

"Nicola? Ethan?" Alex pointed to the bar.

After placing their orders, Ethan went with Alex. But Nicola was coming toward Deacon and her eyes were narrowed and she was going to say something he didn't want to hear. He needed to finish his drink and get out of there.

"Don't give me that look, Dash," she grumbled, kicking his ankle with her stiletto. "I mean, come on. Does Vivienne know *anything* about you?"

"She knows I'm interested." That's all that mattered.

"Interested in *what*, exactly?"

Interested in . . . doing a helluva lot more than kissing her neck. In making her blush. Hearing her laugh. Spending time with—

Dammit. He'd made a big mistake. He was going to tell Alex to leave her the hell alone. He was going to—

Nicola caught him by the sleeve. "Don't even think about it," she bit out. "Don't you dare say a word to Alex if you're not serious. That's not fair to him—or to Vivienne."

As if he gave a shit about Alex. But was it fair to Vivienne?

He was going to end up doing what he always did, wasn't he? Get bored. Fly away. Move on.

"What are you going to tell him when I leave?" Why had he asked that? He didn't want to know.

She glanced back to where Alex was carrying their drinks to the table. He held her gin and tonic aloft, and she gave him a thumbs up. "I'm going to tell him the truth, Dash," she said, her blue eyes wide with sympathy. "That Vivienne is a nice girl, that she's single, and that he should ask her out."

Deacon nodded and turned on his heel, weaving his way through the remaining holiday crowd on his way to the exit. When he got outside, the drifting snow had left a layer of soundproof flakes across the cars in the lot. He dragged his phone from his pocket to check his messages. They were all from Gwen. *Is it tomorrow yet? I miss you! What time do you arrive?*

He cursed himself even as he texted her and said he'd be there by eight.

NINETEEN

"Vivienne?" Emily knocked at her bedroom door. "You okay?"

"Call a doctor. I think I'm dying." Vivienne didn't know what hurt worse: her head or her throat. She'd fallen asleep on the couch last night but had woken up at some point and realized Deacon had left without saying goodbye.

"The doctor's already here."

She hauled herself upright, tripped over some shoes, and jerked open the door. The lights from one of their three Christmas trees flashed in the dark hallway.

With wide eyes, Emily tilted her head toward the living room. "A *Dr. Alex McGee* came to see you." She licked her lips and wiggled her eyebrows.

Alex was in their apartment? *Crap.* She needed to brush her teeth. And put on a bra. "Why is he here?"

"Put on some real clothes and ask him yourself," Emily said with a wink. She was about to leave when she froze, shoved Vivienne into the room, and slammed the door shut behind her. Then she was pulling on the neck of Vivienne's shirt, gasping, "Oh. My. God."

"What?"

"You have a hickey."

"I have a *what*?" She raced to the mirror and—Holy crap. Deacon had given her a hickey. "It's not a hickey," she rushed. "It's a...um...rash? From my fever." She was going to kill him. A gentleman? What kind of gentleman gave a girl a frickin' hickey?

"Girl, I know a hickey when I see one. And that, my friend, is a hickey. Now," Emily drawled, tapping her pink nail against her chin, "the question is: who gave it to you?"

"Shut up."

"I noticed a certain sexy Brit leaving dinner in your company. So I wonder..."

"I'm sick. Take pity on me," she begged, hiding her face in her hands.

"Not too sick to stop someone from making out with your neck."

"Emily!"

"Which makes me wonder if that's all he made out with—"

"We didn't even kiss," she blurted.

She had wanted to. He'd even suggested it. But she had refused because she didn't want him getting sick. Now she would have to wait a whole month to know what it was like to have his mouth on hers—assuming he still wanted to kiss her when he got back.

Crap. She'd made a mistake. She totally should have made out with him last night.

"He certainly kissed something." Emily giggled on her way back to the door. "I'll go entertain your cute doctor friend so you can get dressed. Make sure whatever you put on hides the sexy little hickey Deacon gave you."

Vivienne grabbed her phone from the nightstand and texted the idiot. *WTF Deacon!!! You gave me a hickey???*

Three dots appeared on her screen before a kissy-face emoji popped up.

Dead. When she saw him again, he was dead.

Right. Back to the current crisis: Alex.

Vivienne searched her barren closet for something more presentable. Where the heck was all the stuff she'd bought in

New York? Her eyes fell on her overflowing hamper. She really needed to do laundry again.

Luckily, there was a semi-clean Kensington top discarded over her desk chair and a pair of tights balled up beneath it. Once she dressed, she swished with mouthwash while pinching her cheeks until they were as red as her nose. On her way out of the room, she ripped the last of the tissues from the box on her desk and stuffed them into her pocket.

Alex was sitting on their couch, a brown paper bag on the cushion beside him.

"What brings you out in this blizzard, Dr. Alex from California?"

His face brightened when he saw her. "I wanted to check and see if your taste in pie has improved," he said, standing and straightening his jeans. "And to see if you're in need of my brilliant medical services, of course."

She sneezed twice. "Does that answer your question?"

"Never fear." He handed her the paper bag. "I come bearing gifts."

Inside there was nasal spray, two different types of painkillers, a bottle of honey, and a lemon.

"It's a 'get well soon' care package," he explained.

"This is really thoughtful. Thanks." When was the last time someone had tried to take care of her like this?

"My mom swears by honey and lemon tea," he said, picking up a porcelain angel from the manger scene on the side table.

The heating kicked on, swirling the snowflakes Emily had insisted they hang from the ceiling. Their entire apartment had been transformed into a festive wonderland, with pine trees, pine garland, and pine sprigs, all wrapped in twinkle lights and decorated with colorful ornaments.

"I'll try anything at this stage."

"Right. I had better get back to work." Alex set the angel beside a shepherd and went to the door. "I'm working in the campus lab for the next few weeks. When you feel better, you should swing by, and I'll show you how crazy smart and doctor-ish I am."

The invitation was as unexpected as his visit. But also surprisingly welcome. "Maybe I will."

"It was nice meeting you, Emily," he called toward the bedrooms.

"You too!" Emily stuck her head out of her room and returned his wave.

Vivienne closed the door behind him and carried the bag to the counter. After filling the kettle and putting it on the stove, she acknowledged Emily's giddy smile. "Go ahead and say it."

Emily poked through the paper bag on the counter. "I'd take Doctor Alex's care package any day."

"Emily!" She swatted her with a snowflake dish towel. The ensuing laughter started a fit of coughing. When that subsided, she sliced the lemon and squeezed it into her empty mug. The tangy citrus scent was the first thing Vivienne had been able to smell in days.

"What?" Emily sniggered. "If I had a doctor who looked like him, I could see myself getting sick *a lot*."

"Tell me about it." The kettle whistled; Vivienne lifted it from the stovetop. "My doctor in Ohio was old, overweight, and balding."

"It sounds like we had the same doctor." Emily rubbed her hands down her cheeks. "It's a pity we don't see more stubble in Neverland. Could you imagine Deacon with a beard?"

Deacon with stubble that would scratch her neck when he— Okay. She needed to get a grip. The honey oozed into her mug, and she added hot water before stirring it with a spoon from a set of reindeer cutlery. "Do you think me stopping by to see Alex at work would give him the wrong idea?"

"Define *wrong idea*."

"That I'm interested in him, or whatever."

"Because you're not."

"Definitely not." Vivienne punched a pill from the blister pack. She wasn't interested in him . . . was she?

He was cute and smart and funny and—

Okay. Maybe she was a little interested in him.

By Monday, the care package was empty, and Vivienne could finally breathe through her nose. "Are you ready yet, or do you need to change outfits *again*?" she called toward Emily's room before checking her watch . . . again.

According to Emily, mid-morning was the most unromantic time to visit someone.

Early morning could give Alex the impression that Vivienne had been up all night thinking about him and couldn't wait any longer to visit.

And lunch time breached the no-meals-together rule they'd made over the weekend.

Any later in the day could spill over into dinnertime, and when darkness fell, all bets were off.

Bringing Emily along as her buffer would let Alex know she was only there to thank him again for the medicine and let him know that she was no longer on her deathbed.

"Sure am!" Emily twirled down the hall in a dark blue sweater that made her face look brighter than usual. She tapped her fingers on the ceiling snowflakes. "Does Alex know we're coming or are we surprising him?"

"I'd let him know, but I don't have his—" There was an older man standing in the hallway outside their apartment, squeezing a black baseball cap in his hands. "Can I help you?"

His brows came together and he took a halting step forward. "Is Emily home?"

"Who is it?" Emily said, unplugging the Christmas tree. "If it's Max, tell him—*Dad*? Why're you on campus?" She crossed her arms; it looked like she was hugging herself.

"Come in, Mr. Liller." Vivienne moved aside to let Emily's father into the apartment.

"Em…" He walked toward the living room but stopped before he reached the couch. "You haven't returned any of our calls, and when you didn't show up for Thanksgiving"—his shoulders slumped—"your mother and I were devastated."

"I'm thinking I should go?" Vivienne searched Emily's unreadable expression.

Emily nodded.

She could have waited for Emily, but there was no way of knowing how long her dad would be there—or if she would be in the mood to tag along afterward.

For the first time since she had gotten sick, Vivienne ran down the stairs. The snow from the week before had been shoveled into walls of white along the icy paths. Still, to avoid slipping on what was left, she flew to the Hall. The welcome heat inside left her removing layers on her way to the basement.

The door to the small access room was ajar—and still as creepy as it had been the first time she'd been down there. When she pulled on the cord attached to the light, the blue screen appeared. Vivienne scanned her eyes and waited. The screen turned red.

ACCESS DENIED

How the heck was she supposed to visit Alex if—

ACCESS GRANTED

The wall disappeared.

"Welcome back, Vivienne," Robert greeted, his arms full of files. "Have you changed your mind about giving blood?"

"Actually, I'm here to see—"

"She's here to see me," Alex said from behind him, grinning from ear to ear. "At least, I hope she is."

"Good for you, man." Robert traded places with Vivienne and told them to have fun. The wall moved back into place, and he was gone.

"You're looking awfully doctorly in your white coat, Dr. Alex." However, the Beatles T-shirt beneath wasn't quite as professional.

"I only wear it to impress the ladies," he confessed, straightening the collar.

It was working.

"You look like you're feeling a lot better. Your physician must be pretty amazing."

"And modest too."

He laughed and turned toward the wall of frosted windows. "I work back in the microbiology sector. Follow me."

"Where is everyone?" There was only one other person at a desk in the center of the room, stuffing a bunch of wires into a small metal tube.

"Kensington is a ghost town between now and New Year's." He scanned his hand on a blue screen outside the doors, and when the door unlocked, he held it open for her. "Which means I get a lot more work done *and* I don't have to wait in line for equipment."

Five pentagon-shaped desks with drawers on each side had been spaced evenly around the long room; some had microscopes, slides, and petri dishes on top, others had trays of test tubes and vials of different colored liquids. The furthest desk had a computer screen attached to a box the size of a dryer.

A long counter lit by LEDs wrapped around the perimeter. Part of the counter was covered in glass, with holes at the bottom as wide as a person's arms, while another section housed square devices with buttons and lights and dials—some big, others small, some silent, others humming.

Vivienne had no clue what any of them did, but they looked complicated. "This looks like the set from a crime scene investigation show."

"It basically is." He handed her a lab coat from a hook inside the door. "This'll make you seem more official. Did I hear Robert say you didn't give blood?"

"Yeah." She slipped out of her winter jacket and into the white coat. After rolling up the sleeves, she went with him to the closest desk. "They asked us on day one, and I wasn't so sure about all of this at the time. I don't really see what the big deal is. Emily and Max gave their DNA."

"Yes, but we have very few donors with two PAN parents."

"Why should that matter?"

"Have a seat, and I'll show you." He sat on a rolling stool and pushed a second stool toward Vivienne. She sat down in front of a microscope. "Back in a sec." Alex scooted himself to the printer, grabbed a sheet of paper, and then glided back, sending a cologne-scented breeze over her. "Did you cover genetics in any of your high school science classes?"

"Maybe a bit in Biology." She took a deep breath. He smelled great. "But I don't remember a whole lot."

"You're about to get a crash course from a very smart doctor." He pulled a pen from his lab coat pocket and wrote NN, Nn, and nn on top of the page. The nails on his right hand were painted sparkly pink.

"A very cocky doctor in pink nail polish."

"Do you like it?" He held out his hand to give her a better look. "My niece did them this weekend. She said the color would match everything, but I'm not so sure it goes with these jeans."

"How old is she?" Vivienne asked when she stopped laughing.

"Four and a half. She informed me the half is *very* important."

Thinking of Alex sitting patiently while a little girl with chubby fingers painted his nails made Vivienne's heart swell.

"Right. Here we go…" He scooted closer to the desk. "Your DNA encodes all your genes, and genes come in different forms called alleles. You get one set from your mother and one from your father. The Nevergene is what we call a recessive mutation. It's represented by the small n." He put an X across NN. "If someone has two dominant alleles like this, there's no mutation present in their DNA." He put a check mark over Nn. "In this example, the person carries only one copy of the mutation. Because it's recessive, it's overshadowed by the dominant allele. They can pass it on to their offspring, but there's no chance of activating the gene." He circled the final two letters. "*This* combination is the sweet spot. If an individual has two copies of the mutation, their Nevergene can activate." He looked up from the page and smiled. "With me so far?"

"I think so." She tore her eyes from his and stared at the paper. "Basically, we have to have two of these small n's to have an active Nevergene."

"Exactly. Now…" Alex drew a square on the paper. "This is a Punnett square. It's a diagram used to predict genotypes." After dividing the large square into four smaller squares, he labeled the top two squares N and n, and the two on the left-hand side n and n. "When we combine these genes, one from each parent, we can determine the probability of their offspring carrying the Nevergene." He filled in the squares with the different combinations. "In this scenario, there's a fifty percent chance the offspring will inherit the mutation from both parents."

"And what's the chance the Nevergene will actually activate?"

His smile wavered. "Thirty-seven and a half percent." He looked back at the page. "Your parents both had active Nevergenes." He drew another Punnett square with n on the top and on the left. "There was a one-hundred percent chance you would have a Nevergene." He put the pen back into his pocket. "But what the diagram doesn't tell us is that *you* had a seventy-five percent chance of having an *active* Nevergene."

"Why did I have a better chance than this person?" She pointed to the first diagram he had drawn.

"That comes down to hormones." He sat back and laughed. "Sorry…I'm probably boring you."

"No, no. It's really interesting." Alex raised his eyebrows. "Please continue, Dr. Alex."

"Come this way." He rolled his chair between the desks to the counter.

Vivienne tried to do the same but ended up bumping off every obstacle on the way. "I'm not very good at this." She laughed when she collided with him.

"It takes a lot of practice." He twisted her stool so that she was the right way around.

Next to a stand of empty test tubes, she noticed a graph with different colored undulating lines. "What's this?"

"This is my area of expertise: hormones." He pointed to a black line on the chart. "Everyone produces human growth hormone, or hGh." His finger slid to a green line. "But active Nevergenes cause a mutation in the hGh, producing nGh—or never-growth hormone—which keeps PAN young. When the adrenaline reacts with high levels of nGh—"

"It makes us fly."

"Bingo." He gave her a high-five. "According to the research, when two individuals with active Nevergenes have a child with an active Nevergene, the child produces much higher levels of nGh. And I'm sure you know Neverland's goal is to activate every Nevergene." He handed her the chart. "Right now, we administer a sedative and a large dose of nGh to PAN whose Nevergenes are activating to keep them active."

"Sedative?" She scanned the numbers on the axis, as if she knew what they meant. "Why wouldn't you give adrenaline?"

"Sounds counter-intuitive, right? But the sedative gives the body time for the mutation to...stick. However, I believe adrenaline may be the key ingredient to artificially activating *dormant* genes. It's a matter of finding the right ratio of adrenaline to nGh."

"If you activated your dormant gene, then you could fly too." Vivienne traced the green line on the page.

"Who needs to fly when you have these?" Alex shoved away from the desk and spun in a circle on his stool.

She set the chart aside and leaned her chin on her hand. "If I gave blood, do you think it would help at all?"

"Yes." He used his legs to scoot closer to her. "But that's not why I asked you here."

Vivienne liked Alex.

And if she didn't like Deacon so much, she could see herself *really* liking him.

If giving blood could help Alex and others with lazy Nevergenes live forever, shouldn't she do it?

Neverland had given her so much. It was time for her to give something back.

She slipped out of her lab coat and wrenched her sleeve above her elbow. "It's not why I came."

"You're sure?" He frowned at her arm.

"Positive."

"Wait here and I'll grab some stuff from out front." The

keypad next to the door beeped as Alex pressed buttons. The door opened, and he disappeared.

Vivienne touched the cold glass tubes, then looked into the microscope. The image was blurry, but she was afraid to adjust the knobs.

"Make any ground-breaking discoveries?" Alex asked, returning with a silver tray of medical supplies.

"Not yet."

He washed his hands, then snapped on a pair of rubber gloves and pulled an antiseptic wipe from the packet. "Set your arm up here." He shoved a pile of folders out of her way. The cold wipe smelled like alcohol. "This is going to pinch for a sec."

Vivienne closed her eyes but felt only a slight sting. There was a bit of discomfort when Alex swapped vials, but overall, it was a painless experience.

"All done."

She opened her eyes and waited for him to replace the cotton ball with a band aid. "You're pretty good at that."

He gathered the trash and dumped it into a biohazardous waste bin. "Brilliant doctor, remember?"

Vivienne pressed her hand against her bandage and nodded toward the three vials of dark red blood on the tray. "I hope you can find something in those to motivate your lazy Nevergene."

"So do I." While Alex labeled the vials, Vivienne studied his profile. He really was pretty cute. There was a hint of red in his beard she hadn't noticed before, and when he—

"What're you doing after this?"

If Alex had caught her staring, he had the decency not to say anything. "Nothing."

"Would you like to have lunch with me?"

According to Emily, having food together could give him the wrong impression. But would the wrong impression be so bad?

There were times she had been convinced Deacon shared her feelings—like on Halloween and Thanksgiving. But other days, it felt like he forgot she existed. He'd been gone a few days and had barely texted. What if she was hanging around waiting for nothing?

For all she knew, he could come back after Christmas and stop talking to her altogether. Did she really want to waste this opportunity to get to know a nice guy simply because of what could be a one-sided crush?

"Yeah, okay. Lunch sounds great."

Alex left his lab coat on the back of the chair and pulled a light flannel jacket from the hanger.

"Don't you have anything warmer than that? It's really cold out there." She zipped her coat and wrapped her scarf around her neck.

"I'm afraid my California wardrobe isn't suited to this weather." He buttoned the front of the flannel.

"Take this." She undid her scarf and draped it around his neck.

"Thank you." His lips curled into a smile. Her fireflies rustled a bit. Unsure but definitely paying attention.

Once they were outside, an unforgiving wind cut across her legs, but her top half remained toasty. She would have preferred flying across campus but didn't want to be rude. They passed the empty fountain that had been drained before the first frost. In the shadow on the far side was a wide patch of ice as smooth as a rink.

Alex slid across it then waited for Vivienne on the other side.

Vivienne, not to be outdone, took a running start, but wobbled and landed on her butt in the drifting snow. When she heard a muffled chuckle, she glared at Alex. He hid his smile behind one hand and offered the other.

"Laughing when someone gets hurt?" She clucked her tongue at him. "You have a terrible bedside manner."

"My bedside manners are impeccable," he said with a grin that showcased his dimples.

The fireflies started growing restless.

She dusted the snow from her pants and walked more cautiously the rest of the way to The Glass House. When they reached the stairs, Alex raced to the top.

She caught up with him when he stopped at the entrance. "Why'd you run?"

"You think I shouldn't take part in a Neverland tradition because I'm grounded?"

Crap. She'd offended him. "That's not what I meant," she rushed. "I thought—"

"Relax." He squeezed her shoulder. "I'm messing with you. Come on. It's freezing out here." He shuddered and swung the door open.

"I think they have the right idea." Alex nodded to the lone table of guys in the center of the room. "It'll be warmer if we keep away from the windows." He pulled her chair out for her and waited for her to sit before taking his own seat.

She wriggled out of her coat and took the tablet Alex handed to her. After placing her order, she handed it back. "How long are you staying around Kensington?"

"I usually visit London at Christmas, but I'm not going this year. Depending on how much work I get finished, I may be here until after New Year's."

Vivienne tucked her hands beneath her legs to try and warm them up. "Can I ask you something?"

"Shoot."

"How does it feel? Being around all this, knowing what you know, and..." One look into his kind blue eyes had the words dying on her lips. "Never mind."

He tapped his foot against the leg of his chair. "Are you asking me how it feels knowing I'm going to get old, or knowing I'm going to die?"

"You wouldn't look old if you took that ageless injection." Why had she started this conversation?

"The injection is strictly reserved for individuals who marry PAN," he explained, rubbing the bridge of his nose. "There have never been, and never will be, any exceptions." His smile set off the small wrinkles at the corners of his eyes and relieved some of the tension in her body. "But I'm good with it."

"Really?"

"What's the point in *looking* young if I'm not going to actually *be* young? And as far as dying goes, how long have you known you were immortal?"

She shifted in her chair. "Since September."

"And how much time did you spend thinking about death before that?"

"I never really thought about it." She had been too preoccupied with surviving high school to worry about her own mortality.

"Denial is easy when we're young." He chuckled to himself. "But come back to me in fifty years when you're still a beautiful eighteen-year-old and I'm a wrinkly old man, and I'll probably give you a different answer."

He thought she was beautiful?

Her fickle fireflies started to dance.

Maybe she had been giving him the right impression all along.

Vivienne pressed her ear to the door and thought she heard muffled voices. Instead of barging in, she knocked.

The door opened.

"You live here," Emily muttered. "You don't need to knock." She wasn't smiling, but her eyes didn't look red or puffy, which was a good sign.

Vivienne stepped past her to see a Christmas movie paused on the television. "I didn't want to interrupt."

Emily closed the door and went back to the couch. "My dad left an hour ago."

Vivienne took off her coat and sat next to her. "How was it?"

"It was fine." She pressed play on the remote.

"Emily…"

She paused the TV again. "Hard. But good. I haven't forgiven him totally, but at least we're back to talking. I told him I'd come by the house tomorrow for dinner."

Vivienne put her arm around her shoulders and squeezed. "That's great."

Emily leaned the side of her head against Vivienne's. "How was your non-date? I hope you didn't give Dr. Alex the wrong idea without me there."

"I had fun. He's super smart and funny and—"

"Say no more. He sounds terrible. It's a good thing you're not interested in him."

Vivienne's eyes fell on the angel from the manger scene, and she thought of a guy thousands of miles away, wondering if he missed her at all.

TWENTY

Mid December was cold. And not wear-a-scarf-hat-coat-and-gloves cold. It was throw-on-long-johns-and-buy-another-coat-to-wear-over-your-coat cold. Vivienne was braving the double-coat cold to go Christmas shopping, and since all her friends were busy or gone, she had been forced to go alone.

Leaving Kensington that morning, the skies had been clear and blue, the winds sharp and biting. She had never expected to see her car covered in four inches of snow by the time she got out of the mall.

With the backseat of her rental filled with bags of presents, she double-checked her list while the ice and snow melted from the windshield.

Deacon was the only one without a gift, and she still wasn't sure whether or not she was going to get him anything.

He'd barely responded to her texts since he left, and when he did, they were short one-word replies. This past week, it was like he'd fallen off the face of the planet altogether.

But she couldn't think about that now. It was her first Christmas in Neverland and she was determined to make it memorable.

The heavier the snow became, the more she regretted her decision to drive to Connecticut. But if she wanted to call Lyle, she knew she had to do it far away from Kensington. She turned off the Christmas songs blaring through the speakers and jacked up the heating. Even the windshield wipers on full speed had trouble clearing the chunks of ice and snow splattering the glass as she drove.

Eventually, the weather got so bad, she pulled off the highway to give her bleary eyes a break from the blinding white and to refuel. Rows of Christmas trees filled half of the gas station's parking lot, and a man wearing a snow-crusted Santa hat huddled inside a shed, waiting for someone—anyone—to buy a tree.

Even though it only took five minutes to fill the car's tank, Vivienne felt like one of the icicles stuck to the station's gutters by the time she got inside.

A girl wearing a wilted elf's hat and tinsel necklace looked up from her phone and smiled.

Vivienne stomped the snow from her boots onto the spongy rug. "Do you know when the snow is supposed to stop?" If it didn't stop soon, she was going to have to book a hotel for the night.

"Nope." The girl looked back down at her phone.

Vivienne grabbed a bag of trail mix and two cups of hot chocolate from the machine. She brought them to the counter to pay, then found the rack of prepaid phone cards beside the register. "Do you sell phones too, or just the minute cards?"

The girl dropped her own phone onto her stool. "We have a couple of old phones in the back."

"I'll take the cheapest one you have."

After retrieving the phone, the clerk rang her up. "Do you want to donate five dollars to the Children's Cancer Research Center?"

"Can I use my card?"

"Yeah. I'll ring it through as cash back," she said. The amount on the register's screen went up by five dollars.

Vivienne inserted her card into the reader and typed in her PIN. When the transaction went through, the clerk handed her a silver angel statue for the donation. The crooked halo on its shiny head reminded her of the first time she'd met Deacon.

199

She left the gas station with the cherub in her coat pocket and found herself missing Deacon even more.

She left her purchases in the car, then brought the second cup of hot chocolate to the man in the shed. "I can't believe you're out here in this."

"Me either." The man's nose and cheeks were the same color as his hat.

"I bought some hot chocolate for you." She handed him the cup. "If you don't like it, at least your hands will be warm for a few minutes."

Cradling the cup between his gloved fingers, he thanked her and told her, "Merry Christmas."

Back in her car, Vivienne turned up the heat. With Christmas music playing in the background, she called her foster brother.

"Is this going to become some sort of holiday and birthday tradition, Viv?"

Vivienne grabbed a tissue from her purse and wiped the foggy windshield. "How'd you know it was me?"

"No one calls me but Mom, Nick, and Kevin."

"And me," she said, crumpling the tissue into a ball and throwing it on the floor.

"And you," Lyle laughed. "But you don't call enough. Is there any point in asking where you are?"

She narrowed her eyes at the snowy landscape and the trees for sale. "I'm Christmas shopping."

"That doesn't sound very exciting."

"Why do you think I'm calling you?"

"It's nice to know you think of me when you're bored."

She thought about Lyle all the time. But telling him that wouldn't help, so she said, "You all set for Christmas?"

"I guess. You know we don't do a whole lot to celebrate. Mom is working, and Maren is a pit of despair. You were the only saving grace in this place, but you ditched me."

His accusation made her wince. "Don't say it like that. I didn't have a choice."

"If you say so."

"Have those guys been back since we talked last?"

"I saw them once in November, but that's it."

"Maybe they stopped looking for me." She flexed her frozen hands in front of the vent.

"Does that mean you'll come back?"

"No, but it could mean you can come where I am."

"Which is…?"

She smiled sadly at the snow. "Christmas shopping."

"Hold on a sec, Maren!" he shouted.

"Do you need to go?"

"Yeah. Miss Despair is yelling for me, and you know what happens if she's kept waiting. Merry Christmas, Viv."

"Wait a sec—" But it was too late.

Vivienne dropped the phone on the passenger seat and closed her eyes. Maybe if she met with Paul again and explained that HOOK wasn't looking for her anymore, he'd fast-track Lyle's nomination. She'd organize it in January, after the—

The new phone started ringing.

Lyle was calling her back.

"Why'd you hang up—?"

"Hello, Vivienne."

It wasn't Lyle.

She moved the phone from her ear and saw the words BLOCKED NUMBER on the screen. "Who is this?"

"Lawrence Hooke, my dear."

Vivienne's heart pounded against her rib cage, and she couldn't . . . couldn't breathe.

What had she done?

"Before you hang up, hear me out," he went on. "Despite what you've been told about us, we aren't villains in some fantasy tale."

Her arms were so itchy, but she couldn't scratch them beneath all the layers, and *oh god* . . . What had she done? "I don't know anything about you."

"I find that hard to believe since you ran away from home as soon as we showed up."

"How'd you get this number?" She scanned the parking lot for a place to ditch the phone.

"You're not the only ones who can tap phones."

What did that mean? Surely he wasn't suggesting the PAN tapped phones.

"What do you want?"

"Your parents volunteered to assist us with our research, and I was hoping you'd consider doing the same. We'd prefer you as a willing participant instead of the alternative. All you have to do is come to our office in Virginia for some painless tests and—"

She stabbed the END button, stumbled out of the car, and threw the phone in the trash can outside the gas station's bathroom.

Her parents had volunteered to help HOOK?

But . . . HOOK was a PAN's mortal enemy.

Someone was lying.

And when she got back to Neverland, she was going to find out who it was.

If Deacon had been in Kensington, she would have asked him about her parents. But he was MIA, and this wasn't the type of conversation to have over the phone—especially if they were tapped. Plus, he would have wanted to know how she found out, and telling him she had broken the rules and called Lyle wasn't an option.

A few hours later, she found herself standing in the RECORDS room, watching Martina comb frantically through her desk drawer. "I'm sorry. What did you say your name was?"

"Vivienne. We met last month for my genealogy meeting. Don't you remember?"

The woman adjusted her glasses and picked up her calendar. "I don't have anyone by that name on my schedule today."

"I don't have an appointment."

"Then what are you doing here?" The cuckoo clock played its merry tune in the background.

"Like I said before, I have questions about my parents."

"I'm not authorized…um…just a moment." Martina plucked her cell phone from the desk. "What did you say your name was again?"

"Vivienne."

"Vivienne, Vivienne, Vivienne…" Martina whispered, disappearing into the hallway. After a few minutes, she returned, more composed. "Come with me."

Vivienne followed her into the room where she had first learned of her lineage. The sterile white room felt more daunting than before.

"Have a seat. I'll be right back."

Fifteen minutes later, Vivienne was doubtful Martina planned on returning at all. She moved from her chair toward the door, only to run straight into Martina as she rounded the corner carrying a large box.

Vivienne rushed an apology and asked if she could help.

"Take this," Martina said, handing over the box, "and I'll get the rest."

Vivienne brought the box to the lone desk. Martina disappeared once more but returned quickly carrying a long, white garment bag and an alarming red folder.

"What's in the bag?" Vivienne asked, not ready to read what she imagined was in the folder.

"This was Anne's wedding dress." Martina folded the bag and placed it on the back of Vivienne's chair.

"How did it survive the fire?"

"Anne didn't bring it with her. Most PAN leave this kind of stuff here for safe keeping." Martina put her hand on top of the box. "This is a box of your parents' personal belongings salvaged from the fire."

Was she going crazy or did it still smell like smoke?

Inside was a stack of random objects Vivienne didn't recognize, and two she did: Her father's copy of *Peter Pan* and her mother's perfume. She brought the bulbous, pearlescent bottle to her nose and closed her eyes. With the scent of fresh-cut lilacs tickling her senses, it almost felt like Anne was still there.

"Vivienne?"

"Sorry." She put the bottle back inside and set the box on the ground.

Martina handed over the red file folder. "Here's the file on William and Anne's deaths. Unfortunately, most of the information has been redacted. You would need permission from Peter to access the whole file, but he's not available until after the holiday."

"No, no. This is perfect." Vivienne smoothed her hand over the cover. "Thanks."

"I was getting ready to leave the office when you came. I have a flight to Minnesota at eleven, so I need to go in the next twenty minutes."

Vivienne promised to hurry, and Martina left.

After inhaling a deep breath, Vivienne lifted the cover on the folder. Inside was a stack of papers with black marks over nearly all the details. Her parents' names were at the top.

Paul Mitter's signature was at the bottom of the first page. More black lines obscured the details of her parents' passing as she leafed through the rest of the report.

But the final paragraph on the final page was the most damning.

There, typed in black and white, were the names William and Anne Dunn and HOOK. Next to those words was a smudge of white-out. Vivienne used her nail to scrape away the white and reveal one final word: *Traitors*.

After Deacon and his extended family had their fill of turkey, ham, and spiced beef, they retired to his grandfather's cavernous drawing room to enjoy fragrant mulled wine and sugar-dusted mince pies. The room made Deacon think of centuries past and reminded him of his family's timelessness.

Dark mahogany cabinetry housed countless books, and the same dark wood served as ornate paneling along the walls. The coffered ceiling held shadows this late in the evening that the many candles and side lamps could not dispel.

The family had broken into small groups, each in deep discussion over some aspect of the PAN, leaving Deacon on his own, lounging on a velvet settee. He stared into the flames of the wide fireplace, crackling with smoldering logs, forcing its heat into the space.

Despite the spacious rooms in his grandad's home, he felt

claustrophobic. He attributed the feeling to his diminished physical activity. Christmas in England meant running and flying were replaced by serious conversation, cultured entertainment, and food.

When he left the party, he promised himself he would make the time for a flight.

"How much longer do you have in the field?" his grandad asked, sitting on the settee next to him.

"Ten months." A pang of regret filled Deacon's soul when he thought of leaving the position he loved so much. Recruiting offered him freedom without having to cut the tether that bound him to Neverland.

His grandad nodded, looking across the dimly-lit room to study his daughter Mary. "I thought your mother had some sort of arrangement with you about cutting your time short."

"If she had her way, I wouldn't have worked past my fifth year." It had been one of the few arguments he'd actually won.

"What will you do next?"

"I'm not sure."

His grandad may have looked the same age as Deacon, but the way he reflected on every word before speaking indicated his advanced years. "Would you consider coming to London when you're finished?"

The first thing to pop into Deacon's mind was a brown-eyed girl back in the States. "I'm enjoying life at Kensington for the moment."

"You'd be a breath of fresh air in Leadership, and there may be some more openings in the near future."

"I heard about Tootles." Deacon leaned forward and rested his elbows on his knees. He hadn't seen his great-uncle in ages. "How's he settling in?"

"He's doing as well as can be expected. Unfortunately, he has fewer lucid moments every day."

"And we still don't have any answers?"

His grandad shook his head. "Our immortal bodies don't fail us, but it seems our minds are another story."

Deacon scanned the gathering for the other members of

Leadership, wondering which one would be the next to retire. "How are *you* feeling?"

"As sharp as I did in 1875." He nudged Deacon with his knee. "I hear you went to a meeting at Lee Somerfield's."

Deacon tilted the drink in his hand from side to side; the last ice cube melted into the amber liquid. "I wondered how long it would take you to bring that up."

"Anything good?"

"He thinks Leadership is too concerned with staying hidden to do something about HOOK."

"He's not entirely wrong." His grandad sighed and settled back against the cushion. "Lee's always believed we'd get away with an overt attack, but we know from years of experience that dealing with HOOK isn't a straightforward affair. They have something we need. And until we get it, we have to wait."

What could HOOK possibly have that the PAN needed? Deacon was about to ask when his grandad stopped him with a hand on his knee. "Your mother seems to be enjoying herself."

Deacon's mother laughed at something Curly said and clinked her champagne glass against Slightly's.

"It seems that way." But Deacon knew that she had struggled to get out of bed that morning. The holidays weren't the same since his father had passed.

Bruce Ashford had been the most easygoing human on the planet. Deacon still couldn't fathom how his tyrannical mother had been compatible with the man for so many years. Unfortunately, their mismatched love story had ended two days after his father's forty-third birthday.

There was a photo on the mantelpiece from the celebrations. Deacon's father was front and center with his forever-young wife Mary by his side. Deacon had been fifteen at the time. But he looked nearly the same age as his granddad, mother, and father—thanks to the ageless injection. His aunt Ida, Bruce's younger sister, was there too, her hair streaked with gray. For them, it was a normal family photo; however, an outsider would have greatly misinterpreted the relationships between the subjects.

There was another framed photo of his grandfather, mother,

and Deacon from the day Deacon's Nevergene activated. It looked like a bunch of friends celebrating instead of three generations of family members welcoming the youngest into the fold.

A four-inch metal statue on the mantelpiece next to the photo caught his attention.

Deacon recognized the shape, and he asked his grandad where he got the statute.

"I imagine it was one of Tootles' jokes—there've been too many to keep track of. You've seen my office."

Deacon chuckled as he lifted the tiny metal carving, a perfect replica of Peter's statue in Kensington Gardens. "May I have it?"

"I don't mind. It's serving no purpose here."

"Thank you."

"Consider it an extra Christmas present for my favorite grandson."

"Peter? Could you come over here and settle an argument between the two Richards?" Curly said from across the room.

A flash of mischief crossed Peter Pan's face. He smiled at Deacon as he stood from the settee. "My job is never done."

"Hey handsome."

Shit.

Deacon twisted toward the familiar blonde and loosened his collar. "What are you doing here, Gwen?" He certainly hadn't invited her.

Gwen unbuttoned her coat and let it slide down her pale arms. Her tight black dress accentuated her curves—and Deacon knew how dangerous those curves were. She sat next to him on the couch and dragged her nail down the back of his neck. "I wanted to wish you Happy Christmas." In his ear, she whispered, "And give you your present."

Bad idea. A very bad idea.

When she reached for his hand, he pulled away.

"What's wrong?" she whined.

"I can't go with you." He never thought he would utter those particular words to this particular woman, but here he was, uttering away.

Her full lower lip jutted forward. "Why not?"

He knew better than to tell her the real reason, so he said, "Peter said he wanted to speak to me when everyone is gone."

She traced his collarbone over his shirt. "That could take ages."

"I know." His mother stared at him from the sideboard. He stood to disengage Gwen's curious hands.

She rose without teetering on her stilettos and smoothed her hand down his waistcoat. "Will you text me when you're done?"

He caught her hand before it reached his belt. "I'm wrecked tired."

"Lucky for me," Gwen whispered, kissing his jaw, "I know how to wake you up."

TWENTY-ONE

"You should get some rest, Deacon." Despite the darkness, his mother's disapproval washed over him from the front stairs of her London townhome. "We've had a busy day."

"I'm not tired." He wasn't the first PAN to suffer from insomnia. According to his tests last month, his nGh levels were normal, but his adrenaline was a bit high. He remembered having trouble with his sleep ever since he was a child.

His mother sighed and pulled the neck of her jacket closed. "Be safe, please. And fly low."

"I know the rules," he grumbled. As if he needed the reminder. He walked until he grew bored, made his way to an empty alley, and threw himself into the breeze. Upon entering the world of silence that lived above the sleeping city, he realized the historic buildings and landmarks that so many people stopped to photograph had long since lost their magical hold on him. The only attention he paid them was to gauge how far he had flown.

He found himself landing in Kensington Gardens near Peter's statue. The plaguing mist refreshed him as it drifted over his warm skin.

Being in the gardens made him think of Vivienne, so many miles away, enjoying a white Christmas in a different Kensington. Had she spent the holiday with Alex? The thought made his stomach twist.

He pulled his mobile from his pocket and snapped a photo of the statue. The quality wasn't great, but the flash helped illuminate the figure dancing with his flute at the top. He sent it to her, along with a text. *Guess where I am.*

Why did he miss her so much? The usual distractions hadn't distracted him. And the time had dragged on and on and on, and he honestly didn't think he would ever get to leave this bloody country.

He was good at leaving women behind. At moving on. But for some reason—

His mobile buzzed. *Tell Peter you have to go. It's my turn now.*

Gwen really needed to get the hint. It wasn't like this was the first time he'd avoided her this month. She'd shown up uninvited to his room last week. Telling her to get out was one of the hardest things he'd ever done.

On his flight back to the house, he checked his mobile every two minutes. Vivienne never responded. She could've been busy. Or asleep. Or out with Alex facial-hair McGee.

His original plan had been to respond often enough to keep from seeming rude. That way, life could go back to normal—back to when he wasn't obsessed with a girl he hadn't even properly kissed.

But the more he tried *not* to think about Vivienne, the more he thought about her. It made no sense.

Vivienne had texted him regularly at first, but one day she had just . . . stopped. That morning, she had wished him a Merry Christmas in a group text. Like sending him an individual text had been too much effort. Had she decided he wasn't worth it, or had she found her own distraction?

He had to get back home so he could put himself out of his misery.

Deacon landed around the corner from his mother's townhouse and, once inside, took a quick shower before attempting to sleep. The moonlight fell silver through his window. He studied the beams from the comfort of his creaky, antique four-poster bed and considered his next move.

His mother wouldn't be impressed if he left on Boxing Day, but there was nothing for him in London. He had spent the last month with the same family. They would meet again for another meal and more discussions—he had no desire to attend either. Giving in to exhaustion, he promised himself the morning would bring his return to Worcester.

Deacon didn't rise until after noon. His mother had left him a note saying the pair of them would be attending a show at the West End the following day. While he had no interest in accompanying her, he knew better than to abandon her on such an occasion. She was understandably melancholy this time of year, missing his father more than usual.

He was finally able to leave the evening of the twenty-eighth.

After multiple delays and canceled flights due to bad weather at his destination, Deacon landed in blizzardy Boston late on the twenty-ninth.

He wanted to see Vivienne right away, but after twenty-four hours of travel, he wasn't fit to see anyone. Instead, he went to his home, washed up, and, for the first time in forever, had no trouble falling asleep.

Early the next morning, he drove to Vivienne's flat only to find no one home. If he hadn't forgotten his phone in the car, he would have called her. He gave one final knock in desperation. When only silence answered, he drifted toward the snowy ground.

"Hello?"

He flew back toward the door and gave Vivienne a little wave. She looked at him with narrowed eyes, and he had a sinking feeling their reunion wasn't going to go as he had hoped.

"What do you want?" Her voice was husky from sleep, but it was also cold and detached.

He'd been asking himself the same question for the last month. "I wanted to let you know I'm back."

"Great. Welcome home. Now I'm going back to sleep."

He stopped her from slamming the door in his face. He had assumed she'd be a bit annoyed from his lack of contact, but hadn't expected this. "Look, I'm sorry for not texting, I'm not very good at the whole distance thing and—"

"That's a bunch of crap and you know it," she snapped. "It takes two seconds to send a text message. If you wanted to talk to me, you would have. Simple as that."

"I did want to talk to you," he confessed, rubbing the back of his neck. "I *do* want to, I mean."

"Then why didn't you?"

"It's complicated." What was he doing? He was shit at this. The best thing to do would be to let her cool down. Then she'd get over it, and they could pick up where they'd left off in November.

"Whatever." She tried to close the door again.

He needed to get out of here. To go home. To leave her alone . . . "Can I just come in for two minutes? Please?"

She rolled her eyes but stepped aside and allowed him into her apartment. All the decorations were still up, but the lights in the Christmas trees were off. There was a suitcase sitting beside the sofa. Had she been somewhere or was she leaving?

Vivienne's watch beeped when she pressed it. "You have two minutes, starting..." Another beep. "*Now.*"

She was setting a timer? All right. He needed to get it together. The truth. He was going to tell her the truth. "I didn't text you because I was hoping I would get over whatever *this* is." He gestured between the two of them. It wasn't a relationship. It was . . . he didn't have the right word for it.

She shook her head and sank onto the arm of the sofa. "Why? I thought...I thought you liked me."

"I did—I *do*. But I was hoping that some time away would mean I could clear my head and stop thinking about you all the damn time."

She frowned at the face of her watch and pressed a button on the side. It beeped once. Twice. "Why is that such a bad thing?" she asked quietly, keeping her eyes on her wrist.

"Because it doesn't happen to me, all right? I go out with girls once or twice, and that's it. I don't get into relationships. I don't even go on dates. So I haven't a clue what I'm doing. All I know is that I'm doing it wrong."

There. Now she knew he was a terrible person. That he wasn't looking for anything formal or heavy or labeled. He was looking for something casual and fun . . . but with her.

She sighed and pulled her hair back into a ponytail and chewed on her lip, but she wasn't saying anything. Why wasn't she saying anything? Surely she had *something* to say. An opinion. A curse. *Something*.

"Okay."

That's it? *Okay*? What did that mean?

"You like me, but you don't want to date me," she said slowly, as if processing. "So you're saying you...what? Just want to hang out casually or whatever? That you like me but have no interest in being anything more."

"Yes." That was what he meant, wasn't it? Because it didn't sound quite as appealing coming out of her mouth.

"Okay then."

"You're...into it?"

A shrug. "I guess I'm into it until I'm not." She got up and padded into the kitchen.

"All right." Shouldn't he be more excited about this? He followed her into the kitchen and watched her pull a loaf of bread from the press.

"Do you want toast or is breakfast a no-no in this whole casual, non-dating scenario?" she asked, dropping two slices into the toaster.

"I'd love toast." He'd left his house without eating breakfast, which said a lot about his priorities at present.

She laid out two plates and a butter knife. The delicate sound of her feet across the floor made him smile.

He picked up the snowman salt and pepper shakers. Where did a person get decorations like these? "How was your Christmas?"

Her shoulders stiffened. "How about I don't ask what you did over the holidays and you don't ask me. Because that seems a little too serious for whatever *this* is."

Had she done something that she didn't want him knowing about? "Good idea." He dragged a glass from the press and filled it from the tap. The cold water did little to revive him.

When he leaned against the counter, the present he'd gotten for her jabbed him in the ass. "I got you something."

She whirled around from the fridge, butter in hand. "You did?"

Deacon withdrew the hastily-wrapped statue and held it toward her. "The wrapping is shocking." In hindsight, he probably should have put it in a box.

She wiped her hands on her sweatshirt before accepting the present and unravelling the layers of wrapping paper and tourniquet of tape. "This is amazing," she said, running her fingertips along the delicate carving of Peter Pan. "I love it." She gifted him the first warm smile since their reunion.

The toast popped, and she sat the statue on the counter. "Butter that," she said, indicating the toast. "I'll be back in a sec." Then she disappeared down the hall.

He scraped some butter onto the toast, stacked the two pieces so the butter could melt between them, and threw two more slices into the toaster.

When he finished, Vivienne came back with a small box in her hands. "I got you something too."

He'd barely spoken to her all month and she'd still thought to buy him a gift? That had to be a good sign. The wrapping was impeccable; the seams matched up, and the bow coordinated. He opened it to find a small box about the size of the statue he had given her. Inside was a silver angel.

He twisted the cool metal creature in his fingers and noticed she had written something on the base with a black marker. *A Guardian Angel of your own.*

An angel . . . If only.

"This is brilliant. Thank you."

He made his own toast when it popped and carried it to the table. Vivienne curled onto a chair, one leg wedged beneath her, the other tucked to her chest so her chin rested on her knee. When was the last time he'd had breakfast with a girl?

He couldn't remember.

"So," she began, taking a bite of toast, "did you know that Paul thinks my parents are traitors?"

"I...um..." Of course he knew. But how did *she* find out?

Her eyes narrowed. "Go on."

"I know your parents are alleged to have been working with HOOK, but nothing was ever proven."

She took another bite of toast. Chewed slowly. Swallowed. "And you didn't tell me this because...?"

"I was told not to."

"I deserved to know about my parents from day one."

It was true. But she wouldn't have come if he'd told her. "What do you know, exactly?" He touched the crooked halo on the angel. He hadn't been allowed to say anything before, but that didn't mean he couldn't rectify it now.

"Martina gave me a copy of Paul's report on their deaths, but most of it was blacked out."

Peter would have authorized that, so Deacon was fairly confident this wouldn't land him in too much trouble. "I believe your parents were caught communicating with HOOK. They were scheduled to be brought in front of Leadership for questioning, but they died before they could tell their side of the story."

She picked at the crust on her plate. "In the fire."

"Your aunt Christine died in the fire," he said, waiting for her reaction, "but your parents were neutralized."

The plate rattled. *"What?"*

"Your parents had passed away before the flames or smoke reached them. And, from what I can gather, no one knows where they got the poison—or who administered it." The scandal had rocked the Neverlands.

Her mouth dropped open, but the words were slow in coming. "Do people...think my parents...injected themselves?" she asked between gasps. She shoved her shirtsleeves to her elbows and started scratching. Surely her levels of nGh should've evened out by now.

"It's been done before."

"No. They would never do that to me," she said, vigorously shaking her head. "They never would have left me alone."

"It's still an open case. You should speak to Peter about it when he's in."

She nodded and swiped at the tears welling in her eyes. "Thanks. I will."

He should go. Let her process this on her own. "What are you doing tomorrow night?" Why had he said that? She'd found out devastating news two seconds ago, and he was asking her about her plans?

"What?" she sniffed.

"It's New Year's Eve."

Her brows came together, and she frowned at what was left of her toast. "I don't know. Emily mentioned going somewhere, but I can't remember what it was."

"You should come to my house. Bring Emily and Max. I'm having a party." What was he saying? He wasn't having a party. He hated New Year's Eve; it was a pointless holiday for a community who didn't need to keep track of the passage of time.

"Yeah, maybe."

Was he really going to organize an entire party around a "maybe"? "Brilliant. Party starts at nine." He stood and tucked his angel inside his jacket pocket.

"You're leaving?" she asked, watching him load his plate in the dishwasher.

"I have a few things left to organize for tomorrow night."

Like the whole damn party.

"What are you and Nicola doing for New Year's Eve?" Deacon pressed the button to start his car and adjusted the air so it was blowing on the windscreen. He'd only been in Vivienne's flat for an hour and it had already frozen over.

"Are you back?" Ethan said after a long, drawn-out yawn.

"I got home last night."

"Come over to my house right now."

Deacon shifted into drive and spun out of the driveway. "What's wrong?"

"You'll see when you get here."

Despite morning traffic, he made it to Ethan's bungalow in record time and burst through the front door without knocking.

From the urgency in their earlier conversation, the last thing he expected to see was Ethan lounging on the sofa, watching the morning news with a box of blueberry muffins resting on his stomach. "Hey, Dash." Nonplussed, Ethan took another bite of his muffin. "How was London?"

"All right."

A smirk. "Did you see Gwen?"

He did *not* want to talk about Gwen. "Where's the emergency?"

"That's a yes." Ethan laughed. "You're a glutton for punishment, my friend." He grabbed another muffin and bit into it. Crumbs fell onto his white T-shirt. "Why were you asking me about New Year's Eve?"

The shift in conversation jarred Deacon from his irritation. "Do you have plans?"

"Not sure yet. You know how Nicola is about New Year's. She probably signed me up for something I don't want to do."

Last year, Nicola had paid a ridiculous amount of money for tickets to a swanky NYE party in Boston. The year before that, she'd dragged them to see the ball drop in NYC with a million other people.

Deacon took a muffin from the box and sat in one of the leather recliners. "I thought about having a few people over to my house for the night."

Ethan's eyes bulged. "*You're* throwing a party?" Half the muffin in his hand tumbled onto his lap.

"It's not a big deal."

"Not a big deal?" Ethan waved what was left of his muffin at him. "The fact that you are opening your home to other people to celebrate a holiday you find *utterly ridiculous* is most definitely a big deal." He slipped into what he must have considered an accurate rendition of Deacon's accent.

"I find you *utterly ridiculous,* but still hang out with you," Deacon shot back.

"We'll be there." Ethan rubbed his hands together. "Now, what do you need from us?"

217

That was an excellent question.

"I suppose you should invite a few more people."

"Do I need to invite Vivienne," he drawled, "or have you already extended an invitation of your own?"

"Shut up." Deacon chucked his last bit of muffin at him.

Ethan caught it, considered the morsel, and tossed it back. "Will there be food at this soiree?"

Deacon popped it into his mouth and went to the kitchen for a drink. "Yeah, sure."

"Have you *ordered* food?"

"Not yet," he shouted from behind the refrigerator door.

"Such a festive occasion calls for music as well."

Deacon pinched the bridge of his nose, regretting this already. "I suppose I can throw together a playlist—"

"Are you insane, dude?" Ethan snorted. "Your taste in music is shit. I'll invite Ricky and see if he'd be willing to DJ for us."

"Is there anything else you'd like me to do for *my* party?" Deacon filled a glass with milk and took a drink.

"No way. You'll screw it up. I'll call Nicola and get her on it. What time did you tell Vivienne to show up?"

There was no point denying the fact that Vivienne had been the first to receive an invitation. "Nine o'clock."

"Perfect. We'll be there by seven."

"Now that we've organized the party, what was so important that you needed me to come over right away?"

Ethan sat upright with a groan and put the box on his coffee table. "Come with me."

Deacon followed him to the small attached garage. When Ethan turned on the lights, Deacon stared at the scene in front of him in bewilderment. "What is all of this?"

Ethan flew down the steps and opened one large cardboard box out of a stack. "I got a great deal on these at an online auction." He withdrew a green sleeve of outdoor twinkle lights.

"There have to be...thousands of lights here."

Ethan alighted to the top of an unopened case and grinned. "And the question is: What are we going to do with them?"

Deacon was about to jump off the top of the Empire State Building and fly to the middle of Times Square when his mobile buzzed from his bedside locker. He jerked upright so fast that he tweaked a muscle in his neck.

"Have you checked your messages?"

He fell back onto his pillow and squinted at the clock on his phone. What was Ethan doing calling him at half seven in the morning? He hadn't even been asleep for two hours. "What are you on about?"

"Check out the link I sent you, then call me back."

Deacon opened the messages app on his phone and clicked the link Ethan had sent moments earlier. He closed his eyes against the light bursting from the small screen and nearly fell back to sleep while the clip loaded.

"Authorities aren't sure exactly how the festive perpetrators completed the prank without being noticed. But one thing's for sure: the town of Chambersburg, Pennsylvania has never been as festive ringing in the new year."

For normal humans, encumbered by ladders and a healthy fear of falling from great heights, it would've been a monumental task to light a single church steeple. But for two young men who could fly, they had the sloping roof trussed up like a Christmas tree in twenty minutes. The hardest part had been connecting them to the sockets outside.

Deacon chuckled at the shocked look on the pastor's face during his interview. The fact that he and Ethan had done the same thing to every steeple within a ten-mile radius baffled everyone in the clip.

Laughing to himself, he turned off his phone and went back to sleep. After all, he had a big night ahead.

TWENTY-TWO

The short, black, bell-shaped dress wasn't fancy, but Vivienne felt really pretty wearing it. When Deacon left yesterday, she had decided not to go to his party. But then Emily heard about it and she wouldn't take "no" for an answer. She kept saying Vivienne was destined to have his cute, British babies, and that she *had* to go. Vivienne hadn't bothered telling her that Deacon wasn't interested in babies or relationships or anything more than hanging out because . . . what was the point? It wasn't going to change things.

She'd meant it when she told him that she was into it for now. She was eighteen and wasn't looking for anything serious. But when her priorities changed, she'd have to look elsewhere. At least she knew. And knowing was half the battle.

"I totally forgot you bought that dress," Emily said, looking festive in a rainbow-colored sequined jumpsuit, "or else I would have stolen it from you by now. You look ah-mazing. Deacon is going to want to jump your bones."

That was doubtful. "You're one to talk. That outfit was *made* for New Year's."

"Why do you think I wanted to go so bad? All this bling would've been wasted on any other night." She twirled around like a disco ball. "Do you want to borrow a pair of heels?"

"I wouldn't last an hour teetering around in your shoes."

"They're surprisingly comfortable."

There was no way the three-inch spikes on the heels of Emily's feet were comfortable.

"I don't believe you, and would prefer to *walk* into Deacon's house, not stumble."

"What shoes were you thinking of wearing? And if you say those god-awful Chuck Taylors, I'm going to throw them out the window."

With her foot, Vivienne scooted her Chucks beneath her bed and promised to wear the silver flats Emily had bought her the week before.

A minibus taxi picked up the girls and a handful of Deacon's other friends—all of them women—at the gates and brought them to the address Deacon had texted her the day before. When they pulled up to a large house in a quiet neighborhood, she checked the number twice to make sure they were in the right place.

"*This* is Deacon's house?" Emily asked, her eyes wide as she sat in awe of the impressive façade of the historic home.

"I think so." How the heck could he afford a place like this?

"It looks like the kind of place where a politician lives with his 2.5 children and a retriever named Goldie."

Vivienne laughed as she paid the fare.

"Are we going in, or should we just stare at it for the night?" Emily whispered into her ear.

Vivienne steeled her shoulders and led the procession of teenagers up the steps to the front door. Instead of running, everyone took their time to keep from slipping on the frozen stones.

There was no way to see inside because the blinds had been pulled, but muffled music and shouts seeped through the walls.

The door swept wide, and Ethan appeared, resplendent in a tuxedo jacket, shirt, bow tie, and ripped skinny jeans. Somehow the golden top hat he wore did not look ridiculous.

He handed out random *Happy New Year* hats, glasses, and crowns to people as they passed. "Drinks are in the kitchen, and I'm supposed to tell everyone to stay downstairs." A laugh. "But as long as you stay outta Dash's room, he'll get over it."

Deacon's room . . . where he slept. And did other things as well.

A shiver raced up Vivienne's spine.

The modern interior was a surprise considering the historical exterior. All partition walls had been removed to create clear sight lines and an open, free-flowing space that served as living room, dining room, and kitchen.

After being bounced around like a pinball on the makeshift dance floor, she reached the solace of the kitchen. There were only lower cabinets painted a timeless white with a pristine marble countertop. A line of windows looked upon a snowy lawn lit with strings of lights.

The room was filled with gold and silver balloons. There were so many floating mid-air that she could barely make out the details in the coffered ceiling.

It was easy to imagine herself curled up next to the white-washed brick fireplace with a good book and a cup of steaming hot chocolate at her side.

The French doors at the back of the house opened, and Deacon came in. When he saw her, his lips curled into the most devastating smile.

Casual. She could totally do casual.

"I'm so glad you came." He wrapped his arms around her for a bone-crushing hug. He smelled like cologne and fresh air and alcohol. When he pulled away, he kept his hands on her elbows. "Have you been here long?"

"Only a few minutes."

"You look beautiful."

Those darn fireflies danced around to the beat of the pop music blaring in the background. "Thanks. You're looking pretty good yourself."

Better than good. He wore a gray waistcoat open over a black button-down shirt half tucked into the waistband of his jeans.

His easy smile made her stomach twist. "What do you

think?" He inclined his head toward the party happening around them.

"Your place is amazing. I didn't expect so many people though." She recognized most of the guests from campus, but there were a few new faces mixed in.

"That's my punishment," he groaned, raking a hand through his hair, "for giving Ethan free reign over the planning process."

"He went a little overboard on the balloons too, I see."

"Do you think so? I mean, a ceiling full of balloons is quite practical if you think about it."

"So practical." Her laugh was muffled by the crowd.

"Would you like something to eat? Ethan overdid it on food as well." He indicated the trays of miniature deliciousness displayed atop the island.

The mini egg rolls looked good. "I'll take care of myself." She grabbed a gold plastic plate from the end of the counter.

"Shall I get you a drink? Nicola made some sort of frothy orange punch that's strong, but good."

"I'll try it. Thanks." Vivienne filled her plate, and Deacon returned with a fancy cup brimming with punch. Had he said there was alcohol in it? She couldn't taste any when she took a sip.

Deacon knocked his plastic cup against hers and took a drink. "I'm so glad you came."

"You said that already."

"Did I?" His brows came together and he frowned into his cup. Then he smiled. "That just makes it doubly true."

She ate one of the egg rolls and chewed thoughtfully. "*Why* are you so happy I came though?"

"Isn't it obvious?" He gulped more punch. "This whole bloody party was for you. So if you hadn't come, it would've been a waste of balloons."

"Dash! Come here for a sec," Audrey shouted, waving in his direction.

"I'll be right back." Deacon leaned closer to whisper, "Don't go anywhere. I have plans for you tonight."

Her egg roll fell onto the floor.

For someone who wanted to keep things casual, Deacon sure was making an effort tonight. Which left her more confused than ever. He was talking to Audrey and Joel, laughing and more at ease than she'd ever seen him. When he caught her looking at him, he winked. She felt herself blush all the way to her toes.

She needed another drink. After refilling her cup and draining half of that one, she felt calmer. Not steadier—she had to prop herself up against the island. But definitely calmer. Even more confident. When he came back, she was going to ask him about these "plans" of his.

She ate a few strawberries from the cheeseboard and topped up her punch. Where was Emily?

On the dance floor. Of course. That girl knew how to party. If Vivienne was that fun, she wouldn't be hiding in the kitchen.

"Why the frown?" Deacon asked from behind her.

"I was just thinking I should have more fun."

He put his hands on either side of her, trapping her against the counter. "I'd love to help you with that."

"I bet you would," she teased, hiding her smile inside her cup.

"Hey, Dash?" Vivienne didn't recognize the girl in the skin-tight red jumpsuit waving him over.

"These people need to leave me alone," he groaned. Before he left, he pressed a kiss to her temple.

It was a simple gesture, sweet and innocent and not at all what she expected from Deacon Ashford.

Vivienne smirked at her shoeless roommate as she danced her way into the kitchen. So much for those spikes being comfortable.

"Here." Emily shoved one of two fluted glasses of champagne toward her. "You're gonna need this for the midnight toast."

"Thanks. Have you...um...seen Deacon anywhere?" He had

been talking to Ethan a minute ago. She'd had to pee, and when she got back, he was gone.

"I'm shocked he's not with you. Don't think I haven't noticed him all up in your business all night." Emily knocked Vivienne with her hip. "He'd better get his cute butt back here if he's gonna get your midnight kiss."

Vivienne had forgotten that particular holiday tradition. She and Lyle used to watch movies and the ball drop in New York— if she stayed awake long enough to see it. But there had definitely been no kissing.

"Who are *you* going to kiss?" Vivienne shot back, scanning the crowd for Deacon.

Emily tapped her glittery nail against her glass. "I think I'm going to find some outsider and make his night."

Ethan was jumping around, holding a massive clock with a flashing red countdown above his head. Nicola was laughing at something Joel said. Max was sitting on the back of the couch, drooling over a dark-haired girl in sparkling black hotpants. There was something familiar about her that Vivienne couldn't quite place—

Halloween.

The sexy police officer from Halloween was there. Who had invited her? Had her angel friend come too?

"Right," Emily squealed, squeezing Vivienne's arm, "it's time to find my victim. Good luck finding yours."

Where the heck was—

No . . . Vivienne's whole body started to shake and itch and . . . *No.* Please no . . .

Deacon was in the corner next to the book shelf, making out with a blonde in a strappy red dress. She couldn't see his face . . . but she'd recognize that dark head anywhere.

She needed to get out of here. To escape. The front door would lead her right past *him*, and she did *not* want to see *that* up close.

The back door. The champagne spilled over her hand on her way to the—

"You can't go yet." Cold fingers wrapped around her wrist. "I just got here."

Vivienne froze. Turned slowly. "Alex?" What was he doing there? She'd texted him about the party earlier, but he'd said he already had plans. "I thought you were going to Boston."

"I can do that next year," he said with an easy smile, tucking his hands into his pockets. "This sounded like a fun, once-in-a-lifetime opportunity."

Fun. Right. This was supposed to be fun. She pasted on a smile. "How was London?" He had agreed to come to Emily's for Christmas, but had to cancel to make an unexpected trip to the lab in Harrow.

"It didn't end as I'd hoped." There was a tightness in his voice that she hadn't noticed before. "But we don't have to talk about that now. How are you holding up?"

When she'd called him after finding out about her parents, he'd been so great, offering to bring over Chinese food for everyone in the apartment. It had been a good night. Easy.

"I'm fine."

"Some place, isn't it?" Alex said, nodding toward the party. Vivienne didn't bother turning around. "It's good to be royalty," he chuckled.

Royalty? "What does that mean?"

His brows came together over his wide blue eyes. "You do know Deacon is Peter's grandson, don't you?"

Deacon was related to Peter-frickin'-Pan? That seemed like a pretty big thing to conveniently forget to tell someone. Didn't he trust her? Or was there another reason he didn't want her to know?

"He never told me." She took a drink of champagne to fill the hollowness in her stomach.

"He's always been good at keeping secrets," Alex said, taking a sip from his glass. "Which is why it's so weird he invited all these people to his house."

This whole party is for you . . .

Deacon was so full of it.

If he had done it for her, he wouldn't be making out with someone else.

"So I've been trying to come up with a reason for you *not* to go out with me this week." Alex stepped closer. "And I can't think of any."

The bubbles from her champagne tickled her throat when she took another drink. Alex was cute and smart and funny, and he texted her and stayed in touch and—

Vivienne inadvertently twisted and scanned the crowd. It was easy to locate Ethan in his top hat standing next to Nicola, but there was no sign of Deacon—or the blonde.

"Neither can I," she told him.

The noisy crowd drowned out his response, but he was smiling.

"3, 2, 1...*Happy New Year!*"

One moment, everyone was cheering; the next, they were silent.

Alex stepped closer, and his eyes dropped to her mouth, and she felt her stomach flutter when he said her name and reached a hand toward her hair and leaned in . . .

A surge of anger and adrenaline and alcohol electrified in her veins, and she closed her eyes, wrapped her arms around his neck, and brought her mouth to his.

His beard scratched her chin and he pulled her closer and—

This wasn't supposed to happen. It wasn't supposed to be Alex.

Air . . . She needed to get some air.

Vivienne let him go and sprinted for the back door.

Alone in the darkness, she ignored the cheering and Auld Lang Syne singsong taking place inside and tried to figure out how the night had gone so wrong.

What the hell just happened?

Five minutes. He'd been gone five bloody minutes, and when he came back, Alex McGee's tongue was down Vivienne's throat.

Right in front of him.

At the party he'd thrown for her.

In his house.

There was puke in his shower. His favorite lamp was smashed to bits. There was drink spilled all over his hardwood floors.

And for what? So he could play matchmaker for Alex and Vivienne?

She pushed away from Alex and stumbled for the back garden. And then Alex turned to Deacon . . . and *laughed*.

"Happy New Year, Dash." He clapped him on the shoulder on his way to the front door, and if Deacon had all his facilities, he would've knocked the damn smirk from his bearded face, but what the hell just happened?

He shoved the door to the back garden open and stared at the girl who had ripped his heart from his chest and trampled it with her silver shoes.

Vivienne's long, dark hair fell in soft waves down the back of her black dress. He'd found the simplicity of her outfit refreshing and undeniably sexy in the way it showcased her slim figure. She looked like a fairy's shadow against the sparkling winter backdrop.

The snow cushioned his footsteps as he moved toward her. He should have left her alone, but for some reason, he couldn't.

"Go away, Deacon." She kept her back to him and spoke her words into the night.

"Not until you tell me what that was about. You and *Alex*?" His stomach was in knots, and he regretted not hitting him when he had the chance.

She whirled around; tears shimmered on her cheeks. "You don't get to shame me for kissing someone else. We're keeping it casual, *remember*?" she spat. "Besides, you were too busy making out with that girl."

Girl? What girl? In that moment, the only woman in existence was Vivienne—which was an entirely new concept that made him want to fly in the opposite direction.

"I wanted to kiss *someone* at midnight," she went on, stomping forward until he could see the string lights reflected in her wide brown eyes, "and if you hadn't been so *busy* it would have been you. So if you're jealous, it's your own stupid fault."

"What are you on about?" he growled. "I wasn't—"

"Don't lie to me! I *saw* you kiss her!"

"I haven't kissed *anyone*. I went upstairs to take a pi—to use the restroom. Someone vomited in my shower, so I had to clean up that disgusting mess. And when I came back downstairs, Alex had his tongue down your throat!"

"I-I saw you…" Her brows came together and she shook her head.

"I don't know who you saw, but it *wasn't* me." What a disaster. All this trouble for nothing. This was exactly why he never made an effort. "How many drinks have you had?"

She waved her empty champagne glass in his face. "None of your business."

"You're drunk."

"And you're a jerk. Peter Pan's *untouchable* grandson, all 'look at me in my fancy house with my fancy accent, I can have *whatever I want.'*"

She knew? How did she find—"Alex told you, didn't he?"

"It doesn't matter," she hissed, poking him in the chest. "I should have heard it from you."

"You want to hear it from me? Fine. I'm Peter Pan's grandson…" He leaned so he could say against the shell of her ear, "But I'm not untouchable."

Her breathing hitched. "Prove it."

He wanted to. But she had *no* idea what she was asking. "Vivienne, you're drunk."

"I'm tipsy but I'm not drunk." Another poke. "And I want *you* to prove it."

Prove it.

Prove he wasn't untouchable.

Prove that all of this was for her.

Prove that he couldn't get her out of his head.

Prove that his heart was in bloody ribbons in the snow.

"That's what I thought." Vivienne's lips curled into a derisive smile. "Go ahead and fly away, little boy who'll never grow—"

His lips crashed against hers, and his hands tangled in her hair, and he dragged her back onto the snowy bench. His ass and back were getting soaked, but he didn't give a shit because there was a beautiful girl on top of him, clinging to his collar like her life depended on it. And she tasted so damn good, like champagne and strawberries, and her tongue moved in and out of his mouth the way he wished he could be moving in and out of her body, and if he died now, he would die happy.

And when he thought it couldn't get any better, she shifted so she was straddling him, and if he hadn't invited so many damned people, he would have flown her straight up to his bedroom and proved *exactly* how he felt about her.

He'd missed her and he hadn't even known what he'd been missing.

And now that he'd found her . . . he wasn't letting go.

TWENTY-THREE

S eeing his mother looming over his bed on New Year's Day
did nothing to help the aching in Deacon's head. "Deacon
Elias Ashford, I swear, if you step out of line even one more
time, you'll be shipped off to London so fast..."

"It was just a harmless prank." The pounding only increased
when he thought of the state his house was currently in.

She threw a newspaper on top of his duvet. "When are you
going to grow up?"

"Never. That's kind of the point."

"Do you realize how suspicious outsiders can be?" she said,
stalking toward the window and back again.

As he'd suspected, the headlines were full of theories from
his excursion with Ethan to Pennsylvania. "I hardly think their
go-to theory is that Peter Pan is real and his descendants must
have purchased Christmas lights at a very reasonable price to
illuminate a few church steeples."

She massaged her temples. "What about HOOK?"

"You think outsiders will suspect HOOK did this?"

"Stop being a smartass." She tore the paper from his grasp
and rattled it in his face. "You've drawn their attention once
again."

She really needed to lighten up.

He laced his fingers behind his head and settled deeper under the covers. "If anything, I've moved dear Lawrence's focus toward Pennsylvania."

"That's not how I see it."

"Grandad has done much worse. Do you remember the time he and Curly went to the Tower and—"

"What happens in London is your grandad's concern," she snapped, clenching her free hand in a fist at her hip. "What happens in Kensington is mine. And I hear there's been *a lot* happening when I go out of town."

"Like what?" he asked with a lazy yawn.

"Fist fights, rebellious meetings, ghosts, Christmas lights…" Her eyes narrowed. "Kissing new recruits."

Good news traveled fast in Neverland.

"So *that's* what this is really about." Deacon threw the covers aside and dragged his shirt from the night before over his head. It still smelled like lilacs from Vivienne's perfume. "We have this exact argument every time you think I'm interested in someone." And none of those arguments had made a blind bit of difference.

"Only because you never seem to learn your lesson." His mother poked him in the back. "It's like you hear, 'Relationships between PAN are discouraged,' and think, 'Nah. Doesn't suit me. I'm not going to bother with that one.'"

His eyes met hers in his mirror's reflection. "Hmmm… Perhaps you really can hear my thoughts." He collected the rubbish from his dresser, tossed it into the bin, and went downstairs to survey the damage. It was freezing. Someone must've left the window open.

The stench of cigarettes clung to the cold air. The sofa and chairs that had been relocated to make way for the dance floor were covered with damp stains, upturned plastic cups, and discarded jackets and jumpers—none of which belonged to him.

His mother was on his heels the entire time. "All I'm going to say on the subject is that you need to be careful."

He offered her a look of pure innocence. "That's *all* you're going to say?"

His mother's pinched expression lasted for all of ten seconds. "You know Vivienne is linked to HOOK somehow. And for your own safety, I think you should leave her be until we figure out what the link is."

"I'm perfectly capable of taking care of myself, Mother." The empty trays Nicola had used to collect champagne flutes after the midnight toast were scattered on the island.

"That remains to be seen." His mother stepped over a pile of discarded metallic hats on her way to the kitchen. "But that's not why I came over."

"Is it not?" He navigated the disarray, found two bottles of water in the nearly-empty fridge, and offered the second one to her.

"Ever since that fight a few months ago, your antics have caught the attention of Leadership." She plucked the bottle from his hand with a sigh. "And if you don't stop this reckless behavior, there will be consequences."

That probably should have worried him, but Leadership's penchant for inaction was legendary.

After a century, HOOK continued to terrorize the PAN, the Mermaids were demanding seats in the Leadership Chamber, and memory loss was becoming more widespread. He was the least of their worries.

"I appreciate your concern, Mother," he said, lifting to sit on the edge of the sticky counter and closing the window over the sink. "But I'll be all right."

"I'd prefer if you'd say you'll be good," she muttered, tugging the string of one of the few balloons still milling around the ceiling.

"All right, all right." He slid off the counter, accidentally crushing a plastic tiara. "I'll be good."

"Thank you." She went around the room collecting the balloons. "Whose idea was it for all of these?"

Deacon found a roll of rubbish bags beneath the sink and set out the tub of cleaning products. This was going to take ages. "How do you know it wasn't mine?"

"You're my son. I know you better than you think." She opened her arms to him, and he went to her without hesitation.

"I love you. You make me want to rip out my hair most of the time. But I love you."

With balloons banging against his head, he said, "I love you too."

"For once, will you *please* do what you're told before I'm forced to do something that would make both of us miserable?"

He picked up a wine key from the counter and popped the first balloon. "I'll certainly try."

Max was already in the Aviary when Vivienne and Emily arrived for their first class of the new year. Vivienne waved at him. He returned the gesture, then continued stretching his hamstrings.

"How was England?" she asked.

"Harrow's pretty awesome, but I was only there for a day."

"Where else did you go?" Emily drew her arm across her chest. Her cheeks were pink from the biting cold outside.

"There's a mansion in Scotland where they bring PAN with Alzheimer's. It's kinda like a fancy hospital but doesn't have that weird smell."

"Your dad isn't the only one?" Vivienne held onto her ankle with one hand and steadied herself on Emily's shoulder with the other. She swore she could hear her quad muscle sigh as it stretched.

"I counted ten other PAN. And there are nurses round the clock."

Vivienne switched legs. "What was it like meeting your dad?"

"Like meeting a new friend. We even played a bit of soccer when it wasn't raining. They closed for visitors when it got dark, which is crazy early, like three thirty in the afternoon. When I got there the second day, it was like someone had pressed reset on Dad's brain. He couldn't remember a thing from the day before. I had to reintroduce myself and everything."

Vivienne didn't know how she would cope if she had to lose someone she loved over and over every single day.

"Then the weirdest thing happened on my last day there. My dad actually said my name *before* I did." He took off his hat and threw it on top of his coat in the corner. "The nurses said it was impossible, but I know what I heard."

"Maybe since you saw him every day, something stuck," Emily said.

"That's what I'm thinking. I stayed as long as I could that last day. But as soon as it got dark, they tried to kick me out. I asked Peter if I could stay—"

"You met Peter?" Vivienne rushed. "What's he like?" She used to imagine him with red hair and pointy ears, but now she was convinced his hair was as dark as Deacon's. And he probably had green eyes too. The verdict was still out on the pointy ears though.

"He's cool. A bit odd, but cool." Max stretched his hands to the ceiling. "Anyway, he said I could stay after dark..." His face turned as white as the marble floor. "I should've left."

Both girls stepped closer and asked, "Why?"

"It was like night made them possessed." Max's voice trembled. "They were screaming and crying, and a few of them were doing this crazy, high-pitched laugh."

Emily grabbed Vivienne's arm. "Were you freaked out?"

Max's ears turned red. "Yeah, I was."

Vivienne asked if he was going to go back.

"Peter told me I could do my extraction training at Harrow. It'd be a lot closer to my dad...But it's a big decision."

The main door slammed against the doorstop, and Joel forced it closed. "Sorry I'm so late." He unwrapped his scarf from his neck. "Let's get on those stairs for a good warm-up."

After ten sets of stairs, Joel stayed at the bottom while the rest of them ran ten more.

"What's this for?" Vivienne asked when they finished. A giant silver pillow billowed on the floor below the balcony. She stepped over the extension cord attached to the airbag's humming pump.

Joel circled the trio in the air, like a buzzard. "That's going to help me teach you how to fall."

"To *fall*?" Max scratched the back of his neck with an unsteady hand.

"It's exactly what it sounds like," Joel said, landing next to Max. "Up until this point, when you've jumped off the roof, you've flown. And when you're ready, you come down for a nice, soft landing. But in the field, such ideal scenarios don't exist."

"We've been trained to run or fly away." Emily pressed her hands against her lower back and stretched. "Why would we ever need to fall?"

Joel pulled a quarter from his pocket and tossed it into the air. All four of them watched the coin hit the tiles with a sharp ping. "Falling can be a much quicker escape than flying. And it helps us keep secret the fact that we *can* fly."

Sometime between Thanksgiving and mid-January, the steps for flight had transitioned from a checklist to a reflex. Vivienne no longer had to isolate a memory or ingest a pill to bring about lightness or adrenaline. Now all she needed to levitate was a slight command to her body, and her adrenaline spiked every single time.

"I want you to fly to the first balcony and take turns falling as far as you can," he said, pointing toward the balcony. "It sounds simple enough, but it'll take more focus to go down than it does to go up. There's an airbag ready to catch those of you who make it that far."

Max, Emily, and Vivienne alighted to the first balcony with ease.

Emily called back to Joel, asking if there were any steps they needed to follow.

"Your body has been conditioned to fly, so you'll need to fight against your instincts. Keep your arms across your chest for the time being, clear your mind, and let gravity do its job."

Max volunteered to go first. Joel gave him a thumbs up from below. As instructed, Max crossed his arms over his chest and stood with his back to the drop.

"Have your memory at the ready for when you need it," Joel

said, using his hands as a megaphone. "Now open your mind to the thinness of the air around you, and fall."

Max leaned toward the airbag and dropped for a split second before freezing mid-air like he was taking a nap in the sky.

"Good first effort. Go to the back of the line and try again after the girls take their turns."

Emily stepped forward and mumbled, "I guess I'm next."

"You'll be great," Vivienne said with a reassuring squeeze of her shoulder.

Emily assumed the same position, and when she took the step, she fell five feet before stalling.

When it was Vivienne's turn, she curled her toes over the ledge and stared at the silver cloud below. She crossed her arms and gripped each shoulder with the opposite hand. Her eyes drifted closed, she turned her back to the drop, and her mind cleared as she fell.

Her stomach flipped, and every inch of her body panicked against the nothingness. She fought against rising hysteria and her body's desire to fly. Before she had the chance to stop herself, her weight crushed into the waiting airbag.

Struggling to sit up against the wall of flimsy material, Vivienne reached toward the hand Joel offered and mumbled an apology. She should have stopped herself.

"Why are you sorry?" he asked, shaking his head. "That was unbelievable."

"It was?" She frowned at the distance from where she now stood to where her friends waited.

Joel moved in front of her, blocking her view. "I've never seen a seasoned PAN control herself the way you just did, never mind a new recruit. They always stop. *Always.*"

"They do?" Vivienne's confidence returned. She straightened and smiled at him. "Huh."

Joel returned the look and kicked the corner of the airbag, sending a silver wave rippling through the material. "The closest anyone has come to falling to the ground happened well before my time. And the fact that you *can* fall means you should have no trouble stopping yourself before hitting bottom. Will you try it again?"

"Now?" Vivienne tied her tangled strands into a loose ponytail.

"Now." He turned to where Max and Emily awaited instruction. "Hey, you two. Do you mind letting Vivienne go again before you take your second turns?"

Vivienne flew to where Emily and Max waited.

Joel tapped the corner of his eye with his index finger and told her to keep her eyes open.

Vivienne opened her eyes as wide as they would go, crossed her arms, gripped her shoulders, and stepped backward. She expected the distance to slip past, but hadn't anticipated the way her internal fire ignited the instant she wanted it to, like flicking a switch on an automatic lighter.

"Holy shit," Joel whispered.

She grinned at the ornate ceiling far above her and willed herself upright. "How was that?" she asked, realizing she was only inches above the airbag.

The look on Joel's face made his words redundant. "It was perfect."

Max waved from the balcony. "Can we try now?"

"Yeah," Joel said, his eyes fixed on Vivienne's. "Try to do what Vivienne just did."

At the end of class on Friday, Joel asked if Vivienne wanted to try falling from a higher altitude.

Her eyes flashed to the Emergency Exit sign on the top floor. "Do you think I'm ready?"

"I know you are." Joel took off toward the roof in a sprint, and she raced to keep up. They burst through the door and into the January air. A chill made its way down Vivienne's neck and along her spine. Joel continued to the bronze railing marking the edge of the building.

Vivienne joined him and gripped the frozen metal. "It's quite a drop."

Despite flying from the Aviary every weekday since they had started Aviation, the idea of falling from the same height felt risky.

"The distance of the fall makes no difference." He climbed over the rail. "As a matter of fact, most of us prefer a higher drop to a smaller one. It gives us more room for creativity." Joel launched himself from the ledge and performed a competition-worthy swan dive into the air. He held perfect form as he fell, then flipped so that his feet were poised for landing. Right before he reached the ground, his body slowed and drifted to the gravel.

"I don't think I'll be able to do that yet," Vivienne shouted, ducking beneath the railing. "But I will soon," she whispered to the snowflakes landing on her pants.

"Just do what you've been doing all week," Joel bellowed from below.

Vivienne stood and crossed her arms. Her mind cleared, and she stepped into the welcoming breeze. With open eyes, she knew the exact moment she reached the ground-level windows. Her adrenaline spiked and her internal fire ignited. Upon land-ing, she turned to see two pairs of shocked eyes staring at her in disbelief.

"Holy shit." Deacon's eyes were wide and his hand was over his mouth. "I thought you didn't start falling until after the new year."

Joel gripped the lapels of his jacket and puffed out his chest. "We don't."

"Vivienne has only been falling for—?"

"Less than a week," she finished, zipping her coat to her chin.

Deacon smiled; her body reacted the same way it had the first day she had fallen onto the airbag: with a heady mix of excitement and unease.

"That's amazing, Vivienne." He pulled her in for a tight hug.

She breathed in his comforting scent and enjoyed the warmth of his arms in the frozen air. Then she pushed away.

He gave her an odd look and dropped his hands. "We need to celebrate."

"Celebrate what?"

Deacon put his hand on his head and laughed. "Vivienne, you shouldn't be able to fall more than a foot or two at this stage, let alone catch yourself inches from the ground while on your back."

"It wasn't very pretty," she said to the snow drifts surrounding them. "You should have seen Joel's swan dive from the roof."

Deacon needed to stop looking at her like that. Like he was proud of her. Like he cared.

"Joel was swan diving before you were born," Deacon said, waving away her comment. "This is an accomplishment worth celebrating."

"Maybe another day. I told Emily I'd go with her to the movies."

"I can't convince you to give her a rain check?" he pressed, kicking a loose snowball left over from the snowball fight that had broken out earlier that day.

The frown on Deacon's face left Vivienne wanting to cancel her plans. Then she reminded her heart that he hadn't bothered to come see her since they rang in the new year so memorably together. He'd texted twice. Once to say he had to go to Ireland. And once to say he'd gotten back.

That was it.

He had given her the best kiss of her life at that stupid party. But to him, it was obviously just another kiss.

"Not this time." She took a retreating step, said, "I'll see you guys later," and jogged back to her apartment.

Her cold muscles protested at first, but soon warmed to the movement. The exterior door swung in her direction, knocking her off balance and straight into Alex's arms.

"I've been looking for you," Alex said, propping her back on her feet.

She pulled her coat tighter against the winter wind. "I'm right here."

"And you look like you're frozen." He motioned toward the balmy foyer. "Come in out of the cold."

She stepped past him and used the vent near the stairwell to thaw her hands. "What's up?"

He followed her and held his hands over the vent like it was a fire. "I'm afraid I have to go back to London. But I wanted to come say goodbye before I left."

At least Alex cared enough to tell her goodbye in person. "When will you be back?"

"A few months. I'm going to be helping the lab with the treatment for the forgetful."

Another guy leaving her. Only instead of flying away, this one was walking—

"Would it be okay if I texted you? I'd like to stay in touch."

"Yeah. Okay. That'd be great."

"And don't forget," he said, nudging her with his hip, "you still owe me that date."

"I won't forget." She leaned closer to give him a kiss on the cheek.

A whirl of cold air swirled through the door, and Deacon stood at the entrance. Vivienne jerked away. She shouldn't feel guilty . . . but she did.

"Hey, Dash." Alex gave him an easy wave. "How was Limerick?"

"It was grand." Deacon stomped the snow from his shoes, then came as far as the end of the rug. "Vivienne, may I speak with you for a moment?" he clipped, his green eyes snapping with anger.

Alex shoved his hands inside his pockets. "Did you see Gwen?"

Gwen? Her stomach sank. "Who is Gwen?"

Alex kept his eyes on Deacon when he answered. "She's Dash's girlfriend."

Girlfriend.

Deacon had a girlfriend in London.

Vivienne was such an idiot. Of course he had a girlfriend.

"I don't *have* a girlfriend," Deacon ground out, his hands flexing at his sides.

Vivienne turned toward the stairs, ignoring Deacon when he called for her.

It was no surprise Deacon had failed to mention his girlfriend.

Deacon had failed to mention a lot of things.

TWENTY-FOUR

W hy had Deacon allowed his mother to guilt him into a trip to Ireland so soon after returning from London?

He had said no at first. Then she had reminded him that his father's birthday would've been on Sunday, and he couldn't let her go on her own.

The scent of the lemons and limes Joe was cutting helped mask the smell of cigars wafting from the older gentleman leaning on the bar beside him. Deacon nodded to the old man as he waited for Joel to come back from the bathroom.

Now Alex—and his irritatingly bearded face—had wheedled his way into Vivienne's life. Thinking of how chummy the two of them looked huddled together still made his stomach churn.

And then there was Alex and Vivienne's New Year's kiss.

Deacon's phone vibrated in his pocket; he opened Ethan's message. *Snow's bumming me out. Vegas this wknd with me n Nicola?*

If only. *Can't. Need to stay at Kensington.*

Ethan's response was instantaneous. *Why not?*

Because he needed to fix the damage Alex's snide comment had done to his relationsh—his whatever-it-was with Vivienne.

"I'm back," Joel said, reclaiming the stool next to Deacon. His damp hands left streaks on his jeans. "What were we talking about?"

"Vivienne."

"That's right." The ice cubes in Joel's gin clinked against his glass as he tilted it from side to side. "No one's ever been ready this early, Dash."

"If you don't agree with me, that's fine. It's your area of expertise. But I'm telling you, Vivienne's better at falling *and* flying than most three-year recruits in the field."

Joel set the glass on the bar and wiped at the condensation forming on the outside. A halo of blue neon light illuminated his frown. "What's the rush?"

Deacon rolled his shoulders and took a drink of scotch before setting it back on the cardboard coaster. Instead of telling Joel the real reason, he said, "I'm finishing up soon, and the last two classes produced only one recruiter. Emily and Max aren't interested in recruiting, and we could use someone else in the field."

"Why doesn't she enroll in the recruiter training in conjunction with Aviation? She's nearly finished her high school curriculum, and she'll have a lot of downtime on her hands soon enough."

"You know the rules, Joel. Recruiters have to pass your class before starting their field training." Deacon tapped his thumb against the bar. The PAN and their bloody rules.

"Good point."

"I'm asking you to consider it. If you think she's ready now, another four or five months won't make a heap of difference." Deacon abandoned his argument there, content with the seeds he had planted. "Would you like another drink?"

"Tomorrow's Saturday." Joel handed Deacon his now-empty glass. "Why not?"

Vivienne received a text from Joel asking her to come to class early and meet him on the roof. When she reached the door at the top, she pushed it open and walked to the railing to wait.

"Hey!"

Her eyes darted to the stranger standing in the corner near the door.

"What do you think you're doing up here?" the tall, slender man asked. The dark coat he wore reached his calves. His graying hair was out of place on campus.

"I came up for some fresh air," she lied, gripping the rail at her back.

She needed to get out of here . . . but it was too bright. He would see her fly.

He took two steps in her direction and stopped. "You need to come with me."

Yeah, that wasn't happening. "I'm staying right here."

"I think," he drawled, pushing the bottom of his coat aside to reveal a sidearm in a holster at his hip, "you should reconsider."

She tensed, poised for escape. When she didn't immediately take off, her body didn't seem to know what to do with the excess of adrenaline, and she started trembling.

"Tell you what, how about I *escort* you to where you're headed?" The stranger extended his hand in her direction.

"I'm gonna pass," she said, slowly ducking beneath the railing.

Fall. She needed to fall.

The door to the Aviary was fitted with an automatic lock, so unless she gave him the code, he was stuck on the roof.

The man drew his firearm at the same time Vivienne's heels collided with the lip of the ledge. He lifted the handgun and aimed at her chest, and the weapon discharged just as she fell from the roof.

Gravity wrapped its steely arms around her waist and dragged her toward the ground.

Fly. She needed to fly.

She had too much adrenaline, and her internal spark refused to light, and she was falling too fast; she watched helplessly as the treetops turned into trunks and she closed her eyes against the inevitable crash—

The impact was jolting but embracing and warm at the same time. Soft breath tickled her neck, accompanied by a swirl of expensive cologne. "What the hell, Vivienne?"

"Deacon?" What was he doing there?

His grip tightened. "What happened? Why didn't you stop yourself?"

Deacon was bringing her to the roof.

The man was going to kill him. Kill them both.

She writhed and bucked, but still Deacon didn't let go.

"Stop moving," he growled, struggling to keep hold of her, "or I'm going to drop you."

"There's a man up there with a gun. He shot at—"

"I know," he snapped.

She stiffened, and every fiber of her being wanted to revolt. He knew. Deacon knew. "What do you mean, *you know*?"

Sure enough, the older man was waiting for them. Instead of greeting them with gunfire, the stranger nodded.

Vivienne wriggled free and stumbled toward the door. "What's going on?"

"I made a mistake," he muttered, wiping his hands across his face. "You've been doing so well...I thought you were ready."

"Ready for someone to shoot at me?"

"Don't be daft." He pointed to her would-be assailant. "This was your final exam."

"*Exam*? You mean this was a test?"

A nod.

Joel burst through the door. "I'm so sorry," he rushed. "I told Dash no one could be ready this early, but he insisted."

"Deacon wanted you to get some creep to try and kill me?" Her nerves tingled with adrenaline and her fire returned. Only instead of happy memories, her need for flight was fueled by fury.

"Stop being dramatic." Deacon stomped to the man's holster and drew the weapon. Without taking his eyes from hers, he let off two rounds into the sky. "They're blanks."

She may not have been bleeding, but she felt mortally wounded. "How was I supposed to know that?"

"You weren't," Joel groaned, taking the gun off Deacon and returning it to its owner. "Before a student passes Aviation, he or she has to take off and land while under intense pressure. We send a personalized alert to the student's phone, then Mel here poses as a HOOK agent."

The older man nodded toward her and holstered his weapon for the second time.

"Now I'm afraid we've lost the element of surprise..." Joel muttered, pacing between them. "It'll be impossible to prove you can operate safely in such circumstances."

Vivienne stalked to the door and took out her anger and frustration on the keypad. As she reached for the latch, Deacon put his hand over hers.

"Don't you dare touch me." She shoved him away and ran inside.

"Vivienne, listen to me!" he shouted, clamoring down the stairs behind her.

"What, Deacon?" She whirled around, her hands clenched into fists. "What could you possibly have to say to me right now?"

"I'm sorry, all right." He braced himself against the handrail. "When I saw you falling, I panicked and—"

"I would've been fine," she seethed.

He took a hesitant step toward her. "You were three feet from the—"

"Look." She closed the gap and poked his chest. "I've done it before, and I could have done it again. So, if you'd like to leave me alone now and go back to your *girlfriend*, that'd be great."

"For the last time, I don't have a—" He pushed her hand aside. "Wait. You've done *what* before?"

"When HOOK showed up to my house, I had to escape out the window."

Deacon's eyes ignited. "The window in your room...on the third story of your house?"

"Yes."

"How did you—?"

"Invisible ladder," she shot back. "How do you think I did it? I *flew*. And at that point, I hadn't had flying lessons, and I still kept myself from splattering into a million pieces on the ground." She threw her hands in the air, scattering invisible shards of herself around the stairwell. "I don't need any more tests or exams. Next time, I *will* be fine." She turned and continued down the steps, noticing her footsteps were now the only noise in the building.

Joel shifted his stance in the empty hallway outside of Vivienne's apartment. "Do you mind if I come in?"

Vivienne waved him past and closed the door.

"Is Emily here?" he asked, darting a glance toward the bedrooms.

"No, she's at dinner."

He relaxed a fraction and allowed a small smile. "First off, I want to apologize to you. Normally, we prepare students a bit more for the exam. But for obvious reasons, we can't tell them about the dramatic nature of the test. The emergency simulation is necessary to prepare students for any dangerous situations they may encounter in the field."

"I understand." In the hours since failing her exam, she realized the merits of such a test. She also came to terms with the fact that she wasn't angry with Deacon, but rather at herself. She should have been able to rally despite the dire circumstances.

She should have been able to save herself.

"Dash told me what happened at your home back in Ohio. I wanted to personally let you know you've passed my class." He scratched behind his ear and laughed. "Anyone who can escape HOOK with only a whiff of a flying lesson from him is more than capable of excelling in any stressful situation."

She put her fingers over her lips to hide the surprise there. "Thanks so much."

"There's no reason to thank me. You have more natural

talent than just about every other PAN I've met. You earned it. All I ask is that you don't tell Emily or Max about the exam. The element of surprise is crucial."

"I won't."

Joel held out a golden box the size of his palm, decorated with a red velvet bow. Inside was a flesh-colored piece of plastic that looked kind of like a hearing aid. "What's this?"

"It's your helmet. Clip it around your right ear."

She turned the device over and back again before inserting it into her ear.

"Now, press the button on the back side. It's about halfway down."

When she depressed the indentation, it sounded like a balloon filling around her head. Once the noise stopped, a transparent green screen rolled across her field of vision.

Hello, Vivienne

A woman's voice echoed the words in her ear.

"She has facial recognition, so she knows who you are," Joel explained.

"She?"

"Her name's TINK."

"TINK...I like it." She chuckled. "What do I do now?"

A woman's voice answered, "Give me a command. For example, you can say, 'Locate Kensington.'"

Vivienne touched the earpiece and repeated, "Locate Kensington."

"You are currently at *Kensington Academy*. Is there anything else I can help you with?"

"No, thanks." Vivienne caught a glimpse of herself in the living room mirror. The screen and helmet weren't visible in her reflection. It looked like she was staring through the mirror instead of at it. "How do I turn it off?"

"Shutting down." TINK's green screen disintegrated, accompanied by the nearly imperceptible hissing sound of escaping air.

Vivienne pulled the piece from where it hooked around her

ear and flipped it over in her hands once again. "This thing's amazing."

"I know." Joel removed his own earpiece. "TINK can give you directions, make calls, monitor your vitals and altitude. She's also equipped with night vision for any midnight flights you may take. We recommend wearing her at all times. It can be a bit uncomfortable at night, so it's all right to leave it by your bed when you go to sleep. But you're able to shower with it on so don't worry about getting it wet. She's virtually inde-structible."

She thanked him again and gave him a hug.

"Don't hesitate to come to me if you have any questions about the art of flying," he said, pulling back. "I know Dash is pretty good at what he does, but he's not a flight instructor."

She did *not* want to talk about Deacon right now.

"I'm still planning on coming to classes if that's okay." She placed the empty box on the kitchen table. "I may have squeaked through the final, but I can imagine there's still a lot to learn."

TWENTY-FIVE

E arly the next day, when Vivienne saw Deacon's contrite expression outside the glass door, she seriously considered slamming it in his stupid handsome face. "What would your girlfriend say if she knew you were here?"

"For the last time," he groaned, raking a hand through his hair, "I don't have a bloody girlfriend."

"Yeah, okay." Why else would Alex have mentioned Gwen if there wasn't at least a bit of truth to the accusation?

Deacon swore and kicked the door frame. "I've had an on-off...*thing*...with a girl in London," he ground out. "But she's *not* my girlfriend."

"Does *she* know that?"

"Of course she does." He looked genuinely hurt. "What kind of person do you think I am?"

"Fine." As he flew past her into the apartment, she caught him by the sleeve. "But if you're lying to me..."

He put his hand over hers. "I'm not lying."

"Is that the only reason you came to see me? To say you didn't have a girlfriend?"

"No. I also wanted to give you this." He handed her an envelope bearing Neverland's golden crest that had been tucked into the back pocket of his jeans.

She broke the wax seal to reveal a single page within.

"It's your official letter of acceptance into the recruitment program," Deacon said as she read.

She'd thought she had to be in Neverland for at least a year before she started training. "This says I start class on Tuesday..." Her eyes flashed to Emily's kitten calendar on the wall. "That's tomorrow!"

A smirk. "It's all in who you know."

"Peter Pan's grandson must pull some serious weight in Neverland," she teased.

"There are a few perks."

She could only imagine. "I need to thank you for saving me," she said, tapping the letter against her thigh. Although she was still fairly certain her faulty internal fire would have kicked in before it was too late.

He pulled the letter from her hand and set it on the couch. "I've grown too fond of you to see you splattered on the pavement." He brushed her hair back from her neck and trailed his finger along her collarbone.

He was so close, she could feel the heat from his body warming hers. All she had to do was lean slightly and press her lips against his. She swayed toward him and—

No. She couldn't do this. Nothing had changed, not really. Just because Deacon didn't have a girlfriend didn't mean she should go back down that rabbit hole.

"This is a bad idea," she whispered, her breath mingling with his.

"The worst."

"I can't..." She stumbled back, catching herself on the arm of the couch. "I can't do this."

"Are you...You're serious?" His brows came together and he shook his head.

"I think it's better if we were just friends." Her heart couldn't handle the disappointment.

Deacon nodded once before turning toward the door. But then he stopped and looked like he was going to say something. Vivienne waited, half hoping he'd protest.

Instead, he jumped into the air and flew away.

Recruiter training took place on the third floor of the Hall. Vivienne had never been as excited to run up a set of stairs as she was that afternoon.

Ethan met her at the classroom doorway with a high-five. "I hear you're moving up the ranks."

She slapped her hand against his. "I thought you scouted."

"I switch between the two when we're running short of recruiters." Ethan bent to whisper in her ear, "Be careful with your new nanny." He tapped his own ear. "Leadership uses these little gadgets to keep tabs on us."

Really? "Why would they want to do that?"

"They claim it's so Extraction knows where to find us if things off-campus go pear-shaped...but I don't buy it."

She dislodged TINK from her ear to examine it more closely. "You're kidding."

"It's not something they like to advertise. Take it from me: start complaining about squealing or tell them it hurts your ear. Then, if it happens to shut down"—he made quotation marks with his fingers—"*unexpectedly*, they won't be as suspicious. I never wear the stupid thing unless I have to."

"Are you talking about me again?" Deacon said from behind, draping his arms around their shoulders.

Her adrenaline surged and the fireflies swirled. Friends. They were just friends. Her body needed to chill out.

"Not everything is about you." Ethan shook him loose and stepped aside.

Vivienne reinserted TINK. "Yeah, Deacon. Sometimes we talk about important things."

Inside the classroom were ten desks, a large white screen, and a projector attached to a bar hanging from the ceiling. Vivienne sat toward the front of the room; Deacon and Ethan took chairs on either side of her as four other PAN arrived.

A young man strolled in, exuding the confidence of a tenured professor; Vivienne recognized him from campus but had yet to make his acquaintance. "Good morning, folks. I hope you had a good weekend. Before we begin, I'd like to take a minute to welcome our new recruiter, Vivienne."

Everyone clapped and cheered; the noise echoed in the tight space. Vivienne's face flushed from the attention, and she wished she could disappear until it was over.

"Vivienne, I'm Albert, and I've been the Recruiting instructor here at Kensington for over fifty years." Albert clapped his hands, drawing the students' attention back to the front. "Right, this is going to be a bit repetitive for most of you but bear with me. Recruiting is a simple concept, Vivienne. As you already know, recruiters are responsible for bringing new members into the family once the mark has changed. As a rule, we disclose general, non-specific information to persuade our marks to join us in Neverland. Can anyone tell Vivienne some of the information at our disposal?"

Ethan was the first to speak up. "We share our books to get the conversation started."

"Then we give generic explanations," Ricky said from behind. "The fairy tale is real, we can fly—that sort of thing."

"That's right," Albert said, holding his hands in the air like a crossing guard stopping traffic. "But only in extreme circumstances do we actually fly." His gaze was fixed on Deacon, lounging in the chair to Vivienne's left. Deacon's innocent demeanor didn't waiver.

Vivienne raised her hand, and Albert nodded in her direction. "What if the mark still doesn't believe you after all that?"

"There's little more we can safely do, I'm afraid. The rules are strict and explicit when it comes to coercion. If you progress through the three tiers—books, generic answers, and emergency flight—with a mark, and he or she still does not agree to accompany you, that's it. *Right*, Deacon?"

Deacon gave the instructor a sheepish smile. "That's right, Albert."

Ethan sniggered, earning a glare from both Albert and Deacon.

"Vivienne and Cole, since neither of you have been in the field, I want you to commit to memory three key rules. The rest of you, consider this a friendly reminder." Albert lifted his index finger. "We never, under any circumstances, give the location of Neverland to a mark." He paused, scanned the audience, and lifted a second finger. "We never use our real names. It is essential that you operate under your issued aliases while in the field. Do you understand?"

Vivienne and Cole nodded in unison; the rest of the seasoned veterans mumbled their acknowledgment with varied levels of exasperation.

"Finally…" Instead of marking this point on a third finger, Albert put his hands on the back of his chair and leaned toward the students, a somber look on his face. "If HOOK shows up, you run. Do not engage, do not stay around hoping they will be the first to leave. Abandon your mark and return to Kensington as soon as possible."

"You *abandon* the mark?" she choked.

Albert's face softened as he nodded. "I understand this may be distressing for you to hear in light of your experience." She felt every eye in the room turn to her once again. "But allow me to explain why this must be standard procedure. Our marks don't know any identifying details about us or the Neverlands. For that reason, if HOOK takes them, it is unlikely that they will be subjected to torturous interrogation. For HOOK, a mark is only good for one thing: DNA. And once they have that DNA on file, HOOK should let them go."

Vivienne steadied her trembling hands against her desk. "But they'll neutralize them."

"Most likely. But you must remember, a PAN in his or her infancy will always survive neutralization. But a recruiter, especially one nearing retirement, may not."

Despite her horror, Vivienne realized Deacon had broken every single rule when he had come for her in September.

And she said a silent prayer of thanks for each misstep.

Her eyes flew to Deacon's. "Thank you," she mouthed.

He winked at her and offered a silent, "You're welcome," in return.

"Last week you said we would cover the shot," Cole said, shifting in his plastic chair.

Thankful for the abrupt change in subject, Vivienne tamped

down her rising panic and focused on the most important part of completing a successful mission.

"That's right. Once the mark has his or her episode, you have seventy-two hours to inject them with this bit of magic." Albert picked up a small vial that, to an unsuspecting individual, would have looked like a ballpoint pen. Vivienne recognized it as the device Deacon had used on the roof of the hospital. "It ensures the Nevergene remains active," he explained. "An injection into the thigh is the easiest to take. But you could also inject the subject in the shoulder or somewhere on the arm."

Cole asked what it did.

Ethan made his hands into wings and "flew" them toward the ceiling. "It keeps the Nevergene active."

"I know that," Cole mumbled. "But how does it work?"

"Magic." Deacon waved an imaginary wand and bopped Vivienne on the head with it.

She rolled her eyes. "I assume Peter and the lost boys didn't have that when they turned."

"You're right." Albert spun the injector between his fingers. "We estimate that five percent of PAN have a Nevergene strong enough to sustain the change without assistance." Albert replaced the injector on his desk, using one finger to keep it from rolling onto the floor. "Without the injection, nature takes hold of your mark's fate."

Vivienne drew a handful of consecutive circles on the blank page in front of her. Quietly, she asked, "And if they don't activate, what happens to them?"

The recruiters looked between one another, daring someone else to answer her question.

"We find a different way to welcome them into the family." Albert rounded his desk to stand in front of her. "Kensington College accepts PAN who have not turned and provides graduates with exceptional employment opportunities both within and outside of Neverland, depending on individual situations. We look after our own, even if they're grounded."

A busy January spilled into a busier February. Vivienne found herself enjoying class more when Deacon was in town, which wasn't as often as she had hoped. The two of them hadn't been alone at all since he had come to her apartment to give her the letter.

On the last Thursday of the month, Albert approached her and Cole on their way out of the classroom. "I think the two of you are ready for a round of tag tomorrow."

"Yes!" Cole punched the air, then dropped his hand and bowed his head toward Albert. "I mean, thank you, Albert."

"Tag?" Vivienne repeated, gripping the straps on her backpack to adjust its weight. "Like the playground game?"

"Play is the work of childhood," Albert said with a nod. "What better way to test your skills than a friendly game of tag with your classmates? Tomorrow you'll receive a text with the location and your role in the game as either Recruiter or Agent." Albert pressed a button on his phone and the screen came to life. "Then you'll be given a mission and the name of your partner. The objective is to complete the mission and arrive at the checkpoint without being caught by any of the faux agents."

"That sounds simple," she said.

"Your job as a recruiter *is* simple. You cannot fly in front of a bunch of outsiders, so practicing the skills you learned in your other classes is essential."

"I can't wait." Cole checked his own phone.

"Me either," she said with a grin.

When the text came the next morning at ten o'clock, Vivienne's enthusiasm for the evening's activities quadrupled. Deacon was going to be her partner. They would be playing recruiters at the Walmart on Tobias Boland Way in Worcester at 4:30 p.m.

Shortly after two, someone knocked on the glass door.

"Hey, partner," Deacon greeted, sweeping past her without an invitation.

At least, she thought it was Deacon.

"What in the world are you wearing?" she asked as he walked to the kitchen and sat down at the table.

He was unrecognizable in a pair of slouchy sweatpants and

a heavy, fur-lined coat accompanied by a Red Sox baseball cap over a blond wig. The whole look distracted from his handsome features.

"This is my disguise," he said, removing his hat and wig and tossing them on the seat beside him.

She picked up the hat so she could sit down and traced the white S on the front. "Why do you need a disguise for a friendly game of tag?"

"There's nothing friendly about tag." He frowned at her ponytail and pinched the loose material of her Kensington sweatshirt in disapproval. "You aren't wearing this, are you?"

She swatted his hand away. "I thought I would. But now I feel like I should change."

"Yes. Go change."

She left him in the kitchen to search her wardrobe for an appropriate disguise. "What should I be looking for?"

Deacon barged through her bedroom door, and she fell into the closet in fright.

He was in her bedroom. Deacon Ashford was in her bedroom.

It didn't matter. They were just friends. Friends went into each other's bedrooms all the time.

"This isn't quite the disguise I had in mind," he laughed, lifting a sweater off her head. "Need some help?"

She pushed the rest of the clothes onto the floor and grabbed hold of his fingers. His tall frame made the room feel too small for the both of them.

Aaand he was on her bed. Sitting on her bed. Smiling at her.

"Let's see what you have."

She forced her eyes away from him and grabbed the first thing she saw. "How about this?"

"How is that sweatshirt any different from the one you're wearing?"

She swayed the hanger in front of him. "This one's blue."

He rolled his eyes. "I know it's a different color, but it has the Kensington badge on it as well." From his perch, he was able to snatch the hanger from her and toss it onto the desk. "We need to find something normal that you wouldn't usually wear. Something that won't make you stand out from the other patrons in the glorious Walmart."

She picked up the shirt and replaced it in her closet. "Glorious? Walmart?"

"It's by far my favorite place to play tag." He came to her side and scanned the handful of other options left on the rail. "I have a secret weapon."

When she asked what it was, he pulled a CD from his coat pocket, along with a crumpled receipt, and handed both to her. "Our mission usually consists of having to buy some random object. Most of the time, the agents hang out near the checkout counters. I go in early, buy something, then go straight to the customer service desk to make an exchange."

"Avoiding checkout altogether." She returned the CD and receipt. "You really take this seriously, don't you?"

"It's a game, but it also helps get you into the mindset of a recruiter, knowing your exits and maintaining a low profile. Now, let's find you a disguise." He lifted a neon pink bra by the strap and grinned. "I think we should start with this."

In the end, they settled on a pair of skinny jeans and a short pink sweater beneath one of Emily's down-filled coats that reached Vivienne's ankles. She had borrowed a pair of black snow boots from Emily's closet as well.

On their way out of the apartment, Deacon handed her a ball of knitted fabric. "Here. Put this on."

It was a black beanie. Before she realized what she was doing, she lifted the soft material to her nose and inhaled. It smelled so good. Would it be weird if she asked to keep it? Friends gave friends hats, right?

He tilted his head to the side, reminding her of a curious puppy.

"It smells like you." She bent her head to conceal the warmth rising along her throat and pulled his hat over her hair. "What do you think?"

"Depends." A grin. "Are you wearing the pink bra?"

She rolled her eyes at him and said, "Wouldn't you like to know?"

TWENTY-SIX

A message buzzed through to Deacon's phone as he and Vivienne staked out Walmart from the comfort and seclusion of his car. A moment later, her phone dinged.

"Be sure to turn your mobile on silent," he said, skimming the message from Albert.

Vivienne pressed the buttons on the side. "Done."

"It looks like we just need to buy this shampoo." He leaned over to see a matching photo on her screen.

"Sounds simple enough." She shoved her phone into her coat pocket.

"Yes, but we don't know who we're up against or when they'll arrive." He lifted his hand to tuck a lock of her hair beneath the knitted cap, but stopped. She'd made it clear she wasn't into him anymore. He needed to let it go. "Come on. We should go inside."

Deacon followed Vivienne into the store and straight to the colorful, fragrant aisle. "I've never understood why there are so many," he said, picking up a bottle of purple shampoo claiming to make blonds blonder. "It's just hair."

"Now that you're blond maybe you should buy it." She yanked a bit of his wig.

259

"Perhaps you're right."

"Come on." Vivienne pulled his sleeve. "What we're looking for is over here." She found the bottle with ease, and they weaved their way to the Customer Service desk at the back of the store to swap purchases.

"Keep an eye out for anyone you recognize," he said, pointing toward the cavernous shop. "And let me know if someone gets close."

Deacon handed the clerk the CD and the receipt along with the bottle of shampoo. The transaction took less than three minutes; the entire time, his blood thrummed in his ears and his adrenaline threatened to lift him straight to the ceiling.

He loved playing tag.

"Thank you for shopping at Walmart," the girl behind the register said with what seemed like a forced smile.

He thanked her, took the bag from the counter, and returned to Vivienne's side. "See anything suspicious?"

Vivienne shook her head. The knitted cap slid forward, nearly covering her eyes. She shoved it back. "All clear."

"Good. Let's get out of here." Before he realized what he was doing, his fingers were laced with hers and they were racing toward the nearest exit. When they rounded the corner by the children's bikes, Vivienne froze.

"What's wrong?" he whispered, crouching to untie then re-tie his shoe, scanning the area.

"I think Ethan's by the fishing poles."

He peeked around the tire of a pink princess bike and swore. A man of Ethan's height was wearing a lumpy green army jacket and a pair of tight navy sweatpants tucked into black combat boots. When the man turned his head, Deacon recognized his profile. "Yeah, that's him." He stepped back, and she followed him.

"How do we know if he's on our team or not?"

"We don't."

Her hand came to rest on his wrist. "What should we do?"

Main entrance? Too far.

Garden Center? No. They'd have to pass Ethan to reach it.

The only option was Tire and Lube.

When Ricky wandered into the toy aisle to their right, Deacon knew there was no way they would make it out together.

"Take this and run to the Tire and Lube." He shoved the bag into her arms. "You should be able to get out of the store there."

"What about you?" The worry in her eyes made him want to take her into his arms and kiss her until they forgot the game altogether.

"The more of us HOOK can capture to soak for information and DNA," he said, pulling the brim of his hat lower, "the closer those bastards get to unlocking the key to the Nevergene. We have an experienced extraction team whose sole responsibility is to get us out of sticky situations."

"But this isn't real. It's a game." She pointed to the puzzles across the aisle. "There's no extraction team coming to save us from tag."

He put his hands on her slim shoulders and squeezed. "I refuse to see you lose your first game. When you get out, go to the rendezvous point and give Albert the mark."

"But—"

"Go!"

Once she rounded the corner, he pulled his collar around his neck, tucked his hands into the deep pockets, and walked between the spare tires and life preservers toward the fish tanks.

"Tag!" Ethan jumped from where he had mistakenly believed he had been concealed between a canoe and kayak and slapped Deacon's back.

"Dammit, Ethan, take it easy!" He was unbearable when he won anything. Deacon would be hearing about this for the next year.

"Sorry, Dash." Ethan wrapped his arms around Deacon's chest and lifted him off the ground. "I always knew I'd be the one to end your perfect run."

Deacon pushed free, knocking Ethan into a rack of novelty T-shirts. "I let you catch me."

"Ah, ah." Ethan waved a finger in his face. "No one likes a sore loser."

"I'm not a sore loser."

"Where's Vivienne?" Ethan called to Ricky when the recruiter approached from the opposite direction.

"Didn't find her," Ricky said, putting his empty hands in the air.

Deacon checked his watch. "I imagine she's taking the mark to Albert right about now."

Ethan growled but rebounded quickly. "Ah, well. I guess I'll have to make do with knocking you from your pedestal. Has anyone ever told you that you make a pretty blond?"

"Has anyone told you how obnoxious you are?" Deacon murmured. The two faux agents escorted him to the main entrance near the pharmacy.

"Not today, my friend," Ethan laughed, squeezing Deacon's neck in excitement. "Not today."

Two weeks later, when Vivienne and Deacon partnered for an impromptu round of tag at the mall, she was ready.

The mild weather meant they couldn't hide beneath large coats and winter hats.

"I could get into the redhead thing," Deacon said, pulling a black leather jacket from his back seat.

"I kinda like it myself." Vivienne fluffed the ends of her expensive auburn wig and checked her hairline in the rearview mirror. "Our last game of tag inspired me to get more creative."

"Speaking of creative..." He reached into the pocket of his ripped jeans and turned toward the window. When he twisted back around, he said, "Do you think I can pull this off?"

"Oh...my...oh...no..." Vivienne laughed until her stomach ached. "I can't take you seriously with a mustache."

"Your laugh would give us away for sure." He peeled off the fake facial hair and left it in his cup holder.

"And I'd hate to ruin my perfect record." She tied a light

blue scarf around her neck and climbed out of the car. Before they reached the mall, she asked him the plan.

"Apparently, the perfume we want is only sold in this department store." He pointed to the entrance. "We also need to get that blue tie with silver stripes."

When she suggested they split up, Deacon didn't look happy, but agreed.

"You get the perfume," he said, turning toward the escalator, "and I'll get the tie. I'll meet you back here in ten."

When she made it to the beauty counter, there was only one woman on duty, and she was busy helping an elderly lady choose between three boxed gift sets. The perfume they needed was stored behind the locked glass cabinet.

Instead of waiting, she went to the neighboring jewelry counter to ask the clerk there for help. "Excuse me. I need to buy a bottle of perfume, and I'm kinda in a hurry. Is there any way you could get it for me?"

"I'm so sorry," the girl, who didn't look much older than Vivienne, said. "We're not supposed to leave our assigned areas."

"Thanks anyway." Vivienne checked her watch. Seven minutes. She went back to where the elderly lady had narrowed her choices from three to two.

"I just don't know which one she'd like more." Her wrinkled hands shook as she pulled the boxes on the counter closer.

"Why don't you go with the newer one?" The worker pointed to the red box with shimmering gold lettering.

"Which one is more expensive?"

The woman checked the tags on the end of the boxes. "They're both the same price."

The elderly lady set her black purse on the counter and pulled out her wallet. "How much did you say they are?" She withdrew two twenty-dollar bills.

The worker flashed an apologetic smile toward Vivienne. "They're seventy-five dollars each."

"Oh…"

"Why don't you buy both of them?" Vivienne suggested,

stepping closer to the counter. "Then you can decide when you get home?"

The elderly lady squinted over her bifocals at her. "I don't think I have enough."

"But they're on sale. Buy one get one free...right?" Vivienne winked at the woman behind the counter and took out her own wallet.

"That's...that's right." The worker's eyes were wide with surprise.

"Is this enough or do you need more?" Purple and blue veins protruded from beneath the thin skin covering the older woman's hand as she slid the twenties across the glass counter.

"It's just enough." While the older lady was distracted by the clerk bagging her purchase, Vivienne slipped the rest of the money next to the register.

She checked her watch again. Three minutes.

"Thank you, sweetie." The older lady hooked her bags over her forearms and hobbled toward the exit.

If Vivienne hadn't been in such a rush, she would have offered to help the woman carry her bags.

"You really didn't have to do that," the clerk said.

"It's not a big deal." Vivienne pointed to the perfume cabinet. "Can I have the 100 ml bottle of that?"

"It comes in a gift set too." The clerk turned and retrieved one of the white boxes behind her.

"I don't need the set. Just the perfume."

"Are you sure? The set's actually cheaper, and you get—"

"I'm sorry. I don't mean to be rude, but I'm in a big hurry." Vivienne handed the clerk her money and raced toward the escalator.

"Excuse me!" the clerk called from behind.

Vivienne groaned when she saw Deacon step onto the escalator. Back at the perfume counter, the clerk was holding the box over her head. Vivienne hurried back to collect it, muttered, "Thank you," then made it to Deacon before he stepped off the escalator.

"Sorry for the delay," he said, handing her a small paper bag. "There was a queue in the menswear department."

"I know what you mean."

"Why are you out of breath? Did you see someone?"

"Not yet." She tucked the shimmery perfume box into the bag and followed him to the mall doors.

Cole guarded the exit, scanning passersby.

"Let's go back." Deacon settled his hand on her lower back.

"Isn't that Nicola?" Vivienne pointed across the crowded food court toward their friend. Sure enough, Nicola waved at them from between patrons carrying bags and trays of food. Vivienne lifted her hand to return the gesture.

"Get back here," Deacon snapped, grabbing the back of her sweater and pulling her into a store. They barely escaped a collision with a young mother pushing her infant in a stroller.

"Let go." She straightened her top. "Nicola's not a recruiter."

"That doesn't mean Ethan wouldn't stoop to using her as a scout. I'm telling you, it's not a coincidence she's here."

Vivienne peered around the shelf of handbags and saw Nicola approaching with her phone to her ear. "Fine." She turned back to Deacon. "What do you want to do now?"

"Find a place to hide and hope our patience is greater than theirs."

Cole continued to supervise the main doors, and Ethan appeared from the opposite direction to meet Nicola where she stood by the only other straightforward exit. Short of opening a fire door, their options for escaping without notice were slim.

"If you stay here, then I could—"

Stay here. Take this. Let me help you . . . He needed to stop.

Vivienne put her hand over his mouth. "You've gotta stop sacrificing yourself so I can win. If I'm ever going to be allowed in the field, I'll have to prove I can take care of myself. Let's make it out together this time, okay?"

Deacon pried her hand away. "Hiding it is."

Vivienne was able to walk among the racks of women's clothes without being seen. Deacon wasn't as lucky, and there were only so many times he could stoop and pretend to tie his shoe without drawing more attention to himself.

"Any ideas?" he asked, keeping watch through the tall display of maxi dresses.

Vivienne's eyes darted this way and that as she willed a solution into existence. Then, in the near corner, she saw their saving grace. "Come on." She grabbed his hand and tugged him forward while she collected a random selection of clothes.

"That's grand for you," he said when he saw their destination. "But what am I going to do?"

"Come with me."

His eyes widened. "It's the *women's* dressing room."

"Suit yourself. But if you're not coming, you need to get out of here so you don't give away my hiding place."

"I'd hate to be the one to bring you down," he said thoughtfully.

"Then don't bring me down." When they reached the entrance, the attendant smiled and asked if she could help.

"Can I try these on?"

"Of course," the attendant said, reaching for the hangers. "How many do you have?"

"Five."

The woman counted them twice before handing Vivienne a tag with the number five printed on it. "Here you go. The room on the end is empty."

Vivienne checked the labels on a pair of leggings. "Oh, crap. I didn't grab the right size in these." She lifted the hanger. "Would it be possible to try them in a small? I'd ask my boyfriend, but he'd take forever to find them."

The woman took the leggings. "I totally get it." Was she winking at Vivienne or at Deacon? "I'll be right back with a small."

"Thanks."

The moment the woman left, Vivienne pulled Deacon to the changing room at the end of the corridor. The hooks on the walls of the small stall were filled with haphazardly hung tops, jeans, and dresses.

She dropped a few random items on the floor, then hooked her hangers over the door.

"Climb on the bench so no one sees your feet," she whispered, kicking off her shoes.

Deacon's eyes widened, but he did as she said. "What are you doing?"

"No one's going to come in if they think I'm changing." She tugged a black skirt from behind him.

Someone knocked on the door, and they exchanged worried looks.

"Hello?" It was the attendant. "I have the small leggings for you." The leggings appeared over the top of the door.

Vivienne thanked her, pulled the leggings down, and threw them at Deacon.

"My name's Magda," the attendant said. "Let me know if you need anything else."

Through the tiny gap, Vivienne saw Nicola waiting at the entrance. "Close your eyes," she whispered to Deacon.

"Do I have to?"

She smacked him in the arm, and he closed his eyes with an exaggerated sigh.

Quickly, she traded her pants for the skirt, then walked back and forth in front of the mirror like she would if she was actually deciding whether or not to buy the skirt. It was way shorter than it had looked on the hanger.

Behind her, Deacon started laughing.

"What is it?" she snapped, checking the skirt was zipped correctly. It'd be just her luck to have her underwear hanging out.

Instead of answering, his laugh grew louder.

She put her hand over his mouth and glared at him. "What's so funny?" she mouthed.

He pressed a kiss to her palm, then moved her hand away. "Are you planning on giving me a fashion show while we're here? Because I want you to try that one on next." He indicated the forgotten hangers that she'd grabbed. A frilly black negligee dangled from one of them.

Her face flushed, and she wished the pile of clothing next to her would swallow her whole. "Obviously, I didn't realize what I was taking."

He ran his fingers along the lace hem and raised an arrogant brow. "Perhaps your subconscious chose for you."

"Why are you looking at me like that?"

Deacon thought it best to keep the racier scenarios running through his mind to himself. "You don't want to know."

"Tell me." Vivienne's fists ground into her hips, balled up tight and prepared to strike.

She asked for it . . . "First, I was thinking of how great your ass would look in that negligee. Then I was thinking of seeing that skirt bunched around your waist. And then I started thinking about what color knickers you had on, and then—"

"Okay. Fine. I get it. You can stop now."

"Really? I was just getting started." He loved the way she blushed. And the way her breathing hitched when he said things he probably shouldn't.

"We decided we should just be friends, remember?"

"No, *you* decided that *you* wanted to be friends," he said, reaching for the waistband on her skirt. "I, on the other hand, want to peel you out of those clothes and take advantage of you."

She didn't fight him when he tugged her closer or when he dropped his legs from the bench and settled her between his knees. She bit her lip and watched him undo the bottom button on her shirt. And the next one. And the one after that.

"Deacon..."

When he pressed a kiss to her navel, she sucked in a breath and chills broke out on her lilac-scented skin.

"You can stop me any time you want, *friend*."

Her response was to lose her fingers in his hair and drag his mouth to hers.

He forgot about the game—the whole world—when she climbed onto his lap, molding her warm body to his. His focus was on his hand sliding up the back of her shirt, tracing her spine to the clasp on her bra. And her hands dragging his shirt from the waistband of his jeans and finding the button and—

"I'll be just a sec," a girl in the next stall said. "Wait here for me so I can show you this."

Vivienne stiffened and started to push away.

"No." He didn't care if he was begging. "Give me five minutes. Please." It'd be quick, but he'd make up for it the next time.

"I'm not doing this with you in a dressing room," she hissed, pressing one hand to her forehead and one to her heart. Her breaths were coming in gasps, making her chest rise and fall and rise and fall—

He couldn't think straight with her standing half-naked in front of him, so he squeezed his eyes shut and tried to ignore the sounds of her getting dressed and focus instead on breathing and getting the blood back to his brain.

She was right. She deserved better than this. She deserved more.

"I'm done."

Vivienne was back in her jeans and top, looking perfectly composed except . . . "You may want to fix your hair."

"What?"

He pulled on the end of her displaced red wig. She took it off altogether and shoved it into their bag of purchases.

"Feet on the bench and stay quiet," she demanded. When he complied, Vivienne popped her head into the hallway and called for the attendant.

"Did you need something else?" It sounded like the girl was right outside.

"Do you have this in any other colors?" Vivienne reached toward the pile of clothes behind her. Deacon unhooked the silky black number and slipped it into her hand.

The attendant cleared her throat. "I think we have it in white."

He could see Vivienne's neck turning red. "Can you grab it for me?"

"No problem."

When they emerged from the dressing room, their reflections in the mirror at the end of the corridor looked as haphazard as the clothes in the heaps around them. The only way to keep his hands to himself was by tucking them into the pockets of his jeans. Vivienne kept her eyes forward, ignoring him all the way to the exit.

Screw this. He didn't want to be her friend.

Deacon wanted more.

TWENTY-SEVEN

D eacon had woken up in a fantastic mood. The sun was shining, and in a few days, he would be out of Kensington doing the job he loved with Vivienne as his partner.

Earlier in the week, Albert had asked him to stay behind after class. He had wanted Deacon's opinion on Vivienne's readiness for fieldwork. While Deacon wasn't sure she was prepared to go on an assignment alone, he had made a strong case for her being partnered with someone more experienced—someone like himself.

This mission was the perfect opportunity for him to convince her to give him a proper chance.

On the drive to campus to meet with the Procurement Supervisor that morning, he had found twenty quid in his pocket and only hit one red light. Nothing was going to bring him down.

"You look disappointed."

"No, no. It's just..." Deacon closed his alias dossier and tapped the corner of the file against Michael Theroux's black desk. "I was under the impression that I would have a partner for this assignment." The glossy tile on the fireplace behind the desk reflected the sunlight pouring through the wide, curtainless window.

Michael rubbed his beard and frowned at his laptop. "I'm afraid we're running a bit thin at the moment. Peter was supposed to send some people from London, but I'm not sure when they'll arrive."

"Albert said he was going to release one of the new recruits to help with the deficit."

"He did. Vivienne is going to Maryland."

He stopped tapping. "On her own?"

"No. Your mother paired her with"—he flipped through his master list—"Ethan."

Of course she did.

"Lovely," Deacon said under his breath. He caught himself staring at a brass Charlie Bell clock on the mantle next to a photo of Michael's wife, Liz. Something about its intricate gold face and black roman numerals tugged on his memory. "Did you get that from Peter?" He remembered one exactly like it from his grandad's study.

"Good eye." Michael hooked his finger beneath the alarm's handle and brought it to the desk. "It was a gift to celebrate twenty years in Neverland."

Deacon shifted in his chair, centering his view of the fountain in the window. He could salvage this. He had to. "We've known each other a long time."

The reminder couldn't hurt.

"We sure have."

"I have a favor to ask you," he began, creasing the edge of his file. "Is there any way you could switch the assignments?"

"I know you and Ethan like working together," Michael grumbled, frowning and flicking one of the bells, "but Vivienne isn't ready to go it alone. It's her first assignment."

"I don't want to trade with Vivienne," Deacon said, sliding the folder across the desk. "I'd like to swap with Ethan."

"No way." Michael pushed the folder back. "The last time you went on an assignment with a female recruiter, the two of you nearly missed the mark's Nevergene activating because you were busy"—Michael made quotations with his fingers —"birdwatching."

Seven years later, he still hadn't lived that down.

"Have you ever seen a bowl of roseate spoonbills? Because I have. And they're majestic."

"I feel like you're making all of that up."

"I'm not." Deacon pulled out his mobile and typed *roseate spoonbill* into the browser. When the photo of the pink bird came up, he handed it to Michael.

"Very majestic. But that doesn't change my answer."

"Come on. You know it won't happen again." This time he'd have enough sense not to get caught.

Michael rolled the folder into a baton and looked through it. "And your mother has made sure of it by putting you on a different assignment."

"Help me out. This could be my last mission, *and* you still owe me that favor from London."

Michael squeezed his eyes shut and tapped the baton on his forehead three times. "If I agree to try, you have to promise to never speak of London again."

"Agreed."

He tossed the documents into the dormant fireplace and removed a box of matches from his top drawer. "If you step out of line, your mom will have both our heads."

"Don't worry. I'm always a perfect gentleman."

"That's part of the problem," he muttered, striking a match and lighting the corner of the papers.

Deacon watched as the flames swallowed the pages, and smoke lifted up the chimney. "When will my new alias be ready?"

"All going well, I should have your new identity to you by this afternoon."

Deacon pushed away from the desk and clapped his friend on the shoulder. "I trust this conversation will stay between us."

"Say no more, Dash." Michael tapped the side of his nose. "Say no more."

"You've a busy day ahead of you." Deacon should have looked ordinary in the dark gray Kensington T-shirt and black tracksuit pants, but the way the material fit his toned physique made it look like the finest tailor had worked magic.

"I do?" Vivienne handed him a glass of water before drinking from her own. When he showed up unannounced, she had assumed he'd want to discuss what had happened in that dressing room. Apparently not.

He took a sip, then set the glass on the counter. "First, you have an appointment in Worcester for a makeover."

Makeover? "What's wrong with the way I look?"

"Absolutely nothing." He wrapped a piece of her hair around his finger. "But we don't do wigs and mustaches on missions."

Holy crap! She got to go on a mission? Yes!

Wait. She wasn't ready for this . . . was she?

No. Yes. Of course she was. She could totally do this.

Vivienne launched herself into his arms before she realized what she was doing. "Do I...um...have a partner?"

"I'll be accompanying you," he said tightly, setting her back on her feet, "if that's all right."

The two of them.

On a mission.

Alone.

She had decided days ago that she was an idiot for not exploring whatever was between them. Even if it broke her heart.

This was the perfect chance to let him know.

She rose to her toes and pressed her lips to his. "Does that answer your question?"

"Tell me again," he whispered against her mouth.

He clutched her waist as she kissed him with everything she had, telling herself it would be enough. She could make it enough. His mouth was hungry, his tongue insistent. And she wanted more from him than she had ever wanted from any other guy. More than Deacon would ever be willing to give her.

"What were we talking about?" he groaned when she pulled

away. His forehead fell against hers and his breathing was ragged.

At least their attraction wasn't one-sided.

"The mission," she said.

A chuckle. "Oh, yeah."

She slid her hands over his chest and wrapped her arms around his neck. "When's your makeover?"

"I don't need one." He brushed her hair back from her face and started trailing kisses down her jaw. "No one is looking for me outside of our world."

"That's not fair."

"Don't look so disappointed," he said, rubbing his thumb over her bottom lip. "After you're finished, we get our assignment details."

"Will you come with me for that part?"

"I'd love to." He kissed her knuckles, then let her go. "This isn't over," he said, gesturing between them. "You know that, right?"

Of course she knew. They were just getting started.

"Why do you look like someone peed in your cereal?"

Vivienne snorted. Emily was ridiculous. She tucked her wallet into her purse and grabbed her Kensington hat from the table in case she hated her new hairdo. "I start my first mission next week and—"

"You have a mission already?"

"Yeah. Today's my makeover." She checked her reflection in the living room mirror and pressed some stray hairs back into her ponytail. "But I don't really think I need one."

"Of course you don't need one," Emily said, rolling her eyes. "You're fabulous. But you *get* one because you're lucky! You can't go on a mission looking like yourself. You need to become someone else." She picked up a coffee cup and struck the famous pose from Hamlet.

"You're nuts. You know that, right?"

"You love me anyway." She dropped the cup in the sink. "In

fact, you love me so much, you want me to come with you."

As if Vivienne would say no to her best friend. "On one condition."

"Anything."

"You have to make sure I don't look stupid." If she was going to look different, she wanted to look good.

Emily groaned and rolled her eyes. "As if that's even possible."

Deacon was going to keep his eyes forward. On the blue sky. Or the gravel crunching beneath his shoes. Or the watch on his wrist. He was *not* going to check out the blonde coming toward him.

Vivienne. He was going to meet Vivienne.

And he was going to be on his best behavior, because she deserved—

"Deacon? Where are you going?"

He froze mid-stride. Turned around and—"*Vivienne?*"

She had certainly *sounded* like Vivienne. But where her hair should have been dark and falling in waves down her back, it dusted her collarbone and was platinum blonde. She was wearing glasses and red lipstick and a black one-piece thing he *really* liked. What would she say if he suggested they leave for their mission tonight?

"Yeah, it's me," she laughed.

The melodious sound gave her away, convincing him this trendy blonde was his Vivienne.

No. Not his.

At least not yet.

He cleared his throat and managed to say, "You look..." Wonderful. Amazing. Beautiful. Sexy. Like a total ride. None of those seemed to cover it.

"Weird, I know." She pulled on the edges of her hair as if that would force it to grow back.

He shook his head. "Different."

"Isn't that the point?"

"Yes, but they've outdone themselves this time."

"The hairdresser said he wanted me to look as different as possible to keep from being noticed."

"You mean recognized." Because there was no way she would go unnoticed looking like *that*.

"Exactly."

Deacon accompanied her for the short stroll to the Hall, but he couldn't stop staring. He'd nearly fallen into the fountain, he was so distracted. He said a silent prayer that Michael had come through for him. Because he was *not* letting Vivienne go anywhere with anyone else.

Vivienne followed him down the hallway, past the grandfather clock. When they reached Michael's office, he was waiting for them in the doorway. The tie he'd had on earlier had been abandoned on the glossy black sit-stand desk.

"Long time no see, Michael." Deacon clapped him on the back. He inclined his head toward Vivienne. "This is Vivienne."

"Nice to meet you," she said.

"Same to you." Michael took an exaggerated step aside and waved them into his office.

Deacon crossed the checkerboard tiles to one of the two black chairs in front of the desk, then waited for Vivienne to sit first. Once she was comfortable, both Deacon and Michael sat down.

"Vivienne, since this is your first mission, I'll revert to you when asking questions. At the end of our interview, let me know if you have any of your own. You'll have Deacon on assignment to help guide you, but here's a card with my numbers just in case."

Michael had come through for him. Deacon smiled so wide his face hurt.

Vivienne accepted the card and put it into her handbag. "Thanks."

Michael slid two thick envelopes across the tabletop. Vivienne picked hers up and opened the clasp at the back. Deacon collected his but didn't open it; instead, he scooted closer to catch a glimpse of the contents of her envelope.

At the top of the documents inside was a driver's license

bearing a photo of the newly blonde Vivienne, but with a different name.

"Alice Barnard," she said, smoothing her fingers across the reflective image.

"This is your alias packet," Michael explained. "Inside you'll find your new license, credit cards, and other necessary documentation for you to maintain your cover. Read what's enclosed and memorize all relevant information. When you're finished, destroy any papers containing your backstory."

She leafed through the documents, then straightened the pile against his desk. "Where's the info on my new high school?"

Michael leaned forward, his bearded chin on tented fingers. "You won't be attending school this time."

"Why not?"

"Albert thought it would be best if Deacon acted as the lead recruiter on this assignment. You'll be assisting as his scout."

She dropped the alias packet onto her lap. "You want me to just sit back and let Deacon know when our mark is going to change?"

"No. You'll also be covering the evenings by getting a job where the mark works."

"You will be helping," Deacon assured her, wanting so badly to reach for her hand but knowing Michael wouldn't be impressed if he did. "Evening and weekend coverage can get tricky, and the last thing you want is for the mark to think you're stalking them."

"Yeah," she laughed. "Then they definitely won't want to come." She lifted the packet, tucked it under her arm, and asked if there was anything else she needed to know.

"You should be all set. But before you go, I have one last question for you," Michael said. "Do you have any interest in bird watching?"

"Birdwatching? No." Her brows came together in confusion. "Why?"

Deacon cleared his throat.

Michael shrugged. "I'm just making sure you won't be too distracted to do your job in Maryland."

TWENTY-EIGHT

B irds chirped in the air and searched the ground for wormy sustenance on the short walk back to her apartment. Although there was still a nip to the April breeze, the sun felt warm on her black jumpsuit. PAN sunned themselves on the Hall's roof, two girls had their noses stuck in books on the fountain wall, and every picnic table outside The Glass House was full.

Monday couldn't come soon enough. Thinking of the way Deacon had kissed her in the apartment that morning still made her toes curl. And he kept giving her this strange look, like he couldn't wait to get her alone.

Maryland could be the turning point in their relation—whatever they had going on.

Her hand brushed against his by accident, leaving her with a tingling sensation that rivaled the feeling of takeoff.

"Who do you get to be on Monday?" she asked when they reached her apartment.

"Let's find out." Deacon unhooked the clasp on his alias packet. After glancing at the driver's license within, he handed it to her.

"Philip William Carroll." The picture had to be one of the best license photos she'd ever seen. "He looks like a bit of a womanizer." She handed back the license and unlocked her door.

"Oh, he's a renowned womanizer." Deacon slipped the license into his back pocket and stepped closer. "I heard he once tried to seduce a girl in a department store dressing room."

He wanted to bring this up *now*?

Vivienne shivered. "Sounds like Alice Barnard should steer clear of Philip Carroll."

He grabbed her hand and kissed her knuckles. "Or she could take a chance and have dinner with him tonight."

Dinner? Like . . . a *date*? No. Deacon didn't date. It was just dinner.

"Alice usually avoids womanizers...but the dressing room story has her intrigued."

"I'll collect you at seven?" His whispered words tickled her neck, and he pressed a kiss to the pulse at her throat.

"Seven's good." Vivienne backed into the apartment and closed the door. Was it seven o'clock yet?

"What. Just. *Happened*?"

She twirled around so fast she tripped over her new shoes. Emily and Max were sitting slack-jawed on the couch, staring at her. "How much of that did you hear?"

"All of it." Emily's wide eyes narrowed as her lips curled into a knowing smile.

Vivienne tossed her alias packet on the kitchen table. "All of it all of it, or just most of it?"

"Did he say something about a dressing room?"

Vivienne massaged her temples and said, "You can stop now," even though she knew Emily wouldn't listen to her.

"*Ahhh*!" Emily hopped onto the coffee table and threw her hands into the air. "I can't believe he finally grew a pair and asked you out on a date!"

"It's not a date," she protested, plopping onto the cushion beside Max. Her shaking hands were the only indication that she was mid-freak-out. "I'm sure he just wants to talk about the mission."

"Don't do that," Emily said, wagging her finger. "Don't downplay it."

"I'm not, but—"

"Where do you think you're going, Max?" Emily clipped when he stood up.

"I don't really think I need to be here for this."

She jumped off the table and pointed to the couch. "Sit. Stay."

He dropped back onto the cushion.

"You're a guy," she went on. "What's your Y-chromosome's opinion?"

"Um…" He wiped his hands on his jeans. "I doubt he'd be asking Vivienne out if he wasn't at least a little bit interested."

"Wow." Emily covered her face with her hands. "That was deep."

"I don't know him that well," he said with a shrug. He tugged on the cuffs of his sleeves and glanced back at the door. "But if I liked a girl, I'd want to be near her as much as possible."

"Thank you, love guru. You can go now."

He shot to his feet and ran out the door like he couldn't get out of the apartment fast enough.

Once the door closed, Emily sat next to Vivienne. "Deacon *loooves* you."

"Pump the brakes. We're just grabbing dinner." The thought of love never even crossed her mind. Deacon made her nervous and excited and confused. And, after flying, kissing him was her favorite thing to do. It was one thing to like him as much as she did, but a whole different level of stupidity to fall in love with him.

"If the two of you get married"—Emily bounced up and down on the cushion—"can I be your maid of honor? Oh! You would have the cutest kids."

"Brakes, Emily."

"I know exactly what you should wear." Emily grabbed her hand and dragged her down the hallway to the open suitcase on Vivienne's bed. "When Clinton showed us this, I thought it was fab." She held up a mustard-colored chiffon dress.

Vivienne snatched it from her. "Fine. Now get out so I can take a shower."

The hot water released the tension in her muscles, but not her nerves—and it made her mascara run like black tears down her cheeks. She scrubbed away the blackness, then covered her sore red face with foundation. But when the time came for eyeliner, she was like a toddler with a crayon.

"Emily! I need help with this!" A pile of damp, black cotton balls filled the sink next to the half-empty bottle of makeup remover. She looked like she belonged in an '80s rock band.

Emily danced to the rescue. "Gimme." She plucked the eyeliner from Vivienne's hand.

Vivienne closed her eyes and stood completely still while Emily drew along her lashes.

"There. All done."

"Can I pack you in my bag for Maryland?"

Emily's smile wavered when she snapped the lid back onto the eyeliner. "How long do you think you'll be gone?" She dabbed at the corner of her eyes with a bit of toilet paper.

As hesitant as Vivienne had been at first about the whole living situation, she realized now that she couldn't imagine being in Neverland without Emily.

"A month at the most—two weeks before our mark's birthday, and two weeks after. But she could change sooner."

Emily hugged her tight. "I'll miss you."

"If you make me cry, I'll have to redo my makeup—meaning *you'll* have to redo it."

"It's just..." Emily wiped her eyes again, then balled the toilet paper inside her fist. "Max is leaving for London in June, you'll be off saving the world one PAN at a time, and I'll be stuck here."

"Stuck in the mall, shopping with Neverland's credit card." Vivienne left the bathroom and searched the suitcase for a pair of shoes to match the dress. "You'll be *so* miserable," she drawled.

Emily smiled and handed her a pair of Mary Janes from beneath a turquoise cardigan. "You always know what to say to make me feel better."

Vivienne buckled the strap on her shoes and twirled. "Well?"

"There's something missing."

She picked up her skirt and let it flutter back into place. "I have on the right clothes." She pointed at her red lips. "And we did my makeup. What else is there?"

"Aren't you supposed to wear glasses?"

Right. Alice wore glasses. Vivienne smacked her forehead, hoping the jolt would get her brain working again. She dug her glasses out of her jacket pocket and settled them into place.

"I'm loving the whole sexy librarian thing you've got goin' on," Emily said, her voice bubbling with laughter. "Do you think Deacon will try to check out some books tonight?"

"Oh, Emily..."

At seven o'clock on the dot, there was a soft knock at the main door. Emily let out a squeal, then jumped from her strategic position on the couch and hurried to answer.

"Hello, Emily," Deacon said with a smile.

Emily said, "Hey," and hugged him. From the kitchen, Vivienne watched Deacon's eyes widen at whatever she whispered into his ear. "Vivienne! Deacon's here!"

"There's no need to shout. I'm right here."

The color of Deacon's shirt made his beautiful eyes sparkle, while the fitted dark denim jeans slid low on his hips. His hair was slightly mussed, and his cheeks were flushed. "All set?"

Fireflies were *everywhere*. Like they'd had a bunch of firefly babies and they'd just woken up from a nap.

"Yeah. Let's go." The quicker they got out of there, the less likely Emily was to say something embarrass—

"Have fun on your date!" Emily shouted.

Something embarrassing, like that.

"Sorry about Emily," she blurted, following Deacon down the stairs and out into the cool evening air. "I told her this wasn't a date but—"

"It is a date."

Wait. What? Did he just say . . . "But...you don't date."

"Perhaps I decided to make an exception," he murmured, leading Vivienne to his black car parked in the stone driveway outside the Hall.

An exception? What the heck did that mean? Like ... how

much of an exception was he talking about? Was this just a date or did he want more? Did he want the labels and the relationship and everything that went along with it?

The heavenly smell of leather surrounded her as she slid into the passenger seat.

"Emily is quite protective of you," he said, starting the car and shifting to drive.

Oh no. "What'd she say?"

A smile. "She told me that if I hurt you, she'd cut off my... um...certain parts I'd prefer remained attached."

"Ignore her. She says crazy stuff all the time." She chuckled to herself.

"Like?"

"Like, she keeps insisting we'd have cute kids and—"

"We would have very cute kids."

In order to have kids, the two of them would have to do something else first. Her eyes fell to Deacon's lap before darting back to the window. Why was it so hot in the car? She adjusted the temperature on her side and focused on the classic rock anthem playing in the background.

Kensington's gates jerked open, and the car turned toward the hazy, glowing aura crowning Worcester. The moon followed them down the road like an attentive chaperone.

"Isn't Worcester that way?" Theirs was the only car in the line not turning toward the city.

"We're not going to town," he said, rubbing his thumb along the steering wheel's leather stitching.

With the moon no longer in sight, she became aware of how alone she was with Deacon and had to turn on the AC. "Where are we going?"

"You'll see."

There was something familiar about the neighborhood she couldn't place until Deacon pulled into the driveway of a picturesque two-story house. She leaned forward to look out the windshield, finding the moon waiting for her above the roof.

"This is your place." It looked different without the snow.

"It is." He shifted into park and unhooked his seat belt. "Thankfully, it's a lot quieter than the last time you were here."

Alone. In his house. Together.

She followed him up the stone stairs, breathing through her surge of adrenaline as quietly as possible. The last thing she wanted to do was fly away, but her body didn't seem to know how to process the excess energy.

His keys jingled when he turned them in the lock. Inside, a lamp on a shelf beneath the picture window created a vignette around the otherwise dark living area. Light from a second lamp in the corner reflected off the marble countertop. She could also make out the silhouette of candlesticks between two place settings at the island.

A date *and* a candlelight dinner? Deacon was pulling out all the stops.

"Something smells yummy." She unbuckled her shoes and set them beside his at the door.

"Before you ask, no, I didn't cook any of it." He took her jacket and hung it on the coat rack. "If I had, you'd be eating toast for dinner."

"Toast is good too." She smoothed a non-existent wrinkle from her skirt.

Deacon held his hand out to her. "*Viens avec moi belle.*"

"I didn't know you spoke French." Even after studying the language for three years in high school, her skills were more observational than conversational. But if she ever went to France and saw three small cats, she'd know exactly what to say.

Looking up from their joined hands, he said, "There's a lot you don't know about me," and led her to the kitchen island. "That's why I asked you to dinner."

"Are you going to tell me your deepest, darkest secrets and then bury me in the backyard?" She peered out the back windows before sitting on one of the high bar stools. Remembering what had happened on the moonlit patio that winter made her shiver.

"You have the first part correct." He brought a jug of water and a bottle of white wine from the fridge, then returned for two bowls of salad. "But if I tell you my secrets, will you tell me yours?"

Like she had any secrets worth telling. "Okay. Here's a secret: I don't really like wine." She lifted the glass by the stem and inhaled even though she had no clue what she was smelling. Wine had always reminded her of dyeing Easter eggs in vinegar when she was little.

"It makes the table look fancier," he laughed, lighting the candles with a match. When he blew it out, the smoke undulated between them.

"That smoke smells better than the wine."

He turned the dark bottle and frowned at the label. "I'll have you know this was a very expensive bottle."

She had a taste; it wasn't terrible, but it wasn't good. "You wasted your money. Because I can't tell a difference between this"—she raised her glass—"and the stuff that comes from a box."

"Prepare yourself for my first deep, dark secret of the night." He clinked his glass against hers and leaned close to whisper, "Neither can I."

When he stepped away, he left behind a void.

"Is that eggplant parmesan?" she asked when he retrieved a silver tray from the oven.

"You ordered it before, so I thought it was a safe choice for dinner." He cut two slices and carried them on plates to the island.

"Looks great." She inhaled the steam rising from the plate. It smelled even better. "Where'd you get it?"

"Audrey, the head chef at The Glass House, did me a favor."

"That was nice of her." Vivienne stabbed a piece of lettuce. And she was sure *Audrey* didn't expect anything in return.

"I thought so." Deacon had a few bites of salad, then dabbed his lips with his napkin. "If I asked you some questions, would you answer them honestly? In turn, you can ask me anything you want."

Her lips left red lipstick stains when she took another drink. "And you'll answer honestly too?"

"Always."

She tapped her fork against her salad bowl while all the

questions she wanted to ask came rushing to mind. "Could be fun."

"I hope so." He looked at her over his water. "Relationships based on lies don't work."

Relationsh—Did he just say *relationship*? She pinched herself and swallowed more wine to get rid of the lump in her throat. "You think we're in a *relationship*?"

"Not yet." The corner of his mouth lifted into a half smile. "But we're certainly in something, and I'd like to figure out what it is." He sprinkled a bit of parmesan cheese on top of his dinner and handed her the small grater. "Are you ready for my first question?"

"I feel like this is some sort of final exam." She thought back to the last exam she'd been given in Neverland and set the grater beside the pepper grinder. "No one's going to try and shoot me, right?"

"Not tonight," he chuckled, straightening his spoon against the marble. "All right. First question: do you miss Ohio?"

Ohio? That was an interesting start to this conversation.

"No," she said, "but I miss Lyle." And now that she knew HOOK was tapping his phone, she couldn't even call him. She washed away her sadness with a gulp of wine. "Is this a back and forth thing? Is it my turn?"

He nodded.

"Why didn't you tell me you were related to Peter? You had plenty of chances."

"When people find out about my connection to Peter, most of them change the way they treat me."

She considered her last bite of salad on the end of her fork. "Did I change?"

"You're one of the few exceptions." Rubbing his forearm above his watch, he asked if she thought she'd ever leave Neverland.

"I'm going to Maryland on Monday. Does that count?" Her laugh came out shriller than expected.

His smile was small, but his eyes were serious. "I meant on a more permanent basis."

The flame closest to her flitted when she let out a frustrated breath. But she had promised to be honest . . . "At first, my plan was to learn to fly, then make a run for it."

He stiffened and shifted away from her. "I'm not doing this if you're leaving. I don't see the point in investing in something that's destined to end from the beginning."

"I'm not leaving, Deacon. I have too many reasons to stay."

"Like what?"

She needed another drink. "My friends, recruiting,"—her eyes met his, and her internal fire sparked—"*you.*"

Deacon scratched his cheek and turned back to his dinner. "It's your turn."

She grabbed her knife, sliced off a chunk of eggplant, and stabbed it with her fork. She had made a pretty big confession, and all he wanted to do was eat. "I want to know about Gwen."

The piece of eggplant parmesan on the end of his fork fell back onto his plate with a splat. "What would you like to know?"

"Did you see her at Christmas?" The candles flickered. She shivered as a chill settled over her shoulders.

After clearing his throat, he took a sip of wine. "Yes."

Had Deacon done more than see Gwen? Had they been together?

Deacon's eyes narrowed at her from over his glass. "Did you go out with Alex while I was in London?"

Crap. "Yes."

"Are the two of you—?"

"I'm pretty sure the next question is mine."

He offered her a tight-lipped nod.

"Did you sleep with her?" she asked, her voice barely a whisper.

He winced. "Can I lie and say I didn't?"

The confession wasn't surprising, but it left her feeling hollow. She reached for her wine glass but couldn't remember which was hers. One was empty, the other full. Both had lipstick stains, so she picked the full one.

"I know this is going to sound messed up," he groaned, raking his hand through his hair, "but I only hooked up with her because I thought it would help get you out of my head."

In what world did that make any sense? "That's really messed up, Deacon." And incredibly disappointing.

He rested his elbows on the counter and covered his face with his hands. "I know. I know it is. I told you I'm not good at this."

She had more wine and pushed what was left of her dinner around the plate. It had been silly to hope this was going to be a good conversation. "Are you in love with her?" she asked. If he was, she needed to know before she got any deeper. He'd wanted assurance that she was going to stick around. She needed assurance that he wasn't going to get back with his ex.

"With *Gwen*?" He dropped his hands and his brows flicked up in surprise. "No. I mean, at one point I thought I was. But definitely not."

"Have you—?"

"I believe it's my turn."

She bit her lip and nodded, relieved that he'd stopped her. She'd been about to ask if he'd been in love with anyone before Gwen. But the truth was, she didn't want to know.

"What do you expect from me?" he said carefully, waving a finger between them. "From this?"

Whatever was going on between them was an entirely new experience for her. She'd dated a few guys back in Ohio, but hadn't gotten into anything serious. "What *should* I expect?"

"Honestly?" he chuckled. "Probably not much. I'm shit at texting and keeping in touch, and I haven't led the most… virtuous existence. When I said I didn't date, it wasn't a lie. I literally had to google what to do on a date." He waved a hand at the candles and forgotten plates. For someone who didn't date, he'd done a pretty good job.

"But if we decide to do this," he went on, "I can promise that I will always tell you the truth. And that I won't go off with anyone else while we're together. And that I will try."

What more could she ask of him beyond honesty, fidelity, and effort? But . . . "Why me?"

"Because I can't get you out of my mind, and even thinking of you with someone else makes me want to commit murder, and you call me on my shit, and you don't seem to care about my family, and I'd really, *really* like to see you naked and—Was that enough or shall I continue?"

Watching his lips as he spoke was almost as distracting as feeling his hand drawing circles against her bare knee.

"I think those are some pretty solid reasons."

He rested both his hands on her knees. "What do you say?" He leaned forward until he was only a breath away. "Would you like to try…with me?"

Vivienne wasn't saying anything. Why wasn't she speaking? Surely she had *something* to say. He'd just bared his soul, told her exactly how horrible he was, and then asked her to ignore all of it and try to build a relationship with him.

Surely that deserved some sort of response.

"Deacon…" She sighed, and a wrinkle formed between her brows.

She was going to say no. Of course she was going to say no. Why had he slept with Gwen in December? He'd known it was wrong but had done it anyway. He was some kind of fool. A complete and utter—

"I would love to try with you."

His relieved breath came out in an audible gasp.

Yes. She'd said yes.

Hope built in his chest as he reached for her, and she didn't push him away. She'd really said yes.

Her eyes fluttered shut when he lost his fingers in her hair and crushed his lips to hers. God he loved kissing her. The way she clung to him. The way she moaned into his mouth when he nudged her knees apart with his thigh. The way she wrapped her legs around his waist. The way her body conformed to his in *all* the right places. The way her dress felt like no more than a whisper over her waist. Her hips. Her thighs.

The way her back arched, thrusting her chest forward, making it clear stopping was the last thing on her mind. He especially loved that.

The adrenaline coursing through his veins engulfed him in

unbearable flames, itching to be extinguished. Could she feel it? Did he make her feel the same way? He kissed Vivienne's jaw below her ear, knowing she'd sigh and drag on his hair. His lips moved lower while his hands worked their way back up to her waist. Her fingers fumbled with the buttons on his shirt.

His hands continued their upward climb until they reached her ribs and then her—

"Do you hear that?" she asked in a breathless whisper. Her heaving chest rose and fell when she unraveled herself from around him.

"Hear what?" he groaned, adjusting his jeans.

"The door."

The only sounds he could hear were his own heart beating in his ears and their heavy breathing. "I don't hear any—"

Dammit. Someone *was* knocking on the door.

"Who do you think it is?" She tugged her skirt back to her knees from where it had risen over her thighs.

He shook his head and pushed the fabric higher. "I don't give a—"

The devil's knocking turned to pounding.

"Deacon," she giggled, smacking his hand. "They're not going away."

"All right, all right." He fastened the buttons she'd opened and walked uncomfortably to the door. Whoever was there was about to hear him curse in every language he knew.

"Nice lipstick," Nicola drawled, rubbing her red, swollen eyes with her fingers. "Not sure it's your shade though."

What was she doing here? And why was she crying?

"I'm a little busy at the minute." He used the back of his hand to wipe Vivienne's lipstick from his mouth. "Can you come back later?" Or never. Never was good.

"I didn't realize you had *company.*"

He knocked his fist against his thigh. "If you'd rang first—"

"I called you four times," she hissed, pinching the bridge of her nose and muttering about needing help with Ethan. "He says he's going to another stupid meeting tonight and refuses to listen to me. And when I talked to him an hour ago, he sounded drunk. He's not answering his phone, and he's not at his house.

I checked Lee's but it doesn't look like anyone's there yet. I thought maybe he came to see you."

"Is that Nicola?" Vivienne called from the living room. She'd relocated to the sofa.

"You brought *Vivienne* here?" she snapped in a harsh whisper. "You're an asshole. You know that, right?" She shoved him out of her way and stepped into the house. "Hey, Vivienne."

There was no point in telling her it wasn't what she thought. Nicola wouldn't believe him.

"Hey!" Vivienne waved at her from the sofa, a wide smile on her face. She'd fixed her dress and hair. "Where's Ethan?"

"Your guess is as good as mine," Nicola said, crossing to sit next to her. "I thought he'd be here."

"Come on in," Deacon muttered to no one in particular before shutting the door. He picked up his mobile from the entry table and saw the missed calls. "I'll ring and see if I can get him." On his way up the stairs, he tried Ethan twice. When the calls went straight to voicemail, he made a third call to Kensington.

"Hey, Dash."

"Julie, I need you to do a trace on Ethan." He wiped what remained of Vivienne's lipstick from the corner of his mouth and fixed his disheveled reflection in his bedroom mirror.

Julie's voice dropped. "I told you after the last time that I couldn't help you anymore."

He quickly explained the situation, and Julie reluctantly agreed. She tracked Ethan's mobile, car, and helmet to his house. Ethan might have forgotten one or the other, but not all three. "Thank you, Julie. You're a lifesaver."

"Don't tell anyone I did this for you."

"I wouldn't dare." He checked his reflection once more before going back downstairs to find Vivienne and Nicola speaking in low tones on the sofa.

He shouldn't have left the two of them alone together. "Ethan's at his house," he said, happy to interrupt.

Nicola swore. "Seriously? I was just there."

"He was probably hiding." Ethan had done it before.

"Ugh! He's *so* immature." She kicked the coffee table. "If he goes tonight, I swear I'm gonna kill him."

"I'm so confused," Vivienne mumbled, massaging her temples.

Was she flushed? She looked flushed. If Nicola had upset her . . .

"Are you all right, Vivienne?" he asked, kneeling in front of her. "Do you feel unwell?" From the corner of his eye, he saw Nicola give him a strange look. She could shove off.

"I'm *great*. A *tiny* bit tipsy though," she giggled, reaching for his hand. "Can you tell me what's happening with Ethan?"

Tipsy? Was that why she'd said yes? Would she still feel the same way tomorrow? Perhaps it was a good thing Nicola had interrupted when she did. The last thing he wanted was for Vivienne to regret anything that happened between them.

"Ethan's drunk too," he said slowly, "and liable to do something stupid, like drive or fly." Or attend a rebellious meeting and possibly get kicked out of Neverland.

"Then we need to make sure he's okay."

"I'll go." Nicola dragged her keys from her jacket pocket. "You guys get back to your...*date*," she drawled, narrowing her eyes at him.

"Deacon lit candles," Vivienne whisper-shouted.

"Did he now?" Nicola's brows arched as she took in the scene in the kitchen.

He ignored her and went to grab three bottles of water from the fridge. His relationship with Vivienne was none of her business. "If Ethan's in one of his moods, he's not going to listen to a thing you say, Nicola." Hell, he didn't know if Ethan would listen to anyone at this stage. "I can at least make sure he's not going to get behind the wheel."

"Wait!" Vivienne whirled around and pointed to Deacon. "You can't drive cuz you've been drinking."

He rolled his eyes. "I had two sips at dinner."

She squinted toward the kitchen. "Then why's your glass so empty?"

"You drank it."

"I did? Huh."

After helping her into her coat, he handed her a bottle of water. "I'll drop you home and—"

"I want to come with you," she said, hugging his arm against her chest and resting her head against his shoulder.

Nicola really needed to keep her judgemental stares to herself.

"We'll let you know what's happening in a bit, Nicola," he said, steering his girlfriend—Wait. Was she his girlfriend? *Girlfriend*. Yeah. She was. He steered his girlfriend toward the door and cursed his mates for ruining their first date.

TWENTY-NINE

D eacon pulled into the driveway of a house at the end of a cul-de-sac minutes later. It was a single-story brick home with blue decorative shutters. A cheerful line of colorful blooms edged the sandstone walkway that curved toward a covered porch. A light next to the front door was on, but the rest of the home looked empty.

"Oh! I see him! He's on the swing." Vivienne pointed to the corner of the shadowed porch.

"You don't need to shout," Deacon chuckled. "I'm right here."

"Oops. Sorry." That wine had been *waaay* stronger than she'd expected.

"Vivienne? Is that you?" Ethan greeted her with a smile. A nearly-empty six-pack sat next to him; four of the beer bottles were missing, and a fifth was in his hand. "I'm lovin' the new look."

She reached up to touch her hair. It was *so* short. "Thanks."

"What're you doin' out this late on a school night?"

She put her hands on her hips the way her mother used to when she was in trouble. "Comin' to find you."

"I'm right here waiting, beautiful."

Deacon stepped in front of her, and Ethan's voice lost its jovial tone. "Why're *you* here, Dash?"

"Making sure you're not going to do anything stupid. If you want to go to the bar, I'll drive you there—and bring you back home."

"You know I'm not going to the bar. Now move over so I can talk to my hot friend Vivienne."

Deacon grumbled but stepped aside.

"Take it from me," Ethan slurred, saluting her with his bottle. "Never ever, *ever* drink and fly."

"Don't plan on it." She couldn't imagine flying the way she was feeling right now—and that was after only a couple glasses of wine.

"Nicola came running to you, didn't she?"

Deacon's shoulders stiffened. "She came by my house to see if you were there."

"Yeah, right," Ethan snorted. "Gotta tell ya, Dash, you have the right idea when it comes to women." He shoved a potted plant with his feet, setting the swing in motion. "I'm going to start telling them—"

"Now's not the time to get philosophical." Deacon's eyes flashed to Vivienne before returning to Ethan.

"You got that right." Ethan took another drink, then set the bottle into the dirt with the plant. "It's meeting night. Gotta get to Lee's."

"Is Lee's a bar?" She'd yet to go out in Worcester.

"Never told her about Lee, huh? Typical," Ethan snorted, pulling a bottle opener from his shirt pocket and opening the last beer. He offered it to Vivienne, and when she refused, he took a swig.

"Lee Somerfield," Deacon said, stepping on the bottle cap spinning next to his foot, "is the leader of the resistance against Leadership."

She looked between the two of them for answers, but Ethan was too busy drinking, and Deacon was too busy glaring at him. "Hello?" She waved her hand in front of Deacon's face. "Why would he start a resistance?"

"He didn't," Ethan said from the swing. "Your dad did."

"My dad did what?"

Deacon settled his hands on her upper arms. "Your father disagreed with some of Leadership's decisions and found a group of like-minded PAN who shared his beliefs. When he left Neverland, Lee took over."

"Lee thinks we should stop pretending we don't exist," Ethan said, pushing the swing a fraction higher.

"Sounds a lot easier than trying to stay secret." And if it was her father's idea first, it had to be a good one.

Ethan scooted over and patted the space beside him. "Come with me to the meeting?"

"No," Deacon blurted.

"I was asking *her*." Ethan stomped his foot, halting the swing.

"You're not my boss, Deacon." The reminder couldn't hurt. The springs whined a greeting when she sat next to Ethan on the swing.

"So, you're going with him?" He pointed an accusing finger at Ethan.

"Yup."

"Fine." He threw his hands in the air. "I guess that means I'm going too."

"Great! Dash, you drive." Ethan left his beer beside the swing and extended his hand to Vivienne.

"You don't have to babysit me," she told him on the way to the car.

"I'm not babysitting *you*," he grumbled, yanking her door open, then slamming it shut before going to the driver's side.

Ethan pounded on the car's roof. "My door's locked, dude."

"No, it's not," Deacon called back from his seat.

"Yes, it is."

Deacon shoved out of the car and opened the back door for Ethan. "No," he growled, "it's not."

Ethan slid into the car and swore. "My seatbelt isn't working."

Deacon groaned and put his head against the steering wheel, setting off the horn.

There was a click, and Ethan said, "Don't worry. I got it."

They drove with nothing more than the hum of radio static to break the silence. When they arrived at an unassuming house with white siding, Deacon parked along the street behind a black mustang and turned off the engine.

"Get out." Deacon pushed Ethan's knee. "We're here."

When Vivienne poked Ethan's leg, he slumped against the door and started snoring. "I think he's asleep."

"Brilliant." Deacon turned the engine back on.

"Wait." She took off her seatbelt and reached for the door. "I still wanna hear this guy talk."

"I can't go inside."

"Then stay in the car and babysit him." She pointed to the back seat.

"You're not going on your own."

Deacon thought he was going to tell her what to do? That wasn't happening. "I'll listen for five minutes and come right back."

"I'd prefer if you—"

"There's Max!" She had the door open and was out of the seat before he had time to stop her. "Hey, Max! Wait up." The path wound around the back of the house.

"Hey!" Max stopped next to the basement stairs. "You look nice."

"Thanks."

"Is this your first meeting?"

"Yeah. You?"

"It's my third. Lee has a ton of great ideas." Max nodded to a guy in a backwards baseball cap with a sleeve of tattoos when he passed. "He thinks we should chuck the rule book out the window and get rid of HOOK ourselves."

Vivienne followed him down the stairs. "Outsiders would find out about us."

"So what?"

He had a point. If HOOK wasn't a threat anymore, would it be so bad for outsiders to learn about the PAN?

She had to push her way past a bunch of guys to get into the crowded unfinished basement. When she and Max stopped moving, she found herself standing on top of the floor drain. A bare bulb light with a pull string swung over her head.

"Let's get started," a strong voice commanded from amidst the buzzing crowd. "First, I'd like to thank you all for coming."

She shifted in search of a better view, but she was too short to see. Through the gaps between people, she caught glimpses of a man wearing jeans and a black T-shirt.

"Let's go up front so you can see better." Max grabbed her hand and pulled her forward.

"I know a lot of you, but it's nice to see so many new faces in the crowd. You'll be happy to learn that I heard from Peter this week. He wants to meet with me. It seems they are finally taking us seriously." The delight in the man's voice seemed to resonate with his followers. "Tonight's meeting will be brief. I'm sure all of you have better places to be than in this musty basement on a Thursday night—except for Calvin."

The good-natured jab received a resounding chuckle from everyone, even Vivienne. Max stopped when he reached the front of the crowd. She waved to Joel on her left.

"For those of you who don't know me, my name is Lee Somerfield." Lee had addressed the crowd, but Vivienne felt like he was looking directly at her. "What I'm about...what I'm here to represent...is freedom." He may have been handsome in his younger years, but it was hard to tell beneath his bushy, graying beard.

The group clapped and cheered at the welcome declaration. Their response echoed off the cinderblock walls.

"Leadership wants you to believe being part of Neverland gives you the freedom we all deserve, but I'm here to confirm what you already know: They. Are. Wrong. What kind of freedom requires you to hide away in secret for the rest of your never-ending life? What kind of freedom comes with being hunted like wild animals with *no* repercussions? There are evil people whose only goal is to open us up like frogs and experiment on us until we are no longer useful, or dead—whichever comes first. And yet, *we* are the ones in hiding."

The group muttered in accordance with each point Lee made.

Vivienne remained silent, even though she found herself agreeing with what he had said so far. She couldn't stop thinking of her dad and imagining what he would be saying if he was the one up on stage.

Lee lifted his hand, waiting for silence. "If HOOK was gone, we'd have no more reason to hide. My friends"—he held up a tarnished Charlie Bell—"HOOK's time is up."

The response was deafening.

As people began to filter out, Lee stepped down from the plywood stage directly in front of Vivienne. "You're Vivienne Dunn, aren't you?"

Her spine straightened. "Yeah."

"Boy," he laughed, "you look just like your mom. My brother and I were friends with both your parents."

"Really?"

"It was a long time ago." He nodded toward the handful of PAN still in the basement, speaking in low tones to one another. "Your father started this to protest Leadership's response when my brother and I got neutralized."

"HOOK got you?" Seeing the wrinkles that shouldn't be on his forehead left her touching her own smooth face.

"They sure did." In the crook of Lee's right elbow, his veins looked like someone had traced them with a black marker. "I was young, so I was grounded. Nick wasn't as lucky."

"What'd Leadership do?"

Lee scratched his beard. "Nothing."

"At all?"

He shook his head.

Vivienne touched her own arm. "HOOK tried to get me too."

Lee drew in a carefully controlled breath. "They're so sure we won't retaliate that their attempts to get our DNA are becoming more brazen. Someone needs to stop them."

She stepped close enough to see the sadness in his dark eyes. "Do you really think that's possible?"

"If we can get enough people on our side, we can do anything."

Her phone buzzed in her pocket. *Longest five minutes of my life.*

She'd completely forgotten about Deacon. "Sorry, I gotta go."

"You should come back again," Lee said, extending his hand to her. "It'd mean a lot to have you here to finish what William started."

"Don't worry," she said, putting her hand in his. "I'll definitely be back."

"Five minutes, eh?" Deacon started the vehicle and drove toward Kensington. "I was this close to coming for you."

"Sorry," she muttered, checking the backseat to see Ethan lying face-down. "I was talking to Lee."

He twisted his grip on the steering wheel. "About what?"

"My dad." She smoothed down her skirt. "Did you know Lee thinks we shouldn't hide anymore? He wants us to go after HOOK."

"Right now, we have one enemy, Vivienne. *One.* We know about them and understand how they operate. We win more often than we lose. What do you think would happen if we had hundreds or thousands of enemies? Do you honestly think the world would just accept us and our abilities?" He snorted. "Will HOOK stop their experiments because we come out of the shadows? Or will governments add to HOOK's funding? Will our enemies disappear, or will they grow exponentially until we cannot exist? Outsiders are not as accepting of differences as we would all like to believe."

She thought about what he said the entire drive back to campus.

"I think you're wrong," she told him when he stopped in front of the Hall. "The world would be a better place if people knew how much magic there was in it."

Deacon leaned across the center console, said, "I love your optimism," and kissed her until she forgot about everything.

THIRTY

"Hey, Vivienne. It's Julie. I've got some important paperwork you'll have to sign before your first mission. Could you come by sometime today?"

Vivienne stopped buttering her bagel long enough to check her watch. "How's right now?" Despite going to bed late, she had woken in a tangle of sheets an hour earlier than usual, drenched in sweat. Thinking of her dreams the night before made her blush.

"Perfect. I'll see you shortly."

She turned to see Emily jumping up and down in the kitchen. "What's gotten into you?"

Emily clapped her hands beneath her chin. "I wanna hear all about your date!"

"I'm kinda in a hurry," she said between bites, hoping to delay this conversation for as long as possible. She and Deacon were going to try having a relationship, but they'd gotten distracted before discussing what exactly that meant. "Julie needs me to sign something before I leave for Maryland."

"Give me the highlights. I am *dying* here."

She chewed the last bit of her bagel then washed it down with some water. "We had food, then met up with Ethan."

"Come on, Deacon." Emily closed her eyes and whispered,

"You're better than that." Then she opened one eye. "Did he at least kiss you?"

"Um..." Unsure where to look, Vivienne zipped her backpack.

"That's a *yes*." Emily danced a lap around the table. "Was it one of those awkward first kisses where you go one way and he goes the other"—she jerked right then left—"or like something you'd see in a movie? Is he a good kisser? I bet he's a *greeeat* kisser."

Vivienne tossed her backpack over one shoulder and started for the door. "It wasn't exactly our first kiss."

"Hold it right there." Emily caught her by the backpack. "You're only telling me this *now*?"

"Gotta go!" She twisted free and sprinted for the stairwell.

"When you get back, you're going to tell me everything!" Emily shouted out the door. "And I mean *everything*!"

When she arrived at reception, Julie was busy helping a guy at the front desk. Vivienne waited for her in the oversized wing-back chair beside the grandfather clock.

"I'm so sorry to keep you waiting," Julie said, carrying an olive green folder across the room.

"It's okay." Vivienne tapped on her knees. "I don't have anything to do until ten."

"We've been doing an overhaul of our records, and I'm making sure all my t's are crossed in case Leadership decides to have a look." Julie nodded to someone in the hallway behind Vivienne.

A woman with dark brown hair waited in the shadows. The stranger stepped into the filtered spring sunshine and asked, "Is this Vivienne?" in a crisp British accent.

"It is." Julie handed the woman the folder she carried. "Vivienne, this is Mary."

Mary opened the cover of the folder, then closed it again.

"Hi." Vivienne waved.

Mary tilted her head and smiled. "Thanks for this, Julie. I can handle it from here. Vivienne, come with me to my office so we can get everything squared away for Monday." She turned back to the shadows.

Vivienne followed Mary's rigid frame down the windowless hallway, past a number of tall wooden doors, and into a bright, airy office with furniture that looked like it came out of an IKEA catalogue. There wasn't a single personal touch or family photograph on the desk or bookshelves. The only decoration Vivienne could see was a large, polished hourglass resting near the desk's edge.

Mary motioned to a straight-back office chair across the desk. "Before we begin," she said, taking her own seat, "I must ask if you feel adequately prepared for your first mission." She wiped her hand across her organized desk. "In most cases, we train recruiters for six months before allowing them into the field."

The seat back dug into Vivienne's spine when she sat up straighter. "I'm ready." Her own doubt-filled recruitment experience made her feel confident that she could convince a fellow skeptic to come to Neverland.

"And do you feel committed enough to Neverland to recruit new members?"

Committed? What kind of question was that? "Of course I'm committed."

"Is that so? I have it on good authority that you attended a meeting at Lee Somerfield's home last night." Her voice tightened when she said his name.

"I listened to him talk for a few minutes."

"I understand how...enticing his ideas may sound." Her green eyes narrowed. "But Leadership's official view on Lee and his uprising is not favorable. If you're unhappy about something, I encourage you to bring your complaints to me so that I can take them to Leadership."

"I'm not unhappy about anything."

"That's good to know." She picked a pen out of her top drawer and opened the folder Julie had given her. "I heard you went out with my son last night."

Oh no . . . The bagel in her stomach turned sour. Mary was Deacon's mom. How much did she know? Vivienne decided to play it safe. She shrugged and, as casually as she could, said, "We had dinner and talked about our mission."

"*Our* mission?" Mary's head snapped up. "I assigned Ethan as your partner."

"That's not what the guy said in our meeting yesterday."

"Oh, Deacon..." Mary closed her eyes and shook her head.

"Is something wrong?"

"My son," she clipped, "will *not* be going to Maryland with you." She handed Vivienne a document and pen and told her to read it over and sign at the bottom.

Vivienne stared at the block of legal text in front of her. Was this a foreign language? She couldn't understand a word of it. "Why not?"

"The last time Deacon partnered with a female recruiter, the two of them spent more time in bed with one another than doing their actual job." Her lips pressed into a tight grimace. "Being a recruiter is difficult enough without extra distractions—and unfortunately, Deacon is known for his distractions."

Was that all she was to him? Another distraction? No, no. She was an exception, not a distraction. He wanted to have a relationship with her.

"I love my son very much," Mary went on, "but he doesn't have a very good track record where women are concerned. He tends to...get what he wants," she said slowly, her narrowed eyes conveying her meaning, "and then move on without remorse."

Get what he wants.

Vivienne knew *exactly* what that meant.

She added a shaky signature to the bottom of the page and returned it to Mary. "Is there anything else I need to sign?" She hated that her voice broke on the last word.

"No. You're free to go."

She tore through the hall and nearly rammed into a broad chest in the main waiting area. Thankfully, a pair of strong arms cushioned the collision.

"Good morning, girlfriend." Deacon offered her a breath-taking smile.

"Hey, Dash!" Julie rounded the desk at a clip. "What brings you our way?"

Vivienne couldn't do this. Not here. "Let me go," she whispered.

He dropped his hands and searched her expression. His forehead creased, seemingly with concern. He answered Julie's question, but his eyes remained on Vivienne. "I missed a call from my mother. I was passing and thought I'd stop by instead of calling her back."

"She's free at the moment if you want to see her." Julie ushered him toward Mary's office.

"Thanks, Julie. I'll call over in a bit, all right, Vivienne?" He frowned at her.

Vivienne shook her head and raced to the door.

Something was wrong. Very wrong. Vivienne's eyes had been filled with tears, her face flushed. Deacon was about to go after her when he noticed his mother's office door was open. If Vivienne had been to see her, that would explain why she was so upset.

Inside the office, his mother's back was to the door as she spoke in low tones to someone on the phone. "I understand… Yes…Yes…Are you sure there's no other—" She fell silent. "Yes. All right." She dropped her mobile onto the desk and put her head in her hands.

The way her typically rigid shoulders slumped made Deacon take a step back from his own irritation. "Mother? Is everything all right?"

Her hands fell to the desk, and she met him with tear-filled eyes. "I told you in January to stop your reckless behavior. But you just couldn't do it, could you?"

"I haven't done anything reckless in months." He flipped the large hourglass sitting on the edge of the desk; the grains of sand slipped through with mesmerizing speed.

"What do you call asking Joel to give Vivienne her final exam early?"

He swore under his breath and sank onto the chair. "It was merely a suggestion."

"She nearly killed herself." His mother typed something on her laptop; the printer shuffled through its paper tray and spat out two pages. "But that's not all you've done, is it?"

"Ummm…" He knew better than to incriminate himself.

"I assigned her to a mission in Maryland. But you…" She rose slowly and leaned across her desk. "*You* decided that wasn't good enough, didn't you? You wanted her on *your* mission. I wonder why?"

The sand in the hourglass ran out.

He rubbed the back of his neck. Would he ever live down that mistake? "This isn't like the last time." He knew she wouldn't believe him, but he had to say it aloud.

"You're right. Last time, I was foolish enough to assign you to work with a female recruiter. This time, you went behind my back and changed the assignments yourself." She stalked to the printer beneath the window and came back with the pages. One was thrust in his direction; the second she read over herself. "I told you there would be consequences."

He stared at the British Airways boarding pass dated for later that evening. "I'm *not* going to London."

Then she handed him the second sheet.

"You cannot be serious." Deacon read and re-read the missive. Laughter filtered through the window with the sunshine, but he had never felt less like smiling as despair took root in his gut. "They're putting me on *trial*?"

Vivienne should have known. She *had* known. But she'd ignored all the signs and continued down the path to heartache anyway. The yellow dress she had worn the night before still smelled like Deacon's cologne. She twisted it into a ball and shoved it into her trash can.

Why did his mother's revelation shock her so much? Deacon had done nothing to hide the fact that he wanted to sleep with her. But knowing that was all he was after . . . that was unforgivable.

It was her own stupid fault for thinking that it would actually mean something to him.

That he would still want to be with her afterwards.

He was only looking for a distraction—and she had willingly played the role.

Not anymore.

Someone knocked at the glass door.

Vivienne knew who it was even before she opened it.

"I need to speak with you for a moment."

"I don't want to talk to you right now, Deacon." Vivienne tried to shut the door, but he blocked it with his foot.

"What's wrong?" He pushed his way past her and propped himself up against the side of the couch.

She closed the door and took a few steps toward him. Why did he look like he was worried? Like he cared? He was just passing the time with her. "Did you change assignments just so you could sleep with me?"

"Is that what my mother told you?" he scoffed, his eyes narrowing.

"Answer the question."

He dragged on the ends of his hair. "It was my second assignment, and I was partnered with a girl I fancied. I made a mistake and have been paying for it ever since."

His tortured expression only made her angrier. "That's not what I asked." She didn't want to hear about other girls.

"No," he said through his teeth. "I did not change assignments so I could sleep with you."

"I don't believe you."

He stood, and the movement put him impossibly close to her. "Why would you believe my mother over me? You just met her! She doesn't know what's going on in my life. She doesn't know how I feel about you or—"

"How you *feel* about me?" she bit out. "Deacon, you want to *sleep* with me. And you've made it clear that where sex is concerned, feelings aren't involved. So don't stand there and look wounded when I call you on your shit. That's something you like about me, remember?"

"You think this is about sex for me? If I just wanted to have sex, all I'd have to do is dial a bloody phone number."

"Thanks for clearing that up," she snapped, turning toward the bedroom. Just because he refused to leave didn't mean she had to stand there and listen to his—

"Dammit, Vivienne. Is it that hard to believe that I want to spend time with you?" he ground out. "That I genuinely care about you? That I want to be part of your first mission? That I want to be there if you need me?"

Yes. It was that hard to believe. Because he was Peter frickin' Pan's drop-dead-gorgeous grandson, and she was just an orphan from Ohio with an active Nevergene.

"Get out, Deacon."

"Wait. Listen." He ran his hands over his face. "I didn't mean what I said. I don't want to sleep with anyone else. Vivienne, I—"

"For once, will you just leave me alone?" She dashed at the tears running down her cheeks with the backs of her hands. The mascara she wasn't used to wearing burned her eyes.

The only sounds left to hear were his retreating footsteps and the slamming door.

THIRTY-ONE

Frostburg was a small college town in western Maryland whose population dropped by almost half when college wasn't in session. It was beautiful, quaint, and far from Kensington; everything Vivienne needed to get over Deacon.

"My name is Alice Barnard, and I'm here for an interview with someone named Bill."

A man behind the counter at Luigi's Pizza Parlor dropped the rag he was using to wipe the plastic menus. "That's me," he said, drying his hands on his apron and pulling a pad of paper and pen from his pocket.

"You're the owner, right?" Vivienne, slipping into her role as Alice, followed him to a booth by the window.

"Are you wondering why my name isn't Luigi?"

"I guess I'm not the first person to ask you that."

"Definitely not." He laughed. "Bill's Pizza Parlor just didn't have the same ring to it."

He had a point.

"My interviews are simple," he said, glancing at her bogus resume before setting it aside. "Are you reliable and do you show up on time?"

"Yes."

"Do you plan to work, or sit around scrolling on your phone the entire shift?"

"I'll go with the first one."

"Good choice," he said with a deep, rumbling laugh. "What's your availability like?"

She twisted the watch on her wrist. How did she casually request shifts with her mark? "Whenever you need me."

He flipped through the pad he held. "Can you start today at three?"

"Three works for me." Adjusting the strap of her purse on her shoulder, she asked Bill what she needed to wear.

"I'll grab you a T-shirt. You can wear jeans and any shoes that don't slip."

When Alice returned at three, Bill showed her around the restaurant, kitchen, and back room used for storing dry goods and employee belongings.

"Here's a clean apron." He handed her a black bundle from behind a stack of Styrofoam cups. "Make sure you wash it between shifts. It doesn't look good when there's more food on the waitstaff than the trays."

"Gotcha." Alice tied it around her waist.

"I got you a nametag too."

She thanked him and fastened it to her red Luigi's T-shirt.

"While you're working, food is free. I only ask that you eat it here in the back and that you remember the customers are your first priority." The bell over the door rang, and Bill handed her a notepad and pen. "Looks like you're on, Alice."

She collected menus from the container hanging next to the counter and brought them to the booth. "Hi, folks. My name is Alice and I'll be your server. Can I start you off with something to drink?"

"I want soda. Mom, you promised I could have soda," a boy, about ten years old, said, dragging on his mother's sleeve.

"Calm down." The woman ran her hand over her weary eyes before picking up the menu in front of her. "You can have *one*. When it's gone, you get water. Do you hear me?"

The boy rolled his eyes and let go of her sleeve. "Ugh. Fine."

The woman smiled at Alice. "Can we get one small Sprite and a large iced tea?"

"I want a large one! *Moooom*! You promised."

"Fine. Make that two larges, please."

"No problem. I'll grab those and be right back for your order." While Alice filled sodas at the drink station, her mark came through the back door off the kitchen. Alice gave her a warm smile—which the girl ignored.

After dropping drinks off at her table, Alice met the mark again on the way back to the kitchen. "Hey there! I'm Alice."

"I'm Megan," the girl said, tying her apron and stuffing a load of straws into the pocket.

"I just moved here from Wyoming."

"That's cool." Megan stepped around Alice as she scoured the counter. "Did you take my pen?"

Alice frowned at the number of pens she had unknowingly acquired during her first hour at work. "I'm not sure…"

Megan retrieved the only purple one from Alice's pocket and held it toward her. "This one's mine."

"Got it. How long have you worked here?"

"A year," Megan sighed. "Do you mind getting that two-top that just walked in? I need to use the bathroom."

Without waiting for an answer, Megan went into the ladies' room, leaving Alice staring at the chipped paint on the door.

Sometime after five o'clock, Ethan burst through the door. "Sorry I'm late! Bill isn't here, is he?"

"Calm down, *Jimmy*," Alice said. "Bill left an hour ago, and the night manager, Tory, is too busy flirting with Will the cook to realize you're late."

"Whew." Jimmy pretended to faint on her shoulder. "How's it going?"

She waved her hand at the lone occupied table in the restaurant. "Kinda boring. Tory's nice, but it doesn't seem like she does much when she's here. Will's quiet except when Tory's around."

He nudged her with his elbow. "I'm not asking about work."

"Megan hasn't really talked to me," she grumbled, glancing toward the kitchen door, from where the sounds of chopping and laughter emerged, "but she doesn't seem dizzy or sick or anything."

As if she had heard her name, Megan came out of the kitchen carrying a basket of fried pickles. Her eyes lit up when she caught sight of Jimmy. Alice swore the girl skipped to the table.

After dropping off the appetizer, Megan came over to them. "Hey there. I'm Megan."

He grinned at her. "Jimmy."

"I know," she giggled, flicking her ponytail to the side. "We have second and fourth periods together."

"That's right," Jimmy said, heading toward the back of the restaurant.

Megan stayed on his heels. "Tonight's your first shift, isn't it?"

Alice, feeling invisible, followed them into the back room.

"It sure is." Jimmy put his coat on the hook behind the door and untangled an apron from the pile. "Have you worked here long?"

"I've been here for a year. Bill is my mom's cousin's husband, so he kind of had to hire me."

Alice had been there for hours, and that was the most she'd heard Megan say all night.

"Megan! Order up!" Will called from the kitchen.

After Megan left, Jimmy turned to Alice. "She seems nice."

Megan passed the door carrying a pizza. Jimmy missed the glare she flashed at Alice through the small window. "I get the feeling she doesn't like me."

Jimmy tied his apron and collected a bus tub from the stainless steel table beside the sink. "Really?"

"Really."

As the evening progressed, Alice waited on customers while Megan asked Jimmy an endless stream of questions and followed him and his bus tub from table to table. Jimmy, being well-versed in improv, was quick and creative with his responses.

Alice studied Megan, Megan studied Jimmy, and Jimmy studied the pizzas.

With twenty-five dollars from tips in her pocket, Alice's first shift ended.

Jimmy said goodbye to Megan and Alice with high-fives, then jogged to his Jeep.

"Is that your car?" Alice asked, nodding toward the white Hyundai parked next to her silver Civic.

"Yeah."

"It's nice."

Megan seemed to increase her pace. "Thanks."

"I'll see you tomorrow night?" she called, stopping beneath the lone light post to fish her keys from her purse.

Megan hopped into her car and said, "See you tomorrow," before slamming the door. She was out of the parking lot by the time Alice found her keys.

For some unknown reason, Megan did *not* like her. Which was crazy. Alice had been friendly, offered to help carry food, and tried to talk about Frostburg, but nothing had worked. Defeated, she unlocked her car and sank onto the seat. Jimmy's headlights got brighter as he drove into the space next to her.

"What's up, partner?" he said through the open window.

Partner? She wasn't a partner. She was a hindrance. Alice threw her purse into the passenger seat; everything inside spilled onto the floor. "I don't know what I'm doing here," she groaned. "You don't need me."

"You're right. I don't." His thumb tapped the beat from the oldies station onto his car door. "But since you're here, you may as well stop feeling sorry for yourself and do your job."

"Ouch." Couldn't *someone* be nice to her today?

"You're overthinking this. Don't worry about recruiting or Nevergenes or injections—or rules. You're making a new friend." He removed his nametag and tossed it onto his dashboard. "That's it."

"Megan doesn't like me."

"Then you need to *make* her like you." He leaned out the window and rested his chin on his forearm. "Find some common interest—like manicures or makeup or something—and bond over that."

"I'm not into that stuff." She checked her nails only to find some of the pink paint had chipped. "And Megan doesn't seem like she is either."

"Vivienne may not be, but it looks like Alice is."

"Yeah." She flipped the ends of her hair. "If I was here as Vivienne, I'd know what to do."

"Do you hear yourself right now?" He smacked the outside of his door. "You *are* here as Vivienne. The only thing Kensington changed about you is your hair and your name. Stop trying to be Alice and be blonde Vivienne with bad eyesight."

Laughing, she adjusted her glasses. "I think I can handle that."

When Alice got ready for work the next day, she put on her makeup—but only the bare minimum. After all, she was going to a pizza parlor, not a fashion show. It was only a small change, but when she caught a glimpse of herself in the rearview mirror, she felt more like blonde Vivienne.

Alice waved at Megan on her way to the back room.

Megan peered around the corner with narrowed eyes. "You look...different."

"Yeah. I don't know who I was trying to impress with all the makeup," she said, tightening her apron. "My boyfriend doesn't even live around here."

Megan hesitated in the doorway. "You have a boyfriend?"

"Back in Wyoming."

"You're trying to do the distance thing?"

Alice shrugged. "That's the plan."

"What do you think of him?" Megan nodded toward Jimmy busily clearing a table where two toddlers had used their spaghetti sauce as finger paint.

Alice slid two calzones from beneath the heat lamp onto her tray. "He's cute. But I like guys with dark hair."

Megan nodded, then seemed to notice Alice's full tray. "Do you need some help?"

"Can you grab the parmesan cheese for me?"

"Sure." Megan followed her to the table then back to the kitchen.

"Hey, girls?" Tory called from where she leaned against the prep table behind Will. "Can one of you cut those lemons?"

Megan frowned and said she hated cutting lemons.

"I don't mind doing it." Alice brought the handful of lemons to the drinks station so she could keep an eye on her tables.

Megan handed her a knife and cutting board. "How old are you?"

"Eighteen." Alice sliced a lemon into wedges and stacked the pieces into the plastic container next to the straws. The bell above the door dinged. "Do you want to grab that new table, or should I get it?"

"I can get it." Megan pulled a handful of menus from the holder.

Jimmy came past carrying a full bus tub. "It looks like you made a new friend, blondie."

Alice smiled at Megan's back. "I guess it does."

Megan came back and pulled a tray from beside the soda fountain. "Did you already graduate or something?" She set her pad of paper down and started filling glasses. "There's only one public high school around here, and if you were there, I would know."

"I graduated last year. I'll be nineteen in a few weeks."

"No way! I turn eighteen next Wednesday."

"Do you need help with those?" Alice nodded toward the full tray of drinks.

"Do you mind?"

"Not at all." She transferred three of the cups onto an empty tray.

In the middle of the restaurant, Megan tripped and spilled her tray of drinks across the floor. Alice laid the tray she carried onto a nearby table and rushed for a stack of towels from the kitchen.

"I feel like such an idiot." Megan wiped the stain on her damp shirt with the towel Alice handed her. "Everyone's staring at me."

"If it makes you feel any better," Alice said, collecting the cups onto the dirty tray, "I once fell headfirst into a locker with the entire soccer team watching."

That earned her a laugh and a smile from Megan.

"Let me clean this up," Jimmy said, arriving on the scene with a mop and bucket. "Alice, why don't you get that table new drinks? Megan, I have a clean black T-shirt in the office if you want to change."

Megan's eyes glittered with appreciation. "Thanks, guys."

"I think she tripped over this." Alice straightened the corner of the rug near the entrance.

Jimmy's eyes met hers, and she recognized the excitement there. "That or her Nevergene's activating," he whispered.

"What do we do?" Her adrenaline surged, but she kept her voice low. "Should we inject her now?"

"Go ahead and chase her down with a needle and see how *that* goes." He laughed and dragged the Caution: Wet Floor sign from beside the door.

She smacked his arm. "You know what I mean."

"Could be a fluke." Jimmy and Alice watched Megan come out of the back in Jimmy's T-shirt. "A clearer sign would be if she loses consciousness. She turns eighteen next week, right?"

"Wednesday."

"Then there's only a few more days to wait."

Two hours later, the restaurant was quiet, and Megan seemed much steadier on her feet.

Tory emerged from the kitchen long enough to ask everyone to meet her in the office. "We haven't had any new customers in over an hour," Tory said from behind the desk. "Jimmy, why don't you go home? The girls can clear the tables themselves till we close."

"I don't mind staying."

"Yeah, but there's no sense in Bill paying you to do nothing."

Jimmy shrugged. "Sounds good." He untied his apron and slipped it over his head.

Tory stared at the schedule on the wall and scratched her head with the end of a pen. "How many tables do you have left, Megan?"

"Two."

"Once your last table leaves and you finish your side work, you can head home too."

"Sweet." Megan clapped then rushed out of the office.

Alice found Jimmy in the back room, pulling his coat from the hanger. "Okay. I'm going to go," he said, settling his coat over his shoulders. "But I'll wait outside in the Jeep till you're done."

"Why?"

"In case you need me."

"Just go home." She handed him his keys from the hook. "You were with Megan at school all day. Let me feel like I'm doing something."

Jimmy yawned. "You sure?"

"Yes."

He told her to call him if anything happened, zipped his coat, and headed for the back door.

The bell over the door rang, and Megan yelled for her.

A man in his early forties shook the raindrops from his dark trench coat and read a copy of the laminated takeaway menu. His black hair was cropped short, and his face bore a heavy five o'clock shadow. He looked up from the menu and smiled. "Hello, Alice," he said after studying her nametag.

"Hi. What can I get you?"

Perhaps it was the seriousness in his dark eyes or the forced lightness of his voice, but something about the stranger set her on edge. "What's your secret?" he asked.

She tensed. "What secret?"

He pointed to the ancient backlit sign suspended from the ceiling, boasting that Luigi's was Frostburg's Best Kept Secret. "What makes your pizza so much better than the stuff they pedal at the national chains?"

Alice shrugged and adjusted the glasses slipping down her nose. "Family recipe."

He grinned, baring a set of gleaming teeth beneath his stubble. "I'll have a medium pizza with pepperoni and sausage, please."

"Would you like that to go?"

"Yes."

Alice rang the order in the register, and he paid his bill in cash.

"Hey, Alice! Hold the register," Megan called, rushing to her side. "Can you get me change for a twenty?"

Alice counted out the correct bills and handed them to Megan. "Here you go."

A family of four, with two young kids that kept blowing spit wads at each other and their tired looking parents, paid their bill while Megan boxed up their leftovers.

While he waited, the man examined the small restaurant, from the dropped ceiling to the black and white floor tiles. He remained near the counter the entire ten-minute wait but didn't try to make conversation again. Will rang the bell for the order, and Alice collected the box and handed it to the man.

"Thank you, Alice." He opened the lid and gave the meal an appreciative once-over. "This looks delicious."

"You're welcome." She felt unexplainable relief when he turned toward the door.

As he reached for the knob, he twisted and smiled. "If this is good, I'll have to come back."

Alice gave him an awkward thumbs up.

"That guy gave me the creeps," Megan said, tucking the black cheque book beneath the counter.

"Tell me about it." Alice adjusted the ties on her sagging apron as the last of the customers paid.

"I'm running to the back for some more straws and napkins. Do you mind doing the salt and pepper?" Megan asked over her shoulder.

"No problem." Vivienne collected the shakers from the tables on a tray and brought them into the kitchen. She had finished filling and replacing them before she realized Megan had never returned.

"Hey, Will? Is Megan with you?" she asked through the screen door used for deliveries.

Will took a drag of his cigarette and blew the smoke at the stars. "Haven't seen her."

"Hey, Megan?" Alice called, walking into the back room. "Did you get lost in—?"

Megan's shoes stuck out from behind the rack of straws. Alice raced to find her collapsed on the floor. "Megan! Are you okay?" She dropped to her knees and checked the girl's pulse.

Breathing. She was still breathing.

Vivienne fumbled for her phone in her purse. "Pick up, Ethan...pick up," she whispered. The call rang out. Stupid voicemail . . . "I need you back at Luigi's ASAP. It's happening."

Her eyes fell closed, and she took a deep, steadying breath. "You can do this, Vivienne." The injector pen was in her purse, stuffed under a pile of receipts and gum wrappers. After removing the cap and exposing the needle, she bent to Megan's ear. "If you can hear me, you're going to feel a pinch in your arm."

She inhaled another deep breath, rolled up Megan's sleeve, and jabbed the needle into her shoulder.

Megan groaned when the medicine was injected. "Alice? What're you doing?"

"You're going to be fine. Ethan is on his way in so he can bring you home."

"Who's Ethan?" Megan whispered before passing out again.

Vivienne's phone rang. "Where have you been?"

"I close my eyes for fifteen minutes and all hell breaks loose." Ethan cursed. "And now I've stubbed my damn toe."

Megan groaned, and Vivienne placed a comforting hand on her shoulder. "Megan's unconscious."

"Shit. You still at Luigi's?"

She threw the injector pen into the trash can along with the receipts and wrappers. "Yeah. She's passed out in the back room."

The sound of an engine starting roared in the background. "Did you inject her yet?"

"Just did." Vivienne found TINK in the secret pocket of her purse next to a tampon. She tucked the earpiece in place and fluffed her hair to cover the device. The bell from the front door jingled.

"Alice!" Will called from the kitchen. "Someone just walked in."

"Crap. I'll be right back."

"Vivienne, wait!"

She left her phone on the desk and mumbled a curse toward the clock on the wall. Couldn't these people read the time?

A man, probably in his late forties, stood by the door deliberating over the choices on the menu. He was one of the biggest men she had ever seen—at least six and a half feet tall.

Vivienne startled when she saw him but smiled. "I'm sorry, sir. We're closed for the evening."

"No problem. I didn't realize you closed at nine." He gave a curt nod before going back outside.

"Maybe you should have read the sign on the door," she muttered on her way back to the storage area. "Sorry about that, Ethan." Megan was still passed out on the floor, but some of the color had returned to her face. "A stupid customer came in two minutes before closing expecting—"

"Vivienne, listen to me. You need to get out of there *right now*."

"I can't leave Megan here."

"There's no time to explain, just get back to Kensington. Extraction is on their way and—"

"Extraction? Why are—" The door's bell rang again, and Vivienne could hear Will cursing from the smoking area outside. "I'll call you right back." She ended the call, tucked her phone into her purse, and rushed to the front.

"My friend tells me you're closed already," a man called from the entrance. "Is everything all right?"

"We always close at nine," she said, rounding the corner and loosening the strings on her apron. "Come back tomorrow if you want—"

"I don't want pizza." The creepy guy who had ordered takeaway earlier lingered by the door. "I'm here for you, Vivienne."

Her apron slid to the floor. "Who's Vivienne?"

The man pulled a sheet of paper from his pocket and took his time unfolding it. *Not good* . . . It was a photocopy of her high school yearbook picture. "I really like what you've done with your hair."

He knew. But how? What was she supposed to do? Vivienne collected her apron and moved closer to the counter.

"You're a hard woman to find, Miss Dunn," he went on. "When we spoke on the phone, I thought perhaps you'd see reason and turn yourself in."

Phone? What was he talking—"When did I talk to you?"

"I apologize, we haven't been formally introduced. My name is Lawrence." His lips twisted into a sneer.

The hair on the back of her neck stood on end. "*Lawrence Hooke*."

"Ah, so you *do* remember me."

"What do you want?"

"Oh, we'll get into that later. First, you need to come for a little drive with me."

"Yeah, that's not happening."

His hand flew to his heart. "I apologize for the confusion. You see, it wasn't a request." Through the glass door, she saw three men standing by a black van with the sliding door open.

Leadership's rules required her to run.

She knew too many of Neverland's secrets.

Her skin tingled as her internal flame sparked to life, and she took a halting step toward the kitchen.

Lawrence moved closer. "Or we could ask your friend to join us instead. *Megan*, was it?"

Oh god . . . Megan. Vivienne couldn't leave her. Couldn't let her get taken . . . she was helpless.

Vivienne glanced toward the back room, then back at Lawrence Hooke.

Deacon's mother had questioned her commitment to Neverland, and it was time to prove her wrong.

THIRTY-TWO

They found her.

How the hell had they found her?

Oh god . . . They could be doing anything to her. She could already be—

No. He couldn't think about that.

But how the hell had they found her?

Deacon slammed his battered suitcase on top of the oak dresser and threw his belongings inside. He knew swearing at the luggage would serve no purpose, but he let a string of curses fly anyway.

"I'm so sorry." Ethan's apology crackled over the speaker on Deacon's mobile.

Ethan had left her alone. What kind of fool left a new recruiter on her own? "Do we have any way of knowing if she's all right?"

"All I know is what I saw on the CCTV footage—which isn't much."

"Who's in charge of Vivienne's recovery?"

"Owen."

Owen was the best . . . But that didn't matter. "I'll be back tonight. We'll talk then."

"Do you have permission from Peter to leave London? The trial is—"

"Moved to next week. But none of that matters. Vivienne was taken by HOOK, and we have no idea how the hell they knew she was in Maryland. I'll be useless here until she's safe."

"Actually...um..."

"Actually, *what*?" he snapped.

"There was a video—"

"What do you mean? What video? A video of Vivienne?"

"Vivienne's foster mother offered a pretty hefty reward for information on her whereabouts. It was broadcast on the local news station in Columbus."

Birds sang cheerful tunes in the trees outside the flat. He crossed to the open window and banged it closed. "I want to see it for myself."

"I'll send you the link."

His mobile rumbled in his palm; he clicked the text that brought him to a clip on the WBNS website.

"Vivienne Dunn went missing from her home in Columbus, Ohio on September 25th, the day of her eighteenth birthday," the female voiceover announced. A photo of Vivienne flashed on the screen, and his heart constricted. "Her foster mother Lynn Foley has been worried for her foster daughter's well-being ever since."

Standing in front of a barrage of logo-covered microphones, Vivienne's foster mother and two foster siblings looked appropriately worried. But the moment Lynn started speaking, Lyle started shaking his head in the background. And Maren's worried expression turned to one of boredom about halfway through.

"We've done everything we can to find Vivienne," Lynn said, her voice catching. "If you're watching this, honey, please let us know you're okay."

"Two additional teens in similar situations have gone missing since last year, all before their eighteenth birthdays. Max Burner, pictured here, disappeared from his apartment in Indiana three days before Vivienne Dunn..."

How the hell did they know about Max?

"...and Molly White, seventeen, from West Virginia, went missing from her foster home in early August."

Molly White? Who was that?

"Anyone who has information on Vivienne Dunn's whereabouts, or any of the other missing teens, is asked to contact the number on the screen. A reward of five hundred thousand dollars is being offered for information that leads to locating Vivienne. This is Marilyn Jackson for WBNS, reporting."

There was only one place Lynn could have gotten that kind of money . . . He pressed play again. And again. It wasn't helping, but what else could he do?

He turned it off and rang Ethan. "When did they find this?"

"It was released a few hours before she was taken, but it went viral online."

"There's no way Vivienne's foster family has that kind of money to offer as a reward. It had to be HOOK."

"That's what everyone on this side is thinking."

"They've never done something like this before."

"I know." Ethan's response was hollow.

This shouldn't have happened. There was an entire department dedicated to risk assessment. "What the hell has RISK been doing? How did this slip below their radar?"

"I don't have any answers for you, Dash. But if RISK had the video earlier, they would've gotten to her before it was—"

Deacon didn't need him to finish to understand what he meant.

Before it was too late.

Bile rose in his throat and he swallowed against the rising panic. Why didn't she run?

"I know you're freaking out, man. We're all freaking out. But she'll survive whatever happens in there. You know that's the reason we send new recruits into the field."

"That doesn't make me feel any better," he muttered before ending the call.

Vivienne may survive what was coming . . . but Deacon wasn't sure he would.

Deacon cursed his mother for sending him to London.

He cursed himself for pushing Vivienne into the field so early.

He cursed the seat for being uncomfortable and his seatbelt for being too restrictive.

He also cursed the damned sluggish plane for the entire seven-hour journey back to the States.

Once the plane landed outside of DC, he abandoned his bag and headed straight for the airport's exit. He pressed the button on the side of his ear, and his helmet appeared. When he was clear of an audience, he took off. "Hey, TINK. Call Ethan for me."

"Sure thing, *Deacon*."

His phone only rang once before Ethan answered. "Hey, Dash."

"Have you heard anything?"

"No."

"Do we know if she…is she all right?"

"We don't know."

Dammit. "Do you know *anything*?"

"I know lots of stuff, but it's all shitty." A curse. "They're having trouble finding a way in. Owen thinks we need to stay back and wait for an opening."

"I don't care if you have to bust down the front doors. We are not leaving Vivienne there a minute longer than we have to."

"You gotta let extraction do their job. Nicola thinks you should go to Kensington—"

That wasn't happening. "If I went back to Kensington, I'd go mad."

Ethan groaned. "Don't come straight to the facility. We've made camp about two miles south, in the trees below the ridge-line. I'll send TINK our coordinates."

Nineteen excruciating minutes later, Deacon located his fellow PAN in the forest surrounding the HOOK facility. Ethan and Nicola were deep in conversation beneath an ancient oak tree with two other members of the extraction team dressed in full tactical gear. Deacon bypassed his friends and went directly to the teenager bent over a stump. "Has there been any sign of her yet? Do you know if she's all right?"

The stone-faced PAN with serious black eyes looked up from the schematic drawing of the HOOK building to glare at him. "Who invited you?" Owen was shorter than Deacon, but what he lacked in height, he made up for in ruthlessness—which Deacon had found out the hard way when they had sparred a few years earlier.

Owen was very good at his job.

And he was among those who didn't care for Deacon after the bird-watching incident.

"Owen. Please."

"We know she's inside the building somewhere," Owen grumbled, removing the binoculars hanging from around his neck and setting them into a black bag at his feet, "but we're unable to use TINK to pinpoint her exact whereabouts. They must have some sort of signal jamming tech."

"Is she—?"

"I don't know."

"You didn't even let me—"

"There's no need for you to waste your breath. Whatever you're going to ask me, the answer is going to be that I don't know."

"What *do* you know?"

"I know I've been doing this for twenty years." Owen shoved him toward the others. "And I know that if you don't get your ass back with the rest of the spectators, you're gonna be sorry."

"And in those twenty years," Deacon snarled, jabbing his finger toward the building in the distance, "have you ever infiltrated a secure facility where they know of our existence *and* our ability to fly?"

"Have you?" Owen smirked as he pulled a silver tube from his vest pocket. He pressed a button, and the tube disappeared except for a faint blinking light. When he tossed it into the air, it floated toward the building.

They were wasting time in a bloody pissing match. "How many FAIR-Es have you let off?" The tiny, drone-like devices extraction used for reconnaissance would send video back for analysis.

"That's number seven."

"Is the receiver in here?" Deacon pulled a nickel alarm clock from beneath a pair of night-vision goggles and asked why they'd brought it.

Owen took the antique timepiece and tapped the black and white face. "When we cross paths with HOOK, it's standard procedure to leave them a souvenir. Drives 'em nuts."

Deacon withdrew the FAIR-E receiver and handed it to Owen. Instead of turning it on, Owen set it on top of the blueprints. "What are we looking at here?"

"The smaller buildings in the front are administrative offices." Owen slid his fingers along the page. "Vivienne wouldn't be in there. The larger building is surrounded by CCTV cameras, and it's where most of the employees are located."

"How many entrances are there?"

"Four. The main door has a security guard, and all the others are keycard access only."

This was bad. So much worse than he'd feared. If there was no way in—"Can we get our hands on a keycard?"

"If we do, we have to wait until after it gets dark to use it. The fields around the building are too big to cross in daylight, especially when they know we'll be approaching by air."

Darkness was hours away. They had to get in sooner. "What about windows?"

"If only I had thought of that," Owen drawled, dragging his hands over his face. "Some windows have been left ajar or completely open, but there's no way they're an oversight."

"They know we're coming," Deacon said. The leaves rustled in the evening breeze.

"Of course they do. And at the moment, we can't get a handle on where she is within the building without putting everyone here in jeopardy."

"So, what's the plan?"

Owen exhaled a huff of breath. "At the very least, we wait until nightfall. There are bound to be witnesses, but I have to minimize the damage at the front end in case all hell breaks loose."

The lazily falling sun inched toward the horizon. "And then?"

"Then we need to get eyes on the inside."

THIRTY-THREE

"**N**o one's comin' for you, Viv."

"Who said that?" Vivienne sat up, then collapsed back onto the bed. Why was she so dizzy? She pressed a cold palm to her aching head and turned to see a hazy figure sitting on the chair next to the bed. "*Mom?*"

"*What have you gotten yourself into, honey?*" Anne had a patient frown on her lips.

Vivienne blinked twice but didn't dare move for fear of making the apparition disappear. "Don't worry. Deacon will save me." He was her guardian angel. It was his responsibility to keep her safe.

"*No, he won't. He's gone.*"

"He'll come back for me." Even as she spoke the words, the claim rang hollow. No one would be storming the gates of HOOK to come to her aid. Whatever HOOK had in store for her, she would have to endure it on her own.

"*Do you honestly believe they'll let Deacon risk his life to save yours? You're expendable. He's not.*"

"Were you always this mean?"

Anne smiled, and for the first time, Vivienne recognized a bit of herself in her mother. "*I'm trying to help you, honey. It's not Deacon's job to save you.*"

"Of course, it is."

"*No. It's your job to save yourself.*"

"The window's open. I could just—"

"*If they know your secrets, you'll never escape.*"

Her mom was right. She had to keep her secrets.

Vivienne sat up carefully to study the barren room. Her stomach let out an empty growl. She was starving. And freezing. The cell had a toilet and a single thin cover for the bed, but nothing had been left for her to eat.

Muted beeping sounded from behind the industrial door, and then the heavy metal partition opened.

"Who authorized this?" A man snapped from the entrance. He had strawberry blond curls and wore a white button-down beneath his white lab coat. The red sneakers made him seem more likeable than the man in combat boots beside him.

"Your brother did," combat boots said.

Brother? Did that mean this guy was related to Lawrence Hooke? He looked at least a decade younger.

"My brother isn't in charge of research," red-shoes ground out. "This is *my* division, and he has no say. Got it?"

"Yes, Jasper."

"Can't you tell this poor girl is freezing? Get her a warmer blanket." A keycard jingled on a cord attached to Jasper's pocket when he came over to the bed and knelt beside her. His forehead creased, seemingly with concern. "Have you had anything to eat or drink, Vivienne?"

She shook her head.

He muttered a curse and pulled her wrist toward him, pressing his fingers to her pulse and checking his watch. "I'll see what we can rustle up for you from the canteen. I apologize for the way you've been treated since your arrival. Lawrence isn't known for his bedside manner."

Unsure of what to make of his care, Vivienne pointed to the window ten feet above them. "Will you ask someone to close the window? And maybe you could turn up the heating a bit."

Jasper frowned at her, then at the window. A normal human couldn't reach it without a ladder, but for someone with the ability to fly, it would have been an obvious means of escape. "I'll have someone come in and shut it for you," he promised, offering her a half-smile. "Hang tight and we'll get you comfortable."

Minutes later, the window was closed, and Vivienne was finishing a cold chicken sandwich and lukewarm glass of water. Worry kept her from getting any rest, but weariness forced her to remain huddled beneath the new, downy blanket.

If the opportunity for liberation presented itself, every ounce of energy would be crucial in making her attempt successful.

But before she escaped, she had to prepare for the worst.

Would they hook her up to machines that were little more than torture devices in medical casings?

Would the tests be quick and painless, or excruciating and drawn out?

Would she be able to withstand the pressure?

The door to the cell opened, and Lawrence Hooke stood on the other side.

"Oh, good. You're awake," he said with a congenial clap as he stepped into the room. Two burly men filled the entrance behind him.

"Where am I?"

"Right now, you're at my family's state-of-the-art medical research facility in Virginia."

"Why'd you kidnap me?"

Lawrence's jaw ticked. "Kidnap? Oh, no, no. You have it all wrong. That's certainly not what's going on here at all," he said to the guards. The men laughed with him.

Vivienne crossed her arms and glared at them. "You took me against my will, drugged me, and have me locked in a cell."

"I'm sorry you see it that way." Lawrence pointed to himself with his thumb. "I was merely following procedure."

"Who knew there was a guide? Is it called *Kidnapping for Dummies*?"

One of the guards sniggered.

Understanding she had little choice in the matter, she pulled on her shoes and followed him into the hallway, noting on her way out that both guards had holstered guns at their hips. Lawrence brought her to a small, sterile room six doors down from where she was being held. A young woman in a lab coat sat at a computer in the corner, labeling vials of blood.

"Sit." Lawrence indicated a plastic chair with wide, flat arms.

He sat near the door and opened a fat manila envelope, making a dramatic procession of pulling the documents from within and sifting through them until he found the one he had been searching for.

"Are you going to torture me?"

His laugh sounded forced. "Will it be necessary?"

Vivienne splayed her fingers on the edge of the stainless steel table between them. "I'm just trying to figure out why you took me. Yes, I ran away from my foster home. But I'm eighteen, so it's hardly illegal."

His wicked smile turned into a thin line. "You know that's not why you're here."

"Well, then. Why *am* I here?"

"I'll get to that in a minute. First, do you mind telling me where you've been hiding since you left Ohio?"

"I haven't been hiding anywhere," she said, flicking the ends of her hair. "I've been *living* in Maryland."

"Bullshit."

Oh, Lawrence had a temper. This was going to be interesting . . .

"You haven't been in Maryland," he snarled, jabbing his finger in her direction. "You're lying."

"Okay then," she said with a smile. "Since you seem to know so much, why don't *you* tell me where I've been?"

Through bared teeth, Lawrence said, "You'll talk eventually. They always do." He withdrew a photograph from the folder. "How about you tell me your friend's name?"

"That's Jimmy. He's the busboy at Luigi's. He was working the night you came in—"

"What about her?"

"You know who she is," Vivienne said, sliding the pictures back to him. "Her name is Megan. She's a waitress, like me."

He stuffed the pictures back into his envelope. "Do I look like a total idiot to you?"

"Do you really want me to answer that?"

The woman in the corner snorted, but found her composure when Lawrence slammed his fist on the table.

"What about...him?"

They had a photo of Deacon. It was grainy, maybe from a CCTV camera. Could have been from the hospital since he was wearing his black hoodie. "I don't know. But he's pretty hot."

Lawrence ripped the photo from her hands. "You lying little bit—"

Jasper burst into the room; all heads swiveled toward him. "I told you to wait for me."

"We're just getting started, Lab Ra—I mean Jasper." Lawrence tucked the remaining photo back into the envelope. "Vivienne asked why she was brought here."

Jasper glared at his brother and slid his chair from beneath the table. His look eased when he turned to Vivienne. "When you were in the hospital in September, the doctors had ordered additional tests. You're here so we can administer those tests."

She drummed her fingers on her knees. "And this requires me being held hostage?"

Lawrence kicked the table, making her jump. "For the last time, you are *not* being held hostage."

"Then I'm free to go?"

Jasper gripped his brother's arm. "Calm down, Lawrence. I'm afraid you can't go yet, Vivienne. We believe you have a rare disease that requires treatment."

"Why do you need the armed guards if that's all that's going on?" She aimed a finger-gun at Lawrence and shot him in the chest. His face turned bright red.

"Don't let them bother you," Jasper said, laughing in his

brother's angry face. "They're simply here to keep the facility secure."

"Okay, I'll play along. Why don't you tell me about this disease I have?"

"We aren't sure if you have it." Jasper withdrew a pad of paper and a pen from the breast pocket of his lab coat. "But your parents did, and since the disease is hereditary…"

"You assume I have it as well."

"Exactly." He continued pulling things from his pockets: keys, wallet, another pen, and a pack of bubble gum. "We'll conduct a round of specialized blood tests, and if you don't have the disease, you'll be free to go. Would you like some gum?"

"Sure." She accepted the stick he held toward her and took her time unravelling the silver wrapper. "But what happens if I have the disease?"

"We'll administer treatment," Jasper said, taking the trash from her, "then you're free to go back to Maryland."

"Or you could stay and help us with our research." Lawrence rolled his eyes and swatted the gum Jasper held toward him. "That's what your parents did when they came to us years ago."

"That's not true," she whispered.

"Yes, it is," Jasper said with an easy smile, tucking his belongings back into his pockets. "Before I started here, your mother and father routinely donated blood in exchange for treatment. Right, Lawrence?"

"That's right, Jasper."

Vivienne swallowed. "What kind of treatment?"

Jasper yo-yoed his retractable keycard. "We've developed a miraculous serum that—"

"Enough, Jasper. Just ask her the questions so we can get on with the tests."

"I'm getting to that, Lawrence."

"Get to it *faster*."

Jasper opened the notepad from his pocket and clicked the top of his pen. "Have you experienced any strange symptoms since your time in the hospital?"

"Define strange."

"The most common one we've come across is memory loss."

She tapped her finger against her chin. "I don't remember having any memory loss."

"All right." He chuckled as he jotted that down. "No memory loss." He clicked his pen twice. "Have you had any additional dizzy spells or lightheadedness?"

"Nope."

Jasper wiggled his pen between his index and middle fingers. "Have you ever flown?"

"Like, in a plane?"

"No, as in flying through the air like a fucking bird." Lawrence flapped his hands like wings.

"Lawrence!"

"Do I look like a bird to you?" She lifted her arms to look for feathers. "Are you sure you guys are scientists?"

"Enough with your pointless questions. She's only going to lie anyway." Lawrence waved his hand toward his female colleague. "Marianne will take some blood for testing, and after the results come in—"

"You'll be back to tell me the good news?"

"Exactly," Jasper said, clapping his hands together.

Lawrence glared at Vivienne before pushing away from the table. The Hooke brothers left the room, but the two guards remained outside the door.

Marianne slid across the floor on her rolling stool and told her to roll up her sleeve and lay her arm flat. She cleansed the area with a damp cotton ball and tied on the tourniquet. "Now make a fist."

Vivienne's veins rose, and she winced at the sharp pinch. "Why do you work for these monsters?"

"They're not monsters," Marianne said, her eyes fixed on the filling vial. "HOOK is responsible for groundbreaking genetic research." She unclicked the first vial and attached a second.

"If you say so."

After collecting the third vial, Marianne pressed a bandage over the dark bead of blood in the crook of Vivienne's arm.

Vivienne stood too fast, and her head started spinning. She

closed her eyes against the nausea and collapsed back onto the chair.

"Are you okay?" Marianne steadied her hands against Vivienne's shoulders.

With a deliberately weak voice, Vivienne told her that she hadn't eaten anything.

"Someone should've given you food before I took blood," Marianne grumbled with a concerned frown. "Give me two minutes and I'll be right back. Please, don't try to go anywhere."

Vivienne nodded but kept her eyes closed.

The door clicked closed.

This was her chance . . . maybe her *only* chance.

She ran to the door and peered through the small window. The two guards were talking in the hall, their backs to the room. One way in and out. No window. The vent above her head was too small to fit into.

Think, Vivienne. *Think*.

Right. The desk. She pulled open the drawers and searched for *something* that could help her escape. But there were only notebooks and pens and band aids and medical supplies and . . .

No good.

The blood. If she could make them believe she didn't have the Nevergene, they'd let her go. Right?

There were a bunch of vials in trays, and a few still needed labels. She grabbed her three vials and swapped them for ones in the tray. Maybe that would be enough . . . Hopefully it would be enough.

She slumped back into the chair before Marianne returned with a glass of orange juice and a handful of saltines. "Miss Dunn?"

Vivienne blinked and whispered, "Yes?"

"Have a drink of this." She held the juice toward her. "You should feel better once you get a bit of sugar back into you."

Ten minutes later, Vivienne hobbled out of the room, saying a silent prayer that it would work.

The two guards escorted her through the fluorescent-lit

hallway toward a door that looked like it belonged on the front of a bank vault.

Jasper rounded the corner and his eyes widened when he saw them. "What do you think you're doing, Ted?"

The guards looked at one another, then the taller one answered, "Bringing her back to her…room."

"She's not staying in there. Come with me, Vivienne." Jasper gripped her elbow and guided her down the hall. The guards fell into step behind him. "I can handle things from here, guys."

"Are you sure? Lawrence said—"

Jasper's incoherent grumbling included a few choice swear words coupled with his brother's name. "Vivienne?"

"Yes?" She batted her lashes at him.

His blue eyes narrowed at her. "Are you going to run away?"

"Do I need to?"

"She won't be any trouble," Jasper said with a chuckle. "Take a break, and I'll call you if she attacks me and makes a run for it."

The two guards didn't look happy, but they lumbered down the hall in the opposite direction without another word.

"Please, excuse my brother's need to display power. I'm convinced he's overcompensating for something." Jasper's grip loosened, and his hand fell to his side. "Allow me to take you somewhere more comfortable to wait for your results."

He brought her to a room at the end of the corridor. The glass doors at the entrance made it feel like she was being escorted to a board meeting. Inside was a faded red couch, a water tank, and a long table surrounded by leather chairs.

The far wall was made entirely of windows. The last window nearest a panel of thick curtains had been left ajar. The opening would be large enough for her to—Her adrenaline stirred to life. No. There was something too convenient about the escape. Too good to be true. She had to keep her secrets.

"This should be more suitable," Jasper said, pointing to the couch. "Help yourself to some water if you're thirsty. I'll send someone up with snacks and reading material as soon as I can. If you need to use the restroom, press the call button here and an escort will show you the way." He tapped the silver box next to the door.

She walked to the water cooler but stopped when she reached it. "Why are you being so nice to me?"

"Why wouldn't I be nice to you?" He smiled, nodded, and left.

She filled a glass and sipped slowly, taking stock of the boardroom. Two intriguing paintings, one of a peaceful mountain and another of the tumultuous sea, had been framed and displayed on the gray wall. She was no art expert, but they looked expensive.

A large gilt-framed mirror across the room caught her eye. She studied her haphazard reflection and combed through her tangled hair with her fingers. Her hand glanced over the nearly invisible plastic bit inside her ear. How had she forgotten about TINK?

When she clicked the button, instead of hearing TINK's cheerful voice, all she caught was static. Of course it didn't work. That would be too easy. Frustrated, she pressed the button to stop the fuzzy noise from clouding her mind.

Lawrence came to the door an hour later, and he seemed astonished to see her sitting on the couch, reading an outdated issue of TIME magazine.

She offered the jerk an innocent smile. "Are my test results back?"

Lawrence glanced toward the wall of windows, then back at her. She recognized the moment his confidence faltered. "We're expecting them any minute. Come with me."

He brought her down an elevator and out to the lobby, through an open courtyard dressed in shadows against a pink evening sky, and to a smaller building next to an empty parking lot. He kept checking over his shoulder that she was still behind him. When they reached an office with his name on the plaque next to the door, he motioned for her to enter. "Go in and take a seat."

The door closed behind them with a jarring click.

An urgent knock sounded, and Jasper joined them a moment later, his eyes focused on the papers in his hands. He leafed through the results multiple times, an unreadable expression on his face.

Lawrence pulled a metal tray from a sideboard next to his desk and placed it in front of him. On the sterile silver platter sat a square antiseptic packet, a glass vial filled with greenish-yellow liquid, and a needle encased within a hygienic plastic tube.

Vivienne's heart thrummed in her ears and her adrenaline spiked. To keep the fire at bay, she took a deep, even breath.

Lawrence extracted a pair of blue medical gloves from a box on his desk and placed them on the tray.

"I don't understand it." Jasper scratched his head.

Lawrence groaned, "What now?"

"She showed all the signs when she was in the hospital." Jasper flipped back to the first sheet and began again.

"Don't forget about the Shadow. Why was he in Ohio if she isn't one of them?"

Vivienne was pretty sure she knew who they were talking about. Still, she asked, "Who is the Shadow?"

Instead of answering, Lawrence darted a glance at her. "You're sure she's clean?"

"It appears that way." Jasper handed over the file. "I ran the tests a couple of times and nothing showed up. Have a look for yourself."

Although Lawrence's evil smile had been replaced by a frown, Vivienne knew better than to let down her guard and celebrate the victory until she was back in Neverland.

"Is everything okay?" she asked, setting the Newton's Cradle on Lawrence's desk into motion.

"It appears as though you do not have the disease," Lawrence mumbled, unable to look up from the stack of papers within the folder.

"Then that's good news, right?"

"What? Oh, yes, yes. Very good news for *you*." He knocked the swinging silver balls to the ground.

"Am I free to leave?"

"We don't discharge patients this late in the evening."

Lawrence tossed the file on his desk and wiped his hand across his face. "You should stay until morning."

"I'd rather go home. After all, my boss and friends are probably worried about me." Calm. She needed to stay calm. And stand up. And *walk* toward the exit.

The two startled guards grabbed her when she opened the door, but Jasper stopped them with a dismissive gesture. "Let me walk you out."

He snatched the file and clutched her results to his chest, a dejected look on his face. "Wait here," he said when they reached the glass doors, "and I'll have my assistant drive you back to Frostburg."

"I'd rather wait outside in the fresh air." Instead of keeping her promise to wait, Vivienne strolled toward the parking lot. Fifty feet from the building, she tried TINK again. "Hello?"

"We have eyes on you," Deacon's voice crackled from the earpiece concealed beneath her hair. "What're you doing?"

"Leaving," she said as if her actions should have been obvious.

"They let you go?"

"More or less." She turned in a circle, searching the horizon for signs of him. "Where are you?"

His words were muffled by the light breeze and rustling leaves. "Ridge line, six o'clock"

"Hey, Vivienne?" Jasper shouted from some distance behind.

Her muscles tensed as she twisted toward him. "What, Jasper?"

"First name basis, huh?" Deacon muttered.

"What's your blood type? These hospital records say AB negative..." He turned to the back page of his report. "But the tests we ran today say O negative. There must be...some mistake..."

Lawrence was evil. That much was clear. But Jasper seemed . . . clueless. She would've felt bad for him if he hadn't been trying to murder her.

"It's hard to believe you're this naive," she said with a mirthless laugh, backing toward the parking lot.

Jasper's brows came together, and his head tilted to the side. "What are you talking about?"

"That 'treatment' is poison," she spat. "It *kills* us."

"Us? Wait—" His eyes widened, and he took a halting step toward her.

Fire raced beneath her skin as adrenaline surged through her veins. In one fluid motion, she crouched and pushed away from the earth.

THIRTY-FOUR

Vivienne dipped below the leafy camouflage at the base of the ridgeline as dusk settled over the horizon. A dark figure appeared from the canopy above and landed beside her.

"What are you doing here?" she clipped, hating her fireflies for acting up. This guy was trouble and heartache in one *very* appealing package.

Deacon moved toward her slowly, his face hidden in the shadows of his black hood. "I thought you needed me to save you again."

He may have saved her before. But not anymore. "I save myself."

"I see that." He moved closer, and she could see his mouth was pressed into a thin line. "They didn't give you anything, did they? Pills or injections?"

"I'm fine."

His finger brushed along her bandage, sending chills down her spine. "Then what's this?"

"They just took some blood." She pulled her arm away. "It's not a big deal."

"You're sure that's all they did?"

"Positive." Now that he was at arm's length, she noticed his gray complexion and the dark smudges beneath his brilliant green eyes. "You look terrible."

"Yes, well." A laugh. "I thought my girlfriend was being murdered, so I've been a little stressed out."

"I'm not your girlfriend," she reminded him. Saying it aloud made her feel empty.

"Are you not?" His brows flicked up. "I don't remember you breaking up with me."

"Come on, Deacon. We both know this isn't going to work. We both want different things."

"Do we?" He slipped a hand around her waist and pressed a kiss to her cheek. "What do you want, Vivienne?"

How was she supposed to answer that question? With him standing this close, dusting kisses across her jaw, her neck . . . it was impossible to think straight.

"I want someone who isn't going to break my heart."

"I won't break your heart," he whispered, bringing his mouth to hers, "if you promise not to break mine."

"Deacon, you know it's not necessary for you to stay here for this." Paul Mitter's longing expression faded as he sighed toward the exit.

"I believe it *is* necessary," Deacon said, scooting his chair closer to Vivienne's.

They had gotten back to Kensington an hour ago, and she had barely had time to shower before being called to meet with External Affairs.

Paul adjusted his glasses on the bridge of his nose. "If you gave me a bit of time on my own with Vivienne to—"

"I'm not going anywhere unless Vivienne asks me to," he drawled.

Paul cast hopeful eyes toward her. "Vivienne?"

She smiled politely but knew she wanted Deacon at her side. "He can stay."

"Have it your way," Paul grumbled, flipping open the legal pad and taking the lid off the top of his pen. "Okay, let's get right to it. We know your foster family released a video offering a reward in exchange for information on your whereabouts."

Vivienne clenched her hands together in her lap. "That's what Deacon told me." And the betrayal she felt cut her to her core. They had worked with HOOK—had nearly gotten her killed.

"We have it on good authority that someone in Maryland called the tip line regarding your location. We also believe we know who has been reporting to HOOK."

Please don't say Lyle . . . Please don't say Lyle . . .

"Lynn made the initial call when you went into the hospital," he went on, "and she appears to have been the only one communicating with them."

If Lynn was the mole, that meant . . . "Lyle is clear?"

A nod. "We believe your foster brother has no connection with HOOK."

"I knew it!" She punched the air victoriously. "Can I see him?" Lyle was going to freak out when she told him.

"We'll discuss that in a minute. First, I need you to walk me through what happened Thursday evening."

She relayed every detail she could remember from the night in question. When she got to the point where Lawrence had threatened to take Megan, Paul stopped her. "You should've followed procedure and abandoned the mark to save yourself."

"There were four of them," she said, wiggling four fingers toward him, "and only one of me. I did what I thought was best."

"It was the right decision," Deacon chimed in, putting his arm around her; she leaned into his warmth. "Wouldn't you agree, Paul?"

Paul hummed as he made a notation on his paper. "Did you give HOOK any information regarding our whereabouts?"

Did he really think she'd do that? "Of course not."

"Don't look so horrified. You know I have to ask."

"Lawrence only once asked me where I've been hiding. Then Jasper arrived, and the interrogation ended."

Paul looked over the rim of his glasses and asked why it ended.

She was no closer to knowing the answer to his question than she had been that morning. "I know this is going to sound strange, but it seemed like Lawrence didn't want his brother to hear. He had photos of Ethan, Megan, and Deacon, but he hid the pictures the moment Jasper came in."

Deacon twisted toward her; his brows came together. "Where did he get photos of me?"

"I think they were from the hospital in Ohio. Don't worry," she told him, dismissing his concern with a wave, "they don't know who you are. Lawrence referred to you as *The Shadow.*"

"The Shadow?" Deacon snorted. "Has a nice ring to it, don't you think, Paul?"

Paul grunted and rolled his eyes. When he finished writing, he placed his pen at the top of his notebook and flipped through the pages with a thoughtful expression on his face.

Deacon opened his hand in his lap, and she laced her fingers through his.

"The bad news is..." Paul yawned and removed his glasses so he could rub the weariness from his eyes. It was late, and the poor guy looked tired. She almost felt sorry for him. Almost. "We know Lynn was the one to call HOOK, but we don't understand how she knew to contact them."

"It must have something to do with my parents." Light, reassuring pressure from Deacon's hand gave her the courage to continue, and she explained what Lawrence told her about them.

"If your connection with HOOK goes back twelve years," Paul said thoughtfully, "we need to look beyond Lynn. There's more to this story—and I will find out what it is."

"What's the good news?" After the week she'd had, she could certainly use some.

"The *good* news is, anyone who doubted you before now knows where your commitment lies."

"And Lyle?"

"After things die down," Paul said, putting his notebook and pen into his briefcase, "you should be able to contact—and perhaps even see—your foster brother."

When they were finished, Vivienne and Deacon walked out of the Hall hand-in-hand. Moonlight fell in silver waves over the Kensington campus. The hush of night whispered on the breeze, welcoming her home.

"What now?" Vivienne asked, her eyes fixed on the stars twinkling above them.

Deacon drew her into his arms. She stood on her tiptoes and pressed her lips against his.

"Now," he said, placing a tender kiss to her hairline before resting his forehead against hers, "we get into trouble."

WANT A SNEAK PEEK?

**Read on for a sneak preview of Book II in The P.A.N. Trilogy
(Landing Spring 2021)**

ONE

Jasper Hooke still remembered the first time he saw a human fly. He had been eight years old, and his father had gone on yet another trip to yet another town to help the less fortunate with minor medical issues—pro bono, of course. That left Jasper and his fifteen-year-old brother, Lawrence, with their creepy grandfather in his even creepier house.

Old Edward Hooke never smiled and made no effort to feign concern for his grandsons. Lawrence was his favorite, but that wasn't saying much—Edward seemed to despise them both. While he and his brother were there, his grandfather's housekeeper served as their inattentive guardian. Jasper was used to fending for himself at home, so having very little supervision in his grandfather's cavernous mansion felt normal.

That fateful day, the housekeeper had called in sick.

Knowing better than to leave Jasper in the charge of his irresponsible brother, Edward brought his youngest grandson with him to the office.

The HOOK facility at that time had been located in a retail unit at the end of an ordinary strip mall on the outskirts of town. The waiting room had dingy white walls, a single poster no one had ever bothered to frame—stuck with peeling masking tape gone brittle from age—and an artificial ficus gathering dust in the corner. A bored-looking receptionist manned the desk behind sliding glass windows. Occasionally, a nurse would come out of the back offices, unlock and rummage through a black filing cabinet, then lock it and disappear again.

Jasper had planned on staying put as his grandfather commanded, but eventually he had to use the bathroom. The receptionist tried his grandfather's office extension, but no one answered. Jasper had danced around the linoleum floor, trying to hold it in.

"*Please.*" His eyes filled with tears from the pain in his stomach.

The woman rolled her eyes and let out a disgusted sigh. "Fine. The bathroom is just across the hall. Don't go snooping around, okay?"

"Okay."

And he *had* kept that promise.

It wasn't his fault that, at the exact moment he had emerged from the most satisfying pee of his young life, the door across the corridor burst open. Out ran a wild-eyed young woman, her face as pale as the walls, and her hair plastered to her head like she had been in a swimming pool.

She paused for a moment, undoubtedly shocked by the sight of young Jasper obstructing her path. When a gruff voice shouted for her to stop, she turned toward the red Exit sign illuminating the end of the hallway and ran.

Edward Hooke and a man in scrubs came barrelling out of the room after her and quickly closed the distance. She reached the exit first and threw open the door.

She did not run into the woods at the back of the warehouse or toward the Burger King across the road—but instead shot upward, into the clouds and beyond.

Eventually, Jasper's grandfather noticed him staring out the still open door.

Instead of comforting Jasper and explaining away the confusion, Edward met him with the same unfailing disdain and irritation that defined their relationship. "I told you to stay in the waiting room."

Too shocked by the scene to respond to his grandfather's scolding, Jasper whispered, "That girl. She just…"

"Get back to the waiting room!"

"That girl just *flew* away…like a bird."

"Yes, she did." He knelt to eye-level with Jasper. "But she won't be flying for long."

Twenty-five years later, the small strip-mall office had been replaced by a new state-of-the-art research facility fifteen miles away. Edward Hooke had died the day after its completion. Jasper's father, Dr. Charles Hooke, had concluded that the old man was just stubborn enough to keep the Lord from taking him until the building was finished. Jasper wasn't sure the Lord had been the one to take his grandfather, but had mumbled his agreement with the second part of his father's statement.

After Edward's passing, Charles retired from private medical practice to serve as the President at HOOK, although he still volunteered locally one week every month.

Lawrence had a head for business—and his grandfather's ruthlessness to go along with it. He had been voted CEO unanimously by the Board of Directors. Three years after Edward's death, the company's stock had tripled in value, and they were on target for their best year to date.

Meanwhile, Jasper had inherited his father's affinity for science and medicine. Instead of pursuing a career in a hospital, he had chosen to study molecular biology; Jasper had known it would one day be his responsibility to continue the family legacy of scientific innovation and discovery. Only the year before, Jasper had been named Head of Research at HOOK— although the incident this past spring had nearly put an end to his employment there altogether.

Vivienne Dunn had caught him off-guard. Jasper's father had been enraged when Lawrence broke the news of her escape, and had wrongly claimed that his youngest son had been distracted by a pretty face. Unsurprisingly, Lawrence had been blameless in the matter, but Jasper was well used to Lawrence towering over him on his grandfather's pedestal.

Vivienne had convinced Jasper that her NG-1882 had not

activated. In the time they had held her at the facility, she hadn't made any attempts to escape . . . until she did.

From his desk drawer, he pulled out the old alarm clock that had been left on top of his car the night Vivienne had gotten away.

"I told you to get rid of that thing," Lawrence growled from the doorway. He stalked over and ripped the clock from Jasper's hands. Then he dropped it onto the tiles with a clang and stomped until it was nothing more than a twisted lump of metal.

"You didn't have to break it," he groaned, falling to his knees and sweeping the broken glass into a pile, cutting his finger in the process.

"They've been taunting our family with those clocks for decades. Do you really think it's an appropriate souvenir to remind you how badly you screwed up?"

Jasper dropped what was left of the clock into the trash can. "What do you want, Lawrence?"

"We got a hit on your girlfriend's whereabouts."

Jasper looked up suddenly. Was he talking about Vivienne? "Did someone call the tip line?" he rushed.

Lawrence's lips curled into a sneer. "Let's just say we got a lucky break."

"Are you sure your source is credible?" Jasper sank onto his rolling chair. This was the third time they'd gotten a call about Vivienne, and none had led to anything but dead ends. One woman claimed she'd seen her at a mall in New Jersey. Another at the airport in Arizona. And the last one, a man who had sounded like he was fond of cigarettes, had said Vivienne had been working at his local deli.

Lawrence shoved his phone in Jasper's face. "You tell me."

Jasper squinted at the gritty black-and-white photo of a girl in a convenience store. "I'm not sure that's her." She was petite. Her hair was longer and darker than it had been in April. But her face was turned so that he could only see—

"Your opinion doesn't count."

His opinion never counted. "Are you going to check it out?"

"Dad's out of town this week, so I need to stay here." He

tucked his phone into his breast pocket and leaned across the desk, bracing his hands on either side of Jasper's laptop. "Which means it's *your* job to bring her back."

"We already have her DNA on file." Jasper wrapped his handkerchief around his bloody finger. "What's the point in going through the hassle and expense of travelling to—?"

"We need her *here*, Lab Rat. End of discussion. I'm trusting you to not screw up again."

Again.

Vivienne had fooled them both.

"Last time was as much your fault as it was mine," he ground out.

"I'm in a forgiving mood, so I'm going to let you get away with saying that to me this once." Lawrence kicked the trash can, and the alarm clock let out a final high-pitched chime. "Oh...and one more thing," he said from over his shoulder, "Rhett and Terry will be going along for the ride."

Lawrence had hired new guards after Vivienne escaped in April to help with acquiring subjects for the most recent round of testing—or at least that was what his brother claimed. Jasper couldn't help feeling like the two henchmen who followed him like mosquitos buzzing in his ears were there to keep an eye on *him* as much as his subjects.

A few hours later, Jasper climbed into the backseat of the town car and squeezed between his bodyguards. He nodded at each of them. "Rhett...Terry." When his greeting was met with silence, he found himself looking forward to seeing the shock on their chiseled, scarred faces the first time they saw one of the PAN fly.

ACKNOWLEDGMENTS

First and foremost, I'd like to thank you for reading this book. My hope is that you found yourself as invested in this story as I've been since I wrote it.

I'm blessed to have a husband who is a true partner in every aspect of this crazy, exhausting, brilliant life. I couldn't have written this—or anything—without his willingness and ability to take up my slack. Jimmy, I love you.

Colin and Lilly, thank you for being so good at watching cartoons and for letting me stare at my screen while you fall asleep. I hope someday this story makes you feel like magic is possible.

Thank you to my mom—who also happens to be my biggest fan. All those paperback romance novels (sans front covers) you let me borrow are the reason I fell in love with reading. And thanks to my dad for repeatedly reminding me what it means to be a Hickman. Look up. Move forward. I miss you every day.

Thank you to my sisters who never told me my first drafts were crap. Megan Kitzmiller, Dani Hickman, & Tillie Lee: I forgive you for lying.

I'd also like to thank Phyllis and Shay Fyfe for helping me hit my deadlines by being our go-to babysitters. You've been wonderfully supportive. I feel like one of the family now.

Thank you to Miriam Sincell Burton. You've read every story

I've ever written and have found something positive to say about each one. Everyone should be so lucky to have someone like you cheering them on. And to my neighbor April Drew, you've been an integral part of this journey as a sounding board, a cheerleader, and a *friend*. You inspire me every day to keep going—or to take a much-needed break. If the audiobooks need sound effects, I'll let you know.

Lenka McGurk, Bibi Breen, and Magda Cronin, I want to thank you for forcing me to be sociable even when I didn't feel like it. I'm blessed to have found such wonderful, close, supportive friends at this stage in life.

Brittney Maynard, I'm enamored with the crest you've created for the PAN. Thank you for lending your brilliant artistic ability to this project. And Mila, thank you so much for giving this novel a beautiful new look.

A huge thanks to the experts who helped bring this fantasy a bit closer to reality. Anne Bicker: without your late-night input, brilliant ideas, and genetic expertise, I would've just been making stuff up. And Brandon Stein: thanks for keeping my guy out of jail.

I cannot thank Elle and everyone at Midnight Tide Publishing enough for giving my orphan novel a home. And Candace Robinson, you are an angel. Thank you from the bottom of my heart for all you've done.

And to my editors: Jess Moore, you made me Google purple prose and highlighted my writing ticks and flaws. This story is stronger because of you. Meg Dailey, you pushed me to make this story better than I could have imagined. And your comments/asides in the margins always brought a smile to my face and kept me going when I felt like stopping.

Lastly, I feel it is imperative to thank J.M. Barrie—the genius who created Peter Pan. You gave us magic; you gave us adventure; you gave us Neverland.

ABOUT THE AUTHOR

Jenny grew up in Oakland, Maryland and currently lives in County Tipperary, Ireland with her lilting husband and two tyrannical children. Her love of reading blossomed the summer after graduating high school, when she borrowed a paperback romance from her mother during the annual family beach vacation.

From that sunny day forward, she has been a lover of stories with Happily-Ever-Afters. In early 2008, she wrote her first novel, *The Mirrors at Barnard Hall*. But it was not until she moved to Nashville, TN and met her mentor, Billy Block, that she was encouraged to self-publish the work in 2012.

Seven years, and two additional self-published works later, Jenny is ready to release her next novel, *The P.A.N.*, the first book in a YA Sci-Fi Romance trilogy of the same name.

ALSO BY JENNY

The PAN Trilogy
The H.O.O.K. (Spring 2021)

MORE BOOKS YOU'LL LOVE

If you enjoyed this story, please consider leaving a review!
Then check out more books from Midnight Tide Publishing!

The Girl in the Clockwork Tower by Lou Wilham

A tale of espionage, lavender hair, and pineapples.
   **Welcome to Daiwynn where magic is dangerous, but hope
is more dangerous still.**

For Persinette—a lavender-haired, 24-year-old seer dreaming of
adventure and freedom—the steam-powered kingdom of
Daiwynn is home. As an Enchanted asset for MOTHER, she
aids in Collecting Enchanted and sending them to MOTHER's
labor camps.
   But when her handler, Gothel, informs Persi that she will be
going out into the field for a Collection, she decides it's time to
take a stand. Now she must fight her fears and find a way to
hide her attempts to aid the Enchanted or risk being sent to the
camps herself.

Manu Kelii, Captain of the airship The Defiant Duchess, is 26-
years-old and hasn't seen enough excitement—thank you very
much. His charismatic smile and flamboyant sense of style
earned him a place amongst the Uprising, but his fickle and
irresponsible nature has seen to it that their leader doesn't trust
him.
   Desperate to prove himself, Manu will stop at nothing to aid
their mission to overthrow MOTHER and the queen of
Daiwynn. So, when the Uprising Leader deposits a small unit of

agents on his ship, and tasks him with working side by side with MOTHER asset Persinette to hinder the Collection effort, he finds himself in over his head.

The stakes are high for this unlikely duo. They have only two options; stop MOTHER or thousands more will die—including themselves.

Available
9.23.20

Lyrics & Curses by Candace Robinson

Lark Espinoza could get lost in her music—and she's not so sure anyone in her family would even care to find her. Her trendy, party-loving twin sister and her mother-come-lately Beth, who's suddenly sworn off men and onto homemaking, don't understand her love of cassette tapes, her loathing of the pop scene, or her standoffish personality. For outcast Lark, nothing feels as much like a real home as working at Bubble's Oddities store and trying to attract the attention of the cute guy who works at the Vinyl shop next door—the same one she traded lyrical notes with in class.

Auden Ellis silences the incessant questions in his own head with a steady stream of beats. Despite the unconditional love of his aunt-turned-mother, he can't quit thinking about the loss of his parents—or the possibility he might end up afflicted with his father's issues. Despite his connection with lyric-loving Lark, Auden keeps her at arm's length because letting her in might mean giving her a peek into something dangerous.

When two strangers arrive in town, one carrying a mysterious, dark object and the other playing an eerie flute tune, Lark and Auden find that their painful pasts have enmeshed them in a cursed future. Now, they must come to terms with their budding attraction while helping each other challenge the reflection they see in the mirror. If they fail, they'll be trapped for eternity in a place beyond reality.

Available
11.11.20

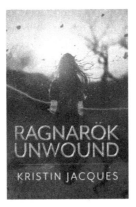

Ragnarök Unwound by Kristin Jacques

Prophecies don't untangle themselves.

Just ask Ikepela Ives, whose estranged mother left her with the power to unravel the binding threads of fate. Stuck with immortal power in a mortal body, Ives has turned her back on the duty she never wanted.

But it turns out she can't run from her fate forever, not now that Ragnarok has been set in motion and the god at the center of that tangled mess has gone missing. With a ragtag group of companions—including a brownie, a Valkyrie, and the goddess of death herself—Ives embarks on her first official mission as Fate Cipher—to save the world from doomsday.

Nothing she can't handle. Right?

Available
10.07.20

CPSIA information can be obtained
at www.ICGtesting.com
Printed in the USA
LVHW091233300920
667416LV00015B/846